"*It Begins in Betrayal* has a wonderfully complex plot with threads that eventually resolve most satisfactorily. The post-war time period is particularly interesting and well captured."
—Maureen Jennings, author of the Murdoch Mysteries series

"Action-packed and emotionally charged from the prologue to the climax . . . it just doesn't get much better than this."
—Don Graves, Canadian Mystery Reviews blog

"I am in love. . . . Brilliant! Absolutely in the spirit of Dorothy Sayers' Harriet Vane/Peter Wimsey mysteries, but smart and fresh in its own right. For lovers of cozy mysteries and British police procedurals—there's even a murder investigation in which evidence includes fragments of a broken tea set—this title will not disappoint. . . . The writing was wonderful, the plotting rock solid." —Kerry Clare, author of *Mitzi Bytes*

"If you're after historical crime with a strong backbone but also an air of genteel cosiness about it, then the Lane Winslow series by Iona Whishaw is just right for you."
—Crime Fiction Lover

PRAISE FOR *An Old, Cold Grave*

"A fascinating picture of a life in which many people spent every waking hour working and a disturbing look at the fate of orphaned children raise this mystery above the ordinary." —*Kirkus Reviews*

"Exquisitely written, psychologically deft. . . . If you miss Mary Stewart's sleuthing heroines, if you loved *Broadchurch* and its village of suspects, settle in, turn off the phone, and enjoy."
—Linda Svendsen, author of *Sussex Drive and Marine Life*

"A debut mystery from an author destined for awards. A setting that is ripe for storytelling and a convincing gift for portraying the painful and challenging life for the survivors of the two world wars. . . . Whishaw is an exciting addition to Canada's fine roster of mystery writers." —Don Graves, Canadian Mystery Reviews blog

"The writing . . . conjures up nicely the ambiance of a 1940s west Canadian locale and develops in depth both the characters and their interactions." —*San Francisco Book Review*

"*A Killer in King's Cove* is worth a look, especially as the author intends to reprise her lead character." —*Seattle Book Review*

"Iona Whishaw brings to life a rural country town from the 1940s. . . . She's created an engaging, quirky cast of characters in the countryside who, some more reluctantly than others, welcome Lane into their circle. . . . Despite Lane's promise to Inspector Darling to not cause any more mayhem in town, we sort of hope she does!" —ReviewingtheEvidence.com

"A simply riveting read by a master of the genre, *A Killer in King's Cove* is especially recommended for the personal reading lists of dedicated mystery buffs, as well as an enduringly popular acquisition choice for community library mystery/suspense collections." —Wisconsin Bookwatch

THE LANE WINSLOW MYSTERY SERIES

———

IONA WHISHAW

IT BEGINS IN BETRAYAL

A LANE WINSLOW MYSTERY

TOUCHWOOD

Edited by Claire Philipson
Cover illustration by Margaret Hanson
Design by Colin Parks

LIBRARY AND ARCHIVES CANADA CATALOGUING IN PUBLICATION

Whishaw, Iona, 1948-, author
It begins in betrayal / Iona Whishaw.
(A Lane Winslow mystery ; #4)
Issued in print and electronic formats.
ISBN 978-1-77151-261-9 (softcover).—ISBN 978-1-77151-262-6
(HTML).—ISBN 978-1-77151-263-3 (PDF)
I. Title. II. Series: Whishaw, Iona, 1948-.
Lane Winslow mystery ; 4.
PS8595.H414I8 2018   C813'.54   C2017-906578-5   C2017-906579-3

We gratefully acknowledge the financial support of the Government of Canada
through the Canada Book Fund, the Canada Council for the Arts, and the
Province of British Columbia through the British Columbia Arts Council and the
Book Publishing Tax Credit.

PRINTED IN CANADA AT FRIESENS

22 21 20 19 18   2 3 4 5

For my father,
bomber pilot, raconteur,
pacifist to his very bones

PROLOGUE

France, April 1943

THE CREW LAY PANTING AT the edge of the clearing, watching, glassy-eyed and stunned, as the roiling orange and red flames engulfed the plane and lit up the night. Thick black smoke rising from the toxic, stinking mess of gasoline, oil, and metal surged into the darkness above the inferno.

"Good work, Skip," Watson managed. "I thought we were done for." The navigator, shaky and exhausted, pulled off his leather helmet and turned stiffly to look at his commander.

Flight Lieutenant Darling grunted, wrenching his eyes away from the obscene horror of the blaze boiling out of his downed plane. Where are the others? he wondered. Are they all here? He knew they'd have to get a move on before shock settled in and immobilized them.

"Report," Darling commanded.

"Nothing major," Watson said. "Trouser leg torn."

"Arm, sir. A scratch," reported Salford, trying to steady his voice. "But the radio's out."

"Sir, rear gunner is looking peaky," said Anthony, his anxiety showing. He and Darling had moved him at a run from where he appeared to have fallen near the plane. The engineer had scrambled over to sit by Evans, who was shuddering convulsively. Darling waited a moment, feeling like he could not catch his breath. Had he heard from Belton, the front gunner? At that moment another violent whoosh of flame enveloped the Lancaster, and the men recoiled, throwing their arms across their faces. Darling saw Belton, ducking like the others, and felt a momentary relief.

"It's going to blow! Move!" Darling yelled. He ran toward Anthony and Evans and then realized with a sickening thud that the enemy was moving in the shadows just behind them. He pulled out his revolver, wanting to shout another warning, but there was no time. He and Anthony hauled the slack-limbed Evans up between them and frantically made for the cover of the woods just as the explosion sucked the air out of them and lit up the forest. In a flash that seemed to hover for an eternity, he spotted a farmhouse at the near end of the field, where a dog leaped and barked as though in a silent movie. The only sound he could hear was the roar of his bomber going up.

Deafened, the men stumbled deeper into the dark. Darling, the blast still pounding in his ears, felt someone tugging on his sleeve. Anthony's face was near his, his mouth moving. His words finally came through: "Bosch, sir."

Darling looked out to their rear, trying desperately to hear, to understand where the attack was coming from.

"Go," he shouted. "Go, go! I'll hold them off!" He turned and looked at them, immobilized in the darkness, and caught their hesitation. "Do as I bloody well say!" Why hadn't he seen Jones?

Gunfire exploded somewhere near them. Darling struggled to see into the maelstrom of forest and fire as he moved forward, keeping low. Dimly aware of a pain in his left leg, he crouched, waiting for further fire from the attackers. A loud crack burst out from somewhere behind him, and then a spray of bullets whipped to his right. Bloody hell, they'd begun to circle! Had his men gotten away? He struggled to see his own way out, but the thundering flames obliterated sounds, obscuring the attackers. If he shot in any direction, they would know his position. He could hear them calling out, moving in a fan, he guessed. He crawled a few feet to the left and looked behind to where he hoped all his men had found at least a tenuous safety and then stood up to go after them. He would sling Evans over his shoulder.

The fire began to abate, and the moving shadows of his men seemed to fade in the direction of the farmhouse. He leaned over, ready to carry Evans, and in a flash of light from the fire finding one more source of fuel, he saw his gunner was dead, sprawled and broken, beyond help, looking in death younger than his eighteen years.

The voices of the attackers were louder, sharper, moving in his direction.

He would have to tell the boy's parents: "Killed instantly"—the usual comforting message. In this case it was true. He could see that. Something . . . but there was another burst of gunfire. He could see a German soldier, ahead of his mates, using the failing light of the plane to find the airmen who had gotten out.

With cold, numb efficiency, Darling took aim, heard his own shot as though from a distance, and saw the German crumple to the ground. After one last glance at Rear Gunner Evans, he bolted into the darkness after his men.

CHAPTER ONE

—————

"**G**OD'S TEETH!" DARLING EXCLAIMED, PUTTING down the receiver. "Ames, get in here!"

Darling's youthful and indomitably cheerful second in command put his head around the door. "Sir?"

"Saddle up, we're off to near Harrop. Local padre has found an old lady dead up behind her cabin in the woods somewhere near there. He said he 'didn't like the look of it.'"

"I don't much like the look of dead people either," Constable Ames commented, turning back toward his office to get the keys of the 1940 four-door maroon Ford they used as a police vehicle, which he treated like a princess.

Darling took his hat and jacket off the stand, straightened up the papers on his desk, and joined his constable where he waited in the hallway. "There goes lunch. Why do people always wait till just before a mealtime to call us?"

"Do I have time to run downstairs to the café for a couple of ham and cheeses? It'd take five minutes."

Darling hesitated. The prospect of spending the whole afternoon in the back of beyond on an empty stomach was daunting. The old lady would not get any deader. "Yeah, go on. Get a couple of bottles of Coke as well. Come get me when you're done."

Darling sat back down at his desk and looked at his list. If the truth were known, he was a bit relieved about the distraction because he had a call to one Mr. Dudley on his to-do list, and it was going to be tiresome. Might as well use this lull to get it done and out of the way. Preparing to be shouted at about the incompetence of the police department, which had not yet found Mr. Dudley's stolen car, and queried about why honest taxpayers should be forking out for his salary, Darling was reaching for the receiver when the phone rang, causing him to jump.

"Darling," he said.

"Sir, there's a gentleman here to see you. Name of Jensen." The desk sergeant was speaking in a peculiarly studied manner.

Darling frowned. "I'm just off to a suspicious death. Can it wait?"

"He's a government man, sir," the sergeant whispered. And then loudly, "Very good, sir, I'll send him right up."

"What?" said Darling, annoyed, but it was too late. He could hear the click of the phone on the other end. He took off his hat and placed it on the corner of his desk and prepared to receive the government man, whatever that was supposed to be, and wondered if it would take long.

The man who presented himself was short and well fed and encased in a dark suit. He had removed his hat, which he now held in his left hand with a sizeable brief-case, revealing thinning, slicked-back dark hair. He was offering his hand. Darling stood up and shook it. He was about to introduce himself when the government man said, "Flight Lieutenant Darling?"

Taken aback, Darling said hesitantly, "Yes, as was. Just Inspector Darling now. With whom am I speaking?"

"Yes, how remiss of me. Roderick Jensen, with the Canadian government." He spoke in a posh British accent and smiled in an ingratiating manner that instantly put Darling on alert.

"Please sit down. How can I help?" Darling went back around to sit on his side of the desk, and waited. "I should mention," he added, "that I am just expecting my constable to return. We are going out of town in a few moments to investigate a death."

"Ah," said Jensen. "How very unfortunate for the poor creature. The difficulty is that I am pressed for time. I need to gather information. You will understand I have come out specifically to depose . . . perhaps that is not the right word, but it will have to do for now . . . you with regard to an incident you will be best placed to provide information for."

"I'm very sorry, but I must give priority to my job. Perhaps we can put it off till later in the afternoon?" Darling said, but he already knew that whoever this man was, he likely had the authority to interrupt whatever he liked.

"I'm afraid that I cannot . . ."

At that moment Ames appeared, holding a paper bag, and then seeing Jensen said, "Oh."

Darling considered the situation. The government man was obviously not going to leave. It was a confounded nuisance. Bowing to the inevitable he said, "Ames, you'll have to go on your own. It appears I might be tied up here."

"Sir?" It would be the first time Ames would respond to so serious a call completely on his own.

"You'll be fine. The van boys will be with you to bring the body back. Just the usual palaver, eh? Picture, notes, interviews. We'll go over them when you get back."

"Yes, sir," Ames said, not knowing if the feeling he was having was excitement or anxiety. He turned to leave.

"My lunch, Ames."

Ames extracted a bottle of Coke and a waxed paper–wrapped sandwich from his bag and handed them to Darling, who knew already it would be a long time before he got near them.

FATHER LAHEY AND Ames, his camera at the ready, stood by the dead woman. Ames glanced around. They were in a dark and deeply wooded area, pines growing close and tangled. Through the trees and to the right of the cabin, a path wound down toward the tiny village of Harrop. The woman was face down about thirty feet into the woods, her arms thrown out as if she'd fallen violently forward and had tried to stop her fall. She seemed to be caught on a tumbling of sharp-edged rocks and torn tree branches that had been blown down in some long-ago windstorm and were now covered with an accumulation of pine needles. She could simply have had a heart attack, Ames thought, which would make it an accident. She looked old enough.

She was wearing street shoes, a blue cardigan, and a brown dress, which had ridden up on one side revealing that her heavy wool stockings were held up with garter snaps. She could have stumbled quite easily in those shoes, so unsuited for rough terrain. The spot was far off the beaten path. Yet, he could see immediately what the priest meant by not liking the look of it. He was no scientist, but if she'd stumbled, her arms might not have been in this position, so violently thrown forward. This looked more like she'd been pushed savagely from behind, with no time to do anything but fling her arms out. He snapped pictures, trying to take in the scene from several angles.

"What is her name?" Ames asked.

"Agatha Browning. A bit of a local character. Comes from the English aristocracy, if you can believe it. At least that's the story everyone seems to believe." The priest looked down nervously to where the late Agatha Browning had left this earth. "I mean, she could have fallen over. She was getting on, and you'd expect someone that age to be more unsteady on her pins than before. But she was very sure-footed for a woman of her years, I'd have said, and I can't think why she'd be this far away from the cabin, and dressed like that. She must have been planning to go to town or somewhere, so why come up here? I had the idea that the only places she went were down to the village shop for a few things every now and then, or, more rarely now, she'd drive that rattletrap of hers into town. In fact, I remember her telling me that this forest up behind her cabin gave her the heebie-jeebies, even after all these years. It just doesn't make sense."

The woman's cardigan was pulled off one of her arms, and her face was turned sideways, and Ames could see that her eyes were open, as if caught in the shocking moment of death.

"How well do you know her?" Ames asked Father Lahey, shuddering slightly.

"Probably less well than most of my parishioners. I won't say she kept entirely to herself, but she was, I don't know, independent, I guess you'd say. Made it clear she didn't really need anyone else. Apparently came out here just after the Great War from the old country and set herself up in that cabin. She was already in her forties when she came. I come over every week to provide services, and she rarely came, not even at Christmas. She was Church of England. Her name was on the parish register when I first came here in '22, back when it was an Anglican church. It's the only church around, and some who aren't Catholic come to Christmas Mass, but as I say, I never saw her in church. I did start going to her cabin periodically, oh, eight or ten years ago when I came in from town. I was worried that she was getting on and would need help to get to the village. I needn't have worried. She was as hale as could be. I thought she'd outlive everyone. She was happy to get the few things I'd bring out for her, though, as I don't think she had much money, and I think her trips to town were getting fewer. I've been expecting that jalopy of hers to break down, but she's managed to maintain it. Does all the work herself. Admirable, really, I wouldn't know a bolt from a pipe on the inside of my car."

"If she was forty-something when she came, then that would put her just north of seventy." Ames looked more closely. Her hair, short and looking permanently unkempt, hovered between fading blond and white. Her clothes were baggy and she looked thin and wiry. He saw what he'd missed before: a stain of blood just near her left shoulder. Opening his bag, he pulled out his camera and took some pictures from where they stood. Then, moving sideways, he carefully negotiated the brush and rocks to where Agatha Browning lay. He stepped into an unsteady tangle of branches and nearly lost his balance. He swore under his breath.

"Oh dear, do be careful. I just can't believe this!" said Lahey anxiously. After a few more shots, Ames lifted her stiff left shoulder and turned her over awkwardly, and then stood up, looking away. He took a deep breath, feeling the beginnings of nausea. Imagining the impression he'd make with this priest and the van boys if he were to vomit on his first solo outing to a crime scene, he willed his stomach to behave. Father Lahey had turned away, his hand to his mouth. She was still stiff, but the blood had dried completely and was caked on like black scabs. Flies were having a field day. He had the idea she had been killed the afternoon before.

"Someone's stabbed her," he said to the back of Father Lahey's head. He knew that was right, but it hardly seemed to cover the gaping wound that started just above her breast and angled downward toward the middle of her chest. The bodice of her dress was slashed and soaked with blood that had dried and hardened with the dry heat of the summer day. She wasn't stabbed here, he thought. He struggled back over to where the priest stood and began to look at the ground. Ames could see that the undergrowth had been disturbed, and cursed that they had disturbed it further. He had followed the priest to where the body lay and now was worried that he'd ruined any evidence. Then he saw a second trampled path coming into the forest a few feet away. Moving slowly, he leaned low and searched the scuffed bed of pine needles, which had been disturbed during Agatha's journey to her final resting place. It came out of the forest not directly behind the cabin itself but from the path at the side of the cabin that she must have used every time she went down to the settlement. The path seemed at one time to have run up through the edge of the forest, but it had evidently fallen into disuse. Had she thought of running down the path to where people might be found and then thought she would be safer running uphill and sought refuge by hiding in the woods? There they were. Stains of blood, smeared along the crushed grasses between the path and the wood. Hard to see, but there. More pictures.

Ames stood up and looked toward the forest. "She wasn't attacked there. Is that her cabin?"

Lahey nodded. "Yes, but why was she up here?"

"I'm going to hazard that she was trying to get away from whoever did this and was perhaps chased and pushed." He frowned. "Why were you up here, come to that?" He asked.

"You know, Constable Ames, I cannot tell you why. I have one or two parishioners I visit during the week in the various towns: Kaslo, Proctor, here. I was here visiting one of my old fellows, and when I was done I had an urge to follow this old path up toward a clearing. There used to be a working mill down along the water in the last century, and they cleared the forest farther up. There's a rumour someone wants to build a new mill, farther up this way, and I wanted to try to imagine what it might be like to have all that commotion in this tiny peaceful place. It's mostly a few old timers and a couple of holiday homes now. Well, I thought it was peaceful, anyway. I actually was trying to think of ways to discourage a new mill. I wandered a little into the forest to see if the lumber was even worth harvesting. Do you ever have a feeling that you are guided to something? When I found her, like that," he pointed to where she lay, "I felt as if I must have been called here by God."

Ames took out his notebook and began to make notes. Was the priest telling the whole truth? Ames had little experience of God or being guided, except by hunger. Would the priest have called the police if he himself had done this? It seemed unlikely and, having spent the last hour with the priest, Ames was convinced the man was sincerely distraught. Still.

"Do you know why she first came out here?"

"Believe it or not, she was prospecting originally. She ran into a spot of bother with a mill owner in the early days, but she kept herself to herself and staked claims well out in the bush. I don't know that they ever amounted to much. To be honest, I think it was her way of pretending she was working. She seemed to have family money to live on, though she lived pretty simply. Usually wore denim overalls and rubber boots, though she dressed up sometimes to go to town." The priest looked at her and shook his head. "I don't know of any next of kin, before you ask."

Ames now hesitated. Mentally he was running over the list of what he ought to do, fearful that he might leave something out and have Darling's wrath to deal with. Was there anything he'd missed? He'd taken pictures, including of the path she'd made in her flight, made notes. He would investigate the cabin, interview people. No doubt their pathologist, Ashford Gillingham, whom no one had called anything but "Gilly" for as long as Ames could remember, would be able to estimate when she'd died, but in spite of the dried blood he could see that she'd not been dead long enough for rigor mortis to have passed.

"I'll need to see the parish registry, and maybe you could make a list of any people in the village I should speak to. When I've got the boys to carry her out to the van, maybe you could show me to the cabin?" Was that all? He looked back at the two van drivers, who had followed them up and were sitting on a log in a clearing, smoking; the unseasonably hot June weather had already made the forest floor tinder dry.

"Bill, Andy. Go get the stretcher, and put those out, you'll set the whole place on fire."

The two men got up slowly and ground their cigarettes into the log. "Who died and made you boss?" one of them muttered.

"I heard that," Ames said. He turned back to the task at hand.

He walked into the forest and stared at the body, trying to see it as his boss might, looking at details. He suddenly saw that it was a miracle they had a body at all. If she'd gotten farther up the hill into this tangle of trees, she might never have been found. The dark lines of trees climbing the mountain behind them were vast and indifferent. She could quite easily have become just another missing person.

When the body had been removed from its awkward position, Andy and Bill put the stretcher down to rest before they made their way back to the van. Ames took the opportunity to look more closely at the victim. Now that he could see her face, he thought she had the deep lines of someone perpetually in a disagreeable temper. Her skin was rough, as if she gave no care to herself. Under her half-closed lids, the old woman had pale rheumy eyes. How well would she have been able to see? He leaned down and looked at her hands and became aware of what he had not initially noticed: the woman smelled as if she had not washed for some time. Her fingernails were thick and chipped. Aha. Blood. Not a lot. Possibly not even from the fingers themselves, but traces of darkening red, as if she'd scratched someone very badly.

"SO, FLIGHT LIEUTENANT, or Inspector, if you prefer it. I'm going to take you through anything you can remember about April 20, 1943. Is this date familiar to you?" Jensen had a notebook open and, with slowness that aggravated Darling's already growing misgivings, was affixing the cap of his fountain pen at the top. "Now then." He looked at Darling, his eyebrows raised expectantly.

"Of course it's familiar to me. One is not likely to forget the loss of a couple of bright young airmen and a plane." He frowned. It was jarring to be suddenly precipitated back into the war. "What's this about?"

"No need for concern, Inspector. I will just want you to take me through the events of that date. I may stop you from time to time to ask questions, or make notes."

"Yes, but why?"

"I, I am afraid, am only the messenger, or the scribe, if you will. It is my understanding that we have had a request from the British government to gather a few facts so that the business can be closed up. Now then, can we start with the mission? What was the object of that day's flight?" He prepared to write.

"What do you mean, 'closed up'? It was closed up when I made my report and spoke with the parents of that unfortunate boy." Darling still woke some nights, jolted into heart-stopping panic by the sound of the explosion and the blinding eruption of flames. It was seared into his brain, he often thought, and he might never move past it, or the cry of Rear Gunner Evans's mother at the news of her son's death. The war office had taken care of notifying Jones's next of kin, since he did not have living parents.

"I'm sure there's no need to be concerned, Inspector. Now, if we could get on. I am scheduled to take the morning train back to the coast for my flight home."

Darling got up and went to stand by the window with his hands in his pockets. He could see the ferry halfway along its little route that linked Nelson with the other side of the lake. He wondered what Lane, across the ferry and thirty miles down that road—which he had come to love for her being at the end of—was doing. At the beach with Angela and the Bertolli boys, he wouldn't wonder. June had been fine and warm. And then with a slight frisson of

16

guilt he wondered how Ames was getting on.

"Inspector?"

It was remarkable how this government man kept any impatience out of his voice. He was like a lizard, Darling thought. Persistent, cold-blooded, patient. He turned and began.

"The morning of April 20, 1943, we prepared for a bombing raid over suspected arms warehouses in Germany . . ."

CHAPTER TWO

FATHER LAHEY WATCHED THE BODY being carried to the van, and only then crossed himself, shuddering slightly.

"So strange, poor soul," he said. "A dreadful, lonely death. I hope she is at peace with God."

"She wasn't exactly alone, unfortunately," Ames remarked. "Let's hope God is in a mood to overlook her failure to attend church all these years."

"Oh, of course, she wasn't alone. How dreadful!" The priest glanced around anxiously and then looked down toward where the few houses sat along the banks of the lake above the railway, which was hidden by the forest.

The cabin belonging to Agatha Browning lay some way up from the village, along the old mill road, now nothing more than a forest path. They made slow progress along the route Agatha Browning took to escape her killer, as Ames walked carefully ahead, scanning the ground for signs of blood or disturbance. The path wound down past the north side of her small log cabin, which had darkened with the years. The nearby forest gave the cabin an aura of forbidding loneliness. A well-travelled trail led from the main route to the back of the cabin. They followed to where it passed by an outhouse set back some forty feet from the cabin at the end of the garden. There the ground was covered in dried blood. Lahey stood some distance away, with one hand over his mouth. Still feeling queasy, Ames took photos, wondering if the stains of blood would show up well enough.

"It must have happened here," he said. He followed the route from the outhouse to the cabin, with the priest tagging nervously behind him.

Though the cabin was heavily shaded by the evergreens, there was a cleared area at the side and back of the property, which was now yellow with sunlight. He had a momentary urge to go toward the back of the house to escape from the gloom of the overhanging forest.

"Had she ever been married, do you know?" Ames asked the priest. He had put out his hand to stop Lahey from going any closer to the house. Ames walked around to what appeared to be the front door of the cabin, but it was clear from the wear marks that she never used that door, but came in and out of her cabin through the back door that led onto the small garden she had created. Who had come up this path to attack Agatha Browning? Had they knocked at that little-used front door? He stood well away and tried to see if the overgrown grasses around the base of the steps had been walked on. Yes, possibly. And when? And for that matter, why?

"You know, I have no idea," the priest responded. "Certainly there was no one since I came. She was older when she arrived after the war. She certainly could have been, perhaps, widowed? I won't say she was completely unsociable . . . she did nod to people when she came to the village store, and as I say, I visited her more lately when I came up from town. We'd sit in her little garden here and chat. But I know I tried to ask about her former life, and she invariably cut me off. 'Let the dead past bury its dead' she used to say. But . . ."

"But what?" Ames asked, pausing and looking at the priest.

"Well, I just thought of this because it was unusual to begin with, and in light of . . ." He waved his hand vaguely in the direction of the spot where they had found her. "The last time I saw her, she said she might want to come to confession this next week. Of course I never ask why. I'm just grateful that people are wanting to square their souls with the Almighty. Especially in this case. I wondered if this was the beginning of her coming back to God."

"But she's been killed before this confession," observed Ames.

"Yes, but I am confident God will take into consideration her intention, may he have mercy on her soul," Lahey murmured.

Mounting the three stairs onto a landing, Ames took out his handkerchief and pushed at the door. It swung open on well-oiled hinges. Behind him, the priest made as if to go in, but Ames stopped him. The room they were looking into was a sharp contrast to the peaceful-seeming atmosphere outside. The cabin had been completely turned over. The one table was knocked on its side, and two wooden box benches against the wall had all their contents—blankets, heavy clothes, books—pulled out and strewn on the floor. Dishes had been flung out of the cupboard by the stove and lay shattered on the floor, buckets were turned over, and a vegetable bin was upset. There was an entrance to a second room, and Ames could already see that it had gotten the same treatment as this one.

"Father Lahey, I'm going to ask you to find me some sort of padlock. I'll need to take a few pictures, but I want to lock the cabin down and return with my boss. We'll need to go over the place thoroughly. I don't want people wandering through here." Back outside, Ames made some notes in his book. "Was she disliked by anyone in the village?" he asked.

The minister was silent for a few moments and then cleared his throat, looking behind him down the path, as if fearful he would be overheard. "Was she universally popular? No. I don't like to speak out of turn, really, and there are, you will appreciate my situation, things I couldn't speak of that will have been shared with me by my parishioners."

"For Pete's sake, Father. She's been murdered. We have no idea whether someone came from somewhere else, or if the killer is still here—a member of this community, even. I would very much appreciate it if you told me everything you know that might have any bearing on her death."

"Yes, I see," Lahey said, but was again silent. After a considerable time, he sighed and shifted his weight. "She lived here for over twenty-five years, Constable Ames. I can imagine in a small community like this there might have been tensions from time to time. I'd best get back and collect what information I can from the registry for you. I can tell you that nothing I have heard from anyone here extends to a murderous dislike of her."

While the priest was gone, Ames, annoyed at what he felt was the priest impeding his investigation, took pictures, walking carefully through the chaos so as not to disturb potential evidence. He saw a picture frame knocked over, glass shattered, on the floor in front of the narrow mantel by the small iron stove that occupied the back wall. He was surprised to see that the frame itself was silver. He knelt down and turned it over. The grainy sepia photograph showed three pretty young women, smiling for the camera and leaning over a fence at the base of a rising field with a few sheep and a whitewashed house with a dark roof along the ridge in the distance. The old country, he thought. It looked to have been taken in the early teens, he guessed. Was one of them Agatha Browning?

Leaving everything as it was, he closed the door of the cabin and went round to the back. He took a deep breath, as if he'd not been breathing properly in the tumult left by whoever had done this. The garden, as the priest had said, was lovely. Ames didn't know much about the names of plants, but he saw what he knew as daisies and some sort of rose bushes and some other tall flowers of a deep blue hue. Lupines? The name leaped at him from a buried memory of his grandmother's garden. There was also a vegetable garden with carrots, beans, peas, and, he assumed, potatoes. There were two wooden garden chairs and a small table against the cabin, and a shed farther into the line of trees. The shed contained buckets, shovels, a scythe, and small hand tools. He wondered, with a touch of melancholy, who would use them now. He sighed. There was no evidence of carnage in this quiet garden.

He turned toward the edge of the garden where the trees seemed to encroach, anxious to get back the space that had been cleared by this pioneering woman. He returned to the outhouse for a closer look. Behind it the ground was trampled and blood permeated the crushed grass. He could see that the trail of blood led into the woods they had just come through. He poked among the grasses and broken ferns for any sort of weapon, and then keeping well to the edge of the disturbed area, he carefully followed the trail back toward where she had gone, imagining her desperate progress into the forest. It appeared to him that Agatha Browning had been stabbed here and then, still alive, made the attempt to escape through the woods. The position of her arms suggested she had not been dumped, already dead, by someone trying to hide the body. Ames sat down on a squat wooden garden chair and began to fill out his notes.

"Constable Ames?" The priest was returning from the village and called out to him from lower down on the path.

Ames finished making a note of his suspicions and stretched his back out. He was tall, and sitting in an uncomfortable wooden chair was a strain.

"I think it's clear Mrs. Browning was not killed outright. She must have run to try to escape and been pushed over." Ames frowned suddenly. "Father, where did she keep this car you told me about?"

"She keeps . . . kept it parked just off the road where it turns down to the village. Now that you say it, did I see it there just now? Well, we can check on the way back down. That poor woman. If she hadn't lived so far out, someone in the village might have heard her scream." He took a deep breath and shook his head. "It's my first, you know. This sort of death . . . usually I attend to people in a hospital, or on their deathbeds at home. Or, even the very worst, a sick child. But never a . . . a murder. It's one thing in detective fiction, isn't it? So horrific to think of someone dying in this desperate and futile attempt to outrun evil." After a moment he held up a padlock and key. "I've brought you the lock, and I'd like to take some time and go through the parish papers more thoroughly. We possibly have more information about where she came from. Perhaps she still has family there."

Ames took the lock and then realized there was no hasp on the door, or any way to affix the lock. He wanted Darling to come and have a look. Could he leave the scene? "Does anyone have a telephone?"

"I'm afraid not. If they reopen the mill, I expect they will have to."

"I need to drive back to town to collect my inspector. Would you be able to keep an eye on the comings and goings of cars into the village from your church? I'd like to try to keep people away till I've come back."

The minister nodded. "I can, of course. How long will you be? I generally go back to town by six."

"We'll be back as quick as we can. What kind of car did she drive? I'll look out for it on the way back to the ferry."

"You know, I just don't think I saw it. So strange." Lahey's eyebrows came together and he shook his head. "It is a very old thing, something from the twenties I'm sure. She must have bought it went she first moved out here. Dark green."

Ames stood on the steps contemplating the silence of the forest when the priest had gone. Sun dappled the ground through the trees, and the scent of the pine needles warmed in the afternoon heat conveyed a sense that nothing bad had, or could, happen in such a peaceful place. He made his way back down the path to where he had parked his car, trying to imagine how anyone could want to live in such utter isolation. The police car was the only one parked on the grassy edge of the road. He looked around and could see no old dark green jalopy anywhere, and yet this must be where she would normally park it. In fact, there was an oil slick just a few feet away, where the grass had given up the ghost. Ames made a note and then got into his car and drove it down the hill, happy to see the cable ferry on the village side.

Once on board, he stepped out of his car and approached the ferryman, holding up his identification. The older man, with an unreadable face partially obscured by a scraggly growth of beard, coughed violently and then waited.

"Has anyone unusual been across in the last twenty-four hours?"

The ferryman turned his mouth down and thought. "They are all pretty unusual," he commented. He took out a handkerchief and wiped his dripping nose. "That old lady, Browning, she went over to Nelson last night and hasn't been back yet. I'd say that's unusual. She usually goes up to town in the morning, back well before three. Anyone in the three days before that I couldn't say."

"What time was this?" Ames asked, surprised. He would have said, at a guess, that the victim had been there at least overnight, if not a little longer.

"Ten, I guess. On my last run."

Ames frowned. "Did anyone unusual come over earlier yesterday, or the day or two before?"

"I couldn't say. Kept to my bed by the missus with this cold. Fat lot of good she did me. Couldn't wait to get back."

"Who fills in when you're sick?"

"Young Nobby from the gas station down the road." With extreme patience Ames established that "Nobby" was not his real name, and that the gas station was all the way down the road in Balfour.

DARLING SURVEYED THE scene in the cabin, now thoroughly dusted for prints. "Do you ever think, Ames, about what could come charging out of the underbrush from your past to lay waste to whatever life you've imagined you've built up for yourself?"

Ames had experienced, if the truth be known, a few hiccups with his penchant for pretty girls, but his romantic life was now nicely settled on Violet from the bank down the street from the police station. He could think of nothing more troubling in his past than the continued cold shoulder from his last girlfriend, April.

"It was a rhetorical question, Ames. Please don't bother trying to dredge up sordid episodes from your dating life. Tell me about your adventures today."

As Ames talked, Darling made a few notes himself, relieved to have something solid and in the present to expunge, at least for the moment, the incomprehensible insinuations of the government man, who in his continued reassurances that this was nothing to be concerned about, raised in Darling the liveliest misgivings.

Ames, he realized with pleasure, was delivering the information he had collected that morning in an extremely organized manner. There was hope for him yet. Darling felt a slight twinge of guilt that he had not noticed in the past how clear a thinker Ames was. After inspecting the cabin, Ames took Darling along the ghastly trail where the dead woman had passed her last desperate moments.

"What do you make of it, sir?"

"What do you make of it, Amesy? This is effectively your scene, and I must say, for a puppy, you've done a decent job."

So few and far between were these overt compliments from his boss that Ames smiled broadly.

"We're not at a comedy review, Ames. Let's have it."

Ames pulled himself together and cleared his throat. "Well, sir, I think the most unusual aspect of this case is the missing car. The ferryman said that the old lady drove off late last night and has not been back. But she obviously did come back, only without her car. Which, since I think she died sometime yesterday afternoon, can't be true. It must have been someone else. Certainly it appears she was planning to go somewhere."

Darling looked down toward the lake. "Why do you say that?"

"Father Lahey. He said she never wore anything but dungarees and boots, but she was dressed up, which, according to him, she only did if she was going into town."

"So she dresses up to go into town, let's say, gets murdered before she can go, and later she drives her car onto the ferry and doesn't come back. I see one or two problems with that scenario."

Ames smiled ruefully. "Sir." They stood silently for a moment. "Unless I'm wrong about the time of death. It could have happened after she got back. She met the murderer, brought him back with her, he killed her and drove her car away disguised as her."

"Gilly might be able to furnish a time of death," observed Darling. "Then we might more logically speculate about the sequence of events. If she didn't drive to town to pick up her murderer, he would have gotten here some way other than by car; if he took Agatha's car, we should be one car up."

"I'll check after to see if anyone has seen a car that they don't recognize sitting around here somewhere," Ames said. "I don't think it was an outright robbery," he continued.

"That's interesting. Why not? The cabin has been searched from top to bottom by the look of it."

"I know, but there was a lot of destruction. It feels, I don't know, angry, as if the person was looking for something and not finding it. I think the victim may have surprised the person and then tried to hide before she was seen, but the killer did see her and found her there, behind the outhouse. I think there was a bit of a battle. I thought I saw blood under the right-hand fingernails of the dead woman. I initially thought the stab wound looked bad enough that she'd been killed outright, but the evidence of the blood by the outhouse and along the underbrush is that she tried to get away."

"Well, well," Darling said noncommittally. "You could be right. And then, you might not be. We'd better go chat with the few residents of this place. I expect Gilly will confirm your suggestion that she clawed at her attacker. It would be helpful to know we are looking for someone with some nasty scratches."

GILLY, THE LACONIC pathologist upon whom the inspector depended, was even at that moment making notes and inspecting the body closely. He knew that Darling would be along demanding time of death details, and he was having difficulty. Anytime in the last forty-eight hours, he'd have said. He made notes and continued. He had recently taken to going out to crime scenes to evaluate the bodies in situ. It was unfortunate that he was absent at a family funeral this time. He would like to have seen exactly how she lay. The van boys had said they had had quite a nervous time of it fetching her out of the tangle of the forest. The area was full of half-buried sharp rocks and torn branches. The abrasions on her face and hands attested to the impact of some of that, anyway, but he would say that the wound, though initially appearing to be shallow, could have caused her to bleed to death. He could not see that her being pushed over alone would do the job, but it might if she was weak from loss of blood. Must have been dashed unpleasant, he thought, washing his hands. He'd go out to the drugstore for a soda to fortify himself for Darling's return.

DARLING AND AMES walked back down to the village and found the priest in a small office behind the altar of the church. He jumped up to greet them.

"I've been going through the records, which are sparse at the best of times as they mainly concern themselves with the ecclesiastical goings on. Births, christenings, weddings, and deaths, and this is quite literally all I can find. I've written it down for you. It is an entry from May of 1922 that a padre called Vicar Derrick made: Agatha Victoria Browning, Whitcombe, Dorset. There's not a single other entry that references her. Of course at the time, this place was a going concern with the mill here. There have been very few entries in the last few years."

Ames took the sheet of paper from Lahey. "We are going to need to talk to the people who live here now. Can you give us their names and tell us where they live?"

"That won't take long! There are not many families here, mostly older people who stayed on after the industry started to die down. It's mostly holiday homes now. A more harmless bunch I think you will be hard pressed to meet. By the way, I didn't see her old car in the usual place. I really don't understand it."

As they approached the first house they were to visit, names and locations in hand, Ames remarked, "I don't think a bunch of harmless older people are going to be happy that there might be a killer lurking around."

"With her car gone, we may be able to reassure them that he's decamped and will leave them in peace. The question still puzzling me is how he got here in the first place."

CHAPTER THREE

LANE PULLED HERSELF ONTO THE wharf and flopped, shivering, onto her towel. "It's always cold getting out no matter how hot the day is," she said to her friend Angela, who was sunning herself on a blanket while somehow managing to keep one eye on her three children. Philip, Rolf, and Rafe were collecting minnows in glass jars along the rocky edges of the beach below the wharf.

"That red bathing suit is very becoming on you. Has the inspector seen it yet?"

"Really, Angela. Have you nothing better to talk about? There's big news in India about their independence, after all. Or, if you prefer something more local, Alice Mather apparently found a bear rummaging through her garbage and didn't shoot it."

Angela sat up and shouted, "Not so far toward the point, boys! I want you where I can see you." She looked with interest at Lane. "Did she? How do you know that?"

"Eleanor of course. I'm sure it will go out with every piece of mail she hands out today."

"I have heard that her mister has locked up the rifle to keep her from any more mischief. She must have been furious to finally have a legitimate target and not be able to get at it. Now, when did you last talk to the inspector?"

Lane knew Angela meant well. It had been Angela's goal for the last year to see Lane happily settled into a romance. She gave herself part of the credit for the budding relationship between Lane and Inspector Darling of the Nelson Police, and she was eager to see how it was progressing. It was not so simple for Lane. Love had been a treacherous road for her, and she had felt acute embarrassment over her own naïveté in the disaster that had been her four-year affair while she was working for intelligence during the war. She had never wanted to be in love again, and yet love had found her unexpectedly, in her new home in Canada. She could not see her very new and fragile relationship with Darling as fodder for light-hearted banter, even with her friend Angela.

She closed her eyes and felt the sun begin to warm her. In fact, though she would never, well, at least not yet, tell Angela this, Darling had taken to phoning her every evening, at the end of his day. She still loved the lift she felt inside when she heard his voice at the end of the line.

"What are you up to?" He had said last night.

"I'm leaning against the wall in my hallway talking to you."

"You should get a new phone. You could be sitting in comfort by your Franklin."

"I never want to give up this phone. Some of my favourite people call me on it." She was, in fact, reluctant to give up her old-fashioned horn phone because she was astonished that an instrument that had been current when her parents were young children could still work.

"Am I?" Darling asked.

"Are you what?"

"One of your favourite people?"

She had wanted to keep up the banter, a safe harbour for them, but had been overwhelmed by a longing to have him there, with her. Then a ferry ride and thirty miles of dusty road between King's Cove and Nelson seemed an impossible distance.

"I wish you were here," she'd said.

There'd been a silence, and then Darling had said, "I'll come Saturday. We'll picnic by the lake. I may even kiss you. I'm desperate to kiss you now."

"Really darling, what will the party-line people think?"

"They will think that I love you. And they would be right."

LANE LAY LISTENING to the gently echoing lap of the water against the posts of the wharf and thought happily about Saturday. Three days away, and they would spend the whole day together. The distance had not begun to rankle completely, but she knew it would eventually. She dreaded that moment because she knew she could never leave her beloved white Victorian house or her endearing and eccentric neighbours in the idyllic peacefulness of King's Cove, and Darling could never live thirty miles from his work as an inspector in the Nelson Police.

SHE GLANCED AT the clock in her kitchen when the phone finally rang that evening, much later than was usual. Ten o'clock. She had nearly given up and taken her book and some cocoa to bed. She could tell instantly that something was wrong.

"What's happened?" Lane asked Darling.

He sighed. "Well, aside from the fact that I have, no, let me be accurate and get used to the idea, Ames has, a rather grisly murder near Harrop, I've had a strange visit today from someone 'in the government.' Frankly I'd far rather be working away on the murder. I'm sure it would intrigue you, though I don't like the parallels. It's an Englishwoman who's been homesteading outside this tiny place since just after the Great War. I imagine she came here to get away from something just like you did."

"Well, I'm not moving into town just on the off chance someone wants to murder me in thirty years! And why is this Ames's case? Not that I'm not pleased for him . . . you never give him enough credit."

"Ames had to go look into it because the government man came just as we were setting out. He managed to convey the message that I'd better stay right there and talk to him. Very peculiar. I may have to go back to bloody England." He recounted his unsettling interview. "He was asking a lot of pointed questions about a crash I had in '43. My plane was shot down at night, and I managed to bump it home in a field just behind enemy lines. All but two of us got out in one piece, but the Germans figured some of the crew had survived and came looking for us. My gunner, a nice, long-suffering young man who was extraordinarily good at his job, was shot and I had to leave him. A second man, Jones, was never found. He went up with the plane. The rest of us managed to get to safety with no small amount of help from a local farmer. We got home, I made a full report, and then I went to the boy's family myself rather than leave it to the War Office. By good fortune, the farmer managed to recoup the boy's body, so the family could have a proper funeral. I admit, I always thought I would have been questioned more closely about the loss of the plane. When it didn't happen before I demobbed, I assumed it never would.

"Suddenly now, this absolute cartoon of a government functionary is making insinuations, but not making them, if you see what I mean. Implying by constant reassurance that this is all procedure, that I am guilty of something. Good God . . . it's the kind of language I use myself with suspects. I can't tell if they think I did something to the plane, or worse. Mishandling the business of the death of the crewmen, perhaps. So many people die around you in war, but that one still keeps me up at night. I think because Evans in particular was so young. I felt extremely responsible. He had a horrible job. A gunner is crammed into a tiny space, generally in the freezing cold. But he never complained. And he was good."

"God, how beastly for you. What is the cartoon saying is going to happen?" Lane was going through an unfathomable series of emotions. They had never really talked about their wars, and this story elicited in equal measure fear for how Darling might have died, and relief that he had not. She also understood his ongoing feeling of guilt.

She often woke up late at night from nightmares, unable to fall back sleep, assailed by waves of guilt . . . about what? She could never really remember in the daylight. And more pronounced than these feelings was anxiety.

She had a great deal of experience with secretive and suspicious deskmen, as she thought of them, who seemed to think themselves capable of monitoring and really understanding what went on in the field. She remembered the uneasy feeling she had sometimes that these people had control of her life in ways she would never understand. She often felt that her very safety could be compromised by some dark, political backroom machinations that people like her could never be privy to. Her relief when the war ended and she had turned her back forever on the intelligence branch had been profound. She realized she had come as far away as Canada to start a new life because she felt that none of it could follow her that far. What seemed to be happening to Darling upended this sense of safety, almost as much as having her wartime handler come all the way out the year before to try to take her back to something like her old job. New enemy, and all the same old deskmen in charge. She had not been interested, and the handler had left angry and disappointed. There was no getting away, apparently. She sighed.

"That's the thing," Darling said. "He ended by saying he would consult with whatever forces of hell sent him out in the first place and let me know, that I might have to 'pop' back to England to just clear up one or two things. I can't help feeling like I am about to be under arrest. The whole thing has certainly shaken my smug policeman sense of superiority. I'm positively humbled. Didn't you mention Kafka to me last year? That's how I feel."

"I'll come up to town," Lane said.

"No, don't be silly. It's late. I won't be fit company. I expect to hear from him tomorrow, and then I'll let you know."

"Listen, darling, if you are going to be tossing and turning anyway, use the time to write down everything that you remember about that incident. Did you keep a copy of the report by any chance?"

She was right, of course. He wouldn't sleep, and he'd be better off trying to organize his thoughts. In truth he'd have loved Lane to come up, but their relationship had not quite reached that footing yet, and he did not want the next phase of it to be dictated by some crisis he was having. "I did actually. We weren't really supposed to, but I made a carbon copy because I wanted to make sure I remembered details if I was asked about it. Of course at that time I expected to be asked about the performance of the plane. My report is in a trunk in the attic. I'd better pull down the ladder and crawl up there."

"Don't fall down."

"Will you visit me in the hospital if I do?"

"I would try to make time, of course. But the lake is lovely for swimming at this time of year. And I'm learning to garden from the Hughes ladies. I wouldn't want to miss my lessons. How is Ames getting on? It must be galling for you to have him out there on the scene without you."

Fighting back the image of her swimming, he said, "You'd be very proud of your Amesy. Very organized. I

suspect with enough dumb luck he could even solve it."
Darling paused and said soberly. "He may have to if I have
to go back to Blighty. I'll tell him to call you periodically
to discuss it. I know you don't like being left out of any
murder investigation."

Oxfordshire, April 1943

"THERE YOU ARE, sir. I think he's right," Jones said, speaking of the briefing officer. "Coming in from the northwest
might give us more of an element of surprise." Jones
thumped his finger on the area on the ordinance map
immediately surrounding the warehouse target. "I have a
photograph as well. It shows exactly what we'll be looking
for. It should be a doddle." Jones pulled an aerial photo
out of a manila envelope and put it next to the map.

Darling leaned in and looked at the photo, fascinated
by its close correspondence to the two documents. "That's
rather good. How did you get hold of that?"

"Frogs, sir. Someone was showing off with an aeroplane
before the war. I managed to get hold of a pile of photos
from this region. I always hoped one of them would come
in handy. The photo people are snapping more pictures
now, but not specifically of this region."

"It means circling a fair way north to come at it as they
suggest. It will add time," Darling said.

"Yes, sir. But it will be quicker if we can reduce the risk
of being spotted coming in the usual way."

The other pilots had already left the briefing room.
Darling and Jones were the last two. The rest of his crew
were preparing in the locker room.

"Well done, Jones. Always have something up your sleeve. Better run along. See you at nineteen hundred."

Darling sat back watching the dusk settle on the airfield outside. He had developed a habit of meeting with Jones for a few minutes so that he could get the sense of the territory he was to fly over. Jones was like a good-natured merchant peddling black market socks at the Saturday market. He always seemed to have something to augment the official maps and photos they were provided, and while curious, Darling had mostly stopped asking how he had acquired them. "A wink and a nod, sir, a wink and a nod," Jones would say.

When Jones had left, Darling used the few moments of solitude he had to go over in his brain what he'd seen, mentally preparing. In another half hour the small convoy of Lancasters would be roaring through the dark in formation, the North Sea a dark and sinister void below them. He thought about how that formation made them seem invincible, tied together as if by invisible cords, a rumbling blanket of destruction fanning out across the dark occupied French countryside.

CHAPTER FOUR

DARLING SLEPT LITTLE THAT NIGHT. He'd pulled the ladder down from the attic and spent a precarious evening avoiding stepping between the beams and going through the ceiling. He moved the trunk that he'd have preferred never to see again to the one small part of the attic that had a proper floor. Even though the war had been over for a little under two years, he felt like it was a distant and alien event, and he was filled with wonder as he pulled his flight jacket from the trunk that he had ever been a part of it. Why had he kept his Thermos and burn gloves, he wondered, or all the other little paraphernalia of his former life? Aside from the camaraderie and genuine love for his crew, and, if the truth be known, his Lancasters, he had found nothing else appealing in his wartime experience. Holding his uniform brought the whole thing flooding back.

He had gotten together with fellow vets a few times at the legion when he had first returned to civilian life. Touching down in his old life had felt alien at first, but he came to realize that for many of them the war had been the highlight of their lives, and they missed a sense, they said, of truly being alive. He could not bear to think that his wartime experience was going to be the one great thing he'd have to look back on, so he tried to throw himself back into his "real" life as quickly as possible. Policing had an intensity of its own, and he saw its advantages. For many of the men, a return to civilian life meant a return to working in mills, on the railways, in farming, or in offices. Perhaps it was harder for them.

At the bottom of the trunk he found what he was looking for. A manila folder full of paper. He took this down the ladder, without falling off, obviating the necessity of Lane having to make a difficult decision between swimming or visiting him in hospital. He switched on his kitchen table lamp and began to reread his notes about the crash landing on that horrible day.

When he had finished, he stacked the papers, squaring the edges, his usual way of aiding his thinking at work. The report was, as he expected it would be, complete and detailed. Was this what he was being called to account for? Surely they had the report. In fact, his superiors had discussed it with him in detail and had thanked him for his thoroughness, remarking, if he recalled, that they wished reports from others were so well done. Certainly nothing was missing in his accounting of the crash, the condition of the plane, their subsequent escape, the loss of one man in the crash itself, or the death of his gunner from German fire. In fact, he thought grimly, they'd given him a medal when the whole thing was over.

He poured himself a Scotch and stood, looking out at the lights of the town below him. Had there been anything unusual about that trip, besides the obvious difference of having crashed? Perhaps the fact of the crash had made any other unusual aspect of that flight so minor that he had forgotten it somehow when he wrote the report.

He took his memory back to before they set off that night. He tried to recall every detail: getting kitted out, whom he had spoken with, what he might have said to the men as they got into position. It was then that he remembered the only anomaly in that mission. Harlow was in sick bay. Some ghastly intestinal thing. Darling had stopped by to see him. Harlow had wanted to come, he remembered, and Darling had told him he certainly didn't want him along making everyone else sick. He'd made a joke about Henry the Fifth's men all having flux at the siege of Harfleur and that he didn't want history repeating itself, which had gone completely over Harlow's head.

"You read history at university, did you, sir?" the patient had said with weary sarcasm.

Neville Anthony had been assigned to replace Harlow as engineer on that mission. Try as Darling might, he could think of nothing else. Anthony had performed admirably, Darling recalled. Showed real leadership in the post-crash mayhem.

The next morning he woke from his few short hours of uneasy sleep still exhausted and vaguely headachy. He looked with distaste at the stale loaf of bread that was the only source of nourishment, and decided he'd pick breakfast up at the café next to the station. He could invite Ames along. His constable could happily eat a second breakfast moments after consuming his first. Darling would focus his energies on going over next steps on the dead Englishwoman up the lake. They should hear from Gilly today about how she died. Happy to have these distractions before him, he scowled at the folder containing his crash report, put on his hat, and went out the door.

"WELL, WHAT DO we think, Ames? Murder most foul, certainly, but with what motive?" Darling drank gratefully from the mug of strong coffee April had placed before him with a large smile. She had no such smile for Ames. Darling whispered, "It's been almost a year. Even I am beginning to feel sorry for you."

Ames, used to his boss's insinuations about his personal life, rose above this remark and said, "I really can't help thinking there was something personal about it. That she knew her attacker. It's what you said yesterday, sir. Something coming out of the past."

Darling drew in a breath to speak, but Ames put his hand up. "I know, sir, before you say anything, I've no real evidence for that, and one shouldn't base any conclusions on feelings."

"As a matter of fact, I was about to say that if, as you say, there was something rather savage about the scene that seemed more than someone surprised in a robbery, then I don't say you should disregard feelings. They are part of a thinking man's toolkit. But one shouldn't try to make evidence fit them."

They ate their scrambled eggs and toast in companionable silence, Ames enjoying, for a record second day in a row, a feeling of being approved of by Darling. As he plopped his napkin onto his empty plate, he was emboldened to say, "I think we should go over the interviews I did again, and see if what Gilly tells us moves this along a bit." Darling looked in wonder at Ames, Lead Investigator, and called for the bill. "I'll get this," he said. "This once!" He added.

BACK AT THE office, Darling made the surprise move of suggesting they meet in Ames's little office. "We might as well. Saves moving your file back and forth. I suppose I'd better bring my own chair?"

Ames had two chairs in his office, but one was always covered in his "out" pile of papers.

"Give me a minute, sir!" Ames exclaimed, darting into his office. Darling moved on to drop his jacket and hat off on the coat rack behind his own desk. He felt his office was still tainted by the government man's presence. His life was upended, and though he knew he was being indulgent to Ames, Darling was going to have to leave this investigation in his hands and wasn't sure how he felt about Ames's abilities when left entirely on his own.

"Why don't you give me the gist of the people you talked to," Darling said, sitting on the now-empty chair. He could see that Ames had taken the pile of papers and files and stacked it on the window ledge, where it now rested precariously. He ought to put in a bookshelf for Ames, he thought.

"There aren't too many people there, sir, as you saw. The good Father," he opened his book to scan his notes, "went up to the forest above the cabin on a whim. I didn't ask if he stopped by Mrs. Browning's or just went directly up along the path. He said he wanted to see where they might put the new sawmill someone is talking about. I suppose he's telling the truth. Man of the cloth."

"Supposing is not always the best strategy for a detective, Ames. You have to know as much as you can, and even then it will still be hard to know what actually happened. Never mind. Go on."

Unsettled and glancing at his boss, Ames continued. "He said he came to see her a few times a month to check in and see if she needed anything. He worried that she was getting older. But he did comment that she was very healthy and sure-footed for her age. I don't really think he has anything to do with it, sir. Why would he telephone us?"

Darling shrugged. "That's as may be, Ames. It wouldn't be the first time. But on principle I agree with you. It isn't very priestly behaviour. Even if he was someone from her past out to get revenge, he's had twenty years to do it. All right, go on."

"I talked to a Mr. and Mrs. Elliot. They live opposite the church. Old as Methuselah. They said they knew Mrs. Browning well enough. Saw her in the store sometimes and exchanged a few words. They didn't see anyone they didn't know that day. They were very nervous and asked me if they were safe. I suggested they keep their door locked at night, in case."

"Yes, well, we don't really know what time this attack happened. Go on."

Ames continued doggedly. "The only other person I talked to was a gentleman who moved recently into one of the empty houses. He's from a forestry company. Says he's here to survey the situation, as they are thinking of building a new mill. He showed me his identification and his notes. He did say he'd seen the cabin because it lies along a route where they might put in access to some part of mill. He had a note that he was going to talk to whoever lived there, but he hadn't had time yet. His company had sent letters to everyone, and she never answered hers, so they sent several more. He'd already spoken to one other property owner near the ferry and hadn't got to Mrs. Browning yet. I suppose wanting the property as access is a motive."

"Usually they offer to buy people out, not stab them and leave them for dead. Well, I had a similar set of unhelpful visits to three other families. They've all been there since the twenties. They worked here on the railway till they retired and are able to scrape by on their pensions. So that brings us to the deepest mystery of all. The car Mrs. Browning drove was not there, and the ferryman swore she herself drove it across yesterday afternoon and has not returned. And he does not recall anyone unusual coming over in the last month, let alone the last twenty-four hours. However, he was not on the job for three days prior. Someone he called 'Nobby,' who turns out to be a young fellow called Nathan Bannon, who normally works at the gas station in Balfour but unfortunately has gone out to the coast for a week to look into going to university. I'll speak to him when he gets back. Oh, and no extra car anywhere."

GILLY'S REPORT WAS, as ever, succinct. "The victim was in her seventies, very thin as you can see, but overall in good health. Quite muscular in fact. It's clear she put up a fight. She was slashed with a kitchen-type knife. Something smaller than a bread knife and larger than a paring knife. The assailant plunged the knife into the space just below the shoulder and then pulled the knife down and across toward the heart. It was certainly not the work of an expert. More of a slash in the end than a stab. At a guess I'd say there was a struggle. The assailant, whom I'll call right-handed, meant perhaps to stab at the heart, but the victim was fighting and twisting, and we ended up with this mess. She certainly bled to death, though there are abrasions on the face and hands, but you found her face down on the floor of a messy forest, so those could have happened when she fell, or was pushed, into it. All happened in the last, I'm going to hazard, forty-eight hours."

"In a way this supports Ames's theory that there was something impromptu and frenzied about the whole thing," said Darling, looking with interest at the woman's face. The vicar had said she was rumoured to come from the aristocracy. Was that something one could see on the visage?

"I wouldn't say 'frenzied' necessarily. That might imply someone stabbing a victim many times, but there is certainly something unrehearsed, as if a fight broke out, and the assailant had the physical advantage. It could certainly be committed by a strong woman, or by a man unused to fighting or violence but roused to sudden anger."

THE LONG SUMMER light was being pushed across Elephant Mountain by the encroaching shadows of evening, and Darling stood at the living room window in his house on the hill, watching the engulfing twilight, feeling it as a metaphor for this moment in his own life. He had not phoned Lane yet with the news, and he had left his bag half-packed on his bed, desperate to see the last of the sun before nightfall. As he analyzed his own feelings, he saw that the worst thing about the whole business was the unknown. He had gone over and over the events of that deadly night in '43 and still could not divine the source of the government man's "unanswered questions."

He turned and sat down at the small table where his telephone was and picked up the receiver.

"Inspector," said Lane.

"Maybe not for long," he said after a pause.

"Whatever is the matter? You sound ghastly! It's not that business with the government man?"

"It is indeed. How perspicacious of you."

"What's he said?"

"I'm off to England. They've 'reopened' an investigation. I didn't know there'd been an investigation in the first place."

"Into the crash? There were plenty of downed planes. Why should yours be any different? Except that you seem to have survived it. That must be unusual."

"I did, yes, thank you for noticing, as did most of the rest of the crew, barring Jones and Evans." Darling trailed off. Was that it? Was it Evans's death they were interested in? The questions he was asked were very oblique, if so.

"What is it?" asked Lane.

"Well, I've been thinking the whole time it's the plane crash they are questioning, but now I wonder. There was an odd question about whether I'd moved Evans's body. A man called Anthony and I moved him just after we got out, to get him away from the plane. He was alive. We were under attack, and I ordered everyone away; I stayed back, covering them, and to protect Evans. He was too wounded to run, so I stayed with him till it was safe to carry him out. When I went to pick him up, I saw he was dead. I felt badly, but I beat a hasty retreat. That was the last I saw of him. Later I learned a French farmer had collected him."

"They are seriously making you go back? Is it the police, or the military police, or even, God help you, intelligence?"

"This is like one of those multiple choice questions in physics where you can't begin to know what the answer is, so you eliminate the least likely. Let's eliminate intelligence. That leaves the police or the military."

"Something that happened has gone into the 'crime' column for some reason. But why you? You'd be the last person I'd look at."

"Thanks for your faith in me."

"A girl knows these things. So, when are you going?"

"I'm going out to the coast by train tomorrow and then flying to Montreal and thence to London."

Lane was silent, her heart sinking. "So soon! Well, I wish you weren't," she said at last.

"I know," he said—so softly that she felt his voice inside her. Another silence.

"Who will I talk to every evening?"

Darling had to pull himself together. "Your irrepressible friend Angela. No doubt she will get to work finding a replacement for me the minute I'm gone. Your friends the Armstrongs, your in loco grand-parentis. You can take up new pursuits instead of meddling with things that don't concern you. Speaking of which, I jokingly told Ames he could call you if he got stuck with that murder up the lake. I wish I hadn't. He'll jump at the chance to speak to his beloved Miss Winslow. You'll not have a moment's peace."

Whitcombe, July 1905

"YOU'RE RUNNING A risk, setting up outside. I don't care if it is his first time here, we'll hardly make a good impression if we drown him." Agatha stood with her sister Mary surveying the tea table, set out on the lawn under the willow at the back of the house. Five rattan chairs were in a semicircle around it, facing the view of the river at the bottom of the garden and the rising meadow on the other side. The air was thick and warm, sun filtering through the leaves onto the table, but Agatha's misgivings were focused on the dense blue-black roll of cloud that was building up beyond the meadow.

"It'll give him a good taste of the mad family he's marrying into. Poor Lucy. She's been in a flap for days. She's terrified we won't approve of him. She's upstairs now making poor Tilly pin and unpin her hair over and over."

"I can't see why. We're not marrying him. Why should we need to approve of him? What's he called again?"

"God, Agatha, you might make an effort! Alphonse Henderson."

"What kind of sadist would name a child 'Alphonse'? I'll bet you any money he's an absolute pillock. Just what you'd expect Lucy to drag home."

"Try to be nice. Father is in the barn. He's going to need to be cleaned up before tea, or Lucy will never forgive him. I'll go."

When Mary was gone, Agatha sank into a chair and pulled her white skirt up over her knees to cool down. The air seemed suddenly close and thick. She was certain there would be a storm. Lucy was so intent on making an impression. What did it matter? Lucy would marry and go off to Yorkshire or wherever the blazes Alphonse came from, and the rest of us will stay on, sinking quietly into spinsterhood. She watched the river through the trees at the bottom of the garden, the water moving swiftly, always hurrying to the sea, always being anchored right there at the end of their garden. Like her own heart, she thought, always away to some far-off place, always stuck here.

The shadow that fell across her face shook her from her reverie, and she looked up to see a young man in a pale linen suit smiling down at her. "I hope you don't mind. The maid told me to come through." He glanced with amusement at her exposed legs. "A casual household. What a relief. I was worried I should have to be on my best behaviour."

Agatha hurriedly pulled her skirt down and stood up. "This is a good start, isn't it? I'm Agatha, Lucy's elder sister. I think you'll find the rest of them much more appropriate, if they ever get out here." She offered her hand. "Please do sit down. I think if we are very, very patient, someone will eventually bring out the tea."

He sat down and stretched out his legs. "It's heavenly here! I'm Alphonse Henderson, but you'll have guessed that already. I expect I'm the chief exhibit here today." He looked at her, tilting his head slightly, and then looked away.

It was his voice, Agatha decided, that was much the most attractive thing about him. It had a deep, soft resonance that carried. She was impressed with Lucy's taste. His dark brown hair was parted on the right side and swept unostentatiously away from his face. He was not fussy, his hazel eyes were direct. What did he do, again? She wished she'd paid more attention when Lucy babbled about him.

"Yes, I'm afraid you are. We'll try to be kind, though you will appreciate our restraint. It is hard not to tease one's youngest sister abominably. Did you have a good journey?"

"Splendid. Beautiful countryside on the way. I feel like I could live with utter contentment in a place like this. Of course for all I know, you're desperate to escape."

"Well, you've found me out in no time! But happily Lucy is not, so you may get your wish, if it's the quiet country life you hanker after."

He turned to her with interest, and Agatha felt the shock of his eyes looking directly into hers. God, we are sheltered, she thought. She'd met young men, certainly, among the scattered local families. But they were as familiar to her as her own sisters. No wonder Lucy fell for him.

"Where would you go?" he asked.

"Somewhere big and airy. The Americas, perhaps. I like a view."

"So not the big city."

"I've been up to London. I felt the world was closing in on me. And it was dirty."

"That's a shame. You must come up and visit me one time. There are some really lovely bits you might have missed."

Voices behind them signalled the arrival of the rest of the family. Their father had been cajoled out of his work clothes and into a suit, and Lucy was looking as lovely and nervous as an eighteen-year-old could look, her golden hair swept becomingly into a knot on top of her head. She wore, like her sisters, a white linen tea dress, though her collar had delicate forget-me-nots embroidered on it instead of lace. Agatha felt a rush of fondness for her. For her loveliness and vulnerability at this turning moment of her life. It was too late for her, at nearly thirty, ever to have such a moment herself, but she was happy that her beloved Lucy did.

THE STORM HAD come in the form of a heavy rain that drove them all, laughing and carrying crockery and damp cake, into the house. But it had come later too, when Alphonse was gone and Lucy lay sobbing on her bed in her darkening room. The storm clouds mingled now with the coming night, and Agatha, who was sitting on the bed trying to console her desperate sister, looked around for the lamp.

"Let me get the lamp. You can't lie miserably in the dark like this."

"I don't want light," Lucy wailed. "Why did he not talk to Father? Why?"

"Darling, I'm sure it means nothing at all. You can't expect he'd do it right at the first visit."

"But he said he would. He said that's why he wanted to come down. He said!"

Agatha had no answer. She sat with her hand on her sister's back, looking out at the storm.

CHAPTER FIVE

THE PLATFORM OF THE NELSON train station bustled with travellers going to the coast. Some stood in awkward silence next to those who had come to send them off, their goodbyes said, the travellers looking anxiously at the train pulling in. A group of young women were talking, seemingly all at once. Lane heard "you'd better get a new hat before he sees you" and looked toward them. Off to join a fiancé? Or better, take up a job in the city? She almost envied the girls' sense of purpose, whatever the cause. She herself felt like a leaf caught in an eddy, swirling uselessly, waiting for Darling who was in the station buying his ticket.

She wore her yellow cardigan over her shoulders. It had been vain of her to wear her summer dress with the calla lilies, and she regretted it now, feeling ostentatious, and wrapping her arms tightly across her chest in a subconscious effort to hide. How had she succumbed to the temptation to look her prettiest for a very new lover who was going away? In a moment he was beside her, dressed in his one brown suit. He put his bag on the ground and stood before her, turning his hat in his hands, his charcoal eyes filled with longing and worry. The train had come to rest and hissed loudly. Travellers moved forward expectantly, waiting for passengers to alight so that they might get the best seats.

"I want to kiss you," he said.

"You always say that."

"I always, every minute, want to. It's probably very unseemly behaviour for Nelson's dour inspector."

"Well, you'd better get on with it, unseemly or not, or you'll be left behind."

Darling put his hat on the suitcase and pulled her close. "I can't bear to leave you," he murmured into her hair.

Lane could feel tears welling up. "Look, this won't do." She kissed him, embarrassed by her own desperation to keep him there, to memorize the softness and passion of his lips. "I'll look an idiot stood here weeping like an ingénue. Get off with you." Anyway, she wanted to say, I'll see you soon. "Wire me as soon as you get there. Promise."

"God, you are beautiful. I will always remember you in that dress." He stroked her cheek.

"For God's sake, Inspector. Now you're being dramatic. You'll be back in no time." How Lane wished that were true, but there was a sinister quality to this sudden polite summons to London that really frightened her.

"Look after Amesy," Darling said, recovering slightly and putting his hat on.

"I'll bake him cookies and knit him socks," she said, wiping away the tear that had escaped.

"I thought you didn't bake. I'll be very cross if I come back and find him with his stockinged feet on my desk and guzzling your cookies." The stationmaster made the last call for boarding. Darling picked up his suitcase and looked at her as if he were memorizing every plane of her face. "I love you."

"Me too," she said. He turned and boarded the train.

She did not stand and weep on the station platform but instead went outside and sat on a bench, watching cars pulling back up the hill, their travellers dropped off and safely away. The idea that had lodged in her head as she waved at Darling, until his face in the window disappeared under the reflection of the sun on the glass, would not now leave her, and it alarmed her. Of course. She could use her grandparents as the excuse; she had not seen them for more than a year. But she was too honest to disguise from herself that she could not bear to see him go. He would be appalled, think her clingy, and might be angered that she couldn't trust him to look after himself. But right at the centre of her mental struggles, one truth stood out. If he was in trouble, the connections she had in England might be able to help him.

She would stop in to see Ames. But first things first. She went resolutely to her car and drove to the post office to write and mail off a letter to her grandmother, announcing that she would be there within the fortnight.

London

THE TAXI PULLED up outside a row of houses and the driver called into the back, "There you are, gov, number five." Darling pushed some coins through. He had spent the ride from the aerodrome at Croydon reminding himself about the workings of pounds, shillings, and pence and staring out at the city he'd not expected to see again for many years. Buildings that had been bombed still lay in heaps, though the roads around them had been cleared, but in spite of the lingering mess, the streets had an air of getting on with things. Their route had taken them through the City, and men with bowler hats were pouring out of buildings, talking and laughing. Young women met on the steps of buildings and lit up cigarettes. He had glanced at his watch. It must be noon. He should have changed it to local time.

"Thanks," Darling said, pulling his suitcase out after himself. He'd wired his friend Rudyard about his visit to London and had been told he was not to think of staying anywhere else. The door opened even before he mounted the steps. A woman of his age, with a great pouf of permanently curled blond hair framing a round and cheerful face, came onto the steps.

"You must be Rudy's friend Frederick. Come in! I'm Sandra Donaldson, Rudy's wife, for my sins." She offered a hand with deep red fingernails. "I was so pleased to hear you were coming over. Rudy talks about you all the time. Here. Give us your hat and I'll show you up." She led him up a narrow flight of stairs to a room at the top of the landing.

"Here you are, then." She pushed open the door to a small, neat room with one window that looked over the narrow back garden. The flowered bedspread and matching curtains gave the room an air of cheerfulness that Darling hoped would be a refuge from whatever decidedly cheerless business brought him here.

"This is lovely. Thank you so much for allowing me to impose on you."

"Oh, nonsense. The loo's down the hall. Have a bit of a wash-up and come down for a cup of tea and some lunch. You must be exhausted."

He was exhausted. He put his hat down on the desk by the window and looked longingly at the bed. He knew if he succumbed and lay down for even a moment, he would be lost to sleep and would wake groggy and disoriented at some inconvenient time. Instead he took out his sponge bag and went down the dark hallway to the bathroom. When he had washed and shaved, he stopped a moment to gaze at himself in the mirror. He could see the bags under his eyes. It was not just the journey over, through most of which he had been unable to sleep. It was the anxiety before he left that had rendered his nights long and without peace. It was leaving Lane, who had become a touchstone, a growing centre around which he organized his sense of self. Now suddenly he was just himself again, alone, self-sufficient. He had not understood how much she had grown to be a part of his world until he confronted the sudden void that her absence left. He turned away and pulled himself back to the present moment, pressing his lips into a grim line. Whatever was about to happen, he knew he would need all his wits about him.

Darling and Donaldson sat in the warm, dim light of the sitting room nursing Scotches. Sandra Donaldson had taken herself off to bed, and the two men occupied matching chairs in front of the fire. They had been friends since flight school, a friendship that intensified as the losses in the air diminished their number throughout the war. Both had been pilots and, aside from the attraction, which had been almost immediate, their deeper understanding of the feelings a pilot developed toward his crew and his plane brought them a level of common experience that infused their understanding of each other. Where they should have been able to sit in companionable silence, this silence was full of anxiety.

"I don't understand, Darling. What's this all about?"

"Hanged if I know. A smarmy party turned up in Nelson claiming to be from the Canadian government, a claim I doubted immediately, given his posh public school accent, and began to grill me about the accident. I agreed to come here on my own for 'further investigation' because I honestly didn't know how much power he wields in his velvet gloves. For all I know he could have had me arrested there and then. For what I am at a loss to explain." Darling swallowed the remains of his Scotch and did not prevent his friend from refilling his glass.

"I mean, what are they hinting at?" Donaldson asked. "Cowardice at the scene of the accident? Fault for the crash in the first place? You lost a couple of men as I recall. Is it something to do with that?"

"I've been through my report ten different ways, I've written out every bloody thing I can remember about that night, and I'm stumped. I feel like I'm playing a game with someone who has half the high cards up their sleeve. They have something on me they haven't deigned to share with me, only since I can't think of a single thing I did wrong, I can't begin to guess what they're on about."

Donaldson got up, put his glass on the mantle, and spoke with sudden decision. "You need a solicitor. My flight engineer, Drake Higgins, was in the law before the show. He's gone back to it. I'll call him first thing in the morning."

Darling wanted to say, "I'm sure it's not as serious as all that," but he was beginning to feel, all things considered, that it was. He leaned forward and took a folded piece of paper out of his wallet. "Listen. If anything happens, I mean, something serious, like I get arrested, I want you to contact this person. She lives in the countryside, but she's on the telephone. But only in extremis. I don't want her bothered otherwise."

Unfolding the paper Donaldson read it and then glanced at Darling. "You're a dark horse. You never told me about her."

"You can stop being coy. It doesn't become you. I met her last year when she came out to Canada from here, as a matter of fact. She's intelligent and deserves to know if I'm not coming back."

"Well, well. I thought after that balls-up with Gloria you'd be off women for a while. Good for you. You deserve someone wonderful. I bet she's a looker, too." Gloria had been Darling's disastrous wartime romance. It was the event that had taught him something essential about himself; that he could never be casual about love.

Darling refrained from discussing Lane's looks, though he felt his heart ache at the memory of her standing in a slant of sun in her sitting room in the house by the lake, her dark hair framing her exquisite cheekbones.

"I DON'T KNOW why we went through all this palaver. He could simply have been arrested by Canadian authorities." Andrew Sims, a detective inspector seconded from Scotland Yard into Special Investigations Branch, grumbled. He was unhappy because he'd been given a cramped office in the basement of the War Office that was at the farthest remove from an entrance to the building, and it had taken him twenty minutes to find it in the warrens that were the corridors of the Horse Guards Avenue behemoth. He wanted the whole business over with and to get back to his office with the window at the Yard.

"Well, sir, we don't strictly know the level of his involvement. He evinced genuine puzzlement when I interviewed him," Jensen said.

"Rubbish. It's open and shut. We have a completely impartial witness who saw him do it. He may have pulled the wool over your eyes with his genuine puzzlement, but it won't work with me. I want him here first thing tomorrow so we can get this business over with."

"I appreciate the severity of the evidence. However, he has a distinguished war record and deserves to have the case thoroughly investigated."

Sims stood up. "If you're questioning my ability to conduct a murder investigation . . ."

"I do beg your pardon, Detective Inspector Sims. That was not my intention at all. Please, let me show you to the canteen, where you can have a decent tea, and I'll assemble all the paperwork and bring it here. Darling knows to come here at nine o'clock. Anything else you require will be at your disposal." Crikey, Jensen thought. At least ten civilian police seconded to War Office work through the war years, and I get the one with the thorn in his paw.

CHAPTER SIX

—————

JANE DID NOT FIND AMES at the police station on the morning Darling left. She collected some packets of chocolate-covered biscuits for the Armstrongs and the Hughes, some milk, a tin of coffee, and just a few other essentials to keep body and soul together until she herself set out to the old country. In the two days that followed, she found her suitcase where she'd stored it in the attic and opened it on the chair in her bedroom, and there her forward motion stopped.

Now she sat, exhausted, at her kitchen table, looking out at the lake, her hands wrapped around a mug of coffee. The morning was ushering in a day of indeterminate weather, and clouds gathered in the folds of the mountains on the far shore. She should really get a wireless, she thought. No doubt they offered news and weather reports. She often found the Armstrongs sitting in their snug kitchen listening to radio dramas or classical music, Kenny's feet up on the fender of the stove, but she resisted the temptation. She found the silence soothing. It felt expansive, like the vast sense of physical space she had found in Canada. The silence gave her a kind of spiritual space.

She drank the last of the coffee and swallowed the anxiety that had been growing in her since her decision to go to home. No, not home. This was home. Her anxiety had manifested itself in being unable to make any decisions about what to pack. Her initial plan had been to go to Scotland to see her grandparents, and this would require warm clothes—wool stockings, her tweed suit, trousers—and she laid these out. But she knew she really wanted to be with Darling in London. She feared that her notion that she could be of help would prove to be ludicrous. She didn't have the least idea of what was happening to him, and she hadn't heard from him. She stood in the hallway and glared at her blameless ancient phone. Ames would know. She had to go into town to pick up her tickets from the agency. She would stop and see him. He had to have heard from Darling. He wouldn't have left Ames struggling completely on his own with a murder case. She tried to dismiss what his wiring Ames but not her implied about her importance to him. She was being small-minded. She tried to remember whether her workmates had been more important to her than Angus, the man with whom she'd had the secret and ultimately disastrous affair during the war, but knew they weren't. But then she had worked in an atmosphere of oppressive secrecy that disrupted normal relations completely. And perhaps it was different for men.

AMES, SHE COULD see, was unreservedly delighted to see her. Had she even detected relief? He pulled out a chair and then hovered nervously for a moment.

"Should I get some tea up here? Coffee?"

"Not unless you want some. I drank a whole pot of the stuff this morning." Ames sank into his chair. She watched him. He had changed. He had a new cast of worry around his eyes. It made him look older and more serious. She wasn't sure this was an improvement on the usual sunny and unwavering optimism with which he approached the world. "Have you heard from His Nibs?" she asked.

"No, I have not. And I can't call him because I don't know where he is. He said he was staying with a friend. Some pilot he was in the action with. He didn't tell you?"

"No." Lane went from a brief moment of relief to a more pervasive worry. It was not like him not to have contacted her, and if she'd been thinking clearly, she would have seen that immediately. "He said he would wire me as soon as he could. Perhaps he's still sorting himself." She did not want to add worry about Darling to Ames's list of troubles.

"How is the case coming? Darling said I should keep an eye on you. But you don't have to tell me of course. Police matters and all that."

Ames looked relieved. "I can't see any harm in it. You've practically worked with us before. And for a change you aren't involved." He smiled and for a moment the sunny Ames was back. "Do you mind if I tell you? I mean, have you got time?"

"I've got lots of time. I have to stop by the travel agency to pick up my tickets, but they don't close till four thirty."

Ames, who had pushed his chair back so that it was on its back two legs, thumped down. "Travel agency? Not you too. Where are you going now?"

Lane realized she hadn't told him, in fact she hadn't told anyone, she was going. Her heart sank at having to tell Angela and the Armstrongs, and anyone else at King's Cove who might care, that she would be away an indeterminate amount of time. She had asked the agent to leave her return ticket open. Though Ames might harbour suspicions, he didn't really know yet that she and Darling were in love. Best to keep it simple; no need to tell him she was dashing back to the old country for Darling's sake.

"I'm off to see my grandparents. They're getting on, and I may not get that many opportunities." It sounded very convincing, even to her. Her visit to the bank had given her another reason to need to see them. Her father had left her an enormous legacy of four thousand pounds, and she had been puzzled and troubled by where he might have accrued so much money in his line of work. She wanted to find out from her grandparents anything they could tell her about a man who had been elusive and forbidding all her life.

"Well, that's dandy! Let's all bugger off to the old country and leave Ames on his own, excuse my French," Ames said. "I better get a move on then, I guess, and tell you about what's going on with the case before you disappear in a puff of smoke."

WITH A CLARITY that impressed Lane, Ames outlined the main details of the case. He did not consult his notes or show her any photos, which she assumed he must have taken.

"Now," he said after a few moments, "I have discovered something else that complicates what seemed to me at first to be a very personal murder. There was an old sawmill there that closed down years ago, and some outfit is thinking of reopening a mill away from the town and up behind where Agatha lived. When I went through her house, I found a letter from a month ago from some representative of the company. It said this was their third time offering her a sum of money to vacate the property, as they need to put a road through to the new facility they are going to build. She'd crumpled it up and tossed it in the garbage."

"That is interesting, certainly. But surely you aren't saying you suspect a respectable forestry company of murdering an old lady to get her out of the way of a road they want to build. I'm sure even in the wilds of British Columbia that isn't a common business practice."

Ames shrugged his reluctant agreement. "Probably not, but the letter has quite a threatening tone to it, legal action sort of thing. It turns out that might not even have been her own land. It looks like she just set up shop on Crown land. The place was practically a ghost town when the original mill shut down, so probably no one cared."

"Where did the letter come from? I mean, is it directly from the company itself, or a law office?"

Ames leaned over and looked through some files he'd placed on the floor to free up the chair for Lane. "Here. Morgan Franklin Limited. It's a name that could cover a multitude sins. The frank on the stamp is smudged, but the return address is in Vancouver." He handed the letter over, holding it carefully in a clean handkerchief.

Using her handkerchief to protect the letter from her fingerprints, Lane looked at it. It was certainly cold. In addition, the writer said, another agent would be coming in the second week of June to discuss the matter. "I wonder if any of the other residents had this sort of letter?"

"I met the agent. He didn't seem particularly threatening. Certainly not as bad as this letter. He was just getting around to seeing people. One old codger who lives near the edge of town had a pleasanter version of the letter saying the company would like to purchase what amounted, he said, to a strip of his land where he plants potatoes. He said he wouldn't mind having the extra cash, so he never received any more."

"So if her cabin is on Crown land, they might have been offering a small amount of money even though legally they would not have to because, in point of law, they could go directly to the Crown to negotiate for the use of the land to put in a road. When she didn't respond, the gloves were off. That is unpleasant, certainly, not to say cruel to force an old woman out of her home, but it does not suggest someone came and killed her."

"No, I suppose not. But here's the interesting bit. A guy called Carter, who lives in the house behind the church, happened to be going to the ferry just a couple of weeks ago. He was passing the place where she usually parks her car, and he said she was standing by her car brandishing a shotgun and shouting at a man who seemed to belong to a fancy car that was parked next to hers. I was a bit annoyed to hear this because, when I interviewed everyone the day I went out there, the forest company agent who has moved there to investigate the viability of the project neglected to tell me about it. I now have to go back and interview him again, and the ferryman, in case it was someone else in a fancy car he neglected to tell me about. Having said that, it wasn't unusual, apparently, for her to fly off the handle if people encroached on her land. I got the feeling the people in the village were a little cautious around her."

"Charming. What are you going to do next?" Lane asked.

"It seems perfectly obvious that someone drove her car away dressed in a manner that convinced the ferryman it was Agatha, and that someone is probably our murderer. I need to find that car, and I need to know how he or she got over there in the first place. I'm going to assume they came by water, which means a rowboat or canoe must have been abandoned on the shore. I'll get the Vancouver Police to check on the agency that wrote that letter. It's a waste of time, but I have to cover all the possibilities."

"The inspector would be very proud of you!" Lane said, getting up. "I've got to be off. I'm leaving in a couple of days, and I have a lot to do."

"You wouldn't be seeing his majesty while you're over there, I don't suppose?" Ames was close to winking, Lane thought.

"England looks small on the map, but it's a long, long way between London and Scotland."

"Hmm. Too bad. Agatha Browning came from some fancy family there, apparently. Someplace called Whitcombe in Dorset. I could have asked you to go and find out what you can."

CHAPTER SEVEN

THE RINGING FINALLY PENETRATED LANE'S consciousness. She was still in the grip of a dream in which the piercing ringing played a part. Sitting up, she pulled the chain on her lamp and then, galvanized by the time—two in the morning—she threw her blankets off and bounded into the hall. Snatching the earpiece she said, "KC 431, Lane Winslow speaking."

There was a silence, and then someone very distant said, "Please hold," and then a male voice she did not recognize. Not Darling.

"Is this Miss Winslow?"

"Yes, this is she."

"I'm sorry, I don't know what time it is over there. I hope it's not the middle of the night or anything. My name is Rudy Donaldson."

"It is the middle of the night, actually. What can I do for you?"

"I am sorry. Only Fred said I needed to contact you in case. I'm not sure he'd want me telephoning you at this stage, but I felt I ought to."

Lane felt herself go cold. "In case what? Has something happened?"

"He was arrested this morning. I've got a solicitor, though. I think he's seeing him right now. He'll be arraigned in a few days."

Lane put one hand against the wall to steady herself. The light from her bedroom made an angle on the wall just past where her phone hung, emphasizing the darkness beyond. "Arrested for what?"

"I think it might be for murder. He's been down to the War Office for a couple of days in a row being questioned about a crash and the death of a gunner. He really hasn't been able to make out what it's all about, but they seemed to really focus on his gunner dying during a crash. I'm sorry. I don't know how much you know. Then today he telephoned to tell me they were bringing him in and that I should get the solicitor."

Murder. A hanging offence.

"Miss, are you there? Hello?"

"Yes, yes. I'm here. They think he's murdered the gunner," she said flatly.

"It looks that way. I don't know what else I can tell you. I'm going to go by and see him this afternoon, bring him his sponge bag and a change of clothes, some books. Can I reach you here most times if I have an update?"

"You won't need to bother, Mr. Donaldson. I'm flying out from Vancouver the day after tomorrow. How can I reach you?"

KENNY ARMSTRONG'S RED truck was at the top of Lane's driveway. He and Eleanor, his wife of almost thirty years, stood with Lane on the front porch, waiting while she turned the key in the lock. The click in the quiet morning had a ring of finality. Kenny reached for her suitcase and started back toward the truck.

"We'll look in, dear. You mustn't worry. No doubt Kenny's dear departed mother will be opening the attic windows to keep the air fresh. I'll close them just in case of rain," Eleanor said.

Lane smiled ruefully at this mention of the resident ghost, assumed by everyone to be Lady Armstrong, to whom her beloved house had once belonged. She was thought to be the one who mysteriously engaged in opening the windows in the attic. Lane, more inclined to believe in faulty equipment, had had the latches fixed, but the window opening persisted. She had come to regard the long-dead Lady Armstrong as a guardian angel. Well, she'd be no good under the current circumstances, Lane thought grimly.

"It's so good of you to take care of things," she said, taking one desperate, longing look around her garden and at the lake beyond. "I was really going to get at the garden this year. You all put me to shame," she added sadly. The day, instead of being sombre as befits a painful parting, was diabolically all golden sunlight, highlighting the deep green of the lawns and playing through the leaves of the weeping willow by her pond.

"Don't you worry, lovie. You have a nice visit with your gran. They'll be so happy to see you. Then you hurry back

74

to us." Eleanor was patting her back as they walked toward the truck. Lane had pulled on her white gloves and hung her handbag over her wrist. She'd not told them about Darling being arrested. She didn't quite know why. There was usually nothing she didn't tell them. Perhaps it was her own fear that if she said it out loud it would make it real, make it rush to its unthinkable and horrific conclusion, Darling hanged for a murder he did not commit. In the middle of her last sleepless night in King's Cove, when she had no defences against her darkest musings, the thought presented itself that he might be guilty after all. What did she really know about him? But in the first grey light of dawn, she knew. She knew as well that there would be nothing she could do by rushing over there, but she could not leave him to face things alone.

"Thank God! I thought I'd miss you!" Angela was hurrying down the road, calling out loudly.

Lane endured the hugs and Angela's tears and now sat quietly in the truck, her heart constricting with pain, looking out the window as Kenny drove down the King's Cove road, past the church, which was bathed in sunlight, and the creek running by that gurgled cheerfully. Eleanor, Kenny, and Angela seemed now to be her three favourite people on earth. It was ridiculous, she knew, but she was in the grip of an almost superstitious fear that she might not come back.

"I've never been back to the old country, myself," Kenny was saying. "It wasn't easy in those days. Once people came out they tended to stay. Not like now, eh? A train to the coast and then a flight all the way."

"You could still go," Lane said, glad of this distraction.

Kenny turned onto the Nelson road, happy to see no one ahead on the road kicking up dust. "Nah. Nothing there for me, is there? My people are all gone. I probably wouldn't recognize the place I was born."

Lane was silent, thinking about her own people, her grandparents who had moved to Scotland after coming away from their home in the British colony in Latvia, their rambling home nationalized by Russians during the war. They would never go home either and had seemed to settle contentedly into their small farm in Scotland. She would, of course, have to, wanted to, see them, but she could think of nothing but Darling, locked up, waiting for a trial that might doom him.

Kenny gave her one last hug and handed her into the train, and now Lane sat, watching the lake, the forest, the mountains, all falling behind her, disappearing as if they had been a dream.

London

"YOU'VE A VISITOR," the guard said gruffly. Darling put down his book, stood up, stretched, and rubbed his eyes. The light wasn't brilliant in the cell, and Orwell's *The Road to Wigan Pier* was hardly uplifting; it bespoke a turn to Bolshevism Darling had not expected from Donaldson, who'd lent him the book. The quiet hum of prisoners and their visitors, unseen in nearby cells, made the grey stone walls seem haunted. He expected to see Higgins, the solicitor, ushered in with his briefcase. His heart gave a leap. It was not Higgins. It was madly and improbably

Lane, holding her handbag nervously in both hands, her face slightly shaded by a pale yellow hat that contrasted with the dark waves of her hair. The door was unlocked, and Lane was ushered in and given a chair on one side of a small table.

"I've only ever seen you in a hat once," Darling said, sitting opposite her.

Lane said nothing but reached across the table to take his hand. The guard behind her moved forward and cleared his throat. She took her hand back and clasped her hands together in front of her.

"I thought I'd better be as respectable as possible under the circumstances," she said.

"Lane, God, I can hardly believe it's you . . . what are you doing here? I issued strict instructions to Donaldson to call you only if things became dire." He longed to take her hand, to kiss her, to stroke that wonderful hair.

"I don't know how much more dire you want them to be. I understand you are being charged with murder. Is your solicitor any good?"

"He seems competent enough. He's gone off to find out as much as he can. I expect he'll be back this afternoon." Darling frowned. "I don't understand how you're here. Where are you staying?"

"Funnily enough in the same rooming house I was in during the war. Mrs. Macdonald seemed happy to see me, and my old room had just come vacant. It takes me back, I can tell you. I keep expecting my flatmate to come and distribute ash all over the floor, but it's very quiet, all things considered, and I have the room to myself. Now then. The solicitor. I don't expect they'll let me hang about when you see him, but I'll wait on a bench in the hall. You have to tell him that I'm to know everything. Promise."

Darling looked at her, wanting to drink in every line of her face. "I don't think you should get involved . . ." Did he really think that? He knew there would be nothing whatsoever she could do, alone against the juggernaut that was the War Office. There would, he very much feared, be nothing anyone could do. He'd already been interviewed once by an extremely brusque and ill-tempered inspector named Sims, who clearly believed Darling had done it and expected to make short work of the investigation and get back to his own office. Sims did not seem the sort of man who could be charmed, even by Lane. "I promise you. There is nothing you can do. The investigator, Sims, a civilian they've roped in from the Yard, is absolutely convinced I've murdered my eighteen-year-old gunner. He must have extremely compelling evidence."

Lane shook her head. "Did you kill your gunner?"

"No, of course not."

"Then you can stop telling me what I can and can't do. I'll tell you what I can't do. I can't sit here and wait for the man I love to be hanged. Have you given the solicitor every detail you can remember? What's his name, I can't keep calling him that."

"Higgins. Am I the man you love?"

"Madly." Much to her consternation Lane teared up. She reached across and took both his hands in hers. The guard pulled himself away from the wall and came toward them. "Blast him," she said. "Have you been formally

78

charged?" She pulled her hands away, glancing at the frowning guard.

"Tomorrow morning I expect."

"Time's up, miss," the guard said.

"Promise me you'll tell Higgins to confide in me," she said, desperately hoping time was not up.

LANE SAT IN the passage, watching the earnest activity of the court hurrying past her. Men in suits, men in black robes and wigs, men in red robes, all about the business of dispensing justice, righting society, cancelling the debt incurred by crime. The bench she sat on was hard, and her stomach was in turmoil. She tried to recall how she practised breathing to calm herself before setting off on a mission. It seemed harder now. Then it had only been her own life she feared for. No matter how dangerous the flight, or the drop into enemy territory, or the possibility of being found out and arrested or shot, she always had the illusion that her life was in her own hands, that she would find a way to survive. Now she felt at one step removed. Darling's life was in the hands of others, people intent on proving he'd willfully taken the life of an eighteen-year-old boy under his command. People intent on righting society by convicting him.

SHE DID NOT know how long had passed when she heard "Miss Winslow?" She looked up to see a man of no great height with receding hair combed straight back off his forehead, and an efficient but kindly expression. He wore a dark striped suit and brogues. A man who was doing well.

"Mr. Higgins?" Lane started to stand.

"No, don't get up." He settled beside her and opened his briefcase. "I understand I'm to take you fully into my confidence. I normally wouldn't. You are not, I understand, married to Flight Lieutenant Darling, I should say Inspector Darling. However, I'm going to say quite frankly that we need all the help we can get, even from someone who is wholly unconnected with anyone in London."

"Thank you, Mr. Higgins." I'm not wholly unconnected she thought, though I would be loath in every way to have to call upon those connections. "What is the situation?"

"Tomorrow morning he will be formally charged with willfully and knowingly taking the life of one Arthur Evans by shooting him in the back during the course of an action in battle. The evidence I have been provided with is compelling in the extreme. The bullet found lodged in a rib has been traced to a revolver of the type issued to Flight Lieutenant Darling. Apparently the others were either unarmed or had a different weapon, so his would have been the only one of that type. And there was a witness, which is perhaps the most damning circumstance. The presiding judge will set a court date tomorrow. I must say that, on the whole, I believe him when he says he did not do it, but the War Office is intent on clearing a backlog of unresolved cases of treason, wrongful death, and so on, and this one has been described to me as 'open and shut.' I would be lying if did not tell you very frankly, Miss Winslow, there is very little hope."

CHAPTER EIGHT

"**B**E UPSTANDING."

Lane, in the gallery, watched as the might of the legal system gathered below her rose. They settled again in a wave of wooden clattering like parishioners in church pews to await the word of God. The judge sat at the bench, shuffling with some irritation through the papers before him and then looked to the prosecution. The charges were read with a finality and gravity that was chilling, and Lane, wishing desperately that she could see Darling's face, watched his back as he stood unmoving below her in the dock.

The judge consulted his papers again and held a whispered conversation with the clerk. "The trial date is set for June twenty-three. Yes?" This question was in response to Higgins rising.

"M'lud. I am requesting bail at this time. My client, Flight Lieutenant Darling, is currently a police inspector in the Dominion of Canada. He is not a flight risk and is fully aware of the provisions of the law."

This brought the prosecution to its feet.

"If I may, m'lud, the prisoner is charged with shooting one of his own men under the cover of battle. A man under his command. A man who trusted him absolutely. It is unthinkable that he should be granted his liberty under these circumstances."

Higgins rose again. "Flight Lieutenant Darling has, despite these wholly spurious charges, an impeccable war record, m'lud, and was awarded the Distinguished Flying Cross for his bravery under fire. And he has not yet been convicted of any crime. Although the circumstances are unusual, I nevertheless crave the court's indulgence, and request bail."

Lane crossed her fingers, frowning anxiously, watching Darling, who suddenly half-turned his head, as if he would search for her among the sparse crowd of lookers-on. The judge, holding his gavel, stared fixedly at the prisoner, as if to read on his face the outcome of any decision the bench would make. With a sigh, he lifted his gavel.

"Bond is set at five hundred pounds. I need hardly remind the prisoner that he'd better be present before me on the twenty-third of June." The gavel came down, only barely obscuring the gasps of the people in the gallery. Five hundred pounds was a staggering amount of money. What one might expect of a judge who had no wish to release a man charged with murder and yet no wish to keep a war hero in prison.

Lane heard a muffled sob and turned for the first time to look at who else was in the gallery. One row behind her, near the door, she saw a couple in their fifties. The woman, wearing a drab brown dress and pinched black hat with one desultory and faded flower pinned to it over her grey hair, was now crying and had a gloved hand at her mouth. The man, Lane presumed him to be the husband, had his arm around her but was staring angrily down on the drama below. As the melee of leaving and conversation rose from the floor of the courtroom, the man stood and pulled at his wife's arm.

"Come on, Mother," he said. "It's clear we'll not get justice in this courtroom."

Lane watched them leave and realized they must be Evans's parents. It came to her forcibly that the profound conviction she had in Darling's innocence was matched in power, or perhaps greater power, by the grief of Evans's parents and their conviction that Darling was guilty. She felt a rush of empathy for them. They had lost a hero son, in battle, they had thought, a loss profound enough, but to learn from the authorities that a murderer had callously thrown away their son's life must be the final devastation. And they had the man they strongly believed might be responsible in their sights, standing trial for their son's murder.

Subdued by this glimpse of a world where either they or she must in the end endure bitter disappointment, Lane waited while Higgins spoke with the bailiff. She would, of course, despite the amount, stand his bail. She had no idea what Darling's resources were, but hers would more than meet the case.

In the cell, Darling shook his head vigorously. Lane sat primly before him, her hands on her handbag, and Higgins stood discreetly by the door. "You are not to do this. It's unthinkable. It's a ridiculous amount. It was meant as a deterrent. Higgins, make her see sense!"

Higgins made as if to join them, but Lane put up her hand. "I'm not having you rot in jail when I have easy access to the means of getting you out."

"No one rots in jail anymore. Conditions are quite hygienic, in fact."

Lane glanced around the cell that smelled of cigarettes and boiled offal and bleach. "Don't talk nonsense. Now, it will undoubtedly take me a bit of machination to get the bank here to release money from my Canadian account. As you know, my father left me quite well provided for. I expect my ferocious old bank manager is still at his post at my London bank. He'll help. No, don't appeal to Mr. Higgins. He has already notified the bailiff of our intention to post bond. It's Friday. I shall go to the bank immediately to set things in motion, but it may take into next week. Try not to rot until then." She smiled brightly at Darling, whose heart swelled at the sight, and joined Higgins at the door.

LANE AND RUDY sat at the small kitchen table, with untouched cups of tea cooling at their elbows. Lane had a pencil and paper and was making notes. She had learned that the bank could get her bank in Nelson to wire the money, but it would take until the following Wednesday. She chafed at the delay but never questioned her resolve when she had first learned of the four-thousand-pound inheritance she had from her father that she would not touch it until she understood where it had come from. There had not been a moment's doubt that getting Darling out of prison, hygienic as it might be, was the correct use for her money. She could not bear to waste a moment of the mere three weeks they had to try to get the evidence they needed to clear Darling, and so had marshalled Rudy to join her in trying to understand what they were dealing with.

"Are we sure we have them all?" she asked. "Watson the navigator; Anthony the flight engineer; someone called Salford on the wireless; poor Evans, the rear gunner; Belton, the front gunner; Jones, the aimer whose body was never found; and Darling himself." Darling had left Rudy this list before he had been arrested.

"That's it. What we don't know is, who among them claimed to witness Darling shoot one of his own men in the back." Rudy looked at his watch. "Higgins will be here any minute. I hope he is genuine in his assertion that he will take us completely into his confidence. And even if he does, I don't see, really, how we can help." As if on cue, the bell sounded, and Higgins, clutching his briefcase, was ushered in. Divested of his hat and jacket, he sat down at the table, pulled a file from his briefcase, and then looked hopefully at the teapot.

"It's good of you to come out on a Saturday. I'll ask Sandra to brew us up a fresh pot. We've just been making notes based on what Fred gave us. Not much, but it's a start." While Rudy was up finding his wife, Higgins took up the paper.

"Seven names—the usual crew of a Lancaster. Ah, yes," he stabbed at the paper with a finger. "There's our witness. Apparently impeccable."

Lane leaned forward. "Who?"

"Neville Anthony, the flight engineer." Lane took the paper from Higgins and stared at Anthony's name as if it would somehow reveal the reason a man of perfectly impeccable reputation would accuse Frederick Darling of murdering a member of his own crew in cold blood.

"Well, we need to trace all these people, interview them. How does this Anthony rate his 'impeccable' reputation? Darling told me he was a last-minute replacement. How do we know he wasn't a plant of some sort?"

Higgins sat silently for some moments, staring at his hands. "A plant for what? To frame Flight Lieutenant Darling for murder nearly two years after the end of the war? That suggests an extremely elaborate and risky conspiracy, and to what end? Miss Winslow, and you will forgive me here, in spite of what you or I may believe, we don't fully know that Darling did not, in fact, commit this crime, do we?"

Lane felt herself colour. "I do know, Mr. Higgins, and if you haven't the faith in his word that you claimed you had, I don't see how you are going to be of any use to us."

Coming back just in time to hear Lane's comment, Rudy said, "How's it all gone west here? I was only gone two minutes."

"Mr. Higgins is not fully convinced of Frederick's innocence."

Higgins sighed. "I am only saying that it would be foolish of us not to take all possible facts into consideration. I do believe him to be innocent, and he is a fellow airman, and I know what we all endured together. I will do my utmost to see that he is not wrongfully convicted. Frankly, all of the forces possible are arrayed against us, and we will have to be absolutely sure of our facts to be successful. I have already contacted the War Office to help me locate the men on this list. They were astonishingly unhelpful, though they have given me an appointment in three days' time. And needless to say, the prosecution will be anxious to keep us away from their star witness. It will be an uphill slog."

"Not a lot of time," Lane said. "I want to come with you to the War Office. We must find those men, including this Anthony fellow. We have to know what happened from every point of view."

Higgins nodded. "You're right. Someone shot Evans. Darling thought that it was the enemy. We have Anthony saying Darling did it. If we could get the story out of each of them, provided they survived the war, we might get a fuller picture."

Lane nodded. "Let's look at it this way. This Anthony claims he saw Darling shoot the gunner. That can be one of two things. Either he thinks he saw Darling do it, or he is lying. If he is lying, why?"

Rudy, entering into the spirit of the thing, said, "Because he did it himself? Or he saw someone else he wants to cover for do it?"

"This is what I don't understand," said Lane, collapsing back against her chair. "Why bring it up now? If he did it himself, he's taking an awful risk by coming out with an accusation like that. Any one of the others could have seen him do it. He must be very confident, either in his belief that he was unseen or that he saw Darling do it. We must get at those other men. Three days is a long time to wait. I'll start immediately by looking right here in the London directories to see if any have fetched up here. In fact, I think we can narrow our search if Darling himself can remember where they came from. I'll ask him tomorrow when I visit again."

As he showed Higgins to the door later, Rudy remarked, "That's some woman Freddie's got himself. She's like a terrier."

"Good-looking too," remarked Higgins, putting on his hat. "I only hope she doesn't get in the way. A hysterical woman about the place will do my client no good at all."

"DARLING, YOU LOOK awful. Are you sleeping?" Lane was once again across from Darling at the small worn wooden table, with a guard nearby, alert for any funny business.

"Not particularly. I admit, in spite of my objections, I can scarcely wait to get out. I wonder if this will give me any greater sympathy for the prisoners I bung up? I wonder if I will live to ever bung anyone up again?"

"Oh, darling, I can't bear to see you like this," Lane moved as if to take his hand, and then pulled it back again.

"I've gone over and over in my head what happened, trying desperately to remember where everyone was, and even when exactly I knew Evans was dead. It's remarkable how unreliable memory suddenly seems. We all act as if we remember things precisely, but when I try to nail something down absolutely, 'I was here or here, Evans was there, the Germans firing from over there'"—Darling moved his finger across the table as he spoke, pointing at remembered positions—"then it all seems to go blurry. There was such a bloody lot of noise. Shouting, shooting, flames roaring. And it was dark except for what was illuminated by the fire. Oh. And flashlights. Someone had flashlights. Did some of my men, to get away? Or was it Germans looking for us? Anyway, I've already told Higgins all of this. It's ridiculous to be going over and over it. Sometimes I glimpse a memory somewhere in the corner of my mind that I felt there was something wrong, but then it was a battle. Everything was wrong."

Wishing now she'd brought her notebook, Lane asked, "Did you fire your revolver?"

Darling frowned. "I did, yes. I took it out and shouted at the men to make a run for it, that I would cover for them. Then I ran forward a bit, toward where I thought the Germans were. I was low, behind bushes. I heard shots and at first I couldn't tell where from, and then one came from ahead of me, so I moved forward and shot into the dark. I'm certain I hit someone. I expect I thought I could draw their fire toward me. I fell back and made to pick Evans up and cart him off in the same direction as my retreating men, but then I saw he was dead. I made a run for it."

"Perhaps Anthony saw you shoot and thought you were shooting Evans."

"But he and I moved Evans there from where he'd stumbled near the rear of the plane. When the fighting broke out I ordered Anthony away. He should have been far away by then, but he stayed a little behind me to cover me. Oh God. It's no good. I'm going round and round in my own brain here." He leaned forward, his head buried in his hands.

The guard came forward, "Miss . . ."

Lane looked up. The guard was young. He did not look, on close inspection, like an unkind person. Perhaps a bemused ex-soldier, happy to find the work after the uncertainties of war. "Look, I have to go. The minute we get you out we'll go over this. In the meantime, I'm going to be scouring the London directories to find anyone I can. Oh, blast. I was supposed to ask you if you remembered where they were from."

"The only one from London was Watson. Adam Watson, the navigator. I remember that because he used to gas on and on about his football team, Tottenham Hotspur. I'd have to think about the rest. But the War Office will know."

"Higgins and I are going to the War Office on Wednesday. And with any luck, we'll have you out by then as well. Yes, yes, I'm off." Longing to kiss him, she took a last look at him, standing by the table, as she went out the door the guard was holding open for her.

CHAPTER NINE

_____

IT WASN'T UNTIL SHE HAD left Darling that she suddenly thought about his father. She was fairly certain he had a brother as well. She knew his mother had died, though she had never learned how. It struck her now how remarkable it was for her, for them, to be so in love and know so little about each other. Both of them were inclined to privacy and a disinclination to divulge, Darling, if anything, more so than her. "She died after an illness," he had said once, but she remembered the expression that flitted across his face momentarily, and she knew that it was a great sorrow he had buried.

That night, settled in her old room, Lane sat on the bed, pillows propped behind her, and looked at her notebook under the same lamp that had illuminated the wartime letters from her lover—which she had been instructed to destroy in her fireplace after she read them—and the instructions she received from the War Office. She leaned back and thought about Evans's parents, her pencil end against her mouth. She knew nothing about Darling's father. Would he want to come out to be near his son? Perhaps Ames would know, though somehow she doubted that Darling tended to confide in an underling. She looked at her watch. It was nearing ten o'clock. She could put in a long-distance call to Ames. No, damn it, it was Sunday. She would arrange it for the morning at the post office. She calculated that she would have to make the call at five in the afternoon to reach Ames first thing in the morning at the police station in Nelson.

It was a fitful night. She dreamed her recurring dream of fire burning all the roads and keeping her from home, a home that, once awake, she could not recognize. She woke at three in the morning, angry that it looked like she was going to have to do with four hours of sleep, knowing that she would not sleep again that night. In the morning, bleary-eyed, she gratefully slurped the mug of hot tea provided by Mrs. Macdonald and was surprised and delighted to see an egg and some rashers of bacon on offer.

"This is nice," she said. "Don't you have to keep to your rations, still?"

"I keep a rooming house. There's a wee bit more leeway for me. And anyway, you look like you could use it. Ah, good morning, Mr. Hemming." A man with a shiny red face and smelling of lavender brilliantine had come in and bowed slightly to greet her. "Mr. Hemming, meet Miss Winslow. She were one of my girls during the war. She's come out all the way from Canada."

Lane greeted the beaming Mr. Hemming and then realized there must be at least three more boarders to come who would occupy her landlady's energies, so she said,

"Mrs. Macdonald, I wonder if you could help. Do you have a London directory? I am trying to locate . . . one of my friends who worked with me as part of the typing pool."

"I can give you what I have, but it will only work if she's on the telephone. If she's living in rooms, you might not be able to trace her. Was she one of ours?"

Damn, Lane thought. It was true. Who knew where the man would be living. "No," she smiled in a way she hoped was convincing. "No, she lived in Shepherd's Bush."

In her room, she studied the directory and saw immediately how difficult her task would be. She counted twenty-five A. Watsons and had no way of knowing if any of them was the one she wanted. Perhaps Darling knew more about Adam Watson than simply what football club he supported. She would find out at her morning visit. Hoping that taking the directory with her would not inconvenience Mrs. Macdonald, she placed it in her cloth bag and set out to visit Darling.

"You think the reading material furnished by Rudy is inadequate?" he asked when she plunked two phone directories on the table between them. He looked better, she thought, more rested. His charcoal eyes had the slight sparkle of playfulness he seemed to reserve for Ames, and more recently, for her.

"There are twenty-five A. Watsons in the book. I thought if you could see the addresses it might stir your memory. I stopped at the post office and picked up a directory for Haringey where that football club you mentioned seems to reside. The London directory doesn't cover it. I haven't looked at it yet."

Reaching for the Haringey directory, Darling opened it and intoned, "Watson, Watson . . . here's a Watson, A. Bromley Road. I remember now. We used to kid him about that bloody football club, and he said he couldn't help it, he grew up right beside their playing grounds, and I think Bromley Road is near the grounds. You might start there. Perhaps his parents live there and can tell you where he is." He looked at her. "You look a bit tired. Are you sure you want to do all this?"

"Thank you very much. I wish I could say the same about you. You look altogether rested."

"I want to kiss you."

"We'll see. Perhaps one day. In the meantime, I have to hurry this directory back to Mrs. Macdonald before she misses it. If you aren't right, I guess I'll just have to troll through this lot. Oh. I'm calling Ames this evening to let him know how I can be reached. I don't think he knows what's happened, and I think he ought to. I'm wondering about your father and brother. Have you contacted them? Would you like me to?"

Darling groaned and ran his hand through his hair. "I don't want them worried, any of them. No. Not unless . . ." he left unspoken the direst thoughts: unless he was convicted and scheduled to hang. How long could he be "on holiday" from his job? If it went beyond a month, the Nelson city fathers would be bound to become involved and bring in some other person to take his job. "Can you just tell Ames I'm still involved in some bureaucratic quagmire without letting on? And ask him how he's getting on with his murder. I don't want him making a mess in my absence."

"I've had to speak to you before about not giving Ames enough credit," Lane said, smiling. "I'll give him your love then, will I?"

AMES WAS FEELING the absence of his boss. The constable had always been the sidekick in the relationship, the one upon whom Darling could test his theories, explore possibilities. He could speculate without being responsible for the conclusion. Now, though he had taken O'Brien, the uniformed officer who usually manned the front desk, into his confidence, Ames very much lacked a sense of his own confidence. And furthermore, he was missing Darling's company at breakfast in the café next to the station. He had, for one morning, thought of simply skipping his scrambled eggs and coffee out of his anxiety about April, who was still giving him the cold shoulder, but she seemed to have established a policy of having one of her workmates deal with him whenever he came in, so they had reached a truce of sorts.

Now, fully caffeinated and fed, he looked at the notes on his desk and wondered what to make of the jumble of information he was gathering. He was becoming aware that, as usual, what ought to be a simple murder was ever-expanding in complexity. He tried to focus on the basics. Who would want Agatha Browning dead? What was to be gained by whoever it was? The first question yielded only one solid answer: the forestry company that was snooping around wanting the land on which her cabin sat. Perhaps the number could stretch to two and include any villager who had had an unpleasant interaction with her, but, and maybe here he was showing a prejudice, they were all over sixty. Though any of them, at a stretch, could have engaged in a spot of frenzied stabbing, would any of them have bumbled through the forest following the victim and pushed her over? And no murder weapon, of course. He'd lay any money that the knife had been hurled into the lake, well out of reach.

He still had a day to await the return of the replacement ferryman, Nathan "Nobby" Bannon. That at least might yield information about someone coming in the few days prior to the murder. Wouldn't there have been evidence at the cabin? There was such a mess he hadn't really thought to try to ascertain if there'd been any evidence of someone staying there besides the victim. It hadn't been cleaned up yet. He'd go back and really sift through the rubble.

He looked again over his new notes and considered the question of who would benefit. He had no real sense of who Agatha had left behind in the old country. The old photo of the three girls smiling over the fence was it. He needed more information about her background. He underlined this and stood, prepared to go back and sift through the cabin more thoroughly, when the phone rang. It was O'Brien.

"Call from afar for you, Ames. Might be the boss."

"Please hold," said a voice. "Go ahead, Britain."

"Constable Ames. How are you?" Lane asked, after a brief crackling sound.

"All the better for hearing you, Miss Winslow. How's the old country?"

"Very old, thank you."

"Raining?"

"Not a bit. It's unnaturally sunny, in fact. Everyone is complaining about the heat. Listen, as it happens, I did run into Inspector Darling." She hoped she would be forgiven for this bit of fabrication.

"How is the old man?"

"He's not so very old. I told him I'd be giving you a call, and he asked me to tell you he's taken up with a bit of bureaucracy here, so he's not certain quite when he'll be back. He's wondering how you're getting on?"

Ames hesitated. "It's not the same without him," he said in a rush of confidence. "I think, well, I think we help each other think. I have got O'Brien as a sounding board, but it's not the same. I'm not sure anyone is comfortable with me being in charge just now, either."

"You know, Constable, I at least have enormous faith in you. I've watched you work, and in spite of Darling's deflating comments, you are full of good instincts and insights. And he thinks so too, or he wouldn't have left you in charge."

"You're very nice to say so, Miss Winslow," Ames said, his smile genuine. "Say, I just thought. I do need some more information about my victim. Is there someplace there where they have family records or something? The vicar said she might be from the aristocracy, so maybe it would be easier to find something about her."

"One minute," warned the operator.

"Look," continued Ames, "I need to know if she had any relatives that might have more information.

"I could certainly go to Somerset House to check the register. That's right here in the city. I'm . . . I'm not sure

I'd have time to go over to Dorset just now." She was aware of the panic in the pit of her stomach. They'd less than three weeks to solve the death of Evans.

"Anything you could do. All we've got is the name, Agatha Browning. I suppose that was her married name. Everyone called her Mrs."

"All right, Constable Ames. I'll do what I can. Agatha Browning from Dorset. That might be enough. Darling sends his best."

"I bet he does," Ames said, laughing. "And Miss Winslow . . . thanks, you know, for everything."

"You're quite welcome. Bye for now." Lane, having feigned cheeriness, hung up the phone, envious of Ames's ignorance of the details of his boss's situation. She smiled as she pushed the money for the call over the counter. The call box smelled heavily of smoke, and she was glad to be out of it. Back out in the sunlight, she sighed and thought about her next move. She was scheduled to meet Higgins at his chambers at nine o'clock the next morning. It was her hope to set out to Bromley Road in Haringey immediately after that, and if there were time remaining, go to Somerset House for Ames.

She had told Mrs. Macdonald she would not be home for dinner. "I've had a last-minute invitation from a friend." Rudy and Sandra had insisted she come to them for dinner, and her memory of Mrs. Macdonald's efforts with any food but that consumed at breakfast decided her in a moment.

Mrs. Macdonald had responded by smiling indulgently and making a shooing motion with her hands, no doubt relieved at the reduction in the washing up. "You run along and have a good time. Remember, the door is locked at ten!"

CHAPTER TEN

Oxfordshire, August 1943

"I'M WEARING TWO PAIRS OF socks this time," Evans declared. "I nearly froze to death last time. Where's Harlow, by the way?"

Jones had his locker open and suddenly looked down. "He's in sickbay with some sort of Delhi belly, and I'm not feeling too swift myself just now." Jones turned and stumbled toward the lavatory.

Evans leaned over to put his second sock on, thinking about the day's mission. He assumed that the tension he felt in his stomach was the usual pre-trip jitters, and hoped it wasn't whatever his mates had. He'd not eaten with them the night before because he'd gone to the pub with some men from another crew. A noise from Jones's locker made him look up in time to get smacked on the head by a cascade of boots, jumpers, and papers that had become overbalanced. Cursing, he leaned over and scooped up the paper and kicked the boots to one side. As he was about to shove it all back into the locker, his eyes lit on a single photograph.

He fished it out and put the rest of the things into the locker. There was a stamp of some sort, like, he thought, what you'd get on the back of a photograph, showing the company that developed it, only this was in German, along with someone's scribbled note. It must also be in German, he thought, because he couldn't read it. Glancing in puzzlement toward the lavatory where he could hear raised voices and men laughing in that slightly overwrought way they had before going up, he looked at the photograph. Curious, he squinted at it . . . something looked slightly familiar. Glancing around he moved so that he was under the overhead light. But of course he knew that couldn't be right.

"Golly. Sorry about that." Jones said. "I always cram too much stuff in there."

"Your bloody locker emptied itself onto my head. I was trying to get everything back in." Evans held up the photograph. "I heard you were clever with getting maps and the like. This looks like a German photo."

Jones laughed, taking the photo and gazing at it almost fondly. "Well, the Bosch are using our stuff. It seems only fair!"

Men were milling near them, pulling on their gear. "It's amazing how you chaps can distinguish anything. It could be Canterbury for all I know!" Evans said, tying his boots.

"They can all look alike. Luckily we've got a bunch of women who know how to read them. It's not Canterbury, it's Dresden. Jerry has kindly made some pics for us that we've got hold of. It makes it easier for me to point, and you to fire away, kid!" Jones tousled Evan's hair, and put things back into his locker, whistling under his breath, "Now let's get a move on and not keep Flight Lieutenant waiting."

Later, alone in the rear gun compartment, watching the darkness that was the North Sea passing below him, Evans would think about how amazingly clever Jones was.

Haringey, June 1947

LANE STOOD ON the doorstep of a house in the middle of a row along the quiet street, waiting. It was Tuesday morning, at a time when she knew that Adam Watson would surely be at work, and very likely not living at his parents' family home. She had knocked and thought she heard something, but then the house was quiet again. Finally, a young man, looking vaguely reluctant about answering the door, put his head out and said, "Yes?" She could hear a shuffling within. The parents?

Smiling her brightest, she said, "My name is Lane Winslow. I'm looking for Adam Watson, who flew with Flight Lieutenant Frederick Darling."

The man looked behind him now, frowning, and stepped onto the doorstep closing the door behind him.

"I'm Adam. What's this about?"

Lane struggled with how to proceed. He clearly seemed thrown by her appearance, or Darling's name, or who knew what. "I'm a friend of Insp . . . Flight Lieutenant Darling's. He's here in London just now and we're going over all the events of the crash of 1943, and we need to interview all the people who were there. I'm wondering if you could spare a few minutes to tell me what you remember?"

Watson shifted nervously and then said, "Do you have

some sort of identification? How am I supposed to know if you are who you say you are? Anyway, an official report was done on all that. It's finished."

This clear shift to suspicion puzzled Lane. "Oh, I'm no one official. I literally am just a friend of his . . ." She could hear how ridiculous she sounded, especially in the face of what increasingly looked to her like fear. What did he know, and why wouldn't he say? She could see he was beginning to back away and she would lose him altogether. "Listen, I'm going to be straight with you. He's in prison, charged with deliberately shooting the rear gunner, Evans. You know him, Mr. Watson. You must know he's incapable of such a thing. We just desperately need to hear from everyone who was there."

Watson's head drew back as if he'd been struck. He put his hand on the door handle. "He what? No. I'm not to talk to you, to anyone." He slid into the house and closed the door. She could hear the bolt being knocked home. She knew from the silence that he was standing just behind the door. Pulling out her notebook, she tore a sheet off and wrote her name and the phone number of the rooming house and then put it through the mail slot and called through the door, "If you change your mind, Mr. Watson, please, please call me here. Darling's very life depends on it. Please." She heard herself sounding frantic and, pulling herself together, walked away, back toward the tube station, back toward London, the sound of the bolt being thrown reverberating in her head.

Feeling she had to do something useful and needing time to try to understand, to grasp the full meaning of her interaction with what she now realized was a very frightened man, she resolved to go to Somerset House and see what she could do for Ames. On the underground, she pulled out her notebook and wrote down the conversation as she remembered it, staring in particular at his words, "I'm not to talk to you."

IN TRUE LONDON fashion, the morning, which had started out cloudless and warm, turned first cold, and then, by the time she arrived at the entrance at Somerset House, clouds had banked, and she just made it in before a sudden and heavy rain. Putting Watson, A., temporarily into the back of her mind, where she hoped something would come to her later, she procured a birth certificate for Agatha Victoria Browning, born to Geoffrey Browning and Cecelia Browning, July 1874, Whitcombe, Dorset. That was straightforward, then. Browning was not a married name.

"Any siblings?" she asked the clerk, who disappeared to the files and returned with four additional papers.

"Two siblings. Mary, 1876, and Lucille, 1887. I've brought the father's and the youngest sister's death certificates as well in case they are of any use. The father, Geoffrey Browning, 1909. And here's one for Lucille Alice Browning, 1908."

"Goodness, she died young. Nothing for the mum?"

The clerk shook her head impatiently. "You did just ask for Agatha Browning." But she procured the information, laying it impatiently before Lane. "Anything else?"

"No, thank you so much." Lane said sweetly. Mother had died in 1890. There. She finished her notes, resolved to dispatch what she had discovered immediately by telegram to Ames at the nearest post office so that she could get on with the problem at hand.

That done, she felt an urgent need to contact Higgins and see Darling to discuss the puzzling behaviour of Adam Watson. The wait until the next day, when the bank manager said her money would be released for Darling's bail, seemed interminable.

HIGGINS, HAPPILY, WAS in his chambers when she arrived.

"Miss Winslow, how pleasant. Please, sit down."

"I'm sorry to burst in on you like this, Mr. Higgins, but I've had a very peculiar interaction with one of Darling's crew members. I managed to track down the one that lives near here, in Haringey."

Higgins folded his hands in front of him on his desk and looked over his glasses. "I see. I wonder if it was advisable for you to . . ." he was going to say, "blunder about," but continued with ". . . begin any research prior to our mapping out a strategy. We are going to the War Office tomorrow. You could, you see, be muddying the pond, as it were." He sounded infinitely patient.

Stung by both his assumption of her dimness and, in fairness, by the possibility that he might be right, Lane sat heavily back in her chair. "Yes, I see what you mean. I did speak with Darling yesterday, you see, and we discovered an address for the one man who lives near here. And, you know, after my experience today, I believe the War Office may not be as cooperative as we hoped."

Higgins smiled wanly. "You will, of course, have had no experience with the War Office, so I hope you will leave that part of it to me when we go there. I suppose you'd better tell me about your conversation with Watson." He pulled a pad of foolscap forward and took up a pencil.

Practicing enormous patience, Lane opened her notebook and recounted the conversation in full. "The singular impression I had, Mr. Higgins, is that Watson, who made us talk on the steps outside the minute he heard Darling's name, seemed to be very suspicious. I wondered immediately why that might be. Secondly"—here she was obliged to put up her hand, as Higgins was drawing in breath to make, no doubt, another ponderous and patronizing statement—"secondly, he seemed taken aback, not to say shocked, when I told him that Darling was in prison charged with Evans's murder. He made a face, shook his head, and looked very frightened. He could not get away fast enough, saying he 'was not to talk' to me, or anyone. I wondered for a moment if he meant me, in fact, or just anyone who came around asking questions. Of course, it would not be me, since no one knows that I exist, or am here."

Even as she said this, her heart sank. That wasn't actually true. Someone could know. He could know the minute she presented her passport when she arrived. She shook this off as highly unlikely. Even if he did know, she'd only been there a few days. She suspected Watson had been warned off before. Long before. Here she mentally took Higgins's advice. Don't muddy the waters. Whatever the director was up to, it would have nothing to do with this. He just kept tabs on her as a personal project. She prayed earnestly to whatever gods monitored this sort of thing that he'd taken her at her word the summer before that she would never again be involved with the intelligence branch, and would not bother her again.

Higgins smiled at this and put his pencil down. "Still. It is concerning, this reluctance to talk. He's been coached, but why?"

"And by whom," Lane added. "It's all part and parcel of this sudden reopening of the crash, of Darling being brought here and jailed. Something happened that set this whole train of events in motion. They, someone, wants a clear and uncontested charge of murder to be prosecuted against Darling. The question is why is it necessary?"

"Well, we mustn't panic." Higgins smiled unconvincingly, as if to assuage his own anxieties, if not hers. "We'll go to our appointment at the War Office tomorrow, and, of course, you'll have Darling out of confinement by the afternoon. And I think I'll have a go at Dunlop, the prosecution chap, and see what he can give me. Will that be all right?"

Lane, who had been poised to combat her own feelings if he said "dear girl," inclined her head and stood up. "Thank you, Mr. Higgins," she said with all the charm she could muster, and extended her hand. "I will meet you on the steps of the War Office then, at nine."

"IT ACTUALLY GETS harder to bear the closer I am to getting out," Darling said, glancing at the guard, wishing for one touch of her hand. He had dreamed of being caught in long webs of torn and dirty grey cloth that was hanging from somewhere high above him, unable to escape in any direction.

Lane would have liked to be breezy, but her interaction with Watson had badly shaken her. "Listen, darling, only one more night. I'll take you out for a bang-up meal." She paused. "I managed to find Adam Watson." Darling looked encouraged. "No, don't get excited. I expected to find him surrounded by his wife and children, but he seemed alone and very, very nervous. It was a very peculiar interaction. The upshot is, he's frightened and has been warned off."

Darling leaned back and frowned when Lane had finished telling him about her visit to Haringey.

"Weirder and weirder. I'm not, if I'm honest, surprised about no wife and children. I don't think he was inclined that way. But what on earth is going on? Jones and Evans are dead, Anthony seems to be a stooge for the prosecution, that leaves only Watson, Belton, and Salford. Have they all been got to?"

"Let's not get ahead of ourselves. Higgins and I are going to the War Office at nine. What a prig, if I may say so, but he has a strong dose of native caution, which is very good under the circumstances. I'm going to the bank at eleven. I'll have you out in the afternoon."

Darling smiled. "Is he being priggish to you? I'm sure you've set him straight."

"Alas, he is not the type to be set straight. He thinks women are dim and should stay prettily out of the way. He's warned me off opening my mouth tomorrow morning."

SANDRA PUT THE salt and pepper on the table and sat down. "We'll be very happy to see him back here tomorrow, I can tell you," she said. She seemed to always dress up for dinner, Lane noticed. Today Sandra had bright red lipstick and an emerald hair band that matched her green cardigan. Did she do it because Lane was a guest, or because she wanted to be a cheerful presence for her husband? I've got a lot to learn if that's the case, Lane thought.

Rudy passed a bowl of potatoes to his guest. She had taken them up on their standing invitation to dinner, promising herself that when this was all over she would take them all to the poshest place in London as a thank you. At the moment, though, it seemed far from being all over.

"What I don't understand is why Watson was so skittish. I'm terrified that the other two will be like that and we will have no witnesses at all. I think we have to assume they have all been got at. What we are going to have to do is go back a step and try to understand why."

"A step at a time, love, don't you think? Perhaps a way will seem clearer down the road a bit," Sandra said.

"I expect you're right," Lane said. But, she thought, what if the road isn't clearer? This is not some story. It is real life, and sometimes things just don't come out all right.

CHAPTER ELEVEN

———————

LANE CAME OUT OF THE Charing Cross station and oriented herself. She was a few minutes early, but it was sunny without the threat of a sudden rain like the day before, and for a change, perhaps because of the proximity to the river, the air was clear and fresh. A few minutes in the sun on the steps of the War Office building in Whitehall would allow her to collect herself for whatever ordeal of silence Mr. Higgins had planned for her. Dressed in a demure grey suit and a small dark blue hat lent to her by Sandra that set off her auburn hair, Lane tried her earnest best to look like the docile little woman, complete with gloves. These she now took off and held in her hand, watching the traffic beginning to build up along Whitehall Road.

THE DIRECTOR LOVED the city in the morning and decided to walk to the War Office for his appointment with General Haight. It was a pity to waste such a lovely day. He was scheduled to meet the general to discuss the possibility of improving surveillance along the Yugoslav border, so he had a light briefcase with him. He made his way along Curzon Street and turned into St James; from there he would walk along Pall Mall. The birdsong lifted his spirits no end. He was tempted to remove his hat. His wife and children had already decamped to their country home, and he was hopeful of getting a week's holiday when this bit of work was done. Sighing in preparation for the job of persuasion required to help the general understand what modern surveillance entailed, he turned the corner and then stopped dead. Instinctively, he turned his back to the figure at the top of the stairs.

How was it possible? There, clearly waiting for someone, was Lane Winslow, as heart-stoppingly beautiful as ever. He walked away, toward the west door, and then turned and watched her from under the brim of his hat. He had the advantage. She clearly had not seen him. Indeed, she was glancing at her watch and looking in the opposite direction for someone she evidently expected to come that way. The director was in turmoil. She was supposed to be in Canada. What was she doing in London? How had he missed it? She must have been in town only a short time. It might take a few days for the reports to reach him of any of his people coming and going through customs.

As he watched, a short man hurried up the stairs and nodded at Lane, and they turned and went into the building. Who was that? He'd seen him before . . . something legal, he was sure. The name Higgins came to mind. A barrister who'd mounted a hopeless, as it turned out, defence of a functionary at the War Office who had mishandled sensitive information, the director now recalled.

In a second, he understood. He mentally smote his own forehead at his stupidity. It was brought on by the shock of seeing her, he told himself. One thing was clear. Things had gone much further than he imagined. His obligation to the general forgotten, he hailed a cab.

"Middle Temple," he said tersely.

"CAPTAIN HOGARTH IS ready for you now," the young man said. Lane and Higgins had been sitting side by side on wooden chairs placed along the wall of a dark hallway. Higgins had cautioned silence once inside the building, and so they had sat like an estranged couple, Lane looking longingly toward the end of the long gallery, where light from the distant square of window made no dent on the murkiness.

They were ushered into a wood-panelled office, where they were greeted by, to Lane's surprise, a woman in a khaki uniform. "Good morning. Captain Hogarth, ATS. Please sit down." She did not offer to shake hands.

Higgins said, "I'm Drake Higgins, barrister-at-law. Flight Lieutenant Higgins."

"I know who you are. Who's this?" she said crisply.

Lane smiled, she hoped innocuously, and said, "Lane Winslow." She prayed she would not have to explain her presence.

The captain looked at her curiously and pursed her lips, and then redirected her attention to the barrister. "So, I understand you need information regarding a couple of airmen."

"Yes, they were members of a bomber crew, and we do need to get hold of them urgently as witnesses in a pending court matter," Higgins said. "I submitted three names when I made the appointment."

"Donald Belton, Harold Salford, and Neville Anthony. I'm afraid I've been unable to find what you want." She looked up at them as if defying them to contradict her.

"The information doesn't exist, or you are unable to provide it?" asked Higgins, but he found the captain's attention was on Lane.

"Courier," Captain Hogarth said suddenly. "I remember now. I thought I'd seen you before. You won't remember me, of course. We never met officially."

Lane looked closely at the woman behind the desk but could not place her. She had said "courier." Was she involved with the air detail that dropped them off in France? She smiled. "Just desk work, I'm afraid."

"Good for you," the captain said, smiling. "My mistake. We meet so many people here. One loses track. Would you excuse me a moment?" She got up and went out the door, closing it carefully behind her. In the silence that followed, Higgins turned to Lane.

"What was that in aid of, I wonder? Have you worked here? You didn't say." He had a slightly aggrieved tone.

"I had a tiny little desk job in the basement of another building. It can have no relevance."

"On the contrary, it could impede our ability to get anything out of these people if it turns out you worked here and they have reason, for instance, to distrust you. Were you sacked? Is that why you said nothing?"

"I was not sacked," she said, her amused smile belying her sudden doubt. Why had it not occurred to her that in a place the size of the War Office there could possibly be someone who recognized her? Of course, it hadn't even been her headquarters for the period she had had a desk job. She had worked at Wormwood Scrubs, but she saw now there must be many people who stayed on, changing jobs and functions to meet the new postwar reality.

"Right," Captain Hogarth said, coming in and standing by Lane's chair. "There really is nothing we can do, I'm afraid." As Lane stood up, Captain Hogarth offered Lane her hand, smiling genially. Lane could feel the small folded piece of paper pressed against her palm and, shrugging with an, "oh well, we tried," expression, pushed it quickly into her handbag and snapped the bag shut. The door behind them was ajar.

"Thank you for trying, Captain Hogarth. We're sorry for taking up so much of your time." The captain offered a quick shadow of a smile. "I'll bid you good day, then." She nodded at Lane's companion. "Mr. Higgins."

"THIS IS A brilliant cup of tea," Lane commented. They had walked in silence toward Charing Cross, Higgins guiding the way, and now sat in a teashop. Lane had the folded paper in her hand. "We'd better see what we have, then." She opened the paper and placed it between them. Three names, three addresses.

Higgins looked at her narrowly. "How, exactly, did you do this?"

"I couldn't say." She couldn't, but she silently thanked Captain Hogarth for what appeared to be her notion of solidarity. She knew it must be because of her war work.

Hogarth could have been part of the ground crew. Lane wished now she'd paid more attention, but she'd always been in the grip of nerves before each flight and had focused intensely on what she was to do and what coded information she had to carry. Lane smiled briefly at the idea that it was simply because they were women, and Hogarth might have had her fill of trying to prove herself to the men around her who, no doubt, expressed surprise that a flighty woman with no head for machinery, or weapons, or whatever she'd been called on to do, could manage.

Higgins pocketed the paper. "I'll get started on these. I understand you'll have the means to get Flight Lieutenant Darling out this afternoon. We'll meet at the Donaldsons' at, say, five?"

Lane nodded, gulping the last of her tea, and then took a handkerchief out of her handbag and wrapped up the remaining scone. "You don't mind do you? It will provide a bedtime snack at the peerless Mrs. Macdonald's rooming house. She shuts the larder up tight immediately after dinner."

LANE HAD COMPLETED her business at the bank, which true to its word had opened up an account for her and issued a draft for five hundred pounds without too much fuss, since she'd been a customer there during the war. She had brought to England an additional hundred for living expenses and in case she had to travel about. The addresses on the paper were local enough. One in Kent, that was Anthony, and one in Sussex, Belton. The third, Salford, was in Norfolk. That was going to be farther away to travel.

As she made her way to the courthouse, she wondered how Higgins would approach contact with the aircrew. She felt the urge to be in charge of getting the witness statements but knew that, in spite of his officiousness, Higgins knew his business. She smiled at the memory of his surprise at the turn of events at the War Office. She appreciated that he made no mention of it but seemed to just take it on board. She felt herself warming up to him slightly—and to everything else at the moment. She'd soon be walking out in the sunshine with Darling. They could pretend, if only for a short time, that they were just a couple in love gadding about London. She put firmly out of her mind the coming ordeal of the trial as she approached the clerk at the prison.

"I have the bond money for Frederick Darling," she said. "His hearing was on Friday."

"Darling, Darling. Yes, here we are. Five hundred pounds." The clerk had an air of complete lack of interest, as if such sums were a daily occurrence.

Lane opened her bag, took out the draft, and slid it forward under the grill.

"No, wait," the clerk said suddenly, looking again at the paperwork. "That bond has been withdrawn." He closed the file and looked up as if he was ready for the next customer. Lane glanced behind her, trying to still the turmoil of anger and fear she felt.

"Withdrawn? What do you mean?"

The clerk reopened the file. "Just what I said. The judge has withdrawn the bond provision. Not surprising, really. It's a murder charge."

Lane shook her head. "Who can I talk to?"

"No one here, miss. You'll have to talk to his brief."

Lane turned away from the clerk and tried to pull her thoughts together. She'd have to see Darling, tell him. Her heart sank. He was living on the hope of getting out. She would tell him that she was going right back to Higgins. He could do whatever lawyers did to right this. She would try to sound hopeful and businesslike. With this resolve, she went to the prison and asked to see him.

"Sorry. He's been moved," the uniformed clerk at the visitor's desk said.

"What do you mean, moved? Moved where?"

"I've no idea. Ask his legal man."

"But he can't have been. He was due to get out on bail today." Lane knew she was beginning to sound pleading. It would do no good with the automatons that seemed to populate the place, she thought, her anger and fear beginning to build. In any case, they had no power to help her.

"Listen, love, I wish I could help. You're a good-looking girl. I bet he wishes he could see you too. But there it is."

You, on the other hand, Lane thought, turning to leave, are an absolute, bloody ass.

THEY SAT IN silence around the Donaldson table. "This is ridiculous," Sandra said. "It's like one of those spy novels Rudy's always reading." She felt a rush of feeling for Lane.

"It's absolutely unaccountable," Higgins said. "I've grilled my chambers clerk, and he swears nothing has come for me to explain this change of status. I shall have to spend tomorrow doing whatever needs doing to track him down. After all, it's Great Britain. Everyone is entitled to due process."

"Are they?" Lane asked. "I've seen more due process in the tiny town I live near in Canada. We'll need to come up with a plan."

"I'm at work the next two days, or I'd be more helpful," Rudy said.

"Miss Winslow. I feel I owe you an apology," Higgins said suddenly. "I confess that initially I thought you might be a detriment. When I examine what information we do have, it seems that most of it is due to you. The fact of Watson's reluctance, the unaccountable release of information from the War Office. Your level-headed response to what must have been a blow to you today is telling. I'm going to have to be occupied with exerting my client's rights, and I wonder now if you might be able to trace these airmen. I've no doubt that they will have been silenced as well, but we must get what we can. Something is very much amiss with this whole business."

"Mr. Higgins, there is no need for an apology. I should have barrelled on regardless, I'm sure. I like your cautious approach, as a matter of fact. It insulates us against too much optimism. The key thing for me right now is that Darling is innocent. There must be a way to prove it."

CHAPTER TWELVE

France, April 1943

WATSON RAN TOWARD THE BANK of trees, following the others, and collapsed with them on the ground, breathing hard. The last to arrive was Darling, who was looking from one to the other and then back toward the wreckage.

"Bloody Germans," muttered Anthony. He got up and moved toward the underbrush, and knelt down. Watson turned his attention back to the skip, who was asking for a damage report. He'd run to this spot. He must be all right. "Trouser leg torn," he said, but swivelled his eyes toward where Anthony stood. He was saying something about the rear gunner. Someone was missing. He sat up out of his slouch and looked more closely in the semi-darkness, and heard himself beginning to count.

"It's going to blow! Move!" Darling's voice burst through the fog, and Watson was on his feet, running. He could hear Salford just behind him, swearing under his breath. The explosion pummelled against them, making Watson feel like a giant hand had squeezed his chest and then hurled him away. He could hear gunfire. He lost track of Anthony, who seemed to have stayed till the end near Darling.

"Allez, vite!" Watson swung around at those words and saw a man in a cloth cap signalling to them urgently. He looked around and saw Darling and Anthony had caught up with them. Darling gave a nod and waved at them to follow.

"Better be a trustworthy frog," he heard Belton say to him.

"Where are Evans and Jones?" he asked.

"Evans copped it. Don't know about Jones. Haven't seen him at all."

They were hurried past the farmhouse, its shutters closed and unwelcoming, to an outbuilding where they were ushered with frantic urgings by the farmer, down a steep flight of wooden stairs into the pitch dark. Watson breathed in a nearly suffocating breath of damp earth and rotting fruit. He could see a match struck, and light suddenly flooded the room, causing him to turn away and shut his eyes for a moment.

"You stay, oui?"

Darling began to talk in French, and he and the farmer had an urgent conversation. Nodding, Darling took the lamp and waited while the farmer climbed the stairs and closed the door above them. He set the lamp on a wooden crate. Watson looked around. There were barrels against the wall to their right, the source of the smell, he realized.

"Well, we'll have something to drink if we get stuck here," he commented.

"He's going to return later with some food when it's quiet," Darling said. "In the meantime, we'll have to figure out how to get back to England. Apparently he can also lay his hands on a wireless. We may be able to arrange some sort of pickup along the coast."

"I bloody hope so," said Belton. "I don't fancy climbing the mountains to Spain."

"I've confirmed Evans is dead. Our host, Gaston, said he'll wait till it's clear and try to recover him. Anyone seen Jones?"

There was a silence after this. Watson thought about the moment they knew they were going down, but all he could remember was his own stumbling trajectory to safety.

"Well, let's hope he got away somewhere safe," Darling said, sounding weary. "Try to get as comfortable as possible. I wish I knew what was bloody going on above ground." He was silent. "Look, can we just go over everything now, while we might remember it? I felt an engine go out. But we must have been under attack because they were there, waiting for us, weren't they? We seemed to be on course, Watson?"

"Yes, sir. We were, sir."

"You're right about the engine, sir," Anthony said. His voice was tense and angry. "It's so bloody noisy in those planes, I heard it the minute it dropped out."

"Jones came to check on me just before it happened," Belton said suddenly, "and then he was on his way to the rear, to Evans. Something about coordinates. If they were both at the rear, I wouldn't give them a hope in hell when we came down. It's a miracle Evans got out. I'd put any money on Jones going up with the plane."

LANE SAT UP late into the night, her mind in turmoil, not letting her sleep. It was all part of the same picture. She turned on her light and went across the room to get her notebook and pencil. Back under the covers with the meagre pillow provided by Mrs. Macdonald propping her up, she began to write. Darling is brought to England and then arrested for apparently shooting his gunner. Watson the navigator is frightened and warned off, good chance the others were too. She'd track them down. Darling's bail cancelled, and Darling suddenly not allowed visitors. Had he been moved somewhere else, or was she being lied to? He'd been moved, she decided. It is messy to increase the number of people needing to lie. The War Office couldn't give them information, except secretly. Lane felt a flood of gratitude to Captain Hogarth and hoped her sudden release of the information they wanted was not also part of some plot. That was it, really. The whole thing felt like a plot, a conspiracy.

She was about to write "why," in big letters, when she wrote instead "what started it?" The whole thing had a wearily familiar tone to it. It was, she knew almost to a certainty, something to do with the intelligence branch. Only they would go to the trouble of manipulating all the players, and only if they had something important to cover up. If whatever situation could have been managed without "handling" it, they would have let natural justice take its course . . . no need to attract undue attention. It must be something big, something that had been lost control of. And it had to involve that plane crash.

She wondered if she should warn Higgins to be careful, but she dismissed this out of hand. It would mean telling him that she suspected the intelligence branch, and that would lead to his knowing she'd been involved with intelligence during the war. Official secrets. She'd be arrested herself if she wasn't careful. No. He had to proceed using the law to protect his client if he possibly could. Who knew, perhaps the judge had not been got at and would object to prisoners, even those up for murder, being disappeared.

She thought about the one person who might be able to find out, who might be able to help, and knew, as certainly as she knew her own name, that she must avoid him. With a sinking heart she realized the impossibility of this. If he had traced her to Canada, he already knew she was back in Britain. God, he would know every bloody thing she did!

With a semblance of a plan and an earnest hope that Sandra was as game as she seemed, Lane finally fell into a fitful sleep.

AMES JINGLED THE car keys at O'Brien. "Want to come for a ride? I've got Maclean on the desk for the time being."

O'Brien didn't have to be asked twice. "What's up, then?" he asked as he climbed into the passenger seat.

"I got a telegram from Miss Winslow with some information about Agatha Browning, but it isn't doing me a blind bit of good. Her parents, her sisters, who died when. But I've been thinking about the mess in the cabin, and I feel like I didn't explore it well enough. It was so destroyed that it was difficult to see past the mess, and Darling's head was somewhere else, so he didn't pick up on this idea either, and that is, where's the evidence that there was someone else there? I fingerprinted the doorknobs, et cetera, and I got nothing, and I haven't found the weapon. The car's gone missing and I've alerted the RCMP detachments, but you could hide a car anywhere in the bush up any logging road and no one would ever see it again."

"So we're going to see if we can pick up any evidence someone else was there?"

"That's the idea." Ames drove on in silence, cursing inwardly that they'd gotten behind a truck that generated a level of dust that forced them to keep their windows shut.

"Wonder how the boss is getting along," O'Brien said. "Must be nice being on a continental holiday."

"I'm not sure how much of a holiday it is. More like official business. I imagine he'll be back soon, and I'd like to get this solved. He might have some respect for me then," Ames laughed. "Here we are." He turned right down the road to the ferry landing, glad to be out of the stream of dust. The ferry was just pulling out from the other side. They had time to get out into the sun and take a breath of air.

The sun, still in the east, slanted onto the lake, creating a canvas of sparkling water. The air was clean, and redolent with the smell of the evergreens that surrounded them and climbed up the mountain slope opposite them. The low chugging sound of the cable ferry making its way to them from the other side of the lake lent an air of an unhurried summer day to the morning.

"Hard to imagine someone slashed to bits like that in a place like this," Ames said, sighing.

The cabin was how he'd left it—broken crockery on the floor by the sink, a bookshelf upset, chairs turned over.

Only the photograph of the three girls was on the table, where Ames had left it after picking it up and righting the table.

"How the heck are you going to find out if someone else was here? It's not like they left a calling card." O'Brien said, toeing a book that had been flung from the bookshelf.

"Well, let's imagine it was someone who came to visit and then the whole thing went off the rails. Would she give him some tea or something? Let's pick up all these dishes, broken or not, and look for signs of use."

They took up a basket that had been sitting on the landing of the rear door and filled it with broken crockery. Anything not broken they carefully piled by the sink.

"Looky here, Ames," O'Brien said suddenly. "Someone's had a tea party." He was holding up a chipped cup in which there was a ring of what looked like dried tea.

"Okay, let's look for another. Either she just never washed her dishes or she did indeed have a tea party." They found another cup, similarly marked, that had slid behind the door in the rampage. Behind the stove was a broken teapot that must have been in bad shape to start with, mouldy tea leaves resting on the side it had lain on.

"So they got into some sort of donnybrook and then whoever it was grabbed a knife and chased her out to the outhouse, and they got into a wrestling match, and mine hostess was slashed. That pretty well it?"

"Yes, and then she tried, wounded, to get away, so she couldn't have been going that fast, and the other party followed and pushed her down. We don't know if the trashing of the cabin was before or after . . . did everything get tossed around because they were tossing things at each other, or did the assailant come later and do over the cabin?"

O'Brien took off his hat and scratched his head. "How old did you say this dame was?"

"Seventy-something. She looks a hundred."

"So, she's old, she's wounded, she couldn't have been moving too swiftly. If a man had done this, he'd have caught her and finished her off long before she got to where she died. Maybe it was an older man, or God help us, a woman.

"Can you see a woman doing this? It's not the sort of thing women do. Trouble is, we got nobody of any description coming over in the three days prior to finding the body. Talked to a kid called Nobby who ran the ferry while the regular guy was off and he says no one unusual came. So let's say it's a woman. She got over here somehow without being seen . . . Can you see a woman rowing across the lake in the dead of night? Especially if she was not bent on murder but was just coming to visit? She had to have come over on the ferry. What we know for sure is she, or he, dressed as the dead woman, drove that car across and disappeared. I've sent a description of that damn car to every RCMP unit in a hundred-mile radius, and nothing."

"Maybe you should concentrate on the car. I'm guessing she ditched it somewhere." They were walking down the hill to where they had parked the car on the grassy slope of the road.

"Needle in a haystack, O'Brien. Needle in a haystack!"

They were just climbing back into the maroon Ford when a man hailed them.

"Hey, you two here about that poor Agatha woman?" An old man walking a mongrel had stopped and was swatting at the grass with a walking stick.

"That we are. I don't remember talking to you. Did my colleague interview you? What's your name?" Ames asked.

"Ernie Jack, and no, I was not interviewed by anyone. I just got back from seeing my boy in Revelstoke. I just heard about what happened. Did you catch the guy?"

Ames shook his head. "Not yet, I'm afraid. I don't think you need to worry too much though. I expect he's long gone."

The man laughed. "I'm not afraid. I got Marky here to watch out for me. Did you talk to that woman from the old country?"

Ames, who had reached into his pocket to take out his notebook to ask a few questions, looked up.

"What woman from the old country?"

"That one I brought over here last week. Found her walking on the road and offered her a ride, just outta town there, near the ferry landing. I couldn't make out where an old woman like that thought she was going on foot. When she told me she was looking for Agatha Browning, I told her I live here myself. Said she was her sister. I didn't get her name."

"Her sister? Are you sure? And you brought her here? Can you describe her?"

"Old. White hair. Kinda thin. Had a little suitcase with her. Blue eyes? Maybe blue. A bit like her sister's. I wasn't expecting to have to describe her to anyone. Nice enough. Told me she'd come a long way to see her sister. Hadn't seen her in over forty years, she said."

"Can you remember anything else about her? What she was wearing?"

"Oh gosh. A dress, a jacket maybe. A hat. I didn't pay attention, if I'm honest."

Very helpful, Ames thought. "Colour of the dress?"

The man twisted his mouth in thought. "Honestly, I couldn't say. I'm not too observant."

No kidding, Ames thought.

CHAPTER THIRTEEN

London, March 1907

THE TEA ROOM AT CLARIDGE'S was subdued and cheerful, and the two or three couples dancing to the palm court orchestra made Agatha feel at once envious and guilty.

"What are you thinking?" Alphonse asked, reaching for her hand.

"That this is so terribly wrong. That we are breaking Lucy's heart."

"Lucy's heart was doomed the minute I saw you. You wouldn't want me to go back to her. It would only make all our lives miserable. In any case, she doesn't really know, does she? Only that I've broken it off."

"God, you're obtuse sometimes! When she finds out, it will be an absolute betrayal!" Agatha looked away from him toward the window. The street, a bustle of horses, cabs, people, hawkers shouting, seemed unbearably noisy to her. It was too late to pull out of it all, and she knew it. She could never go back home where she would have to lie to her father, to her sisters.

Alphonse watched her. The brim of her white hat framed the profile of her face, and he wondered if this was the time. She was distressed about her sister, but surely she could see that he loved her to distraction? He could put it right. He had bought a ring and he had only to pull it out of his pocket.

"Agatha, my dearest, lovely creature. I have something to ask you. Please say nothing until I have finished. I know you are distressed on behalf of your sister. I understand it, but she will come to accept it in time. She will find someone else. There were heaps of young men interested in her when we were up at the MacPhersons' that weekend."

Agatha turned to look at him. "It isn't heaps of young men she wants. It's you."

"But I love you. And you love me. You know you do. Please, Aggy, please say you'll marry me."

Agatha looked down, her face flushing, and then looked up at him. "I came here against my own better judgment because I do love you. But I cannot possibly marry you. I'm surprised you could ask it of me. What would happen? We would settle into your house in Belgravia? And what about my family? I would be estranged from them absolutely when they came to know it was I who broke her heart. I have given you everything already. I cannot throw my betrayal right in the face of my poor sister."

"Agatha, please. You are only making this more complicated than it need be"

"No, listen, Alphonse. It is not just Lucy's heart that is doomed. We are doomed. You can never make an honest woman of me, nor an honest marriage of us. We began in deception, and we will suffer the consequences."

"I say! Henderson! How do?"

Alphonse looked up, shocked by the intrusion, and stood up hastily, dropping his napkin, and offered his hand to the man who had appeared at their table.

"Carruthers. What are you doing up in town? Oh, excuse me. Miss Browning, Mr. Carruthers. We were up at Oxford together."

Carruthers bowed in Agatha's direction. "I say, you aren't related to old Geoffrey Browning, member for Dorset? Only I'm articling with my uncle in the Commons. He's quite a live wire. Always on his feet!"

Agatha inclined her head slightly and glanced at Alphonse.

"We're just on our way, I'm afraid," Alphonse said. "Or I'd invite you to sit."

Carruthers grinned. "I'm late myself. Supposed to meet my sainted mother here. Much rather be at my club, but what are you going to do? There she is!" He waved toward a table across the room and then turned to Agatha, touching the brim of his dove grey hat. "Miss Browning, Henderson." And he was off.

France, April 1943

THE STEADY ROAR of the plane was interrupted. Jones looked back. Evans was peering anxiously out into the night, alert, his arms resting on the gun. Up ahead, Watson and Anthony were hurriedly conferring. In a moment they would be with the pilot. He could hear the engine faltering already. He shook his head. The attack had come like lightning from below them somewhere in the dark. Still.

Darling was good . . . if anyone could get them down, he could.

Darling was shouting now, "Brace, brace!"

Jones leaned over in his seat and put his arms over his head. The impact threw his head back and down again, and he felt like his teeth had gone through his bottom lip. They hit the earth hard, and then the plane began to scream along the ground. The wheels had not deployed. The sound of metal tearing and crashing into whatever was outside reverberated, drawing cries from the crew. Finally, with a thump, the plane stopped. There was a moment of stillness, and then the men began to move. He could hear Darling shouting for them to get out. He looked back toward the rear of the plane. Evans was moving, was jumping to the ground from his perch. Jones stopped, now, momentarily panicked, and then followed him out the gaping hole that was the torn rear gunner station, and into the darkness.

Paris, March 1947

"IT WAS A lovely idea for us to come here for our anniversary," Irene Salford said, taking a conciliatory tone. They were sitting on a bench on the edge of a pond in the Tuileries.

"Well, you say that," returned Salford grumpily, "but you complained about the bed all night, and said the coffee was too strong."

"I know, darling. I'm sorry. You know how I get when I don't get any sleep. As to the coffee . . . well, we probably don't even remember what real coffee tastes like because of the war, so finally getting some is a shock! Anyway,

I'm as happy as a lamb now sitting in the sunshine in this beautiful park. Look at those elegant buildings beyond the trees. It hardly seems like there's been a war."

"Well . . . I have to confess I could use something besides a flakey bun for my breakfast. Still, it will be nice to tell the others when we get home. They'll be dead jealous!" Salford closed his eyes and leaned back, turning his face to the sun, feeling its warmth. He put his arm around his wife and thought how good it was that it was all bloody over.

"Harry, look at that man. Isn't that one of the fellows from your crew?"

Salford sat up and opened his eyes. His eyes were still a little dazzled by the sunlight, and he and tried to focus where his wife was pointing. He could see no one clearly.

"Where?"

"Over there, see, by the kiosk."

Salford finally saw what his wife was pointing at. The shock made him turn away and shake his head, and then look again, his eyebrows knitting.

"Stay here," he said to his wife, and he got up and went across the wide dirt walkway toward the kiosk. It couldn't be him, of course. It couldn't be. But the resemblance was so striking that he thought he even recognized that grim set of the mouth Jones always had.

"Jones," he said, when he got near him. The man, who was drinking coffee from the kiosk, did not even turn his head. He was reading a newspaper.

"I say, Jones, is that you?" Salford said, putting his hand on the man's arm.

At this the man turned and looked at Salford, puzzled. "Oui?" He asked.

Salford stepped back. It was him, he could swear it, but this man did not seem to recognize him at all. "I'm sorry," he faltered. "I could have sworn you were someone I know."

The man shrugged, and gave a rueful smile. "No English," he said apologetically, his accent so thick Salford could barely understand him. The man turned, put down his coffee cup, folded his paper, and touched the brim of his hat. "Monsieur," he said, and then walked away toward the Louvre.

It was three months later that Harold Salford sat down at his desk and started a letter, his second, to his old flight skipper, Frederick Darling.

> *Dear FL,*
>
> *Remember I told you a couple of months ago that I thought I'd seen Jones alive and well in Paris, only to find he was some dead ringer who couldn't speak a word of English? I tell you what. I can't stop thinking about it. I know we all gathered at that church in Fadmore all the bloody way up in Yorkshire for his funeral service, complete with the unhappy father and the weeping wife, but I can't shake the feeling that it was* him *in Paris.*
>
> *I mean, we knew Evans had copped it because we had his body, but we never did find Jones, did we? We just assumed he went up in the plane. I've been racking my brain about those moments before the crash. I remember where everyone was, but I have*

this idea Jones wasn't where he was supposed to be. He passed me going to the back of the plane. I couldn't make out where he was going, especially as we were about to crash land.

I think the bloody bastard deserted, that's what. I think he saw an opportunity, and he left out the rear gunning window. Leaving us to fight on while he buggered off to lie low for the duration.

Well, I suppose there's nothing to be done about it now, but it's bloody annoying. I keep wondering if I should tell someone.

When are you coming over? You've promised before, you know!

Salford

CHAPTER FOURTEEN

———

"**I**T'S SO GOOD OF YOU to come with me, Sandra," Lane said, pulling out her change purse. They were at King's Cross buying tickets to Norwich in Norfolk. "No, no, let me," she added as Sandra tried to hand her money. She smiled at the ticket seller and thanked him. "That's that then. The train will be pulling out in ten minutes. Let's get a nice seat and think about how to approach this."

They walked along the train, checking with the conductor that it wouldn't be splitting anywhere, and picked a carriage.

"Who is this we are seeing first?" Sandra asked, looking at the notebook Lane had in her hand.

"This is Harold Salford. He was the wireless operator. Once we've covered him, we can go to down to Sussex." She became thoughtful. "Higgins believes they'll all have been got at. I hope not."

They had already decided that being direct was the best way forward, so having reviewed how they would approach Salford, they settled in to talk about their own lives. Lane talked about her home in King's Cove, a circumstance that was wondrous to Sandra, who was mostly mystified at Lane's wanting to live so far away from "civilization." Lane was happy to talk about the people she'd left behind in her new community. It took her mind off the crawling fear about what had happened to Darling. She earnestly hoped Higgins was having luck demanding that his client be produced.

The tea trolley further distracted them with strong cups of tea and egg mayonnaise sandwiches.

"Of course, if you hadn't gone out to Canada, you wouldn't have met Frederick," Sandra said between bites. "I'm a terrible romantic. I believe in fate."

Lane smiled. "I don't know that I believe in fate . . . or anything really. The war, I always feel, cannot have been fate. Fate makes things seem inevitable, but surely a devastating war could have been avoided. I imagine even Darling could have been avoided if someone hadn't died on my property."

"Fate, you see. I don't think you could have avoided him. From what I have gotten to know in the few days he was with us before . . . anyway . . . I think he's a perfect man for you. You know how I can tell? He didn't talk about you except to say, in a voice I've never heard from any man, that if anything happened you were to be notified. That you were intelligent and deserved to know. That's when I knew."

"You do talk nonsense, Sandra," Lane said lightly, but all she could feel inside was the terrible fear that her fate was to lose him.

"THIRTEEN, FOURTEEN, FIFTEEN. I think this must be the one." Lane checked the address again. The house was in a row of houses along a still-cobbled street, with little fenced front gardens that seemed to have benefitted from some sort of neighbourhood competition for attractive floral display.

Sandra frowned. "The curtains are drawn. I hope they haven't bugg . . . gone off on holiday or something. As it is we'll have to stay here in town overnight. It would be an awful waste of a trip."

Lane looked at the house. It seemed unnaturally still to her. She had a fancy that the people who lived here had left for some darker reason, but when she applied the dragon-head brass knocker, she was rewarded with a sound from inside. At length they could hear the lock being pulled on the dark green door and the handle being turned. The door opened a crack, disgorging a strong smell of cigarette smoke. A young woman in a black dress with a large men's cardigan wrapped around her came to the door. She said nothing but just looked at them for a moment. Lane felt sharply the contrast between them; Sandra and Lane in summer dresses, standing in a flood of early afternoon sunshine, and this exhausted woman inside the shadows of the smoky house.

"Mrs. Salford?" Lane asked, finally. Lane could see out of the corner of her eye that a neighbour on the way into the house next door had stopped and was watching the interaction.

"Yes?" The woman made no move to open the door but leaned on it instead, as if she could scarcely hold herself up.

"I'm Lane Winslow, and this is Sandra Donaldson. We've come to talk to your husband on behalf of Flight Lieutenant Darling to just collect a few details about a crash they had in '43. Would he have a little time for us?" This explanation seemed desperately inadequate to Lane suddenly. If she were Salford, she'd be wondering why Darling wasn't there himself. Time enough to explain, she decided, hoping it would not make him clam up the way it had Watson.

"He . . ." Mrs. Salford began, and then she closed her eyes. For a minute Lane and Sandra thought she was going to faint, but she only wavered and then put her hand on the door frame to hold herself up.

"Goodness, lovie, you don't look at all well!" Sandra said, taking charge of the situation. She put her arm gently around Mrs. Salford's shoulder and pushed through into the house. "Come on, then. Let's get you onto the sofa. You don't look like you've had a decent meal in days."

The woman put up no objection and collapsed onto the couch, watching listlessly as Lane and Sandra bustled, opening curtains and windows, filling the kettle, looking for something to feed her. Lane saw the neighbour turn and continue into her own house.

Mrs. Salford began to cry, her head down, her hands kneading the edge of the cardigan in her lap. "He's dead," she said, as if saying it for the first time. "He's dead. He was just going to the post office and he walked over the tracks into the path of a train. They tried to tell me he committed suicide. That he was despondent because of a crash he was in. You know that shell shock soldiers seem to get. But he wasn't, you know."

"But when did this happen?" Lane asked, her heart sinking.

"Two days ago. The police came. I haven't even told his parents. I should have. The padre's arranged for a funeral on Friday. It would be horrible if they found out from the papers."

"How dreadful for you! Especially with people saying he did it himself."

"I know he didn't. We're going to have a baby. He was ever so happy about it. He just wasn't like that. He was always cheerful and upbeat. He got a little bit funny after Paris, but he is just preoccupied about his work, especially with the baby coming."

"Look," said Sandra. "Get this toast and egg down you, and then run along and have a bath. Give me your in-laws number, and I'll call them. How about for you? Do you have someone we can contact?"

"No. There's just my sister, but she moved to Australia with her husband before the war. Thank you . . ." her voice faltered. "I didn't know what to say to them about Harry. They doted on him." She began to cry again silently.

Sandra was able to persuade the unhappy widow to go upstairs and was running a bath for her. Deeply pre-occupied, Lane wondered what the death of a potential witness must mean. She could not shake the idea that it was no coincidence that one of the men on the crew had been warned off and another had, possibly, been silenced permanently. She busied herself tidying the kitchen and washing up as she pondered what they ought to do. There was a timid knock at the door. Lane hesitated, suddenly wary, but looking out the window toward the doorstep she saw only the elderly neighbour, looking concerned. She opened the door.

"Oh, hello. I live just next door. I couldn't help seeing you coming into poor Irene's house. She's let no one come near her since the . . . accident. We've been powerless to offer any help or condolences. I just wonder if there is anything I can do? I was so glad to see she let you in."

"That's very kind, Mrs. . . . ?"

"Glover," said the neighbour.

"Very kind, Mrs. Glover. We've only just found out the dreadful news ourselves, but we are visiting from London. I imagine you could be a very great help because you are right here. I think she'll need some support, especially on Friday when the funeral is." Have I said too much? Lane wondered. After all, Mrs. Salford may well despise her neighbours and want nothing to do with them. Indeed, she and Sandra had no standing in this matter at all. But she knew she was right. Mrs. Salford would need support. "May we call on you when we have a clearer picture of the situation?"

"Absolutely. Thank you. She's a sweet woman. I believe they were . . . are . . . expecting."

Lane closed the door. If she was right that Salford's death was no coincidence, was Mrs. Salford even safe? She would suggest to his parents that she go back with them after the funeral. She busied herself cleaning up the kitchen and opening windows and curtains to air out the house. The back garden looked as though it had been well cared for, and, hoping she would not upset Mrs. Salford, she picked a few daisies and marigolds to put into a glass; perhaps it would bring a little joy into the house, she thought.

"All right. She's bathed and I've left her dressing," Sandra said coming downstairs and swishing the teapot hopefully. "She's in an awful state. I mean, it's not just that she lost her husband in this way, she seems actually a little frightened."

"I'm frightened for her myself, but what makes you say that?"

"Well for example, she said she hasn't dared to open the door to anyone. When I asked why, she said someone had been in the house about a month ago. Her husband told her he felt someone had come in and gone through his papers. At first he was surprised because nothing seemed to be missing, but then he discovered he was missing a letter that he'd been writing to Frederick . . . oh!" Sandra put her hand to her mouth. "What if there was something in the letter that has to do with Frederick being charged in that ridiculous way? Was he warning Frederick of something?"

Lane sat down with a thump. It was another coincidence that she couldn't overlook. She had asked herself what event could have precipitated this whole business. A stolen letter from one of his crewmen meant for him would certainly qualify.

"It's maddening not to know what was in that letter!" She exclaimed. "I'm certain he hadn't received anything earth-shaking from any crew member, or he would have said." Or was he, she wondered, keeping things from her? Why not, especially if it had to do with the war? She kept things from her past from him.

DARLING WOKE UP feeling disoriented. He had to look around at his cell to try to place himself. The cell was significantly different from the previous one. Smaller, though a window high in the wall let in more light. He must be in a cell on an outside wall. He was grateful that it was summertime. There was a clamminess to the cell that suggested it would be icy in the winter. He stood up and banged on the door. He had no idea what time it was or how long he'd been there. He only remembered a hasty removal from London in a windowless van, and a trip that must have lasted three hours. He struggled to remember what kind of facility would be that far away.

"Hello! Guard!" He banged again. Crestfallen at the lack of response, he was about to turn and go back to sit on the cot when he heard footsteps. The metal plate covering a small window on the door was pushed open.

"Yes?" He could see just the puffy face of a middle-aged man, a face not improved by the dull green cast of light emanating from the hallway outside his cell.

"Yes. Hello. Is there any chance I can talk to my lawyer, Higgins?" He kept his anger, which was fuelled by real fear, under wraps. No good antagonizing one of justice's foot soldiers.

"A Yank, then, are you?"

"Canadian. Can you ask someone for me?"

The guard shook his head. "Not in my remit," he said.

"Then can you get me someone whose bloody remit it's in?" Darling said.

"No need to get charry. I have my orders. Feed you, water you, take you out for a stroll about the yard. No doubt someone will come along in due course." The guard said. He began to close the metal window cover.

"Wait," Darling cried. "At least tell me where I am!"

"No can do. But I will say this. It's not a million miles from Nuffield." At this the guard chuckled and snapped the window to.

Darling sat on his bed and leaned against the wall, his feet up on the blanket. He could feel the metal wiring of the bedstead through the thin mattress. Nuffield indeed! In a country that had a million villages, Nuffield could be just about anywhere. He closed his eyes and tried to imagine what on earth his next thought ought to be. He had a natural disinclination to fully take in that he was powerless, and yet, by jerks and judders he could feel himself sinking into bewilderment and hopelessness. Bewilderment was nothing new. He was a detective, after all, but hopelessness was, and he was beginning to feel frightened by it. What would Lane do if she were in bloody Nuffield?

This thought of Lane gave him a start, and he opened his eyes, his sense of his own powerlessness dropping another precipitous mile. What if she was in danger somewhere? She'd been getting money to get him out on bail, and no doubt having heard whatever the authorities would have told her, was banging about the countryside looking for him, or talking to his airmen, stirring up whatever nest of hornets had put him here. He had no doubt now that she was in danger, and he could do nothing to protect her.

Ignoring the voice in the back of his head that told him that he was kidding himself that he ever had any ability to protect her, he went back to his original question. What would she do? She'd make a list, draw a map. Gather as many facts as she could and see what they looked like. In fact, he realized that aside from the map, her own peculiar specialty, it's exactly what he would do and should be doing now. He started with the most central fact: he did not shoot Rear Gunner Evans.

CHAPTER FIFTEEN

AMES SAT AT HIS DESK, banging his pencil rhythmically on the one visible corner of wood that wasn't covered in papers. It was of little comfort to him that there was no Darling to shout at him from the next office to stop making a racket and go make himself useful. Mrs. Browning's corpse was being kept cool pending the outcome of the investigation into her death, and he was beginning to wonder how long a corpse would keep under those circumstances because, though he now had a potential murderer in the sister, he didn't know where she was. She could have driven the car all the way to the coast and got on an aeroplane and be safely in her kitchen in Dorset drinking cocoa.

He and O'Brien had established that two people had had tea before Agatha was slashed and left to die, and that perhaps the cabin hadn't been turned over as a result of the fight between the victim and whoever it was, as there was no blood inside the cabin. Had the sister, for want of another suspect, begun to throw pictures and china around, and overturn furniture before she killed Mrs. Browning? And

"Missus" was a misnomer for a start . . . her maiden name was Browning, a fact he knew thanks to Miss Winslow's visit somewhere or other to get information about the family.

He took a piece of paper and tried to figure out how to take the few facts he had and establish a probable sequence of events. Drawing a line down the middle of the paper he wrote:

—One day before the body is found a woman gets a ride across the lake saying she is Agatha Browning's sister. No one else in the village sees a stranger.

That wouldn't be unusual, Ames thought. The person could have made her way directly to Agatha's cabin without meeting anyone in that tiny place. She would have been told by her ride how to get there.

—Two people have tea.
—Agatha is slashed with something the size of a kitchen knife (from her kitchen?) near the outhouse . . . evidence of the blood.
—Agatha, bleeding, is pursued into the forest, where she falls, or is pushed, and dies.
—The cabin is turned over.

He was going to write "in a rage," but stopped himself. He did not know that. Perhaps the person was extremely calm and on a deliberate campaign to destroy everything Agatha owned.

—The ferryman says Agatha took the ferry in her car late in the afternoon away from the village.

147

He thought for a moment and then felt safe enough to add:

—Agatha's car stolen by the murderer, who leaves the scene disguised as his or her victim.

He crossed out "his" and left "her." He felt fairly certain he could put among the facts that the murderer was a woman, and that woman was likely Agatha's sister—if she really was the sister.

Ames reached under some loose notes and picked up the one thing he'd taken from the scene after he'd gone back with O'Brien: the smashed picture of the three young girls leaning on a fence in England that he'd found on the floor. It reminded him that he knew something more.

—Youngest sister named . . .

He consulted the notes he'd made talking to Miss Winslow.

. . . Lucille, died at the age of twenty-one.

That left one remaining sister, Mary. The person who claimed to be Mrs. Browning's sister could have been telling the truth. He gazed at the picture, trying to imagine which one was which. One of them looked much younger than the other two . . . closer to sixteen in this picture. Could that have been Lucy? Let's say it was. That left the other two, and of these, which one would be Agatha? It was nearly impossible to transport the wrinkled and weathered visage onto the face of either of these carefree and pretty girls.

Writing "FACTS" on the top of the page of notes, he tore that page off his pad of foolscap and began another page, which he labelled "POSSIBLE SEQUENCE OF EVENTS." He tapped his pencil frenetically for another few moments and wrote:

—Mary Browning comes to the cabin of Agatha Browning, June five, having gotten a ride from someone going to the village and is dropped off. She asks for directions to the cabin and goes up the hill to see her sister.

He stopped again. The next part is fuzzy. Was she there to kill Agatha? If so, why be seen getting a ride and announcing she's the sister? If she had meant to kill her, would she be travelling around with a knife? Why not a revolver? Those were easier than candy to get . . . especially if she'd come over from England. Okay, let's say no. She's just coming to do her sisterly duty and visit her last remaining relation.

He continued:

—An altercation breaks out, Mary Browning grabs a kitchen knife and . . .

Wait. No. They were having tea inside and there is no blood in the cabin. Something must have got them outside. Did Mary lose her temper and begin to throw things around, causing Agatha to run outside to get away from her? Or did Mary grab the knife and pursue her sister, who ran outside to take shelter in the outhouse, catching her before she could lock herself in?

—Mary Browning slashes at her sister and, still in

*a rage, goes back into the cabin and begins to throw
things around, or look for something.*

Wait. She would have blood on her hands with all that
messy slashing. There would have been blood on anything
she touched. So she must wash her hands outside somehow, and then go back, leaving her sister bleeding.

*—Mary washes her hands, goes back into the cabin.
In the meantime, Agatha, bleeding badly and fearing
for her life, begins to run up the hill.*

Why up the hill? Why not down the hill toward the
village where help is available?

*—Mary finds or does not find what she is looking for,
sets off in pursuit of Agatha, finds her exhausted from
lack of blood, pushes her over, and then throws the
knife far into the bush where it can't be retrieved. She
then changes into Agatha's clothes, finds the key to her
jalopy, and drives away.*

Well, if this were really the sequence, it left some serious questions, the most pressing of which was, where was
Mary Browning now, if it was she who did it, with Agatha
Browning's car? He would have to ask the vicar how far
he thought the car could get. Could it get to the coast?
His second question was why had Agatha run farther away
from help? With these questions written, he slammed the
pencil down on the desk and sighed. His watch told him
it was near his usual quitting time, and Vi was hoping to
be taken to the pictures.

Ames was uncertain suddenly. He usually left the office before Darling, unless the inspector had him tracking down something. But what would Darling do? How late did he stay when he was on a case?

He reviewed what he'd done; he'd put out the information about the car and its driver to the RCMP and the Vancouver Police. Was he likely to get a call after 6:00 p.m.? No. The pictures it was then.

Anchors Aweigh provided entertainment that delighted Violet and should have provided at least some distraction for Ames. Mid-picture he looked at his watch in the flickering light of Gene Kelly in a sailor hat: 7:30 p.m. What time would it be over in England? He would have to phone the police there. It's what Darling would do. If he phoned over at 8:30 in the morning, he should get the police by 4:30 in the afternoon, provided it wasn't too complicated and time consuming for the exchanges involved to put the call through. If Mary Browning had made it back, she would have gone to her own home, wherever that was.

LANE AND SANDRA sat in the tea room of their hotel having lunch. Salford's parents had arrived by the morning train and were staying with his wife. They had promised to take her away with them when the funeral was over.

"I somehow feel we ought to stay for the funeral," Sandra said. "That poor woman seems to have no friends."

Lane shook her head. "That neighbour spent the night with her so she has someone. Every day matters right now, and anyway, her in-laws are there now. I think we should go to Sussex as planned to see Belton, the front gunner.

And then, and I know this is probably illegal or something, I think we should track down Anthony to find out why he thinks Darling killed Evans! Oh, damn."

"What?"

"I meant to ask Mrs. Salford why her husband had been preoccupied since Paris. It might throw light on why he killed himself . . . if he did. I'm beginning to imagine he was pushed, that somehow the other side, whoever they are, are going around nobbling the witnesses to secure a conviction. That, if nothing else, proves Darling is completely innocent."

"Oh. I actually did ask her that when we were upstairs packing her suitcase. She kept going on about how she couldn't imagine him killing himself, and I said, 'But you did say he was preoccupied after Paris,' and she said 'Oh, that. No. That was nothing. He just thought he saw someone he knew, only it wasn't him.' Or some such thing. She got upset, though, and suddenly said that the whole thing might be her fault because she was the one who pointed the man out because he looked just like a crew member from the war."

Lane put her cup down. "A crew member? She said that?"

"Yes. Oh, that's important, isn't it?"

"Yes. Yes, I think it is." Lane tried to keep the desperation out of her voice. "It could be terribly important. The whole thing turns around that damn crew. If Salford thought he saw a member of his crew and came home preoccupied, it could have . . . I don't know . . . precipitated a series of events. Did she say which crew member?"

"No. Only that it turned out not to be him."

Lane sighed. "No, of course. He'd know if someone was or wasn't a crew member. It just doesn't explain why he'd be preoccupied. Of course he could have been preoccupied by the size of the hotel bill, and come home worried about money and not told his wife. Do you think he told her which crew member? It would be odd if he didn't."

"No. I got the feeling she didn't know them except by sight. Do you want to go back and ask her? I think we just have time. Our train doesn't leave for another three-quarters of an hour."

"Oh, yes. Do let's. It will just niggle at me ever after if I've missed something important."

They walked back along the street, still cool in the morning, though already the sun was promising a hot day ahead. They passed a few shoppers. One man coming toward them stepped off the pavement to let them pass, glanced at them, and then touched the brim of his hat. Lane saw his brown eyes light up momentarily and the flash of a flirtatious smile, and then he moved on, a brief-case in hand with a rolled up newspaper, ready for the commute on the train.

"He's probably married with three little kiddies," Sandra whispered. "Behaving like that!"

IRENE SALFORD, LOOKING somewhat more rested for having her mother-in-law fussing over her and making sure she ate some regular meals, nevertheless bore the burden of her grief in her eyes. "No, I don't remember—if he even told me his name. I tell a lie . . . he might have. Something very forgettable. He was a bit superstitious and wanted to keep his flying life from his home life. I didn't know the names of any of them, but I'd seen them when I went to pick him up on leave. Is it important? Do you think it would explain . . . I mean, he seemed very surprised, and he was a bit moody for a while afterward."

Lane tried to sound comforting. "No, I'm sure it's not important. It's just that we are wanting to talk to as many people who flew with Darling as possible. If one of them is in Paris, of course, it would mean a longer trip for us." Lane squeezed Irene's hand one more time, and she and Sandra set off for the station.

"You know," Lane said, getting up off the wooden bench at the station and brushing off the back of her skirt. The train was rounding the bend, the billowing smoke carried aloft by the breeze. "I think it may be very important, this business of Paris. It happened three months ago, if what she says is right. What if it was a member of their crew who didn't want to be recognized?"

"But that doesn't make sense, does it?" asked Sandra. "Two of the crew are dead, and we have the addresses of the others. In fact, you've already seen one of them."

"Three."

"Three what?" asked Sandra.

"Three members of the crew are dead. Evans, Jones, and now poor Salford, who supposedly threw himself under an oncoming train right here." Both women looked nervously toward the pedestrian crossing that had been blocked off with barricades since the accident. It was no accident, Lane thought.

They settled in the nearly empty train, Sandra began

to doze under the influence of the gentle rocking of the carriage. Lane envied her. She herself had barely slept. She looked out at the passing countryside, the green beauty of which was providing very little in the way of comfort. Now alone with her thoughts, she could only dwell on the sick fear about what was happening to Darling.

CHAPTER SIXTEEN

Whitcombe, October 1907

"**H**ONESTLY, LUCY, THERE'S NO POINT in moping about. You haven't been out of the house in days." Mary sat in a wingback chair by the window, looking out at the landscape that had transformed itself in the last week from summer to autumn. She watched a small coterie of leaves, the sun captured in their oranges and yellows, break away and descend in whirls and curves to the ground. She was desperate to get outside. She loved this time of year, the air crisp and full of promise. Instead she felt bound to be with Lucy, who could not seem to shake her misery at being thrown over by that absolute pig, Alphonse. Where was Aggy when she was needed? She could be helping instead of swanning off to town to visit friends.

Lucy, in a chair by the fire that was usually occupied by their father, had been making a pretense of reading and now let the book, Tennyson, fall onto the floor. She looked at the fire and could feel the tears welling again. She wanted to say something but could not think what. Nothing made sense.

Mary got out of her chair, stifling a sigh, and came and knelt by her sister's chair, taking her hand. She didn't approve of Tennyson in this crisis. All that romantic tragedy.

"Look, it is beastly, what's happened. I can't even pretend to know what it feels like. I'm much too self-centred to love anyone, but you are a warm-hearted and loving girl, and he . . . well, he is a fool. You have done nothing wrong but give your love to the wrong person. He wouldn't have deserved you. What if you married him, and then he left you like this? How much worse would it be? Please, darling, try to snap out of it. I miss the old you. Daddy misses your dear, cheerful self."

Lucy clutched her hand and finally looked at her. "I don't understand it, that's all. I lie awake all night, going over every minute, from the moment we met, and I know he loved me. It was like we had discovered a missing half of our own selves. That's exactly how he put it. I never knew such happiness was possible. Every time we met, at the MacPhersons', at Hermione's, at that dinner at the Harveys', we were so happy. At the dinner we found time to sneak out to the garden and sit in the darkness on a bench, looking at the house full of people. He said to me, "They've no idea what happiness is, do they?" And then he kissed me. It was then he said . . . she burst into tears.

Mary took Lucy in her arms. She had never felt so absolutely powerless. Well, if Aggy wasn't coming home, Father was, at least. "He deceived you. He hoodwinked all of us. Look, darling, just come with me for a little walk. We can go meet Father at the station. Hastings can bring his bags back, and we'll walk with Father over the top path. It will make him so happy. Please say you will?"

Tilly, more nurse than maid in these circumstances, cast a relieved glance at Mary, took Lucy's jacket out of the cupboard, and buttoned her into it. The sisters set off arm in arm along the drive toward the shortcut to the station that lay through the neighbour's field, now stubby and shorn of barley.

Tilly sat with a thump on a wooden chair by the kitchen table when the girls were finally dispatched. "I feel that bad for her," she said to the cook.

Cook, who had tried every remedy within her power in the form of making all of Lucy's favourite foods, now harrumphed. "If she had something real to do, she wouldn't have time for all this tragedy. Who hasn't been disappointed in love? I was. No doubt you will be. But do we crumble to pieces? No, we've got work to do, and we get on with it. And she's been overindulged. Typical youngest. She should be more like her sisters. They wouldn't be making such a fuss."

Tilly sighed. She herself risked a bit of disappointment because the boy from the post office who rode his bike around the village and environs making deliveries had recently smiled at her more than once. "But she's in love," she said.

"Don't you start! I've seen that boy making sheep's eyes at you! If they've gone out, you'd best go clean up and air that girl's room. It's the first day she's been out of it in a week."

"THERE'S FATHER," MARY said. The door of the carriage near the far end of the platform had opened, and their father had gotten down the steps and was now pulling his bag after him. "He looks tired, poor dear. Darling, please, let's try to cheer him up a bit. It would make him so happy to see you in a better frame of mind." She pulled Lucy along the platform and took her father's bag. "Hello, Papa. We're making you walk home. I hope that's all right. Hastings has the trap here, so you won't have to carry your bag."

Mr. Browning looked at them both and tried with all that was in him to smile. He was, after all, glad to see Lucy out of the house. He kissed her cheek with a little extra tenderness. Perhaps the fact that she'd agreed to walk to the station meant that she would be able to bear up, though he himself could scarcely imagine how he was going to.

They were on the upper path near the crest of the hill that had the views that swept all the way to the sea. The wind had picked up a bit and seemed to be carrying the clouds away so that the water glinted in the distance like a rim of silver along the earth's edge. Lucy had gone ahead to the top and now stood, her arms wrapped tight around her, gazing out at the view.

"Father, what is it?" Mary asked. She'd pulled him to a stop and turned him to face her.

Browning looked at the ground and shook his head. "Not now. Later. When she has gone to bed. It is worse than you can imagine."

"Worse? Worse? What is? Father, you are really frightening me. Has something happened to Aggy?" She clutched at him, this new idea filling her with horror. Ahead they could see that Lucy had now turned to look down the path toward them.

"Are you two coming, or what?" Lucy called.

Mary felt a momentary sense of relief . . . she was seeing a tiny glimpse of the normal Lucy, but then turned to her father again and whispered, "Father."

"Aggy is fine. That is . . . please, not now. Poor Lucy."

He pulled away and proceeded up the path, leaving Mary filled with misgivings. She could see him take Lucy's arm and kiss her again, and watched Lucy reward him with a little smile. She should be happy, Mary thought, but she could make no sense of what her father was saying. Aggy was all right, but not all right? And why "poor Lucy?"

HIGGINS WAS IN the judge's chambers, pacing.

"It's no good Higgins. I agree with you completely that your client has some rights even if he did shoot his gunner. I've gone all the way up to Sir Denton in the Home Office and asked him what we just fought a bloody war for if people can just be spirited away and their rights denied. He was not to be drawn. He reminded me that your client is not a citizen of this country, and it is a matter of security. And before you ask, I haven't the first foggy clue what he meant by that."

"Then, m'lud, I'm going to the Canadian High Commission. They can take it straight to the Home Office."

"I wish you luck. Your client is facing a heinous crime of murdering one of his own men in the middle of a battle. A young man of eighteen. I shouldn't think the Canadians will be in the least bit interested in pulling him out of the soup."

"What about the court date?" Higgins demanded.

"I am assured the client will be present."

"I have a right to receive his instructions and plan his defence." Higgins said.

The judged winced nearly imperceptibly as if he found the lawyer's persistence in bad taste. "Higgins, you do go on about rights. There are things that may trump some rights. I'm not privy to them, but there you are. I'm assuming you are looking into his defence even without him, and he will get a fair trial with an impartial British jury. I can't think what more you want. If you will excuse me, I'm expected for the afternoon sitting."

Higgins stood on the street, his jaw working. Should he go to the High Commission? Was the judge right? His Honour was clearly not partial to his client. Should he be asking for the judge to be recused? Perhaps he'd better go see Donaldson and find out how that Winslow woman was getting on with the witnesses.

DONALDSON OPENED THE door. "You'd better come in," he said to Higgins. "I'm skipping tea and going right to a drink. Care to join me?"

"Why? What have you found out?" Higgins asked, stowing his hat on the shelf and putting his briefcase on the floor.

The two sat glumly in front of the fire with glasses of Scotch, as Donaldson relayed what his wife had told him on the telephone about their misadventure.

"There is something very dark going on here," opined Higgins. "I've just appealed to the judge to have whoever moved Darling away to produce him, and he told me he'd tried. He's been warned off, I think. Sir Denton mentioned 'security.' With witnesses dying all around us, I can't see who is secure."

"I don't want Sandra out there. It was all a bit of a lark, the two of them going off to find a sympathetic witness. She thought it was anyway. I wasn't convinced, but I let her go. Now look. And she as much as told me on the phone I could go fly a kite, she wasn't coming home till they'd seen the last man in Sussex. They're seeing him tomorrow, evidently."

Higgins, who was unmarried, did not approve of spirited women. "She seems to be under the influence of Miss Winslow. That woman is alarmingly determined to save Darling. Her faith in him is touching, but I fear she is in over her head on this one. And it wouldn't be the first time a man has deceived a woman."

Donaldson looked up at this. "You think he might be guilty?"

"Well, of course, I accept my client's version of events. But someone is making a great effort to confuse the matter. Mind you, that doesn't prove in and of itself that he isn't guilty of something."

"I wouldn't have thought it of him, Higgins. Fred has always been a very straight shooter. Honest, forthright, practical, perhaps a little trusting. There was a business of a woman during the war. He was too guileless to see he was being played. But he'd never shoot one of his own men. Never."

Higgins got up and stood with his back to the fire. "Trusting. That's interesting. Has he trusted where he shouldn't? I've read that damn report he submitted on the crash over and over. He is extremely clear, he takes responsibility for being shot down, for God's sake, and he takes responsibility for the loss of his men. Then he gets a Distinguished Flying Cross for getting the rest of them to safety. The whole report is exemplary, but now that I think of it, it is entirely from his point of view. Well, of course, it has to be, but what I'm getting at is this: what were his men up to? Maybe one of them saw how Evans died. Maybe one of them did it, for all we know."

"Really, Higgins. You're grasping at straws. It was a crash situation. They'd all be bracing and hurrying to save themselves if they survived. Why has no one brought up the obvious? That Evans was shot by the enemy. After all, they came under fire. It's inconceivable that a young airman, by all accounts popular with everyone, and respected—he was good with that gun—would be killed by one of his own crew members."

"No. Of course. You are right. I am grasping at straws, but I just thought, you know, what if one of them was a bit mad and saw it as a way to get out of the whole show and needed to kill Evans so as not to be seen? An 'I'll get out in the confusion' sort of thing. You've seen some of these men with shell shock and battle fatigue. They don't think straight, some of them."

"Even so, why would that lead to what's happening now? It's like somebody knows something, and now people are trying to engage in a cover-up by pinning it on Darling. If it's just about an airman trying to go AWOL, it doesn't make sense. And I wish bloody Sandra was back. I don't like this one bit."

163

CHAPTER SEVENTEEN

AMES STOOD IN FRONT OF the church in Harrop. It was another beautiful day, and the white church gleamed in the sunshine. For a moment he wished he were a painter, catching the thin line of shadow that delineated the lower edge of each wooden siding board. He looked at his watch. It was 12:10. How long would a Mass last? The burble of the creek splashing cheerfully over the rocks on its way to the lake drowned out the sound of whatever might be happening inside. He was hoping to again meet the man who had given Agatha Browning's sister a ride to see if he remembered anything else, and was also hoping to catch Father Lahey to see if he could think of any reason she might have run away from the village rather than toward it.

Vastly unfamiliar with the notion of churches in general, Ames was wondering if the proceedings, which according to the sign began at 11:30, would take an hour, in which case he had twenty minutes to stroll down to the water's edge and admire the lake, when the door of the church opened. A few elderly people, some of whom he'd interviewed, hobbled down the stairs clutching the banisters and nodded at him warily. Ames waited for the first of them to descend and then started up the stairs into the church.

"Morning, Constable. Any luck so far? Did you talk to that lady?" It was the very man he wanted to see, who was retrieving his hat in the vestibule.

"You know, we haven't been able to find her. Can you think of anything else she might have said? How long she was staying, where she lived, anything?" Ames asked.

The man shook his head. "We had plenty of time in the car getting to the ferry and coming over. I know she told me she hadn't seen her sister in forty years, and I might have said, 'Why so long,' or something. What did she say to that? I know! She said, 'It took a long time to find her.' Of course I was dying to ask why she'd lost her, but it didn't seem to be any of my business. I just said, 'Well, you've found her now, and I can point you right to her cabin.' She did say she'd come from the old country, but not where exactly."

Ames found Father Lahey in a room behind the alter hanging up his cassock.

"Ah. Constable Ames. I didn't see you among the congregants."

Ames laughed. "No. I'm afraid I'm a godless Anglican."

"Some of my best friends are Anglican," Father Lahey said. "I'm sure to God it is all the same."

"No. I'm really godless. This is the first time I've set foot in a church since my cousin's wedding." He followed Father Lahey as he completed his rounds for locking up the church. "Father, I did want to ask you something. What strikes me as very odd is that Mrs. Browning, having been wounded by the assailant and apparently having enough time to attempt something of an escape, even in her condition, decides to head away from the village, instead of toward it where she might have raised the alarm and gotten some help. And up a hill for that matter. Can you think of any reason she might have done that?"

Father Lahey stopped midway through straightening the alter cloth and looked perplexed. "I hadn't thought of that. It's very strange, all right. Perhaps she was just in shock and dazed from the attack, not knowing what she was doing."

"Yes, I suppose that's possible . . . I've never been in that kind of shock, but I can't help thinking some survival instinct would come over you, and you'd run to safety, not away."

"Maybe, for some reason, she thought she would be safer doing what she did. Hiding, for example. The woods are denser. Running toward the village, she'd soon be in the open." Father Lahey mused.

"But she'd be more likely to meet someone," Ames said.

"Have you seen anyone wandering around here the times you've been here? You could shoot a cannon down the street at any time of day and get no one. They stick pretty close to home, the few people that live here."

"Perhaps you're right," Ames said. "I think I'll wander back up to the cabin and just have another look around."

"I'd go with you," Father Lahey said, "but I've got a one o'clock in Kaslo. Good luck."

Ames turned to go down the stairs and was just passing the priest's car when Father Lahey called out.

"Constable. I was just thinking, if I were attacked by someone bent on robbing me, say, here in the church, my instinct, I'm almost certain, would be to protect the host at the altar. It is the most sacred thing here. I know it wouldn't really save it, especially if I'd been wounded and was bleeding to death, but it made me wonder if she was protecting something? Let's say that because she finds she's not so badly wounded she can't run away; she runs toward something she wants to protect."

AMES STOOD IN the thickly wooded place Agatha Browning had died, thinking again how lucky they were to have found her at all. The underbrush was so dense that few people would attempt it. Sighing, he began to look around. Would she have staked a claim around here? If so, where? Would it be an actual stake, saying "Browning's Claim"? He would have to find something out about how people stake a claim. Probably you registered it somewhere. He would have to check at the mining office in town. Father Lahey had said he didn't know if she ever did anything with her claim. In any case, a claim was really a bit of ground, so you wouldn't be able to "rescue" it. This forest and the surrounding land possibly belonged to the company that was considering reopening, so she might not have been able to claim anything here.

He pulled up a piece of grass and, speculatively chewing on the end of it, walked back through the silent and shadowed forest to his car. No signs of the deadly drama disturbed its cool and fragrant stillness, as if the crime had never happened.

Back in town he greeted O'Brien at the front desk. "Any calls?" he asked, as he pushed the swing gate into the main part of the station.

"Nope. It's Sunday. Who's going to call you? I'm assuming you mean someone from England. But this came for the boss." He held up a letter. "When's he coming back, by the way? Not that we don't trust you!" O'Brien added with a wink.

"Mail on a Sunday?" Ames asked. The letter appeared to come from England. One of Darling's vet buddies, probably.

"Not the mailman, actually. A guy came in with it about an hour ago. Apparently he lives a few doors down from the inspector, and he was tearing up an old catalogue from the winter and he found this letter stuck inside. He brought it here because he hadn't seen any lights at Darling's house and assumed he's been away. Anyway. You can throw it on his desk."

Wondering at the vagaries of Royal Mail Canada, Ames looked at the envelope. It looked like it had been sent back in March. Definitely from a buddy, but Ames didn't recognize the name. He put the letter into Darling's in-tray, and then went into his office and put his feet up on his own desk, after only a momentary temptation to put them up on Darling's desk.

LANE AND SANDRA got out of the train in Victoria Station. It was bustling with Sunday day trippers. The weather had been fine, and people looked happy and carefree. Lane longed to feel carefree—anything but this gnawing fear. To get to Sussex, they were going to have to change in London. "Let's just go home," Lane had said as the train trundled through the outskirts of the city. "I think I need to meet with Higgins. I'm really frightened by what happened to Salford. I know it may have nothing to do with this, but I keep having this fear that something we may do in the way of talking to one of these people would put them in danger."

Sandra had been relieved. She had told Rudy, her husband, that she was going to see it through, but she wasn't feeling as plucky as she'd let on. "We could drive to Horsham in the car. I'm sure Rudy would drive us, and he'd feel better if he was with us," she'd said.

Agreeing to meet the next day as soon as she had contacted Higgins, Lane now lay on her bed in her old room staring at the ceiling, her feelings in turmoil. It suddenly came to her that she had lain in this same spot, brokenhearted, when she had heard reports of Angus's death four years before, reports that had been deliberately planted to deceive her. Now she was again in a state about someone she loved, on the same bed, staring at the same ceiling. Only Darling was alive. He had to be. She sat up, her breath caught. Could he too have been killed? No, she told herself, willing herself to control the panic she was feeling, Salford, after all, had committed suicide, or could even have simply tripped and fallen into the path of the train. And yet, she thought, the whole thing had the same whiff of deception.

She looked at her watch. Only ten in the evening. An unbearable number of hours till Monday morning when she could call Higgins at his chambers. She cleared off the small writing table by the curtained window and took out her stationary. Map time. What places and people were involved? France somewhere; the plane crash; London; two crew members, Watson and Anthony; Norfolk; Salford, recently dead; Belton in Sussex. She stopped, wishing she had index cards she could write on and move around. She started again.

At the top of a page she wrote "France 1943" and under-lined it. Underneath she wrote,

> *Plane crashes, two crew members die. Evans after getting out, of gunshot wounds, Jones in the plane, body never found.*

She underlined "gunshot wounds."
On another page she wrote "London" and under that,

> *Watson alive, but warned off.*

She reviewed her interaction with him. Had he seemed surprised when she said Darling was being accused of shooting Evans? He had. That was something anyway. Neville Anthony. Says he saw Darling shoot Evans. Why? And why wait four years? Could she get to him to find out?

On the third page she wrote,

> *Norfolk, Salford. Letter to Darling missing. What was in the letter?*

Having written this, Lane sat back. Of course. This was key. She hadn't really taken it in when they were with Salford's widow because his death and her condition took precedence. Sandra had said it must have been the letter that brought Darling here, and in her own confusion, Lane had thought Darling had received the letter, but never told her. But of course, it wasn't the letter that brought him here. It was some arm of the British government.

She continued the Norfolk entry.

Salford killed by a train, apparent suicide. Wife said he was troubled, but not troubled enough for suicide. Accident? Suicide? (Why?) Pushed?

Halfway down the page she wrote "Sussex" and underlined it and then added "Belton." She hoped she would have something of purpose to put there. She sat back and moved the flowered curtain slightly to look onto the street. It was quiet. Most people would be home listening to the wireless, preparing for an early bed for the resumption of their working week on Monday. A man stood on the street smoking and talking to a woman, who laughed at something he said and leaned in to get a light. Perhaps they were lovers, lingering for extra moments before she had to go home to her parents. It looked continental somehow, not English. She frowned. What was it about him? And then, deciding she was being paranoid, she closed the curtain.

She turned back to her papers. Paris, of course! She wrote "Paris" on the top of a fourth page, feeling a surge of hope. Paris was where Salford saw someone who looked like a fellow crew member, only to discover it wasn't, but he was "preoccupied" for some time after.

Was there a time sequence here? Of course, the plane crash starts it, 1943. Then the trip to Paris, three months ago, Sandra said, so in March. Letter stolen in May? Someone was watching him. Was it because of what happened in Paris? Lane contemplated what was fact and what was supposition. She took another sheet of paper and wrote "Timeline:"

—1943: Crash of Lancaster in France. Death of Evans and Jones.
—March 1947: Salford sees what he thinks is a crew member in Paris. He's wrong. (Is he?)
—May: A letter goes missing from Salford's desk.
—June: Darling summoned to England, accused of killing Evans in '43.
—June: Salton commits suicide.

Written like that, the events seemed to Lane to be connected. She thought back to what she had said to Higgins. Something started this sequence of events, and she believed it was Paris. There was, she thought, a strong suggestion of a cover-up. Impediments to their trying to help Darling began to loom large in her mind. Watson refusing to talk to her, the War Office seeming unwilling to give them information, except for the sudden change of heart of someone who thought she knew Lane (Could this be an unwitting ally? Could she be of help again?), Darling not only being denied the bail that had been agreed to, but also being moved away, and finally and horrifically, the death of Salford.

It was past midnight, and she began to feel an awful combination of being desperately tired and completely wound up. She put her pencil down and stacked the papers. She would let the information percolate and then see Higgins first thing. God, she hoped he had news of Darling. She settled into bed and turned out the light. She tried to let the darkness and her own tiredness take her into sleep, though she could feel her mind churning. She prayed she would not have one of her bad nights, disturbed by panic and nightmares.

With a rush of adrenaline she sat up, her heart pounding. But it was not the rush of formless anxiety that sometimes assailed her. It was a cold, solid, concrete thought. All her vague suppositions that intelligence could be involved crystallized. The only entity that had the capacity for this kind of cover-up, for this kind of deadly intrusion into people's very homes and lives, was Special Branch.

CHAPTER EIGHTEEN

HIGGINS SAT GAZING AT THE papers Lane had presented and pursed his lips. After a very long interval he said, "This is very serious, what you are suggesting."

Lane knew only too well how serious it was.

"I mean," continued Higgins, "I see how you reach that conclusion, but we have to be very careful, don't we? We neither of us know anything about the activities or methods of the intelligence branch, and if they are involved, we have very little hope of penetrating their reasons for this particular activity."

I know! Lane wanted to scream. I know all about them. But she could say nothing. She was bound, yet again, by the Official Secrets Act, which forbade her to even reveal that she herself had been in intelligence. She tried to be patient before Higgins's patronizing remarks on the subject. He was right about one thing though: they did have to be careful.

"If not intelligence, then who? I ask myself," Lane said.

"Well, some ordinary criminal could be trying to cover up a crime, I suppose."

"An ordinary criminal would not have the power to spirit away the accused, overturn a judicial order for bail, indeed, compel a completely innocent man to cross the bloody Atlantic and then bung him in jail on trumped-up murder charges. And possibly nobble and murder witnesses. It's absurd." Lane got up and paced, stopping to look out the windows onto the staid and ancient beauty of Middle Temple Lane, busy with barristers to-ing and fro-ing, nursing and shaping the fallout of a thousand dramas that had been acted out in the streets of this old city.

"And I ask myself, Mr. Higgins, I ask myself, would they be able to solve their problem by eliminating Darling?"

"Surely not, Miss Winslow. You seem to be taking this whole thing to an unnecessarily dark and overdramatic place. I told you, the judge himself assured me that Darling will be produced on the trial date. There must be something much simpler at work here."

She turned and looked at him. "Yes. You're right. It is simple. We mustn't lose sight of that. All of this is to obfuscate one thing. But what is that thing? And why do they need Darling to be the villain of the piece?"

THE WINDOW SNAPPED open and the same guard who had spoken with Darling earlier said, "Visitor."

Darling stood up and stretched, and then moved his fingers through his hair. He'd been allowed to shave under supervision, but he nevertheless felt stale and unkempt, outside and in. He tried to clear his brain to respond to this unexpected circumstance. "Who is it?"

"Am I your social secretary? No idea. You're to come

with me." The guard was obviously in a less jocular mood than he had been. He pushed the window shut again, and Darling heard keys clanging against the lock as the guard wrestled the door open. Darling felt a momentary lift at the idea of getting to walk somewhere, anywhere, but he was not a man for unnecessary hope, and knew that his visitor was unlikely to be either his lawyer or Lane. He found himself, after all too short a walk along a semi-darkened corridor, in a small room with a table and two chairs on opposite sides, one of them occupied by Sims, who was thinner than Darling remembered and looked like he was a martyr to indigestion. He was frowning at some papers. He barely glanced up as Darling sat down.

"I have one or two more questions."

"Good afternoon, I think. I've rather lost track in here."

"I still don't completely understand why you shot your gunner in cold blood. According to the witness, you began to pull him to safety, and then when there was a burst of enemy fire, you shot him and made a run for it. I'm trying to understand that behaviour. I just want you to explain it."

Darling sat back and rubbed his eyes, unsure of what to say to this declaration.

"Nothing to say?" Sims said. "Hardly surprising. Indefensible, what you did. His parents will be happy to see a conviction. Feeling very betrayed, they are."

"I hoped after our last conversation that you'd have found out more about why this is happening. I'm disappointed that apparently you've either not tried to, or you tried and could find out nothing. The fact remains that I did not shoot Rear Gunner Evans."

A dyspeptic smile crossed Sims's face momentarily and then it was gone. "You can say that all you like, but I have a witness statement that is irrefutable. And a bullet matching those in your revolver. I was really hoping you'd tell me the truth—it's the least his parents deserve, don't you think? Let's say you weren't just trying to save yourself. Any number of other possibilities might, in a certain light, be convincing. For example, he might have been insubordinate, done something to jeopardize the other men. Or, you could have deemed him too injured to save and wanted to put him out of his misery. That would not be first time on a battlefield. Or was it something more personal? Had he insulted you, or slept with your girl?"

Darling closed his eyes and then opened them again. Inspector Sims sat opposite with an expression that mingled certainty and contempt. It was clear to Darling that Sims believed he had killed Evans. It meant that he believed his informant's information to be unassailable, or, for reasons best known to himself, he had to get a conviction quickly.

"Inspector Sims, as handy as these excuses would be, first of all, it is very unlikely I would shoot a man in any of those circumstances, and second, and more importantly, I did not shoot him at all. That business of the bullet coming from my revolver, for example, is nonsense. I shot once during that skirmish and hit an advancing enemy soldier."

Sims rapped the table in front of him impatiently with his knuckle. It must be abundantly clear to this man, Sims thought, that he was not going to get out of this, and yet, here he was, clear-eyed and calm, repeating the same old line. Sims was convinced of his guilt, but it rankled that he could not fully understand the motivation. A crime was incomplete for him when he couldn't understand why someone committed it in the first place. If he could not understand it, it was, in his mind, a denial of justice. It meant that crime was random and could not be defended against. Perhaps he could get at it if he got the whole story again. Darling might slip.

"Look, why don't we just go through the events again. Start again at the beginning and just tell me everything you remember."

Even knowing that it would likely do no good at all to either question this man or tell him a story that would contradict his version of events, Darling knew he must make an effort on his own behalf. He went through, for what seemed to him the hundredth time, the events on the night of the crash. He tried, as he told the story yet again, to see if there was anything new in it that he had forgotten, left out, or thought was trivial, especially with regard to Evans. Darling was at the front of the plane, trying to control the landing, minimize the damage. He had no knowledge of how Evans had gotten out, though it was obvious it would have been through the gunner cage.

Darling concluded, "I was told that he'd been injured, and I wasn't surprised. Any crash is the most punishing on that rear section. I was happy to see him still alive. We, that is, Anthony the engineer and I, moved him away from the plane, near where the other men had gathered, and then we came under attack. I shouted at the men to run and stayed back to hold off the Jerries. I fired one shot, and I felt that gave me time to leg it and join the others. I wanted to put Evans over my shoulder and take a chance at escape, but I saw that he was dead. I hadn't much time, but I'd seen already when we moved him that he'd been shot, and I thought he must have succumbed or been shot again in the attack."

"That's a fine tale, I must say. Only trouble is, you've again left out the bit where you shot Evans, and you haven't told me why. So, why would a commanding officer shoot his own man? That's the thing that keeps going around in my head. Here's an idea: Did you deliberately bring the plane down and he knew?"

Darling ignored him and frowned. "That's what puzzled me on the night! I remember now. I expected Evans would have been in bad shape because he'd have been banged up by the accident, but I could see that he had a bullet wound when we first moved him. It just didn't register till now. The Germans didn't start firing till after. They must have seen us in the light of the explosion and realized we'd survived."

Sims leaned forward on the table, clasping and unclasping his hands and regarding Darling. "So, let me get this right. You're claiming someone else shot him? And you've just 'remembered' this?"

"Look, Inspector. I can see that you really believe I did this thing and that you would believe it only if you had evidence that has convinced you of it absolutely. I've been in your shoes countless times, believe me. And mostly I've been right, as I'm sure you have. But sometimes I've been terribly wrong. And you're wrong now. I didn't shoot him, but someone did, and I thought that someone was a German. It was too dark to analyze where the shot had come from, but I didn't question it. We were under fire."

"The problem is that it was one of ours. The bullet. And you were the one seen firing it."

Darling sat silently, the ramifications of what he was saying slowly dawning on him. "One of ours? Are we certain? That opens up the unthinkable possibility that one of the men on the flight shot him."

"Well, 'Inspector,' good to see you're finally catching up."

"I'm catching up on why you think it was me. But the bullet was not mine because I didn't shoot him, and the witness statement is either false or mistaken. If you are the man I believe you to be, you will make sure you have it right. You will make sure you find the man who shot Evans because, if you don't, I will be hanged, and whoever did do it will walk out scot-free. I don't think an error like that will sit well with you."

Sims opened his mouth to speak. This time Darling put up his hand.

"And I don't think you will like learning that you have been made a dupe. If I didn't shoot him, someone else did, and someone, somewhere, is trying to bring the full extent of the law to bear on pinning it on me. I don't believe any of the men on that flight have the power or the means to engineer what's happening to me. That means someone higher up is involved. What you need to find out, Inspector, is who, and why you have been dragged in to help with a cover-up of something higher up the chain."

Sims stood up, shaking his head. "Unbelievable," he said, and went to knock on the door of the room. The door was opened, and he turned and looked at Darling. "Just answer me this, Darling. Where was Anthony?"

"I thought he'd taken cover with the rest, but he was quite near me, covering me. We got away together. First-rate man. Why?" But that was a question he would be left to fester over back in his cell because Sims put on his hat and left without another word.

Oxfordshire, April 1943

"THIS LOCKER FREE?" Anthony said. He was leaning against the wall with his arms folded across his chest looking at Watson.

Watson glanced around, but the others had already started up for the briefing. "What are you doing here, then?"

"One of your mates is sick and they picked me. Doesn't that take the biscuit?" Anthony smiled and reached over to touch Watson's fingers where his hand was now tensely gripping the door of his locker.

Watson snatched his hand away. "For God's sake, not here! You don't know me, do you understand?"

"All right, all right, keep your hair on." Anthony turned and pulled the door of his locker open. "It's a turn-up, though isn't it? We always said we'd die together, and this might be our chance."

Watson, his head hidden by the locker door, suppressed a giggle and then he closed it and looked at Anthony, a begrudging smile animating his face. "Did you bring enough smokes?"

"That I did," Anthony said. "We better go get briefed. I've heard Darling's the bee's knees, even if he is Canadian."

"That he is," said Watson.

LANE SAT IN the Circle Line underground, rocking sideways as the train took a curve. She was on her way to the Donaldsons', leaving Higgins to petition the Canadian High Commission. Her plan had been to follow up on Sandra's suggestion that they go see Belton in Sussex, but now she wondered if they should just focus on finding Anthony. If intelligence was behind what was happening, they must already know that she was trying to get more information. They'd probably been following her right from when? The War Office? Someone there would have reported to them that she and Higgins had been there. The woman officer who had helped her? Had she been instructed to play along with whatever she asked? She shook her head at this thought. She was certain that she'd been ready to send them away with a flea in their ear, but something changed her mind. She knew Lane, had seen her during the war, something. And now in the daylight, Lane could not disregard her uncomfortable thought the night before that there was something about the man outside her window.

Someone at the War Office, then? Report any funny comings and goings with regard to these ex-airmen. To whom? And the ever nettlesome question, why? They had to decide if they should try to outrun the long arm of the intelligence branch, or go right into the maw and try to find out what was happening. What if she and Sandra and

Rudy did fetch up at Belton's door? If they were being followed, would they be arrested? Or worse, would something happen to Belton himself?

Perhaps finding Anthony was the right idea. The train slowed as it approached Euston. She would get off and walk the rest of the way. Once on the street, her brain was whirring. What if they bought train tickets to Sussex but sneaked off in the car to wherever Anthony was? There was probably a rule about trying to track down and talk to a prosecution witness, but they had to find out why he was saying Darling killed Evans. If they were being followed by Special Branch, they could get them to follow the wrong lead by pretending to go on the train to Sussex. Oh my God, she thought. I'm mad! I'm beginning to think like them again. In any case, it was nonsense. They had no idea where Anthony was, so that was hare-brained to start with. But she couldn't let it go. By the time she arrived at the Donaldsons', she was clear.

"We have to find Anthony," she said, putting her handbag on the floor by her chair and taking off her gloves, looking more full of purpose and certainty than she felt. "But, we have to be careful. It's possible we have been watched. It's possible our finding Anthony won't be safe for him."

CHAPTER NINETEEN

"WE HAVE TO FIND HIM, that's all there is to it," Lane said. She and Rudy sat at the kitchen table. Sandra was preparing dinner. She turned and leaned on the counter.

"We aren't going to attempt Belton, then?" she asked Lane.

"The trouble is . . ." what could she say? She'd said out loud that she was beginning to think they were being followed, which, said out loud, sounded ridiculous. But she couldn't bring herself to say that she thought Special Branch was behind whatever was happening. She'd seen someone outside her window, after all, casually talking with a woman. It was the woman, she realized, that made her dismiss her momentary worry. Now she reassessed this. The woman was a prop, or, she thought suddenly, the watcher. "The trouble is that the one person who can tell us anything is Neville Anthony. He's the one who has convinced everyone that he saw Darling shoot Evans. He either believes he saw it or he has made it up. We have to find out why. Anyway, the way Darling tells it in the report, Belton was already retreating to the farmhouse. He might not even have seen what Anthony thought he saw. He might be a waste of a trip when we have so little time."

"Do we know where Anthony is?" asked Rudy.

"No. Apparently Higgins tried to get that information but was unsuccessful. We may have to go the old-fashioned way. Telephone directories for a start. Have you got the London directories?"

The London phone books provided a number of Anthonys, though only two Nevilles, one in Putney and one in Shepherd's Bush. Resolved that they would tackle the visits first thing in the morning, they turned instead to the unresolvable problem of where Darling might have been taken.

AMES PUT THE phone down and scribbled some notes. It was five in the morning, and he was desperate for coffee. The night man, not O'Brien, who didn't start until eight, had been surprised to see him coming in at twenty to five and had offered him coffee, but they had run out of cream and, more importantly, sugar. Ames leaned back and looked at his watch. The café next door would open at 6:30 for the early shift workers. After much difficulty and three false starts with different exchanges, he'd managed to get a call put through to a police station in Dorset nearest Whitcombe. There he had learned that a spinster called Mary Browning did reside in the family home.

"No, I don't know if she's there right now. Am I really talking to someone all the way over in Canada?" The man answering the phone had said his name was Terry Fripps.

"Yes, Mr. Fripps," Ames had said patiently. "Do you think you could find out for me and call me back? What time is it there right now?"

"It's gone one. Just finished my lunch. I can motor over and try to get back to you in an hour. I'll probably wire you. I'm not sure how easy it will be to put a call through. Why? What's happened?"

"Her sister Agatha has died. If you find her at home, could you notify her? We have no other way of contacting her, and I believe she may be the only next of kin." Might as well not say that he suspected Mary Browning of being involved.

"Agatha Browning? Are you sure? I never knew them, mind, but there's certainly a story around that she died back in the teens. Well before I was born, but it's by way of being a local legend."

"What do you mean, she died back in the teens?"

"I'd have to ask my mum. She knows the story. Bit of a scandal I think. Anyway, Mary Browning lives in that massive dilapidated old house all on her own. This person you think is Agatha, what happened?"

"She was murdered. She lived out in the boonies and the local priest found her. She'd been stabbed."

Fripps whistled at the other end of the wire. "Murdered! You don't say. Now that's something. That's really something."

Ames, feeling a slight impatience brought on by his lack of coffee had said, "Yes. It is. We're reasonably sure it is Agatha Browning, so unless you have a grave or a death certificate over there, let's assume it is. Can I expect your wire in an hour?"

"Right. Make it two. I think I'd better get the story from Mum as well."

"Good. I'll be here. If you opt for the telephone, get your operators to put you through to the Nelson, British Columbia, detachment. Ask for Ames."

"Right you are. Murdered. Mum's going to have kittens!"

Ames, feeling very grown up after his first long-distance call to the police in Britain over his very own murder case, was at the door of the café when it was opened by April, who gave him a cool smile.

"Good morning, April." Time to bury the hatchet, he thought cheerfully. He would no longer be daunted by her unfriendly reception of him. "I need a giant cup of coffee and something to take away. I'm expecting a long-distance call in a couple of minutes."

"You're lucky you're the first one here, then. I'll tell Jane. She can do you scrambles and toast. That do?"

As a peace offering it was as good as any. "Wonderful! And I see you have a fresh pot of coffee. I'll have a gallon of that while I wait." Darling, when he gets back, will be disappointed that April and I are friends again. He will not be able to make fun of me, Ames mused while he lapped up the life-restoring coffee. Ha!

He'd just finished his breakfast and put the paper plate into the garbage by his desk when the phone rang.

"England on the line, Constable," said the deskman.

"Ames here."

"Hello, Constable Ames. It wasn't easy, but I've got you on the line. Can't talk long. Three minutes. You've

187

given me quite an afternoon, I don't mind telling you. First off, Mary Browning is not at home. I was pretty sure she doesn't have a motor, so I decided to follow up and ask at the nearest station, and discovered that she took a train to London two weeks ago. There was no return on the ticket as far as the stationmaster could recall, but that wouldn't be unusual if a person wasn't sure how long they'd be away from home. But more the point is that her going anywhere is extremely unusual. She doesn't even get much mail. Quite a solitary figure. An older woman called Tilly Barnes comes to visit from time to time. According to Mum, she used to be a housemaid or something to the family before the Great War. She must have married well because she does have a motor. I can go and find out more from her if you want. She may know. She lives about twenty miles away, so it won't be till tomorrow."

"That would be great, thanks, Mr. Fripps."

"Sergeant" said Fripps genially.

"Sorry, Sergeant Fripps. I can arrange to be here any time. It's eight hours earlier here."

"I better tell you what Mum said, as well. She was that interested, I can tell you. It was quite the gossip when she was a young girl."

"Go on," Ames said. Were all Brits this voluble?

"Apparently there were three of them, Mary and Agatha and a younger one called Lucy. I tried to get Mum to just tell me what she remembered that was factual, instead of confusing it with what all the gossip was. So for sure she said that Lucy had intended to be married, and she was jilted. She died a couple of years after, and the rumour was that it was suicide, but that's not known for sure. Their father was the member for this district, and he retired shortly after and was quite broken up over his daughter's death. I believe he had heart trouble. He died in about '09. Now the story is, and Mum wanted to make clear no one knew this part for sure, that shortly after Lucy was jilted, Agatha left the family home and was never seen again. She remembers, Mum that is, going through the society pages with her friends to see if Agatha had run off with the man and married him because they convinced themselves that that's what had happened. They never did see anything. As far as she recalls, the man married someone else and that was that. Sometime, and she can't remember when, it got about that Agatha had died, which is why she'd never come back. They thought it was a motor accident in the city."

"Your mum is a gem. Does she remember the name of the man?"

"Three minutes!" Said a voice.

"Oops. Gotta go."

"Thanks, Sergeant. This is helpful. And thank your mum for me."

"She'll be chuffed to be thanked by a Canadian copper! Should I give you a ring if Mary Browning turns up?"

"Sure thing. I'd appreciate that. Just remember the time difference."

"Right you are!"

"Hey, Sergeant. Could you track down that Tilly person and see what you can get out of her? If she was a servant to the family, she might be able to fill out your mother's story."

There was nothing but silence, and Ames suspected his English colleague did not hear any of his last communication. His day, as it happened, had also been made, but by the cessation of hostilities with April. Feeling slightly smug, he contemplated his new notes. The one thing he could hang on to is that Mary Browning had left her home with a ticket to London and had not yet returned. That made it much more likely that it was Agatha's sister Mary who came to see her, just as she had said. It also vastly increased the chance that it was her sister who killed her. The big question was why. The rumour that Agatha had run off with a younger sister's beau? The trouble with that was that the jilting took place—Ames did a quick calculation—thirty-five or forty years before. He should have checked with Fripps about the exact date of the jilting. Why come now? If she did kill her sister, it must be something that had just come up recently. The trouble was, what? And when the hell was Darling coming back? Ames asked himself, tossing his pencil onto the desk and putting his feet up. But it was not to be. He'd no sooner put his hands behind his head to gaze at the ceiling for a few restful moments when O'Brien appeared from downstairs.

"Remember that car theft from a couple of weeks ago? Well, the owner is downstairs, and he's as sore as a wounded bear. Said he was sick of getting no action and he wants to talk to someone in charge."

TWO PHONE CALLS established that neither Neville was the one they wanted.

"Somerset House?" suggested Lane.

"There must be scores of people. You can't just wander in and say 'Neville Anthony.' You at least need a date of birth," Rudy reasoned.

"He must be around Frederick's age, mustn't he? Or yours for that matter," Sandra said, lighting a cigarette and looking at her husband. "Oh, Rudy, can you get that? I don't want to drop ash on the carpet."

Rudy got up and disappeared into the hallway where the phone was ringing. Lane smiled at the memory of the double ring, and in the next second felt a lurch of missing her own dear old phone, with its counted rings and its party line. How would they all be at King's Cove? The Armstrong and Hughes gardens would be in full bloom. Angela would be ignoring her garden, content to spend the days at the wharf with the boys. How innocent and far away that life seemed now. A dream of escape that was shattered by these inexplicable events that had brought her back to all she'd hoped to leave behind.

"We can stop trying to find Darling, anyway," Rudy announced when he came back into the kitchen. "That was Higgins. He went to the Canadians, and they hummed and hawed, but promised to call him if they came up with anything. They called him just now. Luckily he was still in chambers. Apparently Miss Winslow will have access to Frederick."

"What?" Exclaimed Lane. "Are you sure?" Her heart soared with sheer relief.

"Yes I am, and you could tell Higgins was none too pleased. It is, he said, an extremely unorthodox move for someone not directly involved with a case in any way to gain access to a defendant without his brief. You are to go to the War Office, of all the places, for two in the afternoon tomorrow, where a meeting has been arranged."

CHAPTER TWENTY

INSPECTOR SIMS SAT AT HIS unsatisfactory desk in the government office and ate the last crumbs of the admittedly excellent Welsh cake he'd brought from the tea room. He glared darkly around the office and then slung his arm over the back of the chair. He'd had a storied career as a no-nonsense policeman who, while efficient, had made it an article of faith that he did not knowingly or carelessly convict the wrong man. He'd seen the undignified scramble of fellow officers on the make to convict quickly, only to find they'd ignored or even manufactured evidence and, in the effort, jailed, or worse, hanged, the wrong man while the right one carried right on committing crimes. It seemed to him that there was little point in being a "law man," as he'd heard it called in American movies, if he wasn't capturing and bunging up the right people.

Part of him wished he'd never asked to see the defendant in this case again because there was something about him that he liked. He would have said, had he met Darling anywhere else, that he was as straight as an arrow. And, though he did not like to admit it, Darling had gotten to him. Sims did not want to be anyone's dupe. The very reason he'd asked to see the prisoner was to make sure he'd got all the information available to ensure a conviction. He had a momentary flash of guilt about badgering Darling, but quickly dismissed it. He badgered people. That's how he shook them loose. Not pretty, but it worked, and he'd been absolutely certain of Darling's guilt. But instead of being rattled, Darling seemed to condense into a ball of calm, clarity, and certainty, not only claiming his innocence, but also suggesting he, Sims, was being used. And, he could not help admitting to himself, even if the bullet came from a British gun, it was still only circumstantial as evidence. More importantly, if it wasn't Darling's gun, whose was it? He had taken at face value the military's assertion that the crew carried different weapons. Now he wondered if he could trust absolutely what he was being told.

Shaking off the useless emotion of anger at the thought of being used by shadowy forces somewhere up the chain of command, he got up and went in search of the pretty woman who worked at the desk. He'd been told to ask her for anything he needed. He needed the file with the original statement from that airman, Anthony.

Two Months Earlier

"YES?" THE MAN at the information desk in the War Office raised his eyebrows inquiringly and still managed to look uninterested.

"I need to see someone," Neville Anthony said in an urgent whisper. He looked nervously around, unsure that this was even the right place.

The deskman hesitated. The person before him seemed very agitated. Could he be an ex-soldier with the shakes, intent on making trouble? "What about, please?" the deskman asked.

"I need to report a crime."

"Ah. I see. There is a police department right near here. If you go back out the door and turn . . ."

"No, no, no! A war crime. A battlefield crime."

"The war is over, you know. What sort—"

Neville Anthony slammed his fist on the ledge of the booth. "I know the bloody war is over! Now are you going to let me see someone, or do I have to make a scene?" His voice was rising steadily, causing the soldier on guard at the entrance to turn around and frown. Should he intervene?

"All right. Pull yourself together and sit down. I'll call someone." He took up the telephone receiver and watched as Anthony took a step away from the window. In a moment the deskman put his hand over the mouthpiece and said, "What was your name again?"

"Flight Engineer Neville Anthony," he said, his voice calmer.

The deskman conveyed the information and then nodded into the receiver. "Someone will be down. Please sit over there." The guard at the door watched as the man moved more calmly to the bench. No need to get involved. A uniformed officer summoned Anthony more quickly than he expected.

"Right, Flight Engineer Anthony. I'm Corporal Edwards of the crimes division. Please have a seat. How can I help?" Edwards had his hands folded on a pad of foolscap and looked as benign as he could. He'd heard that this man seemed close to making a scene, and Edwards didn't completely trust that Anthony wasn't an escapee from the local nuttery.

Anthony drew in a breath and closed his eyes. He had to get it right. He looked up at the corporal and then at the paper he was resting his hands on, as if to say, "Are you going to write this down or not?" Seeing no move in that direction, he started. "I was a flight engineer. In April of '43 I was assigned to Flight Lieutenant Darling's plane. Someone had gotten sick. I didn't usually fly with him. I was glad of the assignment; I'd heard Darling was a good man. We were over France . . . no . . . wait. I should say that the mission that day was to get at some arms factories reputedly operating in the north, in Germany. Anyway, I heard one of the engines drop out, enemy fire, probably at the same time as Darling because he sounded the alarm and told us all to brace. He managed to bring the plane down, and we made a run for it. We were missing one man, and another was badly wounded. Darling and I pulled the wounded man, that was Rear Gunner Evans, nearer to where we were gathered, and then two things happened. The plane blew, and we came under fire. Are you going to write this down?"

Edwards pursed his lips. This man said he was reporting a crime. It had been his intention to listen to the story and assess whether a crime had been committed.

"I will as I deem it necessary. Could you go on with your story, please?"

"Anyway, when we came under fire, Darling shouted at us to make a run for it. We were on the edge of some sort of wood, and there was a farmhouse nearby. He might have said to make for the farm." He frowned at this and looked down. Was that right? "I saw that he was going to try to hold them off. The Bosch, I mean, and I stayed a bit behind to cover him. When it seemed that the others had gotten away, I saw Darling lean over Evans, trying to pick him up. Then there was a barrage of Bosch gunfire and he just dropped him. He . . . he . . . pointed his revolver down and shot him where he lay."

Edwards sighed and tilted his head, as if scrutinizing Anthony's face. "Why have you waited till now, nearly four years, to come with this story?"

To Edwards's amazement, Anthony's eyes filled with tears. "I haven't been able to sleep; I can scarcely work. I've started to drink. I think I've been trying to forget it, but I can't anymore."

"Has anything happened recently that brought it to mind again?"

Anthony started. "No, why do you say that?"

"Calm yourself, Airman. This is an extremely grave business. You are accusing a senior officer of the most serious crime possible. We have to make sure you are . . . remembering it accurately. If you are suffering from battle fatigue, for example, your memories could be confused . . ."

Anthony stood up, his chair sliding backward and nearly tipping over. "My memories are not confused! You don't forget something like that!" He sobbed and turned away, wiping his eyes with the back of his hand.

SIMS PUSHED THE file away and wiped the weariness out of his own eyes. He'd read all this the first time. The witness, who had been compelled to go over the story twice and then sign a statement, seemed certain. Sims had talked to Corporal Edwards and questioned him closely about the condition of the witness. Anthony had been described as extremely agitated in a way that convinced Edwards of his veracity.

Sims suddenly realized that he himself, annoyed at being seconded to the War Office, had displayed a streak of laziness. So that he could get back to his own desk at the Yard, he had been convinced by the corporal, by the statement, by the War Office Johnnies who wanted a conviction and had wanted to bring the case to a close as quickly as possible by putting the civilian police stamp of approval on it. He could not escape what he now knew—that he would have to interview Anthony himself. Sims knew already it would be pointless, but he could not live with himself if he didn't.

"I'm going to need to see the witness, that airman Neville Anthony," he said, when he'd tracked down the corporal.

"Is that entirely necessary? We have a few cases on the books and we need to get on with things. We can't be wasting time on the ones that are sure," Corporal Edwards said, his annoyance barely under control. Why did they have to have these bloody civilian policemen involved in this sort of thing?

"Because, Corporal, I'm not entirely sure." There he had said it. Until that very moment he'd not completely known that about himself. He was no longer sure. If pressed, he would not have been able to offer any explanation that would satisfy this man. A feeling. He suspected the military were not big on "feelings."

"We have enough to get a conviction," Edwards was using his insistent voice.

"What if you don't? What if your witness, who strikes me as a tad unstable, comes apart?"

"Surely you don't . . ."

"It's up to you. You drag me here to do your dirty work, so I'm doing it. Thoroughly."

"Very well. We can bring him in. I'll contact the Crown."

"If it's all the same to you, I'll see him on my own, and at the Yard."

GOD, SIMS THOUGHT. This man's a mess. "So this is your complete statement?"

"Yes. Yes, it is," Anthony said, his voice shaky. "Why am I having to do this all again?"

"I'm wondering, you see, if there's any chance you shot the gunner," Sims suggested.

"No! Why should I? I didn't even know him. It wasn't my regular crew. Why would you suggest such a thing?" Anthony could feel the sweat gathering under his arms and could hear his inability to control his voice. They promised the first time it would be over after he signed. Now this policeman was accusing him of shooting Evans!

Sims shrugged. "A man will likely be hanged on the

basis of your statement. We like to make sure he's the right one."

WATSON PULLED THE door open, searching Anthony's face. "I've been frantic!" He said, pulling Anthony in.

"It's all right. God, I thought my heart would stop when that policeman turned up at the door. They just wanted me to go over something again. From the war." Anthony collapsed onto the couch. "Any chance of a drink?" Watson glanced at his watch, and then went to the decanter and poured two glasses of single malt. He didn't like to splash around this ambrosia from his last trip to Scotland, but the need, or the relief maybe, was great.

"Going over? Going over what? I don't understand. And why the police for God's sake?" Watson said. He knew, had known for a while now, that Nev was keeping something from him.

"Look, it's nothing. It's done. Can we just drop it?"

Watson looked at him. They'd known each other since grammar school. "Nev. What's going on? You've been a wreck for weeks now. All this mysterious business of statements to people. What are you not telling me?"

"I've told you. Drop it. It was about an incident early on, '41. I thought I saw something."

"You didn't have an 'incident' in '41. You would have told me."

"I don't tell you everything, you know." Anthony snapped. "I'm going out."

Later, listening to Anthony stumble in and settle in the spare room, Watson lay staring at the ceiling, faintly illuminated by the street light that cast a glow over the top of the curtain. The conviction had come over him, and he could not now shake it that all of this might have something to do with Nev warning him off discussing their plane crash. Why? He could not make sense of it. Neville had always told him everything. And then why had that woman come to the door a few days back with that ridiculous story about Flight Lieutenant Darling?

INSPECTOR SIMS PACKED up his files and looking longingly at his desk, which he suspected some swine had taken over during his absence because it was nearer the window, and went out the door. The inspector had Neville Anthony's new statement. He walked along the river, taking the long way back to the War Office. So their tea room was a little better; he'd stick with good old Yard tea and good old straightforward Yard cases. With a rebellious impulse, he sat on a bench and watched the river traffic, the people going by, busy, with that peculiar mix of dress so characteristic of a people who don't know if it will rain before they get wherever they are going.

There was nothing to complain of, really. He'd done what he had to. The two statements were identical. He contemplated stopping at the pub, but he had War Office documents and thought better of it. That was the problem, really, he thought, preparing himself for whatever came next: the statements were identical.

LANE, DRESSED IN her blue summer dress with the calla lilies and with her yellow cardigan on her shoulders, saw her reflection in a shop window just before she turned to cross the green to the War Office. Her auburn hair fell to her shoulders in a great wave. She should have tied it back and worn a hat, but she felt like a bride on a summer's day. She paused outside the door she'd been shown to, her heart beating, a smile of sheer happiness on her lips. She pushed open the door and stopped as if she'd had the breath slapped out of her.

"You!" she said.

CHAPTER TWENTY-ONE

Whitcombe, October 1907

"**I**'**VE DONE IT, ALL RIGHT?** It was deucedly difficult and it goes against everything I believe, getting people to keep secrets. I could scarcely look the man in the face, but he's promised. He'll be married quietly in the New Year. There's some woman his mother's always wanted him to marry. Luckily he and Agatha had kept a low profile, didn't go into society, so no one really noticed what was happening. She lived discreetly in rooms in Knightsbridge." Browning looked across the vast room at where the decanter sat and then reached up and pulled the bell.

Poor Papa, Mary thought. He looked tired, and his skin was ashen, as if he had been indoors suffering a long convalescence. "Why on earth did they go into Claridge's? Everyone would have seen them. It would have been all over town."

"That's what's so mystifying. By then he'd decided he was going to marry her. He took her there to propose. She turned him down flat." Hastings came in and waited for instructions. "A whisky please, Hastings. I'm sorry I dragged you all the way up. I'm done for. Mary?"

Mary shook her head. She was nearly hopping with impatience to see Hastings gone. The news that Agatha had been offered a proposal of marriage and had turned it down shocked her. How could a woman turn down a proposal from a man with whom she has practically eloped, which would legitimize her position in society and go a long way to erasing the defeat their father was feeling now.

"Papa, what do you mean, she refused him? How could she have?"

"According to Henderson, she said she could not do something so hurtful to Lucy, to force Lucy to live with her betrayal right in front of her face her whole life. He said she charged him with not understanding how very much Lucy had been hurt, and that his lack of understanding persuaded her she could no longer be with him. When I asked where she was, he told me he had no idea. He'd gone to Knightsbridge the following day to try to patch it up with her, and she was gone. He thought she might have come back here, but didn't want to pursue her to Dorset for fear of seeing Lucy."

"What a dreadful, bloody awful coward," Mary said. She turned away, her hand at her mouth, and looked angrily out the window. "Agatha was right about him, anyway. He was not worthy. He would have made a disastrous husband for poor Lucy, only she can't bring herself to believe it. God, I wish she'd snap out of it! I can't bear to see her like this!"

"CONSTABLE AMES? HOW do? It's Fripps across the pond."

"Sergeant, good morning, or afternoon as the case may be."

"I'd best be quick. This will be costing a fortune! I got hold of Tilly Barnes and went up to see her in Shaftesbury. She married someone who did quite well in the auto business and lives in great comfort in a house near the town. She was a little reluctant to talk to me at first, till I mentioned Agatha. They all believed Agatha had died in 1907 in a motor accident, and they were sworn to secrecy about Lucy being stood up, but she had heard a couple of weeks ago from Mary that Agatha was alive. Apparently Mary was beside herself."

"So she knows something about Lucy at least?" asked Ames.

"She does. She said she felt that bad for the girl. Lucy was very much in love with the bloke, called Henderson, evidently. He'd come out for his first visit with her father and had told her he was going to ask her father's permission to marry her. Apparently the visit happened, only he didn't ask her father anything, but just disappeared and never came back. So Lucy went into a decline after this, and everyone was desperate to try to coax her back because she'd always been a sunny little thing. Youngest girl, did I mention that?"

"I knew that. But then what happened?"

"Well, according to Mrs. Barnes, Agatha left, purportedly to visit a school friend in town, and just didn't come home. Then old Browning came back from town at the end of a sitting some months later, and had the news that the man, Henderson, had been seen with Agatha around town. That sent Lucy into a tailspin that she never recovered from, and her body was found at the bottom of an escarpment sometime in '08. Everyone assumed she'd done away with herself. The father left his seat in parliament and died a year later. Apparently had a bad heart."

"How did the story get around that Agatha Browning had died in an accident?"

"Oh, right. Tilly Barnes was that surprised that Agatha was still alive in Canada forty years later. According to Tilly, the servants were all lined up one day and told that Miss Agatha had died in a motor accident in London, and that was that. The family provided no details and never mentioned her name again. That was just before Lucy died. Tilly did say she wondered if the father knew she wasn't coming back, and having her dead in an accident was a way of getting her out of their lives."

"I wonder if it was only the servants, or if Lucy and Mary were made to think she was dead as well?" said Ames.

"Hmm. Tilly didn't say directly," Fripps continued, "but I got the feeling the girls didn't know the truth either. One thing that surprised her was that there was no funeral. Agatha was left for officials in London to deal with. They wouldn't go see to it. It was like they cut her out of their family then and there."

"I see," Ames said. Then how had Mary Browning suddenly got the idea to come all the way to Canada and, possibly, kill her sister?

As if reading his thoughts, Fipps said, "Tilly did say that the thing that enraged Mary was that Henderson apparently left Agatha some money. After she got over the shock of learning her sister wasn't dead after all, she was in a tailspin about the money. She felt that it should have belonged to poor dead Lucy."

"Aha! Could this be about money after all? So Mary was angry enough to come to Canada to have it out with her sister. Thanks for this. It's really helped."

"Think nothing of it, Constable Ames. You've given me something besides stolen motors and sheep-killing dogs to deal with. I'll keep my ear to the ground for you. Cheerio!"

INSPECTOR SIMS WAS not to be gainsaid. "I don't care if I've seen him, I need to see him again."

Corporal Edwards looked darkly at Sims. "I can't think why you are making such heavy weather of this. 'Open and shut,' isn't that what you said?"

"I daresay I did. There's something about the statements I need to double-check."

"Oh, for God's sake! It's a confounded nuisance. Why couldn't you get what you needed the first time?"

"Look, you are the people who dragged me here because you said you had to investigate a crime committed in battle. Well, I'm investigating. And while we are in an inquiring sort of mood, why has Darling been carted off to a prison miles away? This city is full of perfectly good prisons."

"Look, I don't question Spec . . . the czars of the War Office. That's where he is. I suppose if you must go, you'd better bloody get on with it, hadn't you. Try to do a professional job this time!"

Sims thought about the case as he drove along the winding road to Nuffield. Uppermost in his mind was that he was certain Edwards had slipped and nearly said "Special Branch." If Special Branch was involved, then nothing about the case was going to be straightforward. If Special Branch is involved, he thought angrily, then he was more than likely the very dupe Darling had said he might be.

DARLING HAD BEEN allowed some books. They'd been a new form of literature for him. Detective potboilers. They'd filled the hours in a most unsatisfactory manner, both as to style and accuracy. He had just closed his eyes and was imagining himself in a dark coat and hat, brandishing a revolver at some miscreants cowering over stolen treasure in a damp basement somewhere, when the metal window was opened.

"Visitor." It was a new guard. Presumably his jocund friend was on his day off.

Darling got up, slipped his laceless shoes onto his feet, and ran a hand through his hair.

"Inspector," he said when he was shown into the interview room. "This is a surprise."

"Don't have time for small talk. I want you to walk me through part of your story again. Now, as I understand it, plane's gone up, Jerries are shooting, and you've sent your men to take cover. Where again?"

Darling was surprised by this question and by the tone in which it was delivered. Gone was the needling superiority of a policeman who thought he knew the defendant was guilty. What had happened? The change in Sims gave Darling a slight upswing of hope. "There was a sort of forest behind us, and along at one end I'd seen a farmhouse. Often the locals were not sympathetic to the German occupation, so I told the men to make for the farm, while I stayed back to provide some cover."

"And the engineer, Neville Anthony, stayed as well?"

"Yes, though I didn't know it at first. I didn't see till I'd turned around to bolt myself."

"And, very carefully, mind, what happened before you bolted?"

Darling shook his head, his lips set in a grim line. Finally he spoke. "I knew Evans was badly injured, and I worried that getting him out of there could possibly kill him. I think I was leaning over to look at Evans, thinking about how I might carry him to safety, when I saw someone approaching from the line where the Germans had been firing. I took aim and fired. He wouldn't have seen me, I don't think. The bushes screened me. He went down, and I turned back to deal with Evans. That's when I saw Evans was dead, and as I told you, I didn't think it at the time, but something subconsciously registered that he'd been shot, and I was surprised. At that point, I turned to follow the men, and that's when I saw Anthony had stayed to cover me."

"Did you say anything to him?"

"Well, the conditions were hardly conducive to chit-chat, but I probably said something like, 'He,' or 'Evans,' maybe, 'is dead. Let's move it.' I don't think he answered. We both just made for the farmhouse."

"And did you speak of it again when you'd gained the farmhouse? Or at any subsequent time?"

"You mean, with Anthony? No. I told the others when we'd been hidden in a cellar of sorts. No. I just assumed Anthony had seen what I had. He helped me move Evans the first time. He would have seen what kind of condition he was in."

Sims sat back in his chair and looked at the ceiling, and then leaned forward, his hands clasped in front of him. "I'll tell you what's bothering me, Darling. Anthony gave a statement that was written down, and then when I went to see him he told me the same thing, practically verbatim. I find that odd. Unusual, you might say. I also got no satisfactory answer about why you're being held miles away, causing me to have to drive all the way to Oxfordshire, and, though I'm certain I should not be saying it, I have reason to believe Special Branch is involved in some way."

"Oxfordshire is it?" Darling said. He'd been stationed at an airbase in Oxfordshire during the war. There seemed to be some special irony about that. Though he felt a wave of anxiety at the mention of Special Branch, he stilled it. He did not, and could not, know what that would mean to his case, and he wanted to worry only about things that would be fruitful. "I imagine it was to keep me from seeing my lawyer or my friend who was providing bail money for my release until trial. I'm not terrifically impressed with the British justice system just at the moment."

CHAPTER TWENTY-TWO

FIGHTING A WAVE OF RAGE, Lane stood in the doorway and breathed to try to still her pounding heart. Angus Dunn was standing in front of the window so that he was more shadow than man against the light.

"Well, Miss Winslow, you'd better come in, hadn't you?"

"I was told I would be seeing Inspector Darling," she said tightly, not moving.

Dunn moved to one of two armchairs on either side of a small round occasional table. He waved his hand, indicating a chair, and sat then down himself opposite. "Yes, yes. We'll get to that. Do sit down, please. And shut the door behind you. There's no need to conduct our business for all to hear."

Your business is always conducted in secret, she thought. "You've had me followed." She shut the door and moved to the desk and sat on a wooden chair.

"Don't be ridiculous! Why are you so difficult? What's happened to you? We were such good friends."

"You're lying. I've seen your man twice now. Why am I here?" She was damned if she was going to engage in his disingenuous conversation about what they used to be to each other. You happened to me, she thought, with your lies and manipulation and easy disregard for the feelings or lives of anyone else.

"It's all business with you, isn't it? Well, that at least hasn't changed. It's why we valued you so much. It's why, Lane, we want you back. If I'm honest, I hadn't read properly how things stood between you and Darling. I could almost feel envy. Anyway, when you came haring over here to save him, I must confess I was surprised, but I saw immediately how it might be an advantage to all of us. First, I have not had you followed. Second, I have a proposal. You won't perhaps like all the terms, but one of them might serve your own purposes."

Lane watched his face, feeling suddenly vulnerable in the sunny clothes she had dressed in to see Darling. She wished she were in her dark functional tweed suit, armoured against Angus Dunn and all his manipulations, protected against her own growing fear that whatever he had in mind, she and Darling would be the losers. She waited, and said nothing. In the back of her mind she weighed his assurances that he'd not set someone on her. If not Dunn's man, then who?

Angus crossed his legs and tented his hands in front of his chin as if contemplating what he would say next. "Darling has been arrested for a capital crime. A crime that, in this still vulnerable postwar period, when families have sacrificed so much, most people will view with horror. He shot one of his own men on the battlefield. He is unlikely to escape hanging."

"Darling did not shoot him. He is being framed. Seeing you here today, it is quite clear to me that you and all the dark forces at your command have engineered this."

"Goodness. Such loyalty. How can you know? We have an eyewitness. Very good chap. He was quite shaken by the whole thing."

"I know Darling," she said simply.

"You thought you knew me," he pointed out.

Lane sat and looked at him, silent as he landed his arrow. How could I have loved him? she asked herself.

"I do. You're a bastard," she said.

"Yes, you've called me that before. I dare say I am. I'm the bastard who holds all the cards just now. Here's the thing. If you agree to my proposition, Darling can escape the noose, and perhaps, when the dust dies down and Evans's parents have gone home, we might even quietly let him go and spirit him out of the country back to that wilderness you call home."

AMES REREAD HIS notes. He had asked Fripps to keep an eye on the Browning manor house and call him the minute Mary Browning made an appearance. What would be the procedure if a foreign national came to Canada to kill someone? Was she brought back here for trial? He pursed his lips, feeling inadequate. It would no doubt require government involvement, jurisdiction, and who knew what complications. Feeling a desperate need for the commanding reassurance of his boss, he looked at the time. Could he get Miss Winslow on the phone? No. Clearly the middle of the night over there. If he phoned at midnight, or one, he could maybe catch her before she went out for the day. No. Of course not. He wouldn't be able to reach her. He would have to send a wire to get her to call him. With a sigh he closed the file and prepared to go home and change to take Violet for dinner and a film.

To his amazement, as he walked up the hill to his rooms, he suddenly realized he'd rather just go home and settle in with a book. This must be how Darling feels, he thought. It's the responsibility of it all. When Darling was in charge, he always stayed late, while Ames would leave the office with his hands in his pockets and a tune on his lips.

"You're a real drag," Violet said over their dinner at a small restaurant below the courthouse. "You've barely said a thing all evening."

"I'm sorry, my sweet. I think being in charge of this case is getting to me. It's suddenly gotten really complicated. The guys at the station aren't helping, either. I know it's a joke when they call me 'boss,' but I'm starting to feel all the responsibility with none of the power. They are just waiting for me to make a mess of things. I can feel it."

He was surprised when Violet took his hand. "It's not like you to be like this. You're the sunny optimistic one, remember? Who helped me when I got fired from the bank that time? I'm the one that's supposed to be moody. Anyway, whether they like it or not, you are kind of the boss, and I'm sure you're really good at it."

"Do you think so? Even I feel like I'm on the verge of messing things up. I really want to solve this murder before he gets back. I want him to see what I can do."

"How many times has he given you one of his back-handed compliments? He has a lot of faith in you, even if he doesn't always tell you. I can see how much store he puts by you whenever I see you together. And I put a lot of store by you." At this Violet leaned over and kissed him softly on the lips. "There now, let's eat up and get to the pictures. I don't want to be late. You're bound to get some ideas from Humphrey Bogart!"

The Maltese Falcon, while entertaining, did not give Ames any new ideas about his case. He was more relaxed, and rather buoyed by the new supportive and affection-ate side of Violet. He nearly thought better of contacting Lane, but he really did need to know when Darling was coming back, especially if the case was going to take on complicated international ramifications.

THE MORNING AFTER was lovely and fresh, with a dewy green smell that had the effect of energizing Ames after a shaky night of sleep. He decided to walk to the train station to send the wire rather than calling it in from the station. He had to repeat the address twice to the young man in the window. "Please telephone stop." He counted back the time difference and added "six p.m. your time stop."

Having evaded the telegraph boy's curious questions, Ames hurried back in the hopes that Lane would get the telegram and be able to call that very day, or the next. Much to his amazement a call was put through to the station by quarter after nine that very morning. Delighted at the modern world that allowed such ready communica-tion with a place so far away, or perhaps at the prospect of talking again to Miss Winslow, he said, "Miss Winslow, is that you?" He was shouting a bit he realized, and then wondered if he had to. Something about England being so far away.

"Constable Ames, how lovely. How are you? How's the case coming?"

"Well, that's sort of why I need to talk to you. I think it's about to get very complicated, and I was wondering about when His Majesty is coming home."

Evading the question about Darling, Lane asked "Complicated? In what way?"

"I'm pretty sure the victim was killed by her own sister. That middle one, Mary. An old lady claiming to be Agatha Browning's sister was given a ride to the village, and then the ferryman said Agatha herself left that afternoon in her car and hasn't been seen since. Anyway, I've managed to get hold of the police in Dorset, and they confirm that Mary Browning left her house some weeks ago and hasn't been back. They're going to telephone me when she turns up. That's where it get's complicated . . . I imagine all kinds of government types would have to be involved to get her back here to stand trial."

"Goodness. You have been busy. I wish I could help you, but I know absolutely nothing about extradition."

"Do you know when we might expect him back, Miss Winslow?"

Lane leaned against the wall in the post office where the phone rested on a table. She wrapped her free arm around her waist. She mustn't cry. "I . . . I think it won't be long, Constable Ames. Still one or two things to tie up."

"Oh, good. It's funny him being over there, and a letter from one of his chums over there is sitting on his desk over here," Ames said.

Lane stood up straight. "A letter? Do you know from whom?"

"Dang. It's sitting on his desk and I can't remember. Man's handwriting. The funny thing is the neighbour brought it in because it got delivered to him by mistake and got stuck in a catalogue. He nearly threw it away."

Was this important? It might be only one of a steady stream of letters from old mates for all she knew. "Ames, could you do me a favour? Could you open the letter? I'm certain Darling wouldn't mind. He's trying to get around to see all his old pals, and there's one he's had trouble locating." Sort of true, she thought guiltily. We do need to find Anthony. "That letter might be from him. I wouldn't normally advocate reading someone else's mail, but it would really help him. He's outside of London just now, so I'll call him to give him the information if it is from that one buddy of his."

"Two minutes," intoned a disembodied voice.

"Yes, yes, operator. It will be longer. I'll need to hang on. Ames, can you get the letter?"

"Okay. Don't go away!" Ames put the receiver down carefully, hoping that in the time it took him to bolt upstairs to Darling's desk where he had put the letter, they would not be disconnected.

CHAPTER TWENTY-THREE

London, April 1947

LOUISE FREEMAN, NÉE HENDERSON SAT, dumbfounded, holding her mother's hand. The oppressive dark oak of the room they sat in seemed to press in around her. "I don't understand. Half of everything goes to some woman none of us has ever heard of?"

"Yes," said Benjamin Morris, the family lawyer. He was a man who viewed the assets of his clients as so many movable bricks. He had little emotional attachment to the meaning these assets may have to the people who owned them, or stood to inherit them. He was not an unkind man, but he offered no sympathy. Bricks had been moved from this pile to this pile. It was his job to indicate these facts to his clients.

"Who is she?" Louise addressed the lawyer, and then turned with an air of accusation to her mother. "Mother?"

"Oh, do stop making a fuss. There's plenty of money. I don't need much. We don't even have to give up the house. I'll move to the lodge, and you and Darren and the children can have the house to yourselves."

"That's not the point, though, is it? Who is this woman?"

In answer her mother stood up and pulled on her black gloves. "Thank you, Mr. Morris. So helpful as always. Will it take long to settle this matter?"

"It may take some time to find the legatee, Agatha Browning. I understand she lives abroad. But in terms of the assets that remain with the family, there will be no difficulty. I have already begun to arrange the paperwork and will have my clerk bring it round for signatures."

In the car Louise looked darkly at the crawl of traffic in the City, and answered the question her mother had just asked. "I don't want to have tea. I want to go home. George is going back to the uni this afternoon and I don't want to miss him."

"If that's what you want." Her mother leaned forward and said to the driver, "Just take us home, Crawford." She leaned back on the seat and shut her eyes.

"Why are you being like this?" her daughter demanded, her voice rising. "How can you just . . . I don't know . . ."

"Because, darling, if you've lived for forty years with a man who, as kind as your father was, loved someone else, it's rather liberating to be free."

"You knew about this woman?" Louise's outrage climbed.

"It's old history. I don't care, and I don't see why you should." Seeing her daughter draw in breath to have another outburst, she continued: "It was someone he met and fell in love with when, ironically enough, he was about to become engaged to her sister. There was a bit of a scandal that ended with the young woman he jilted committing suicide. They were a prominent family at the time. Their father was the sitting member for wherever it was, but after the death of the daughter, he quit and disappeared, and the whole business ended for us when your father and I married. I bore her no ill will. I was in love with your father and thought he'd come round. He never really did, though he worked hard all our lives together not to visit the effects of his unhappiness on you or me. I won't have you demean him by making this undignified fuss. Your father was an extremely honourable man, and this final provision in his will proves it."

MARY BROWNING SHUFFLED downstairs to the kitchen, put the kettle onto the stove, and then, tying the belt of her frayed silk robe around her thin waist, made for the front door. The newspaper had been delivered, as it was every morning, by a boy from the village on his bicycle. He'd had the decency to put it under the overhang above the door for a change, as the winter rain was pounding down incessantly. Back in the kitchen she put the paper on the table and pulled open the cupboard where she kept a tin of tea. Frowning, she shut the cupboard. Blasted Tilly had been in and tidied up again. What would she have done with it? Cursing about meddling women, Mary launched a search, finally seeing the tin on the counter by the stove, ready with her brown teapot, the sugar, and a cup full of spoons. She harrumphed dismissively.

Mary lived alone in the house she had inherited when her father and sister died. At first she'd kept the servants on and tried to keep it up, but now, in her sixties, she had shut most of the rooms and confined her activities to her bedroom just up the stairs, the kitchen, and a small sitting room facing the back garden. She knew already that she would probably move her bedroom down to the first floor and convert the old dining room into sleeping quarters. No one came to visit, except their old maid, Tilly, who had left service when she married a man who owned a garage and had left her quite well off. Tilly's son had taken over the garage and had expanded it as he took on war work, providing upkeep for military vehicles. Tilly, though nearly in her fifties at the start of the war, had volunteered to drive and worked for the land army driving a delivery truck. Now she had a very smart grey Vauxhall saloon of her own, and she used it to visit her erstwhile employer, whom she now considered her friend, though patently someone who needed help keeping organized from time to time.

The hot water sorted, Mary, with the newspaper under her arm, took the tea on a tray into the little sitting room. Bowed windows flanked by faded floral curtains that she never closed showed yet another front of grey weather encroaching on them from the sea. She was grateful that in spite of the loss of people she loved, and all she might ever have hoped for herself, her view, down the now-overgrown garden to the river and across up the field, had not changed. She scoured the front page and, though relieved now that the war was over not to have to read endless stories about the progress of the imperial army against the enemy, she nevertheless found herself equally reluctant to witness the downfall of all that was civilized in the growing number of stories of more and more Nazi atrocities being unearthed, and the growing restiveness and violence in India. Would the world ever be normal again?

She skipped over the page designed to help housewives cope with the continuing rationing with recipes for delicious cakes made with beets—"He won't spot the difference!"—and felt a slight relief from the pressures of a collapsing world when she arrived at the society pages. "Mr. and Mrs. Duncan are pleased to announce the engagement of their daughter Pauline to the Honourable John Simpson." Pauline Duncan was shown smiling demurely at the camera, wearing a twinset with pearls, her blond hair set in a becoming pageboy. Mary guessed that the twinset was some dusky rose colour.

"Good luck to them," Mary muttered, drinking her tea. She did not favour any of the vast collection of porcelain teacups they had accumulated since her mother was chatelaine of the house, and that now lived in glass-fronted cupboards in the closed off dining room, but instead used a mug because it held a decent amount of tea. It was down at the bottom of the second page of the society pages, a small item she would never normally have bothered with, but for the fact that it was her own surname that leaped out at her. The headline, in a departure from the usual sober manner in which all things in the paper were announced, read MYSTERIOUS WOMAN CLAIMS INHERITANCE

> *The recent death of the financier Alphonse Henderson has unearthed an intriguing mystery from the earliest part of the century. It is reported that the contents of his will stipulated that a significant portion of the*

deceased's fortune was left to a mysterious woman instead of wholly to his wife and daughter. This reporter has ascertained that the legatee is called Agatha Browning, and she is the eldest daughter of a once-prominent family that has since faded into obscurity. She has been living in obscurity in the Dominion of Canada for nearly forty years. The widow has not contested the bequest.

Mary sat frozen, staring at the paper, seeing nothing but the reels that played in her own head. Father sitting them down, telling them Agatha had died. She turned her head and stared at the settee where she and Lucy had sat, remembered her shock and sadness. Remembered her utter confusion about how to respond because of how Lucy had been so monstrously betrayed by the sister they had loved. She heard the faint sound of a motorcar on the gravel. Tilly! She threw the paper down and went back down the hall toward the front door and threw it open, surprising Tilly who, dressed in a neat wine-red suit and blue hat, was a stark contrast to the dishevelled and wild Mary, still in her nightwear, her hair out of its pins and streaming down her back.

"Tilly! Oh my God, Tilly!" Mary was crying out, her voice breaking. "She's alive!"

June 1947

LANE WAITED PATIENTLY in the post office for Ames to return with the letter, avoiding eye contact with anyone who might want to use the telephone, and thinking about her meeting with Dunn. She felt as she had sometimes after a mission in which she had had very little sleep. Dazed and emptied. Her initial despair had turned to a dull grey ache that permeated every part of her body. She could not seem to muster a single thought to save herself. It had seemed utterly clear when Angus was talking, persuading, his voice and manner all reasonableness. His deep timbred tone delivered a message of such inevitability that her anger just washed against it like waves against a rock cliff. She played through her interview with Dunn over and over, as if sooner or later some gleam of hope would shake loose.

"It would be just a short-term assignment. We're hardly asking you to go under as a spy. We just need someone who can make a few contacts inside for us. You'd be quite free when the job is done."

Lane doubted that. "Why can't you leave me alone? I'm asking you again, have you engineered this ridiculous business with Darling just to get at me?" She had felt rage, fuelled by a growing sense of her own powerlessness.

"Don't be absurd. That is another matter entirely. Here's the thing, Miss Winslow"—he had said this with an exaggerated show of courtesy—"the Soviets will trust you because of your father. During the war, when we were all chums, he had contacts that were quite high up. It would be dashed useful to cultivate some of these relationships."

Lane had been silent. She was being asked to exchange her freedom for Darling's. She had heard her father's clipped and superior tone in her head: "You should try to develop the seat your sister has. She's magnificent on a horse." She felt herself being pulled down and down, back into the Special Branch, back into the tension of a life she had chosen only because it was her contribution to the war effort, back further, to the father who had disliked her and preferred her sister. A sister who was now living a life of her own choosing in South Africa. The utter unfairness of it all had struck her forcefully.

"These charges against him are nonsense. Where did they come from?"

"My dear," Dunn had said, shrugging, "quite legitimately from a man who saw him do it."

"You're lying. It's got your greasy fingerprints all over it. You're using him to cover something up."

"Goodness, you are sharp. I'm quite pleased, really. We need girls like you." His voice had hardened. "I'll give you a day or two to think about it, and then I'm afraid I'll need a definitive answer if I'm to find a way to help him out of his little troubles."

"I want to see him. Where have you taken him?"

"I'm afraid that won't be possible, but, as usual, you are engaging in an overdramatic interpretation of events. I haven't taken him anywhere. His legal man and the police have perfectly good access to him, and are continuing the dance of defence and prosecution so necessary in our great judicial system." Dunn had stood up and taken out a card. "You can reach me here on, say, Friday?"

She thought about the card, now sitting like a bomb in her handbag, and felt as unwilling to touch it as if it were coated in cyanide. Then, she realized, something had shaken loose. Higgins and the detective . . . she struggled to remember his name, Sims, that was it, had access to

Darling. Higgins she knew had nothing, but Sims . . . she had not met him. He could be just tightening up the case against Darling . . . why not? What had he got to lose? Or he could be someone who really wanted to get it right. She had not been encouraged by Darling's description of his first meeting with Sims. He'd come in utterly confirmed in his belief in Darling's guilt. Either way, she would have to find him and talk to him.

She would make notes of questions she would put to him, and anything she ought to share with him from her visit to Norfolk with Sandra . . . perhaps a witness dying mysteriously would interest him.

LANE WAS RECALLED from reliving her ghastly visit with Dunn by the sound of Ames on the line. "Miss Winslow, Got it! I haven't opened it yet. I thought I'd better do it in your presence, as it were. Would you like me to read it to you?"

"Fire away, Constable."

CHAPTER TWENTY-FOUR

"BELTON, IS THAT YOU?" WATSON had pulled the telephone receiver into the sitting room and was watching the street cautiously from behind the drapes. Anthony had gone to work, but he was nervous. He had to try to make this call after Belton got home from his job, whatever it was, but before Anthony got back.

"Yes."

"Watson here."

"Ah. I thought you sounded familiar." He was suddenly cautious. "What is it?"

"I'm not quite sure how to put this. Has anyone been to see you about the crash?"

There was so long a silence at the other end of the line that Watson was going to ask if Belton was still there.

Finally, "Why?"

"Well, someone has been to see me. And I think someone's talked to Neville Anthony. I saw him for a drink the other night. He's not saying anything, and I was told not to say anything. Not to anyone, not even a member of our crew."

"Yes." Belton was non-committal.

"Well?"

"Well, what?" Belton asked. He sounded nervous.

"Oh come off it, man. Has someone seen you or not? I don't like all this secrecy, especially since that girl came round. Neville is sitting on something as well."

"What girl?"

"A nice-looking girl. Said she was looking for information about the crash because they were reviewing the file or some damn thing. I asked her for identification, and then she just blurted out that Darling had been charged with murder and she was trying to reach everyone who was there that night."

"What? The skipper?" Belton asked.

"She never came round to see you?"

"Certainly not. I would have sent her away with a flea in her ear, I can tell you. What a ridiculous idea. Who's he meant to have murdered?"

"Evans. See, I thought that as well. I thought Evans was badly wounded. Neville helped drag his body back to where we were. He would have seen. Damn. I should have asked him, only . . ." It didn't do to let on that Anthony actually lived on the Bromley Road with him. Or, and it came to Watson just now, that Nev had said nothing when he'd reported his outrage that Darling had been charged with Evans's death. Hadn't Nev seen how badly Evans had been hurt? He could set them straight. But Nev had said nothing and was increasingly away from home, drinking Watson knew not where.

There was another silence at the other end of the line and then the sound of a chair scraping along a wood floor.

"Something is wrong. I had some man come round a few weeks ago and bring that damn crash up right out of the blue. Said I was not to discuss it with anyone. When I asked why, and what the hell it mattered after all this time, he said it was confidential, and I was obligated under official secrets to keep quiet if anyone came round. I agreed because he looked official, but I was pretty puzzled about the whole thing. Why should this be coming up now? Didn't Darling do a report on it?" Belton asked.

"I had the same visit," Watson said. "We must all have. Anthony, you, me, probably Salford. I should ring him. It's ridiculous we can't talk to each other. The man really put the wind up me, I can tell you, with his official secrets. Said I could be arrested. I was really frightened when the girl came round. How long has it been? Nearly four years now, and suddenly all this hush-hush business. And now I am beginning to think there's someone following me. I think I will give Salford a call."

"Too late, I'm afraid. I saw a notice in the obits. He died less than a fortnight ago. Some sort of accident." Belton said.

"Good God, I hadn't heard. Poor devil. He was married I think, but I don't know of any children."

"I don't want to sound ridiculous," Belton said nervously, "but should we be worried? I mean, what sort of accident, I'm wondering now."

Watson had looked away from the window and now looked back and saw Neville approaching the house. What had Belton said? Well, it didn't matter. "Someone's at the door. I have to go." He hurriedly went back into the hallway and hung up the receiver just as the key went into the door. He went across into the kitchen and leaned over the sink, trying to catch his breath. He remembered now what Belton had said. We should be worried, he thought, we absolutely should.

"YOU'RE LIKE THE flaming king of England," the guard said. He didn't even bother with the cell window, but opened the door right up. "Another visitor. I never thought Canadians could be this much trouble. Thought you were a mild-mannered people."

"We are, but only in our native habitat. Who is it this time?"

"Might be your brief. Short man. Can I have that book when you're done?"

"You can. Shall I tell you who did it?"

"Very funny. I'll give you an extra fifteen minutes."

HIGGINS WAS LOOKING more worried than usual. "Ah. Thank goodness. You're alive anyway," he said, shaking Darling's hand.

"I should hope so. I'm mighty relieved to see you. That inspector came to see me twice. Once to try to bully a confession out of me, and then again asking me to go through the whole crash. I must say I felt a bit hopeful about that. Has something developed? Is that why you've been allowed to see me?"

"I'm not sure. I went to the Canadian High Commission to ask them to pressure the Home Office to tell us where you were, and I just got a note delivered to chambers saying I could see you here. It's a blasted nuisance to have to motor all the way up here."

"Have you talked to that inspector, Sims?"

"No. I telephoned him and left a message, but he's apparently relocated to the War Office. They'll pass it on. I expect I'll get a call late today or tomorrow. I hope you're right about him. Right now we've not much to hang on to."

"What about Miss Winslow? Will she be allowed to see me?"

"I thought she had been. She got notice that she could see you. She hasn't been?"

"No. When was this?"

"A day ago or so. Oh, and of course, you weren't to know. She and Mrs. Donaldson went to see Salford up in Norfolk, but he'd died. Some sort of rail accident. Apparently his missus was a mess. A bit paranoid. She thought someone had been in the house. Probably nothing taken, thought she thought a letter was missing. Miss Winslow made much of something she said. Apparently the Salfords had been in Paris in the spring, and he thought he saw a fellow crew member and was very surprised. Then it turned out it was just someone who resembled him. According to Miss Winslow he got a bit funny after that. Anyway. We'll never know. Poor fellow got knocked over by the local train."

Darling frowned. "That by itself might not mean much, though I'm sorry to hear it. He was a good man," he said. Why hadn't Lane been to see him if she had received permission? Then he looked intently at his lawyer. "Higgins, you've got to keep her from meddling. She'll put herself in danger before you know where you are."

"If I'm honest with you, I don't see how anyone can stop her. I confess I was a bit worried she'd be in the way, but she's been very resourceful. We were turned away from the War Office empty-handed, and the woman officer we saw slipped her what we came for on the QT, the addresses for the other airmen. Can't think why, but there you are."

"She said she was going to find people the minute they got the addresses, but this thing with Salford dying puts a new complexion on it."

"She did get a start on it but was cautious enough to take Mrs. Donaldson with her. She was a bit shaken about Salford. She put it together with Watson behaving so strangely. I still think she's making a bit too much of these circumstances."

"Don't be so sure." Darling stood up and paced, his hands in his pockets. "She's got good instincts. She's . . . she's helped me with one or two things. But she will absolutely go haring off if she thinks she can help me. You've got to stop her. She'll put herself in danger without thinking twice about it. I mean it."

"I understand your concerns, Darling, but we've got bigger problems if we can't find a way to get you off. If you're going to be fussing, I'll make sure she's got me or someone else with her. How's that? It sounds like I should find Sims. What you've said about him is the only sliver of light we've had. I'm assuming there'll be no trouble with me coming here again. Though I wish they'd move you closer. The petrol alone . . ."

"Yes, sorry about that. Don't come unless you absolutely have to. They've been feeding me and giving me ghastly penny dreadfuls to read. I won't say I'm not worried, I am. But I just can't, I suppose, bring myself to believe that they'll hang me for something I didn't do." Darling stood up as Higgins was collecting himself to leave. "Well, thanks, Higgins. If there's a light at the end of this tunnel, I'm sure you'll find it."

"Humph. At this rate it'll be . . ."

"I know," sighed Darling. "The train."

LANE LEANED AGAINST the rail across the street from the War Office. She was holding the letter, which she had copied verbatim, asking Ames to stop and repeat several times, and now she looked at her watch. It was nearing four. Would he come out by the main door? She did not want to go in, fearful of meeting someone she knew. She hoped to waylay him as he went home for the day. She shook her head. It was ridiculous. She had no idea what he looked like. Should she try to find Captain Hogarth? It was a risk. Anyone new brought in to a situation, the full dimensions of which she could barely understand, would be a risk. Finally identifying that her real fear was another meeting with Dunn, she cast that aside. He did not have offices here, and she hadn't got much time.

"I'd like to see an Inspector Sims," she said to the man at the reception window. He glanced up at her, lingered for a moment, and then looked down at his list.

"I'd like to help you, love, but he's not on my list."

"I believe he might be one of the men from the Yard that's been seconded over here. Is there a set of offices where they work?"

He shook his head and smiled genially at her. "You're a pretty little thing. Can anyone else help you? Me for example," he looked her up and down.

"I'll see Captain Hogarth, please," she said, ignoring him.

The man looked down his list and then picked up the phone, winking at her. "You can sit over there."

Relieved to be out of leering range, Lane sat and reread the letter. This was it, really. This is what had begun it all.

Dear FL Darling,

You'll be surprised to hear from me. I've not contacted any of the old team since the war ended. I just wanted to get on with my life, if I'm honest. The thing is, I've had a very odd thing happen, and I knew you'd want to know because I know how broken up you were about Jones and Evans. I know you blamed yourself, though certainly no one else did. The thing is, I was in Paris a couple of weeks ago with the wife, and I could swear Jones was in the Tuileries drinking coffee. It was an awful shock, I can tell you. I went right up to him and said, "Jones, is that you?" And the man just looked at me with a blank stare and came back at me with French.

I tell you, Darling, it was him, large as life and dressed in a very expensive suit, what's more. I know him as well as I know my own name. I beat a polite retreat, of course. He must have his reasons. I wondered if he'd had his memory knocked out of him in the crash and wandered off in the wrong direction, and the French picked him up and he just lived on, being someone else. I haven't told anyone else. It's his

business if he wants to be a frog now, but I thought
you should know. It might be one less thing you have
to feel bad about.

I hope you are well, old chap. If you ever come
back across the pond, I hope you'll come visit. The
wife has heard every story about you there is to tell.
She'd be thrilled to meet you!

Until then, very best
Harold Salford, wireless man, as was.

"MISS WINSLOW?"

Lane looked up at Captain Hogarth, who was smiling down at her. She jumped up.

"Captain Hogarth. Thank you for remembering my name. I don't think I gave it to reception. I'm sorry about being unannounced, only I . . ."

The captain was shaking her head, and pointing toward the door into the main offices. "Come in. We can discuss whatever it is in private. He's an awful piece of work, isn't he?" She whispered as they passed the reception window. "It's only because I outrank him by several layers that he treats me with any respect."

"I suppose men have had a hard time accepting women into the officer's corps, or the ranks, for that matter," Lane observed.

"Oh, they're all right, most of them. Good thing about the army is that your rank must be respected. Of course some resent it. But men died in the war, and we moved up." She ushered Lane into the office they'd occupied the week before. "Now, how can I help?"

"First I must thank you for your help the other day, I . . ."

"Rubbish. Think nothing of it. I could see that pompous little man you were with wasn't going to let you peep. I suddenly thought, why not. I'll show him. Besides . . . the work you did . . . But there, we'll draw a veil, shall we? Now then."

"It's really not worth my having bothered you, I'm so sorry. It's just that there's an Inspector Sims from the civilian police who has been seconded by the War Office, and I urgently need to see him. That ass at the front desk says he's not on any list, which I suppose makes sense."

"No trouble at all. I gather he's working on the same thing you saw me about before?"

Lane desperately wanted to trust this woman, but the fact that she knew and understood what she'd done during the war, and knew not to talk about it, made the woman more suspect, potentially more involved with intelligence or Special Branch. She could even be in with Dunn. Lane had only a couple of days to try to get one jump ahead of the director, to get Darling off by the normal legal channels, before Dunn closed all those down as well.

"Oh, I just have a bit of information to give him," She smiled warmly.

"Right you are then. You sit here and I'll totter off and find him for you. I know where they've put those poor chaps in a sort of cubicle in the basement. You won't get a moment's privacy, so I'll find a room for you."

"You're so kind," Lane said, sitting and pulling off her gloves.

CHAPTER TWENTY-FIVE

June 1947

AGATHA WAS OUTSIDE IN THE garden when she heard the banging on the door. She was kneeling on the edge of the bed with a small-pronged trowel, scraping weeds from around the carrots. She ignored the sound at first. Beastly priest, no doubt. Pious bastard. More banging. Agatha finally pushed herself up and walked stiffly around the side of the cabin to see who was on her front porch. She frowned. It was an old woman whom she'd never seen in her life before. She walked into the open.

"Yes?" She'd had to clear her throat to scratch the word out.

The woman turned and looked at her for a long time before she spoke. "I suppose it's you, is it Aggy?"

Agatha dropped the trowel. "Mary?" She looked around her, as if trying to understand how her sister could suddenly appear out of nowhere. Then she caught sight of the small suitcase Mary had set down beside her on the stair. "You're not planning on staying are you? I haven't got room."

"After forty years that's the best you can do? Can you boil water in this godforsaken place? Let's just start with tea, why don't we?"

Inside the cabin, Mary looked around, barely aware that she was breathing as lightly as possible, as if to block out the stale smell. The single bed, unmade, pushed into a corner by a wood stove, the sparse furnishings of a table with two chairs, and some sort of bedraggled armchair with a stool in front of it. A kerosene lamp stood on the table next to it. There was a basket of firewood by other side of the stove. At one end, where Agatha was now, still wearing her Wellington boots, there was a cupboard with some crockery in it, a shallow chipped enamel sink with a copper faucet, and on the other side, a cupboard with foodstuffs.

Behind the chair, under one of the two small windows that let meagre light into the room, a bookshelf held more books than Mary would have expected. But it was not the books that drew her interest—Agatha had always been a bookworm—it was the photograph in the silver frame. She took off her light coat, dropped it onto the chair, and picked up the photo.

"You haven't forgotten us completely then," she said. "How innocent we look!"

Agatha had put a blackened kettle on the stove, and now opened the stove door and shoved in two more sticks of wood. She turned and looked at Mary. She hadn't aged well, she thought.

"How the blazes did you find me? What are you doing here?"

"Thank you, I will sit down," Mary said, pulling out one of the two chairs at the table. "I found out from Henderson's lawyer. He had to go to a lot of work to find you. He wasn't supposed to tell me, but I convinced him we all thought you were dead, you see."

Agatha refused to sit.

She glowered at her sister. "Why should I be dead?"

Mary didn't answer this question but instead observed, "I live in only two rooms of the house now. Can't be bothered with the rest."

"I suppose Father's gone," Agatha said. She checked the water and brought a cracked brown teapot to the table.

Mary looked around the cabin again. "I can't understand what you've done with all the money. You live like an indigent." She picked up the cup that had been placed before her and inspected it carefully.

Agatha poured water into the pot and put the kettle back onto the stove, and finally sat down opposite her sister. "I don't have any money. You look old. Did you marry?"

"No. Father died in '09. He gave up his seat, of course, after what happened, and his heart gave out. I just stayed on in the house. Tilly stayed on after the others left, and then she married a rich mechanic and moved off. She deigns to come visit me once a week. Very kind, really. 'For old time's sake' she tells me."

Agatha stirred the tea and then poured it. Mary watched as unimpeded tea leaves poured into the cup. No sugar and no milk she wagered. But there was sugar. Agatha produced it from out of the cupboard.

"Priest visits every now and then and brings it. Seems to think I'm some sort of charity case. Sorry about milk. I go up to town once a month for supplies, but don't bother with milk. Can't keep it, you see."

"Why don't you have money? He left you a small fortune," Mary said.

Agatha frowned. "Who left me a small fortune? Daddy?"

"Henderson. Are you seriously telling me you don't know? You would have had a letter."

"Why on earth would Henderson have left me money? In any case, if notice came in a letter, I'd never have seen it. I never read official-looking letters. Some busybody is trying to get me to leave here so they can put a road through. I shove 'em in the fire."

They drank in silence. Mary thought about her sister, so changed after so many years, and yet so intimately familiar to her, as if she were slipping into a relationship she'd only just slipped out of the day before. Finally it was Agatha who spoke.

"What about Lucy? You haven't said. How is she? Did she and that pillock Henderson have children?"

Mary put down her cup and stared at her sister, speechless. Then she got up and looked around the cabin, a blue hot fire burning inside. She took her own chair and flung it aside. It clattered across the floor and banged up against the stove, where it came to rest. Agatha jumped up, suddenly afraid, and grabbed at the teapot, retreating toward the sink. Mary turned the table over and then stood over it, glaring.

"You disloyal bitch! You killed her. You killed the only sweet and lovely thing in our family, and now you're here sitting on money that should be hers!" Mary lunged at her sister and pulled at her arm so that Agatha was forced to look straight into her sister's face.

"Do you know how she died? Do you want to know? She threw herself off the cliff on the upper path. We couldn't find her for two days." She yanked hard on her sister's arm, causing Agatha to cry out and try to free herself. Her fingers scratched fruitlessly at Mary's hand.

"The doctor thought she might have taken a day to die. A day, broken, alone! Can you imagine that? Can you?" She'd let go of Agatha's arm and now had her by the hair. "Where's the money? You shouldn't have it. It belongs to that pathetic woman he married. She lived with him for forty years knowing he loved you."

Gasping at the sudden pain of her head being wrenched back, Agatha croaked, "I don't have any money, I told you!"

SIMS LOOKED AT the woman sitting in the room he'd been shown to and only just stopped himself from whistling aloud. Now she was a beauty! "Good morning, Miss. I'm Inspector Sims. I understand you want to see me?"

Lane stood up and offered her hand. "Good morning, Inspector. My name is Lane Winslow. I am a friend of Inspector or, if you will, Flight Lieutenant Frederick Darling."

Are you indeed? thought Sims. "Right. Please sit down. What can I do you for?" He threw a pad of paper onto the desk and waved her to the chair.

Lane remained standing. "I know I am taking a risk in coming to you, but time is running out, and I have information that may be useful, though you seem to have locked up the case and are quite content to see an innocent man hang." Damn, she thought. I've insulted him. Not a way to win friends. "I'm sorry," she added. "That came out wrong. I . . ."

To her surprise, Sims made something of a smile. "I can see why you two might be friends. Darling has charged me with the same thing."

"You've seen him?" Lane felt her heart pounding, and sat down.

"Yes. Just yesterday. He's fine, but claiming to all and sundry he's innocent." Sims pulled a chair away from the table and sat down himself. "It's a long, tall claim, under the circumstances. And he's had the brass to call me a dupe."

Lane pulled herself together, her relief at knowing for certain that Darling was alive and accessible to someone giving her wings. "Where is he?"

"I'm not at liberty to say. He's been moved to a place about three hours away. I don't understand it, and it's a nuisance. And I'm going to be honest with you, I'd have said the case was a lock, but he's claiming he's innocent, and now you're here. I have a witness statement that I'm not sure about. It's all adding up not quite right."

Lane looked at him. She saw in his face something that gave her hope. She saw doubt, a good honest man's doubt. "He's a lot like you, you know. He'd never let a column of facts add up wrong."

Sims emitted a big sigh. "Be that as it may, the circumstances are not in his favour at the moment. What have you come to say? If it's a fervent plea for his innocence from the little woman, I'm afraid it will do us no good. We need something solid."

"Well then, how's this for solid? I've been trying to understand why this whole thing started in the first place. I started by trying to trace the surviving airmen who flew with him, and things got interesting right away. The first one I talked to, a chap called Watson, refused to let me into his house, and told me he was to talk to no one on the subject of the crash in '43. That wording struck me as odd. Who told him to 'talk to no one'? Secondly . . ."

"Sorry, Miss, could you hold on a minute? I'd like to write this down." He took a fountain pen out of the inside pocket of his jacket. "Right. Watson. He was the navigator, I believe."

"Yes. So I went to Norfolk with a woman called Sandra Donaldson—she's the wife of a fellow pilot of Darling's—because I wanted to talk to a man called Salford, who operated the wireless. Only when we got there, he was dead. A train hit him the week before. The wife's been told it was suicide."

Sims looked up. "You don't believe that?"

"It could have been. I don't want to unnecessarily complicate things, but it seems singular that one man has been told to keep quiet and another has suddenly died. In any case, I learned from his wife that they were in Paris in March, and he saw someone he thought was a member of their crew, someone he hadn't expected to see by the sound of it. He got preoccupied after that. She said she believed someone had been in their house, in his office,

243

but that might be just a kind of paranoia on her part, I don't know. She thought a letter might be missing. I felt anxious enough about her safety that I suggested that after the funeral she go and stay with his parents for a bit."

Sims leaned back, his expression puzzled. "Now that's odd. Why should you feel she was in danger?"

"That question is immaterial, Inspector. I just did. And I was right, I think, given what I subsequently found. When the plane was shot down in '43, two people died. Evans, whom Darling is accused of shooting, and the map reader, a man called Jones, who was believed to have gone up with the plane. There is a very clever policeman who works with Darling back in Canada, and he accidentally found something very much to the purpose. It turns out that Salford wrote a letter to Darling shortly after the Paris incident, and the letter never got to Darling. It got stuck into a catalogue the neighbour received, and he's only just found it." Lane opened her purse and took out her transcript of the letter, pushing it over to Sims. "I had Constable Ames read it to me over the telephone. Here is the transcript. In it, Salford tells Darling he thinks he's seen Jones in Paris. The man doesn't recognize him, and claims only to speak French, but Salford cannot shake the idea that it is Jones. He wonders if Jones has lost his memory and decides to leave him to it. He wrote to Darling to let him know, because he knew Darling felt really dreadful about the loss of his two crew members."

Taking the paper Lane handed him, Sims read the letter, his lips in a grim line. "It's interesting, I suppose. But I don't actually see how it is to the purpose. It does not in any way touch on the death of Evans. It does not, in fact, move the case forward one bit."

"Look Inspector. It's another number you have to add to your sum, along with Watson keeping shtum and Salford being dead. Where are you going to put them, how are you going to squeeze them in so they add up to Darling being guilty of something he didn't do? I was going to see the other airman, Belton, but I became afraid that something would happen to him too. Now I want to see Anthony. I want to know why he thinks he saw what patently didn't happen."

"You certainly have a lot of faith in Darling. How do you know it is not misplaced? If I were facing a hanging offence, I'd be protesting my innocence as well."

"It is not misplaced. I believe it's possible some sort of crime has been committed, and this is an attempt by someone to cover it up."

Sims was silent. Corporal Edwards, he was certain, had been about to say, "Special Branch," when he talked to him. "That's . . . a leap, Miss Winslow. I've already reinterviewed Anthony, before you ask. His story is identical to his original story that led to Darling's arrest. Identical."

Lane was alert. "You say 'identical' with some emphasis. Do you think it's significant?"

Sims was silent again.

"Please, Inspector Sims." Lane tried to keep the desperation out of her voice, but knew she was failing. "I've . . . we've very little time. If you think there is something not right, you must act on it! I will not stop, I can tell you that. I want Anthony's address. I want to talk to him myself." Lane stood up, glaring down on the inspector.

"Sit down, Miss Winslow," he said, resignation deciding him. "If you want to know, I was troubled by Anthony's story being identical. It was identical to the last syllable, as if he'd memorized it. He was terribly careful when he spoke, as if wanting to make sure there was not a word out of place. I was convinced by the army's evidence right from the beginning, based on that statement. The man was described as extremely distraught, saying he'd lost sleep because he could not shake the image of Darling shooting a man in cold blood, and he finally had to come forward to someone. But I said to myself, if a man were pouring out a story in a distraught state, it would be all over the map. Okay, so when he signed off on the story, they'd organized it into something coherent, I understand that. Why then is he giving me the same exact wording so long after the fact?"

Lane sat down and put her purse down beside her. She had a little over a day before she had to give Dunn her answer. "What are we going to do?" She asked simply.

Sims gazed at her. Lucky, lucky Darling, he was thinking.

"WHAT'S UP?" AMES asked O'Brien, when his desk phone rang.

"A citizen is complaining about a car. She thinks it's been there a couple of weeks, and she wants it moved."

"Been where for a couple of weeks?"

"Oh, sorry. She lives along Lakeside, and there's a kind of path that goes past the back of her house along the lake, and it's blocking her view."

Ames ran a mental scan of the city. "Below the station. All right, I'm on my way. For a moment I worried that man was back about his stolen car." Ames thought again about what Darling had to put up with. Maybe this was the man's bloody missing car. Or maybe, and here he brightened up, it was Agatha's car. They'd certainly had zero luck finding it anywhere, even with the help of the mounted police. One could always hope.

It was nearing ten, and the train station was busy with people being dropped off for the ten o'clock to the coast. Ames walked past it and onto the quiet treed street that ran at an angle along near the edge of the lake. It made him think of a small village. The woman, a Mrs. Thomas, was happy to show him through her fenced yard to where the car stood, indeed blocking her view, and a good portion of the grassy path.

Ames saw immediately that it was not the tiresome man's late model Dodge, but what it was set his heart aflutter. He turned to the woman. "Do you remember seeing who might have been driving the car?"

"I don't spend my time mooning out the window, Constable. I have four children and a husband to attend to. All I know is it was not there one day, and there the next, and it's been there over a week and no one's come to move it."

"Not to worry, ma'am. I'll get the towing company to move it right away." Well, that was something, anyway, thought Ames, gazing at the dark green 1927 Ford. Right here in his own backyard. And not before time. He had a summons to the municipal office, and he was pretty certain he knew what it would be about. They'd want to know how he was getting on with the murder up the lake. He ordered the towing and then stopped in at the ticketing office at the station.

"YES, I AM the guy who usually sells tickets here, and no, I don't remember an old lady buying a ticket a week ago. I remember dozens of old ladies buying tickets. We don't take their names and addresses, you know, they give us money and we hand 'em a ticket." The man in the ticket booth now looked past Ames at a couple lined up behind him, as if he'd like to get on with his work.

"This one would have had a British accent," said Ames.

"Do you know how many people here have accents? British, Russian, German, Lower Slobovian . . . Now will you let me get on with my work?"

Ames knew he was being dismissed and could think of nothing else to ask him. He had no idea how Mary would be different from any other old lady in the manner of dress or appearance. "Thanks anyway," he said.

Musing on his ill luck and the upcoming interview on the progress of the case, Ames made his way back up the steep hill and wondered what his next step would be. The only possible avenue of action would come if Fripps called him back from England with news that Mary Browning turned up there. It was when he was just going through the station door that he suddenly thought, what if Mary passed herself off as her sister? She'd stand to get the money then. They looked similar enough in their youthful picture. Had they become more alike as they aged?

"Ames," called O'Brien, as Ames burst through the swinging gate.

"Not now!" Ames exclaimed, taking the stairs two at a time. He went into his office and pulled out the envelope with the developed pictures he'd taken at the scene. He finally found what he was looking for, a photo of just Agatha Browning's face. A bit banged up, but it might be enough. Glancing at his watch, no trains coming or going for the next two hours, he shoved the picture in an envelope and hurtled down the stairs again.

"Hey, Ames," O'Brien called again. Ames waved him off and set out back down the street.

"SHE DOESN'T LOOK too healthy," the ticket man commented through a mouth full of scone. He was using a slight respite to drink tea from his Thermos and have a little snack. Then he put down the top of the Thermos and leaned in. "Now, wait a minute." Then he sat back and shook his head. "No. It wasn't this one."

"I know it wasn't this one," Ames said, "This one is dead. Did you see someone who looked a little like her?"

"That's what I'm wondering. There was a lady who bought a ticket but then came back, wanted to know if she could use it on a later train. Could have been her. Same kinda skinny face."

"What day was this? Did she say which train she wanted to take instead?"

The ticket man took another bite of his scone, and followed it with a slug of tea with the air of a man who could not stop the business of the moment with idle talk. "I don't think I remember what day. A week ago, maybe? She didn't ask about a train that day. Seems to me she wanted to travel another day. I told her she could travel any damn day she wanted. Like you, she was keeping honest travellers from buying tickets by holding me up."

"So, you're saying she didn't travel that day?"

"Look, Constable, all I know is what she told me. She could have gotten on the train, in fact, I thought she had, or she might not have."

BACK IN HIS office, Ames ran a handkerchief over his brogues, admiring again the long slender line and the perfect detailing across the top of the toe. His meeting with the deputy mayor was in half an hour. He would have to convey some sense of competence. What would he get asked? But he could guess the answer to that: "How close are you to solving the murder of the old woman up the lake," with some variation of "We can't have vulnerable senior citizens being murdered willy-nilly in their beds." He imagined he would be badgered. People in positions of power always like to make out that underlings are incompetent. How could he get out of city hall unscathed? It was clear: focus on the progress he had made. With a sudden uplift of spirits, he realized that it wasn't strictly true that he hadn't solved the murder. For all intents and purposes he had; he had the name of a very likely suspect. All that was really lacking was having that suspect in hand. Much cheered, he took up his pencil and began to prepare his notes for the meeting.

Moments before he needed to leave for his meeting (Would it do to be a few minutes late? It would convey the impression of busyness. No. Darling emphasized punctuality and direct honesty), the phone rang.

"Towing company, 'boss,'" said O'Brien.

"Cut that out. Put him through."

"Constable Ames? This is Jim at Regal Towing. Where'd you say that car was?"

"Just behind number fifteen on Lakeside."

"Well," said Jim, "It ain't there. I'm going to have to charge for the call out, you know."

"What do you mean, it ain't . . . isn't there? I saw it myself less than two hours ago," Ames said, his brow furrowing.

"Ain't there, is what I mean."

AMES, HIS CONFIDENCE shaken by this development, walked out of the building toward city hall, wanting more than anything to tell the city fathers to go fly a kite, and get back to work. The disappearance of the car was a confounding occurrence, and he didn't want to waste time trying to convince a bunch of skeptical men, who were doubtless looking to demean his efforts, that he'd all but solved the case. He hadn't, and he needed to get back to the impatient housewife, Mrs. Thomas, to see if she saw who took the car. Then, with a sinking heart he thought, it might not even have been Agatha's car. It was an unusual dark green colour to be sure, and certainly over twenty years old, but there were scores of cars from the twenties. Money had been tight before and after the war. Men held on to their vehicles, keeping them in garages and working on them by hand to keep them going. His next thought stood out with such lucidity that it nearly made him stop.

Men, he thought. Not women. Plenty of women drove, he knew that, but still lots depended on their husbands, especially older women. This woman not only drove, however, but the priest described her as able to repair her own engine. Cursing city hall, he looked at his watch: 3:00. Too late. But he could get England if he called at midnight. Hoping Darling wouldn't balk at the long-distance telephone bill, Ames proceeded to city hall, feeling something he'd never felt before: sudden and absolute mental clarity. He hoped it wasn't just because he was hungry.

CHAPTER TWENTY-SIX

WATSON LOOKED AT ANTHONY, SLUMPED in his chair, a Scotch untouched on the table beside him. He hadn't touched his dinner either.

"Nev, this nonsense has to stop. I'm going to tell you something now. I talked to Belton. I phoned him when you went out. We both had the same experience: someone coming round and telling us not to talk to anyone about the accident in '43. Some rot about it being reinvestigated and the Official Secrets Act. Belton was threatened, he didn't tell me how, Salford is dead, and now we're wondering if it was actually suicide. I was threatened, Nev. You can guess how. And you were threatened in the same way. I'm right, aren't I?"

Anthony looked at Watson and shook his head. "It would mean the end of everything. Do you understand? We'd lose our jobs, we'd face imprisonment. I could bear it for myself, but not for you."

"I see," Watson said. He got up and went to the decanter and poured himself a stiff drink. "You'd better drink up. Recently you've been popping in and out of the War Office like a jackrabbit. No one has called on me or on Belton since the first time. But you seem to be rather special. Why, I wonder?"

Anthony took up his glass at last, and drank thirstily. "I can't tell you. That's all there is to it."

"Does this have anything to do with Flight Lieutenant Darling being accused of shooting Evans? Because that's what that girl told me. I nearly dropped where I stood! He never did, nor ever would do, such a thing. But you've been behaving like a stranger since the day she came. I admit I was frightened. I was told the only way I could protect you was to refuse to talk to anyone, including you. But look at you. You're a wreck. Whatever secret you're sitting on, it's bigger than mine, and it's killing you. And us, for that matter."

LANE PACED, UNABLE to settle. She had come home early because she wanted to be alone with her thoughts, to come up with some plan that would save her, save Darling. Tomorrow was Friday, a thought that made her feel completely ill. Mrs. Macdonald had invited her to listen to a drama on the wireless in the sitting room, but Lane rejected the invitation as politely as she could. She looked outside, expecting to see some mysterious figure lurking around, but the street was quiet. Well, there was no point in Dunn having her watched now; he had her in his web. She had to pull herself together, be pragmatic. She at least had the power to save Darling. If she could get him free, get him to leave the country, she could work on how to extricate herself. Maybe it would only be "a simple mission," or whatever dismissive way Dunn had phrased it. She heard the phone ring downstairs, felt her stomach lurch, and then heard Mrs. Macdonald come partway up the stairs.

"It's for you, lovey, a Mr. Watson."

Astonished, Lane bounded down the stairs, past the startled Mrs. Macdonald, and took up the receiver. "Mr. Watson. Hello!"

"Miss Winslow. I'm sorry. It's late, I know. But can you come out here to see me, us? Tonight, like? There's something you need to know." He sounded completely different from when she'd met him. The man on the line was determined and decisive.

"I'll be there as soon as I can. I'm leaving now."

SHE WASN'T SURE when the last train ran. She glanced at her watch and started toward the stairs at the Holborn tube stop. It was still light outside, but it was nearing nine o'clock, and there were only a few stragglers going home. As she turned to descend, she felt a frisson of fear. She saw a man step suddenly behind the building. She seen him for a fraction of a second, but it was him. The same man she'd seen outside her window that night. The same man who'd passed them on the street when they'd gone to see Salford. She continued into the tunnel without pausing and stepped behind a newspaper kiosk that was shuttered for the night, and waited, trying to control her breath. A few people passed her and went toward the train entrance. Where had he gone? And then he too went by, walking quickly toward the turnstile. Hovering in the shadow, she waited until she'd seen him go through and disappear, and then she bolted up the stairs to the other side of Kingsway.

When she arrived on Bromley Road, she stopped and looked in all directions. She was certain she'd lost him by going to the Leicester tube station, but she had to be sure. Seeing the coast clear, she hurried up the street and knocked on the door quietly. She would warn them to be on their guard.

"FRIPPS HERE."

"Sergeant, good whatever the hell the time of day it is over there. Ames here."

"Constable, good morning! How can I help? We've not seen hide nor hair of Mary Browning yet, before you ask," Fripps said.

"No, that's all right. I need you to find out something for me. Maybe that Tilly person could tell you."

"All right then. I have a pencil at the ready." It was clear from Fripps's voice that he loved these international calls with a policeman all the way over in Canada.

"I want you to find out if Mary drove, or owned, a car. Unless you already know that?"

"No, can't say I do. But I've Tilly Barnes's telephone number, so I'll do that right now. My mum says hi."

"Say hi right back. And thanks for the wire! Very helpful."

LANE HAD GOTTEN back very late from Watson's house on Bromley Road. She was grateful Anthony drove her because she was exhausted and wrung out. The streets were nearly empty at two in the morning, so they sped back into

256

town. She'd made a few notes and then fallen into bed, spent, wearing her slip. It was an unconscious reflection of how she used to sleep, on the run, a few hours a night, ready to up and leave at any minute. It was as if her body already knew what her mind had decided.

She got up, put on a tweed skirt and a white blouse, slipped on her stockings, and tied her shoes. A cardigan should be enough, she thought, unless he's planning to ship me to Vladivostok this afternoon. She looked around her room and then chided herself. She knew she'd be back later, but there was a sense of finality about what she was about to do.

They had arranged to meet along the river, on a bench nearest the Blackfriars Bridge. She sat down on the bench next to a man reading a newspaper.

"Were you followed?"

"For God's sake, Angus. Who would follow me besides you? Who was that man who followed me last night?" Lane crossed her legs angrily and glared out at the people walking by.

"I've told you, already. I have no one following you." It was the second time Lane had mentioned this. Dunn was uneasy. He'd like to dismiss it as hysteria, but Lane had never been a hysteric. He'd have to look into it. He couldn't stand uncontrolled loose ends. Well, it wouldn't matter now, anyway. "So, what's it to be then?" He continued, glancing sideways at her, but not taking the paper down.

"I'm here, aren't I? When will Darling be released?"

"You appreciate we have to go a step at a time. It has to look like some sort of process has been followed."

"I appreciate no such thing. You are talking gobbledy-gook. I want a commitment, a day."

Dunn sighed and folded up the paper and stared out across the river. "I've arranged for you to leave for Berlin early tomorrow. You will meet your driver across the street from the War Office. You'll receive instructions just as you leave. There will be an envelope on the back seat of the car. It contains all you need. Documents, money, instructions."

She turned to look at him. "You arranged all of that already. You were sure of yourself."

"I was sure of you."

"I want you to leave those men alone," she said. "And I don't want them hurt. One of them is dead. I doubt that is a coincidence."

"Aren't you just the Sister of Mercy? Well, they didn't take long to spill the beans. Glad they weren't working for us during the war." He was working to sound uncon-cerned, but the fact of Salford being found dead on the railway track worried him. He certainly hadn't ordered it. He would look into it directly when Lane was dispatched.

"No, they had legitimate jobs flying bombers. They are harmless and you've made their life a hell."

He inclined his head with a shrug. "They are breaking the law," he pointed out.

"You are absolutely without any moral centre, aren't you? They aren't going to talk. Just let them get on. They want to move to Yorkshire, and you should let them."

"I have what I want. It wasn't what I started out to get, but it, you, are oh, so much better."

"Is that a promise or is it not?"

"If it works out, I suppose I can oblige. What did you tell them?"

"I told them absolutely nothing, as you well know. It's what they told me that I find so disgusting. How they've been tormented and manipulated. It must have been your finest hour. Do your wife and family know what you do for a living?"

For a moment Dunn was silent. She was certain she saw a slight wince. Finally he said, "In the morning then, what?" And he got up and walked away without a backward glance.

AMES PULLED THE maroon Ford out of its parking place and drove slowly along the street. The town was busy in the morning, with trucks making deliveries and cars crawling along looking for parking. It was a beautiful Saturday morning, and people were on the move. He drove up and around the curve below the hospital, and arrived at the ferry landing, where he had to park behind at least ten cars. He hoped he would get on. People seemed to be leaving the city to picnic or fish along the many coves of the lake. He had never followed any of these recreations himself, and wondered if he ought to start. Working and going to the movies with Vi suddenly seemed to him to be a limited life. Perhaps he should learn to fish. If he got married and had children, he would need to know a few skills to teach them. Fishing? Hunting? He couldn't imagine Vi wanting to gut fish or dress game. Baseball, then. Curling in the winter.

The ferry went off without him, and he turned the engine off and hung his elbow out the open window. He thought about what his dad had taught him. Not a whole hell of a lot. He'd worked in the CPR freight-dispatching warehouse until he'd had a heart attack and died. He had never seemed to like being at home. Ames's mother still kept a photo of her husband, young, excited, ready to fight just before he'd shipped out for his stint in the Great War. That had been before Ames was born. His mother had told him that he reminded her so much of his father before the war. "It changed him," she'd said. "Knocked the laughter right out of him."

It must have, Ames thought. He didn't recall ever hearing his father laugh. He had increasingly felt bad about his own high spirits, but his mother always told him not to change a thing. There was a brief period when he wanted to sign up when he came of age in the second year of the war, in 1940, when his mother had gone fearful and silent. She'd never asked him not to, but she was relieved when he'd been told he was needed for police work at home. Darling, he thought, was as close to a father as he had ever had.

The ferry was back and disgorging its town-bound vehicles. He turned on the engine and slipped the car into gear. He'd like to get this murder right, even if Darling would likely downplay it.

AMES HAD NO wait with the ferry crossing at Harrop. He didn't recognize the operator, so he wasn't tempted to exchange any small talk, which suited him fine. He wanted to think about the murder, to cast out his preconceived notions about what had happened that day. He drove off the ferry and along the road to the village, the car windows down to let in the smell of the forest. It sure didn't smell like this in town, where a shift in wind sometimes brought the acrid smell of the sawmills. It was another spectacular afternoon, still early enough in the summer that everything was still green and new. He drove past the village and up the hill to where he had parked his car on his other visits.

"Well, well," he said, pushing open his door. There, next to him, was a dark green Ford, no doubt right where it always used to be parked. He took off his jacket and tossed it onto the passenger seat of the police vehicle, and then walked slowly around the green jalopy, looking in the windows.

He made his way along the path to the cabin and then stood outside it. Was she in there? Pushing open the door he heard nothing but silence. "Hello?" he called. A quick glance told him that no one had moved anything. He closed the door and went round back to the garden. A woman sat motionless in one of the wooden garden chairs. She did not look up when he approached her.

Ames spoke very quietly. "Hello, Agatha," he said.

LANE WOKE EARLY and hastily wrote and addressed a note to Higgins. She packed enough for several days and then went downstairs. Setting her suitcase down in the hall, she put her head into the kitchen. "I'm away for a couple of days, Mrs. Macdonald. Some friends wanted a quick visit to Paris, so I'm off with them."

Mrs. Macdonald looked up from where she was frying eggs and bread for her two current houseguests. "That's lovely, that is!" she said. "You have a good time, and be a good girl!" Here she winked so broadly as to nearly wipe out the impression she had made so forcefully on "her girls" during the war on the subject of men.

On the way into the underground that would carry her to where Dunn said she would be met and taken to Croydon Airport, she stopped at the post office and sent the note off to Higgins. She reckoned he would get it by eleven. She glanced up and down the street opposite the War Office and finally saw a man leaning against a black sedan, smoking. He flicked his ashes onto the sidewalk but did not look around. When Lane approached him, he stood nonchalantly away from the car and, taking her bag, went around onto the street to open the rear passenger door, as if it were his object to have his passenger sit as far away as possible from him.

"There's an envelope there. You're to go through it. Any questions, I can try to help. Your flight out is at ten." As Lane settled onto the seat, the driver took her bag and stowed it in the trunk of the car. The envelope had everything Dunn said it would. She opened the passport. He'd found a photo from three years before when she'd had one taken for a mission that required Belgian papers. She threw this into her handbag and slid out the rest of the paperwork. Where she was to go in Berlin, whom she was to contact. There was a Russian double agent who would get her into the other side, introduce her to people.

She settled back in the seat and watched the city become poorer and more ragged as they drove out toward Croydon. She tried to ascertain what she felt, and realized it was just a cold anger. She did not want to let it go. If she did, it might allow in her fear at being in this car, going on this "mission," or her fear for Darling, for what might become of them.

CHAPTER TWENTY-SEVEN

"**H**EY, MATEY, THE MOVING VAN is here." The guard threw open the cell, and Darling got up from the cot, putting his latest potboiler aside.

"What?"

"Look lively. Throw them clothes in this bag. Your valuables will be transported to the new place, so don't concern yourself about them."

Darling could scarcely remember what he had of value and so did not concern himself. "But where am I going?"

"How should I know? Are you taking them books?" The guard waved at the pile that had accumulated on the one chair in the room.

"No. They're all yours." Darling was tucking in his shirt and slipping on his shoes, feeling . . . not hopeful exactly. More like a kind of relief that he'd get a change of scene. "Do you have any idea why they're moving me?" He asked.

"Listen, how many times? I'm not your ruddy social secretary."

Darling took the bag that was being held out to him, folded his sweater and jacket, and placed them in the bag. Then he stopped in front of the guard and held out his hand.

"I'm sorry, I don't even know your name, but thank you. I've appreciated your . . . well, your good cheer, I suppose."

The guard, surprised, said, "Joe Bean. That's decent of you," and gave his hand to Darling. "And if anyone asks, I don't think you did it. You ain't the type."

Darling smiled gloomily. "Perhaps you can come along and be a character witness for me."

HIGGINS WAS IN an uncharacteristically optimistic mood. His complaints to the Canadian High Commission had borne the initial fruit of getting him a meeting with his client, and now he had received word that Darling was to be brought back into the city and housed at one of the local prisons. Miss Winslow and his friends would certainly be pleased about that. So much for the High Commission not wanting to act on behalf of a Canadian accused of a heinous act of violence. He doubted not that in due course, Miss Winslow would be allowed to visit Darling again—though Higgins was puzzled that she had not visited him when given permission. This tiresome interruption to the preparation of Darling's case over, Higgins could concentrate on building a defence.

Short of willing fellow airmen to testify to what happened on the day of the crash, Higgins thought that his best course of action would to build up doubt in the minds of the twelve good men and true, that an outstanding and decorated Royal Air Force pilot would go around shooting his own men.

The clerk came in and dropped several letters on his desk. His mind only half on the task, Higgins went through them, tossing them aside one by one, and then he came Lane's note. He took his letter opener, an ivory and brass affair given him by his grandfather, who had been out in India, and of which he was inordinately proud.

> Mr. Higgins,
> I find I must be away for the next three or possibly four days. I know that you are working to navigate through the evidence in the hope of engineering the best outcome. I will be in touch as soon as I can.
> Yours,
> Lane Winslow

The lawyer read through this missive twice and then turned the paper over as if there might be something to explain it. The first thing that came to mind was what an absolutely redundant message to be sending, and the second was, where was she going, suddenly, when things were beginning to look up? He felt a slight deflation; he had been looking forward to producing the news to Miss Winslow—as if he were conjuring a very large rabbit out of a hat—that she might soon be able visit Flight Lieutenant Darling right in London.

He put her note with the other letters and began a note to Lieutenant Dixby-Brown, who had retired to civilian life following an injury during an air raid on the city and was now running the family haberdashery. He asked if the lieutenant could call on him at his earliest possible convenience, and then called the clerk to make sure the note was delivered by hand that very day. Stretching to take the tension out of his shoulders, he took up his pad of paper and fountain pen and began a series of questions he might put to Darling's immediate superior with a view to ascertaining if he might be a suitable witness as to Darling's character.

Lane's note lay open next to his hand. Frowning, he put down his pen without capping it and took up the letter again. Why would a seemingly intelligent woman, who had been, let's face it, all "go" to clear up Darling's name, suddenly disappear like that? And why write this inane note? He reread it and something struck him. She was intelligent, and she had not done a single thing since he'd met her that was not to purpose on this business. This note had to fit what he had come to know about her. He read it out loud and got only as far as the word "navigate" when he thought he understood. He read on and stopped at "engineer." Of course. She was signalling to him that he needed to talk to the navigator, that was Watson, and the engineer, Anthony. Even her last words, "as soon as I can," suddenly read to him as, "as soon as you can."

He took up the envelope, and where he had only glanced at her name on the corner of the envelope, he now saw that the return address was on the Bromley Road. He smiled briefly and shook his head. He knew her rooming house was in the centre of town, near Covent Garden. Wondering at the need for such secrecy and obfuscation, and hoping that he would find both Watson and Anthony at the address she'd provided, Higgins pulled on his jacket and took his hat off the hat stand, and went out into the clerk's office.

"I'm off to the Bromley Road."

"A spot of football, sir?"

"Very funny. I expect to be back in a couple of hours."

LANE DISEMBARKED, STEPPING out into a sunny afternoon. I'm breathing the air of Germany, she thought. Two short years ago this was the air of our fiercest enemy, and now we are to be friends again. She walked across the tarmac, thinking of Luftwaffe planes flying from this aerodrome to bomb London or Portsmouth, and bombers dispatched to Hamburg and Dresden by the British. Inside, she was directed to passport control and handed over what had been made up for her. She wondered why she wasn't able to use her own passport. They certainly hadn't bothered to change her name. The agent took her passport and leafed through it, stamped it loudly and then asked, "Is this the first time you travel to our country, Miss Winslow?" in a soft German accent.

She smiled and said, "Yes, it is."

"Purpose of your visit?"

"I am here to meet a friend I was at university with before . . . in 1937. This is the address."

"Her name?"

"Inga Meyer."

He looked up at her and, at last, smiled. "Have a good holiday, Miss Winslow."

Trying to control the relief in her breathing, Lane stood waiting for a taxi. When one came, she gave an address very different from the one she had given at passport control.

London, April 1947

"I'VE BEEN SEEN."

"Bloody hell. How? By whom?"

Jones sighed and looked at the back of his hand, as if assessing a manicure. "One of the crew of the Lancaster. A fellow named Salford. Came right up to me in Paris, asking if I was Jones. I pretended not to hear him at first, and then not to know him. I don't know if he was convinced. I'm not sure I would have been, under the circumstances, but there you are. I thought it was more urgent to let you know this than continue on to Berlin."

The director paced, stopping to look out the window, a prey to dark thoughts. He turned. "It's not the only problem we've got," he said. "A bloody hysteric called Neville Anthony came to report a wartime crime. He came to report he'd seen you shoot Evans. Said he just remembered, hasn't been able to sleep. He said he was sure you had died, but he couldn't rest. It was referred to me almost immediately. We're having him back in. Well, we'll have to now, won't we? More the problem is, what is Salford likely to do? And before you suggest it, we are not going to "neutralize" them. That would raise the alarm like nothing else. We need to be more subtle. What do you know about either of them?"

DUNN STOOD GRIMLY at his window looking out at the bustle of Whitehall. He checked his watch and shoved his hand back into his pocket. He should have been here by now. He'd made it perfectly clear what was to happen, and yet there was already one dead body. The possibility that his agent had gone rogue began to take hold, and with it the fear of what might happen next. Had he been following Lane? Was he following her now? He went to his desk and barked into the phone. "I need to send a wire!"

AMES WAITED, STILLER than he ever remembered being. Finally the woman looked up.

"I tried to make a run for it. Thought I'd go back and take up my old life. Ridiculous, really, when I thought about it. I imagined it would be like it had been. The three of us again. But I destroyed all that. I suppose you'll want to arrest me."

"I do, yes. When I do, I'll put handcuffs on you and take you into town where another policeman and I will interview you. I think you should pack a bag. Change of clothes, toothbrush, that sort of thing."

"Haven't got much, but all right." Agatha Browning pushed herself out of her chair and stretched her back, causing Ames to think that that sort of chair did no one any good.

"How did you know it was me?"

"I thought it was Mary, for the money, but your sister couldn't drive. I talked to a policeman called Fripps in your hometown."

Agatha stood in the doorway, surveying the cabin. "This has been my home for longer than that 'hometown,' as you so quaintly call it, was my home." She moved to a trunk near her bed and pulled out a nightdress, and then by the sink she found her toothbrush and tooth powder and pushed them all into a cloth bag hanging on the wall, out of which she dumped an onion onto the rough wooden counter by the sink.

Ames handcuffed Agatha's hands in front of her and, taking her arm, walked her down the hill, holding her sparse belongings in the bag. A car came along the road from the ferry and slowed down marginally to take a look, but Ames did not recognize the man driving it. Perhaps it was someone visiting a local. When he glanced at Agatha, he saw that she was gazing up at the tops of the trees.

"IT'S A QUESTION of loyalty, really, when you get right down to it, isn't it?" Watson opined primly. He, Belton, and Anthony had all gathered at the house on the Bromley Road. Higgins sat with them. He'd thought of bringing Sims along, but not knowing what would come out of this meeting, had decided against it. If it in any way exonerated Darling, he could bring Sims in later.

"I'd prefer this didn't get out," Anthony said to Higgins. "I just want to set the record straight. For the skipper," he added, glancing at Watson.

"Look, if you are about to tell me something that in anyway removes the suspicion from Flight Lieutenant Darling, I shall need you as witnesses. I don't see how I can avoid that."

"Can you not find another way to, say, get at the same information? We've all been . . . well, threatened, I

271

suppose. I don't think that's too strong a word," Belton said. "They told me they could force me to close my shop. Well, my dad's shop. They said it was official secrets. I didn't think anything of it, really, until I heard this rubbish about the skipper. But the point is, I don't suppose it's true, but I don't want my dad's shop closed either. And if it's true about poor Salford . . ."

Of the three, Higgins thought, Belton looked the most carefree. He was tall and muscular with a mass of waving black hair and a moustache, under which he chewed on the end of an unlit pipe. "Well, I'd better hear what it is you have to say. We'll see how we go from there, shall we?"

A nervous silence followed this, and then Anthony spoke. "I suppose I'd better go first. I feel like I started it. I began having nightmares about a year and a half ago." He looked at Watson. "I suppose you hear about that sort of thing after a crash and whatnot. But mine kept going over and over this one moment when I was crawling out of the plane. I should have gone out with Darling, at the front, but I went through to the back. I . . ." He stopped. "I wanted to make sure everyone was out. And so I had to make my escape following Evans and Jones. And one night I realized what it was I was seeing over and over. It was Jones with a gun out and running in the opposite direction from the rest of us. Skip and I found Evans and dragged him away from the plane. I thought he'd been injured in the crash, but then I saw a clean wound where he'd obviously been shot."

Higgins interrupted. "Excuse me, but what part of what you are telling me is dream, and what part is memory?"

Anthony shook his head, as if to clear the cobwebs. "That's the thing, really. I had no memory of this until the nightmares started. It's like it had been wiped out. But once I started having the dreams, I began to put it back together. Does that make sense?"

Higgins, who didn't believe in the hocus pocus of modern Freudian thought, and liked to have facts about him when he stood up in a courtroom, shrugged. "It might. We shall have to see. Go on."

"Well, it clicked one night a couple of months ago," continued Anthony. "I knew that I'd seen Jones actually shoot Evans. When the plane exploded, I just felt like my brain had been blown apart. I went into a kind of shock, and I could only focus on getting out of there. I suppose that's why I didn't remember it."

"What I don't understand is why you suffered in silence all this time and didn't tell me!" Watson said.

"I don't know. I think I just thought it was mad, that I was going bonkers."

"Then what happened?" asked Higgins. "How did this go from you thinking Jones shot Evans, to Darling shooting him?"

"I really felt I was beginning to lose my mind, and I thought . . . I don't know . . . I think I thought that if I could talk to someone, that they could deny it. I thought maybe someone at the War Office already knew about this, had filed it somewhere and dealt with it. I thought some-one would say, 'Oh, that. Not to worry. We know about that.' After all, Jones is dead. Well, that was me living in a dream world. I went there, I was shown in to someone who took notes and kept saying 'I see' in a way that made me feel like they thought I was lying."

"Well," said Watson, "if you burbled on about dreaming it, I'm not surprised."

"But I didn't, you see. By then I was pretty clear in my mind. And when he asked me why it took this long to come forward, I just told him I had blocked it out. Once that was done, I did feel better. I got it off my conscience and I started to sleep a little better. The nightmares stopped. But then after a week or two, someone delivered an official looking envelope to me at work, and I was asked to come back. It scared me half to death." Anthony stopped and took a drink.

"And there's been a little too much of that, lately, as well," Watson said, nodding at Anthony's glass.

"Listen, if you'd been in that room, you'd be drinking too!"

"What was the substance of this second interview?" Higgins asked, hoping to curtail a domestic fracas.

CHAPTER TWENTY-EIGHT

"**D**ID YOU HAVE A GOOD flight, Miss Winslow?" The woman talking to her appeared to be in her late thirties and had a kind of dark Russian attractiveness though her face was very thin and lined in a way that made her look older. Her nearly jet-black hair was cut short, practical, but becoming. She was wearing a dull brown suit, the jacket of which she'd taken off and hung on the back of a chair, revealing a tired beige, short-sleeved nylon blouse. She had wiry and muscular arms. She walked to the window and looked down toward the street, scrutinizing the nearby buildings.

They were in an apartment the exterior of which looked so banged and shot up that Lane had no hopes for any comfort inside. She was pleasantly surprised, however. The sun slanted in the tall elegant windows that spoke of the building's more aristocratic history. The dark cadmium yellow paint on the interior walls, while it had seen better days, amplified the warmth. It was a small sitting room that had been divided from a larger one that now belonged to the next door apartment, but a faded rug and a couple of comfortable chairs gave the room a snug feeling. Olga Valentinova had prepared strong black tea with rock sugar and provided a plate of sugar-sprinkled pastries. She put the cups on the table and then went to the window and lifted the sash slightly to let in a welcome burst of fresh air. She looked again onto the street in both directions.

"These are a bit like what they call donuts where I live in Canada. Thank you. I was famished." Lane devoured the jam-filled confection and drank down some tea. She forgot for a moment her underlying anxiety about what she was letting herself in for.

"I'm sorry I don't have anything more substantial, but we must go across. I have arranged everything for three o'clock." Olga spoke in thickly accented English. "There can be no delay."

"Would you rather we spoke Russian?" asked Lane.

Olga smiled. "Yes, I was told your Russian is very good. No. Not here. Save it. You will need it. We are going to stick as close to the truth as possible. I will introduce you as a woman who was brought up in Russia and wishes to work on behalf of the people. You are horrified by the decadence and duplicity of the West, the unfair treatment of workers and war vets, and so on."

"Is that your cover?"

"I am horrified by the failures of the revolution, if the truth be known. They took my family, my parents, to Siberia, they tell me. They think this is what holds me. But I know my parents are already dead. My brother was killed in the siege of Leningrad. There is nothing to hold me. And so I work for your British government. I am an engineer.

I work designing aircraft in the East and have become a double agent thanks to a wartime encounter with a lover. I work with my counterparts here in the West, and I keep the Russians happy by taking plans across to them from time to time. Then I bring back what the Soviets are up to. There are some differences in accuracy of what I take back and forth. It keeps the West up to date on developments in my small area of expertise."

"You are not afraid of being found out?" Lane contemplated what it would be like to live her entire life in the small, claustrophobic corridor of deceit this woman was describing.

Olga shrugged. "I don't really know. I will either go on forever, or I will be found out. I will either be able to flee to the West when that happens, or I will be arrested and die in Siberia, where at least I will be near my parents. It's immaterial. You yourself could be the agent of my downfall."

"You won't need to add me to your list of concerns. This is a small job. I will do it and get out."

"What is the job?" Olga asked.

Lane looked at her watch. It was ten after two. "Could you show me to the bathroom? I'd better splash up a bit before I take on the Soviet empire."

ANTHONY WAS TAKING so long to respond that Higgins now wished he had brought Sims with him. The thought of making this man squeeze out his story a second time seemed daunting.

"I was made to talk to a man whose name I never got. He just called himself 'the director.' He was extremely pleasant, like a friendly insurance agent. All ordinary language. Was I sure? Could I just go over it again? Had I seen anyone else? Where was the flight lieutenant? He just kept on and on, and I began to get muddled about the answers. He managed to convince me that I was not completely sure about what I saw. Then he stopped abruptly and began to talk in this chatty way about what I had been doing since the war ended. Didn't I live with Adam Watson? Taking a bit of a risk, wasn't I? But he admired my loyalty. It would be awful if it got out, didn't I think?

"Then he went back to the questions and began to posit the idea that Darling had been responsible. Had I actually seen Darling before he and I began to move Evans? But by this time, you see, I was sick with fear because I knew he knew about Adam and me. He didn't have to say anything really. I just knew what he meant. The next thing I knew he was producing this statement, already written out, in which it was the skipper who shot Evans. 'I can't sign that,' I told him. 'It's not true.' He started in with some flannel about how I'd already said myself that I wasn't sure, which wasn't true either. I was sure. I'm still sure. Then he said, 'I like you, Mr. Anthony,' just the way he said it made my hair stand on end. He said he couldn't expect me to understand, but the security of the country depended on getting this 'right,' and he'd hate for me to get caught up in a scandal that could end with me, or even Adam, being in prison. The way he twisted the truth made my head spin, I can tell you. He told me to memorize it and to sign it. I admit it. I'm a dreadful coward, and I couldn't have Adam dragged in. I signed."

"So, let me get this right," said Higgins. "You are telling us that an agent of his majesty's government forced you to perjure yourself?"

"I suppose that's right, yes."

"Well, that's against the law, for a start," Higgins remarked, underlining something in his notes.

"Sooner you than me going up against that man. All I know is the skipper is facing a capital offence, and probably treason for all I know. Adam and I discussed it. That's why we called Miss Winslow."

"I'm very glad you've seen it that way. Will you be prepared to testify to this at the trial?"

Neville Anthony hesitated. "No. Absolutely not. For one thing the lawyer will do to me what that director did. He'll twist my words, say I was unsure about what I saw. I'd be a lousy witness. And for another, I can't. The risk is too great."

Higgins felt his case, suddenly so certain, in danger again. "All we have to do is establish doubt. If their lawyers say you were unsure about seeing Jones shoot Evans, I shall counter with reminding them that that cuts both ways . . . you also could not be sure of seeing Darling do it either."

HIGGINS WAS COMPLETING his notes when the clerk put his head through the door. "A double-barrelled squadron leader here to see you, Mr. H."

Glancing at his watch, Higgins waved his hand, "Bring him through, thank you."

A dapper man in a tweed jacket was shown in. He had a bad limp and carried a cane, which he now shifted to his left hand, offering his right to the lawyer. "Mr. Higgins? I'm Dixby-Brown."

"Ah, Squadron Leader. Thank you so much for coming in after what must have seemed a rather peremptory summons. Please, sit down."

"No bother. I was intrigued. The governor is as old as Methuselah but won't give up control of the family business. Said I should get out from underfoot because I'm always looking for things to improve in the office when I've time on my hands. What's this to do with, then?" Dixby-Brown settled in the chair offered and straightened his leg with his hands. Higgins saw now that there was a fair bit of scarring along the right side of his face. Burns most likely, he thought.

"Got this in a bloody raid right here in the city, instead of like a good honest airman, in battle," Dixby-Brown said.

Higgins smiled. "I understand you were Flight Lieutenant Frederick Darling's commanding officer."

"Yes, that's right." He frowned. "I thought he'd buggered off back to Canada and was busy solving crime in some backwoods town."

"Can you tell me a little bit about him? What was he like?"

"Well," said Dixby-Brown, making an expansive gesture with his hands. "He was impeccable. An excellent pilot, well-liked by his men. Very well liked, I would have said. He never pandered to them. In fact he was inclined to seriousness. Had a kind of dry humour that the crew members were often the brunt of but seemed to make them like him all the more. Nothing's happened to him has it?"

"I'm afraid something has happened to him. He's being charged with murder."

Dixby-Brown started. "Murder? Impossible! I mean, I should have said that was the least likely thing in the world."

"I'd better explain," said Higgins. He spoke in his usual measured manner, consulting his notes, outlining the events that had brought them to the present time. He did not discuss Darling's having been granted and then denied bail, or his having been moved out the city and then back into it.

At the end of his narration, Dixby-Brown sat back in his chair and said, "What you are telling me absolutely beggars belief. I remember that incident particularly well, partly because he managed to get most of his men back under nearly impossible circumstances, and because we lost two people. He saw that Evans had been shot and believed it had happened when the Germans came after them. He didn't see Jones at all. Wasn't at roll call, as it were. He went up with the plane. No. I'm sorry. This is some sort of rubbish. And why is this coming up all this time later?"

"If I'm honest, we aren't entirely sure. It is certainly in someone's interest to have him in the frame for this. I've felt an unseen hand interfering at every step. We've been having some difficulty getting hold of his crew, but I was able to speak to two of them today, but only because they overcame their fear and sought me out. I'm convinced that there's some funny business going on. Anthony was forced to sign a declaration that he'd seen Darling shoot Evans."

"Forced? How forced? I wouldn't have believed it of him. Now mind you, he didn't know Darling as well as the rest. He was a last-minute replacement, it seems to me. I think he knew one of the other fellows, Watson. Watson was a good airman, if bit of a pansy . . . ah. I see. I'm guessing Anthony will have been protecting him, perhaps. Well, well. Never thought the wind would be blowing that way. The point is, they were excellent airmen, fought a good war, and I say live and let live. Who the blazes forces people into this kind of situation? Why should anyone have shot Evans anyway? The woods were full of Germans armed to the teeth."

Higgins took up his notes. "According to Anthony, someone did shoot Evans, all right. It was it was the map reader, Jones."

"Jones? What madness is this? Why would Jones want to shoot a crew member? And he's dead. If he did shoot Evans, and he copped it too, wouldn't that be case closed?"

Higgins shrugged. "The point really is, Lieutenant, and why I've brought you in, is that I may not be able to get Anthony into court, and even if I did, I'm not sure how he would stand up. He and all the other men were warned off discussing the situation with anyone, and one of the airmen, a chap called Salford, died a week or so ago, under possibly mysterious circumstances, so they're understandably nervous. They have a great deal of loyalty to Darling, but anything they do will imperil them. What's happened has enormous legal ramifications. Anthony has lied, and the consequence is likely to be Darling put away or hanged. Whoever is doing this has gone to a lot of trouble, and Anthony, even if he were prepared to risk nearly everything to go into court, could also face charges for lying about the death in the first place. I think we can trust that whoever is behind this will never be taken to task. I'm going to have to go to creating doubt, and that will involve finding credible people who can speak to Darling's character."

"Well, you can count me in. I can probably find some other fellows if need be."

"Thank you, Lieutenant Dixby-Brown. I shall contact you as things become clearer."

When his guest had gone, Higgins put in a call to Sims. He hadn't had lunch and so arranged for them to meet at the Queens.

Sims listened to Higgins without interruption and then took up his ale. "What you are telling me, Higgins," he said, wiping his mouth, "is that they don't have a case. I mean, I'll have to speak to those men myself, of course, but if what you say is true, I can't say I'm surprised. There's something about Darling that I just trust. And he said I might be someone's dupe. I didn't care to be told that, I can tell you, but I can see now he's likely right. There's been something fishy about this from the beginning. I was getting a fair bit of resistance from the military when I wanted to reinterview people."

"Do you think we have enough to petition the court to have the matter dropped?" asked Higgins. "I mean from your point of view as a policeman."

"We don't really know what game is being played here, do we? If it were something straightforward, out in the real world, I'd have the charges dropped. Nothing in 'em. I've a good mind to go back to the War Office and tell them I won't push through this charge, that I've looked into it, and I know the statement of the chief witness to be extracted under pressure. Any judge would throw it out. As I said, I'd have to complete the investigation, take in this new evidence."

"They'll be nervous about speaking to the police is the problem," Higgins pointed out.

"Didn't you say the statement was extracted under the threat of exposing him as a fairy?"

"Yes."

"Well, there you are, you see. You can't go around arresting people on the basis of people's say so. The military made the insinuation but never did anything about it. I'd have to have proof before I could act on that sort of thing. And I don't. I've made those sorts of arrests before, but I'm not keen, if I'm honest. There's plenty of good honest crime on the streets to deal with—people being mugged, war profiteers to track down. It's a waste of my time."

"Good. Then you'll finish your investigation and, if you're satisfied, let them know they haven't a leg to stand on? I've told the airmen to expect you, though I warn you, they are unwilling at the moment to testify."

"We'll see about that. I'll let you know how it goes. I'm sure the army doesn't like being thwarted in its little machinations, but I don't like having my time wasted."

"What I still can't make out is why it's so important to have Darling be the culprit here. They've gone to all this trouble to make a man perjure himself. Who would do this?" Higgins asked.

"Wait a minute," said Sims. "What if what Anthony says is true, he saw Jones do the shooting, and that's what they're trying to cover up? Miss Winslow brought me the text of that letter that Darling's constable in Canada found. I didn't think it forwarded the situation at all, but now, wait, let's see. If Jones is still alive and pretends not to know his old pals, then he's up to something, surely. And if he was the one who killed Evans, then someone is going to throw suspicion in another direction." He slapped the table. "I've thought all along that Special Branch is in this. That bloody corporal almost said those words to me and then pulled back. This makes the whole business a lot more complicated."

CHAPTER TWENTY-NINE

OLGA DROVE WITH CONCENTRATION AND both hands on the steering wheel, freeing Lane to look silently at the passing city. They were in a small, beat-up, pre-war Opel, the gears of which were offering some problems. Lane had been able to roll the window down a few inches, and a warm breeze and the sound of the city traffic wafted in. She had time to think about Olga and the wartime lover she had mentioned. Is that how it always was for women? Well, it hadn't been for her, or she had thought not. She had joined through a normal recruitment. The manipulations of the lover had been entirely hidden from her.

They pulled up in front of a building that, like many she had seen, was battered. Next to it was a pile of rubble that must have been the result of the Royal Air Force counterattacks against Germany. A sagging wire fence meant to keep people off had long ago given up its purpose, and children now played on the piles of stone.

"We're here? I thought we'd have to go through some sort of control," Lane said, surprised.

"No, we are free to go back and forth. I don't know how long it will last. I am sure the Soviets are tired of having a Western-controlled Berlin in the middle of their territory. Now look, I will come with you to introduce you to my friend Andrea. She takes over from here. She is the secretary of this business office. The business, which manufactures farm machinery, is a cover. What happens after this, I do not know. But before we go in, I want to wish you luck. You have chosen a difficult role, believe me."

Lane experienced a sinking feeling at this speech. She knew, of course, that she must navigate whatever was about to happen on her own, but even in the short time with Olga, Lane had seen her as an ally, a bulwark against the certain loneliness of living the lie required of her now. She had felt this aloneness before, every time she had set out on a mission during the war, and had become used to it, had developed an internal mechanism for dealing with it. Just at this moment however, she could scarcely remember what that was.

"Thank you. As I said, it will be short." Lane mentally crossed her fingers as she said this. "Will I be likely to see you again?"

"I don't think so. The right and left hand, you know. I learned this expression, and I think it describes the whole thing so well, don't you? 'The right hand doesn't know what the left hand is doing.' So apropos!"

Lane laughed. "It's from the bible originally. Matthew, I think. I don't find it the least bit reassuring." She didn't add that she was beginning to think the entire enterprise was run by a group of men who had never advanced past the age of thirteen.

They walked through heavy wooden doors into a spacious foyer with a wide, echoing staircase. The banisters were broken in places, and the paint was peeling and discoloured. It must have been a grand building, once, Lane thought. It reminded her of her uncle's beautiful apartment in Riga. A building from an expansive and self-assured imperial age. It made her think of the entire Nazi reign, so confident and violent, decaying from within. On the second landing, Olga rang a bell at an office with an ornate sign in German. A young woman opened the door, ushered them in, and told them to wait. She disappeared into an office down a hall, and moments later another woman strode toward them, tall and blond, dressed in a grey suit. She looked to be in her early forties, Lane thought, and had a strong face that could have been called handsome, were it not carved into severe lines of purpose and seriousness.

"Andrea, how are you?" Olga said in Russian. "This is the Englishwoman I told you about. Lane Winslow. She, of course, speaks perfect Russian. She was born in Latvia." Lane glanced at Olga. She'd not told her that. Of course, the director would have left nothing secret.

Andrea looked at Lane and nodded. "Miss Winslow."

Lane had been going to offer her hand but saw it would not be the proper form, so she too nodded, attempting a slight smile, though she was as far from feeling friendly as it was possible to be. Olga turned to her and, with a quick bow of the head, said in Russian, "Goodbye then," and turned to go.

Righty ho, thought Lane. That's that. She turned her attention back to Andrea, whose last name had still not been offered and who looked as if she would begin to trust Lane when hell froze over.

"Do you wish for something to drink?" Andrea asked.

"No, thank you. What is to happen now?"

"You will be interrogated, I expect. We know nothing about you. I am to arrange for you to go to Potsdam. Someone will meet you there."

Lane's heart sank, and the anxiety that had been gnawing at her innards began to grow into real fear. Potsdam! Farther east, farther into the maw of the empire. And what would this interrogation amount to? She suddenly realized that the game was nothing like what she had been tasked with during the war. Then it was simple; they were at war. Deliver this message, these weapons, those radios. Explain them. Get out. She had been equipped to pretend she was an ordinary French girl, but had mercifully never been called on to play a double role. This new and murky world frightened and, yes, she decided, offended her with all its pretense and untruths.

She spoke now in Russian. "When will I leave?"

Andrea looked at her appraisingly. "I am not sure. I have a room here where you are to wait. Are you sure I cannot bring you tea?"

How long would she have to wait? Perhaps she ought to have the diversion of tea. It might help her stay alert. "Yes, then. Thank you."

She was ushered into a room on the floor above. It was panelled in dark wood, and the window overlooked the wall of the next building. Lines of washing hung out of the windows across from where she stood, struggling to dry in the sparse sun that shone into the space. Two children were kicking a ball in the tiny courtyard below, their high-pitched shouts magnified by the enclosed space. Lane put her handbag down and removed her hat and jacket. The afternoon was warm and the room slightly stuffy. After standing at the window watching the children, she settled into the collapsing settee that was against a wall under an empty bookshelf.

Whose house had this been? She had heard that Jewish properties had been taken by the Nazis, their owners had fled or been deported to death camps, their contents taken as booty. Her own grandparents had left their house in Riga when it was taken by the Soviets. They had tried to stay on but had been confined to two rooms, as the house was filled with military offices and an officer's club. Finally they simply left and went "home" to Scotland. The utter impermanence of the structures people build around themselves came to Lane forcefully. What had her ancestors left when they went east to Latvia from Scotland to build a new life? How certain she had been as a child that what she knew would last forever. Still, she thought sadly, she had gone off to Canada, undaunted, to take another kick at permanence. Now look at her. Sitting in some stolen house in Berlin, waiting to be interrogated.

She had no sooner settled than she was obliged to stand up again, as the door opened and a tall, very good-looking man in his sixties swept in. He was impeccably dressed in an expensive dove-grey suit with subtle fawn-coloured stripes. A young man bearing tea and cakes followed him and placed the refreshments on the table by a lamp, which was lit to give the room a warmer feel. The older man nodded his thanks, and the younger one withdrew with a slight bow.

The man advanced toward Lane with both hands out, as if he were a favourite uncle, Lane thought, rather than an interrogator. "Miss Winslow. At last! I am Viktor Aptekar. Please, please, sit down and enjoy this refreshment with me. These cakes are from the finest baker, who sadly is in the American sector. If this city is ever divided, they will be lost to us!"

Lane retrieved her hands from his grasp and sat with a thump in the chair held out for her at the table. Viktor Aptekar. The name, offered in so friendly a manner, made her blood run cold. It was he who had sent her a letter a few months earlier in the winter begging her to come and work for Russia, indeed, had been responsible for her being kidnapped and very nearly killed. The man who claimed to know her father best. This was the man who now had her life, and Darling's, in his hands.

"THERE HAVE BEEN some developments," Higgins said, flopping his briefcase down on the table in the interviewing room of Wandsworth Prison. Darling was looking thinner, he thought. For the first time Higgins felt a surge of rage about the situation. It was a bloody shame to frame and lock up a good man, especially if the "good guys" perpetrated the crime.

Darling smiled wanly and waved his hand to indicate the room. "It's a new development that I've had a change of scene. I got a nice ride in the back of a prison van from what I now know to be Oxfordshire. The countryside there is lovely. I was sorry not to be able to see it. Beggars can't be choosers, I suppose."

"I hope you won't be a beggar much longer. We know who shot Evans, and it wasn't you."

"Brilliant. I could have told you that. In fact, I did. Why isn't he in here instead of me, then? Who was it by the way? I always thought it was Germans, though, as I said, I felt there was something not right about the direction of fire. In a battle situation, it's easy to confuse things."

"Let me start at the beginning. I was able at long last to interview Anthony. Not strictly true. Watson finally contacted Miss Winslow, and she did the initial interview. She put them on to me just before she left. I've spoken to them, and it is clear that Anthony was certain he saw Evans shot all right, but by Jones."

Darling frowned. "Jones? Why ever should Jones want to shoot any of us? It's unbelievable. And even if it were true, he's not here to ask."

"That we don't know. And the reason that you're still banged up in here is because the complications are overwhelming. Anthony has been forced . . . blackmailed wouldn't be too strong a word . . . into signing a statement about that trumped-up business of you shooting Evans and is absolutely unwilling to testify at the moment. They're afraid that the consequences would be too great because Salford has been killed. Watson and Anthony have evidently been . . . you know . . . living together for some time. The consequences are ghastly. Sims, I should mention, is having a go at them. He's furious to be made a fool of and can't see why people just can't get on the stand and tell the truth. I've decided to go for creating doubt that you would do such a thing. I've spoken with your commanding officer, Dixby-Brown, and he's prepared to stand up for you in no uncertain terms, and can collect some more witnesses to do the same."

Darling shook his head at this bewildering barrage of information. One thing, however, was clear to him. "You are not to compel Anthony under any circumstances. I won't have it. You must carry on with your strategy of casting doubt in the minds of the jury."

"I thought you'd say that. By the way, I realize you were not to know this. Jones is likely alive and well, and living in Paris pretending to be someone else. Apparently Salford sent you a letter about it that got lost. One of your neighbours brought it to the police station in Nelson, and Miss Winslow was able to get the text of it, and she brought it to Sims."

"God, you've lost me completely now. Jones shot Evans and isn't dead, but he can't be produced and put on trial for the murder. Why would he shoot a crew member and then go into hiding? How? If he got out of the plane alive and for whatever reason shot Evans, he'd have to have run in the same direction as the rest of us to escape the Germans. They were right behind us." He put his hand to his mouth. "Oh my God. He ran to them on purpose, knowing he would be protected. He was a bloody German spy. Evans must have found out!"

"And there you are," said Higgins. "Only Jones is officially dead and can't be found, and someone in our own government is trying to cover that up and pin the thing on you. Anthony was forced to sign that statement because he'd gone to them to say he remembered seeing Jones do it. They must have been afraid that would get out, hence this ridiculous charade. I think it's ever more significant that the one man who's dead is Salford, who was the one who saw Jones in Paris."

"If, and I say 'if' because I can't believe what I'm about to say, someone in the government had a British citizen murdered because he thought he saw Jones in Paris, then they are protecting Jones. Jones is very likely an agent. He was then, and he is now. And it's a sure bet he's not 'Jones' now. Jones is conveniently dead, since I declared him so in my report about the crash, and he's someone completely else, completely untouchable. I'd say that my prospects are bleaker than ever under the circumstances." Darling wanted nothing more than to put his head down and close his eyes.

"Now then, Darling. No need to throw in the towel. My appeal to the Canadian High Commission has borne some fruit. You're back in London, and I expect your friends will be allowed to see you. In the meantime, don't underestimate Sims. He doesn't like being messed about."

"Atta boy. Look at the silver lining. By the way, what did you mean about Miss Winslow when you said, 'before she left'? Left where?"

"Ahh. Yes. I don't actually know. She scribbled a hurried note and had it delivered saying she had to go away for several days."

"What's she up to then? Does she understand how dangerous this situation has become?" Darling asked. "Damn!

Listen, Higgins. You need to find out. You need to let me know the minute she is back!"

Over France, April 1943

JONES SAT WITH a map he was not looking at, focusing all his energy on the pressing of his leather helmet against his ears. It was a problem he had not anticipated. It was a problem he could not turn away from. It was a problem he had to solve before they got back to base because he had no idea what Evans would do. Jones was absolutely certain that the security of his mission demanded it.

It seemed to him later that he felt the danger a moment before it happened. He looked up, his eyes wide, and in the next second felt the plane being hit.

"We've been hit! Brace! Brace!" shouted Darling. Jones crouched where he was, hands behind his neck and waited for the impact, but when it came, it was as if giant metal hands were clawing at the bottom of the plane. The sound was terrifying and seemed to be going on forever, and then the plane stopped and tipped forward, the tail lifting, and thumped down with a force that threw Jones, like a loose barrel, against the narrow sides of the rear of the plane.

In the momentary silence after impact, nothing stirred, and then Jones could see his crewmates begin to move. There was already a smell of burning from somewhere. He could see that the gunner window had smashed, and somehow Evans was still alive. He was beginning to stir, was crawling on his hands and knees through the opening. Jones followed him. He felt the acridity of the smoke burning inside his nostrils, and he held his breath as he scraped through the opening, ignoring the dangers of shattered glass and ragged metal.

The ground had been scraped clean, trees broken like twigs. They had landed at the edge of a field. The dark outlines of a wood were just to the left. They would go that way. Evans had gotten to his feet and had begun to stumble forward. In an instant, Jones knew now was the time. He pulled out the revolver and fired one bullet, and then turned toward where he thought the Germans must be.

ANTHONY SAW THE gaping hole in the tail, saw Evans and Jones get out. He should follow. Darling was shouting something. Where was Watson? Had he gotten out with Darling and Belton? A fire ignited to his right, licking up through the torn metal. He plunged forward and scrambled on his behind as he tried to orient himself. The wood was a dark line, and he could see figures moving toward it. A shot rang out just ahead of him, on the right. One of the figures went down. He whirled, trying to see where the shot had come from. A man stood, his revolver in his hand, and then turned and ran back toward the plane. In the flickering light of the fire, Anthony was certain he'd seen Jones. Who had he shot? He must have seen Germans approaching. Anthony ducked and looked wildly around. Why had Jones run back to the plane? He'd be killed.

"Hell!" It was Darling, just ahead, leaning over. Anthony got out of his crouch and ran toward where Darling was. "It's Evans," Darling said. "He's still alive. Let's get him to safety." He began to pull the wounded man by the arms.

Anthony took up Evans's feet and they made for the wood, stumbling on the raised furrows of the field. "I think the Jerries were waiting for us," he panted. He wanted to look back, to see what had become of Jones, a part of his brain struggling with why he'd gone back to the plane. Did it mean someone was still there?

When they reached the others, they laid Evans down carefully. Anthony looked around anxiously and felt a flood of relief when he saw Watson, unhurt and sitting against a tree, breathing heavily.

He threw himself down on the ground next to Evans.

"Report," he heard Darling say.

CHAPTER THIRTY

KEEP YOUR HEAD, LANE THOUGHT. Keep it and be as truthful as possible. "Mr. Aptekar. Good breeding requires that I say that I am pleased to meet you, but I confess, I am not all that pleased."

Aptekar laughed. "Your father failed to tell me what a very beautiful daughter he had!"

"The truth is, my father never thought very much of me," Lane said with equanimity as she stirred sugar into her tea. Strong Russian tea was all very well, but she'd become used to the English way.

"No, my dear! It is not so. Your father admired you very much. He often spoke of you."

"Mr. Aptekar. If we are to get on, then I must insist on there being truth between us. So far I am offering truth, and you are offering nonsense."

He smiled again. Lane thought how very charming his smile was. If he had worked with her father from the beginning, then his chief weapon, surely, was this devastating charm. It was a shame it had not rubbed off on her father.

"Well then. Let me put it this way. You surprised him. You surprised him with your courage and the work you chose. This much he did tell me. I think surprising Stanton Winslow is a great achievement, is it not? He was a very courageous man, your father, but even he would have balked at jumping out of an aeroplane."

"How astonishing. He called me a coward once. I am gratified he changed his view somewhat."

"I see that you are . . . I will not say bitter . . . but perhaps distant from him, and I don't blame you. For all his sterling qualities, he would not have been awarded father of the year. He was focused on his work, which he did brilliantly. His ability to work with the various permutations of government in Russia continued after the revolution. He was a genius at reminding us all that pragmatism trumps politics. It would not be an exaggeration to say that the ties he kept between your government and ours made our alliance against the Nazis possible."

"I'm sure it would be an exaggeration; however, I have never doubted my father's work ethic. And, in truth, I am glad to hear that his work made a difference. I suppose it is all any of us wants," she stopped, hesitating before she spoke again. "There is one thing that I would like to know about that worries me."

"Please, my dear, you have only to ask!"

Feeling that she could so easily fall under the spell of his avuncular manner, she nevertheless proceeded. "My father left me and my sister, who lives in South Africa, quite a sizeable sum of money. Some went as well to my grandparents, which was generous, and I want very much for them to have a secure old age. My trouble is that I do not know where it came from, and I am reluctant to use it."

"Goodness me! You are an upright young woman. The more I see you, the more I am grieved to think that Stanton had no idea whatsoever what manner of daughter he fathered. If it is of any consolation to you, I can tell you. As a matter of fact, he and I spoke of the will before his unfortunate death. And I should say if he had a soft spot for anyone, it was your grandparents. They were, after all, the parents of the woman he loved. I feel somehow that he never got over her loss. He was grateful, I know, that they looked after you and your sister, as he knew himself well enough to know he would never be able to put his heart, or his time, as it turned out, to the task. You need not worry. The money was very honestly come by. Your father's family had quite extensive holdings in the form of properties and business. After the revolution, his contacts and his usefulness to the new revolutionary government allowed him to sell all these at perhaps greater advantage than others. Or perhaps because he was English, I do not know. But he collected the money and invested it, and that is the result. It was not a vast fortune, all told. When I say he sold at an advantage, it was nowhere near the full value. In my view, my country still owes you money, but you will, I am afraid, never see it."

Feeling at once relief—together with a sinking feeling that depending on what happened to her now, she might never get to use the money anyway—Lane said, "Thank you. I hope what you say is true. I am relieved for my grandparents. It is a vast fortune to me."

"I can't think what you imagined about where he got it! He was a spy, after all, not a gangster. I'm afraid it is a game that does not enrich the practitioner. In fact, it is often tedious, dirty, and tiring work, conducted in secret and on a knife's edge. Adventure, perhaps, one could hope for, but riches, never. Now then, to the matter of spies. I wonder how it is best to proceed . . .?"

"SERGEANT FRIPPS. HELLO. Ames here."

"Hello to you! How are things in Canada?" asked Fripps. Things were slow in Whitcombe.

"Surprising. I think you'll be surprised by what I'm about to tell you. Agatha Browning is alive."

Fripps was surprised. Gratifyingly so. "Come again? Then who is your body?"

"I hope you're sitting. It's Mary Browning."

Fripps whistled. "No wonder she hasn't come back. How do you know?"

"Agatha Browning told me."

"Well, how did you people get the wrong end of the stick?"

"Good question. Fair question. The thing is, the only Browning people here have known is Agatha, and she and her sister, while similar looking as younger women, were difficult to tell apart as they grew older. Agatha had been planning to go back and settle in Mary's place over there, but realized, I think, that people would know immediately she was not Mary. Mary was pretty battered up, and no one thought for a minute that it wasn't Agatha. In fact she'd lived here for over thirty years, and no one knew much about her. I found her back at the cabin, revisiting the scene, as it were. But she really had nowhere else to go, and I think it was just beginning to sink in that she was going to have to turn herself in."

"But what happened?"

"She hasn't told me everything yet. She was tired and hungry from hiding out, but she did say it was really a bit of an accident. We've taken an initial statement, but I'm giving her a couple of days to rest and eat a bit before I make her go through the whole thing. I did pick up that Mary turned up because she read in the paper that Agatha had been left a small fortune by someone. That's how she discovered her sister wasn't dead. Of course, Agatha was engaged in a war of sorts with a local mill and had taken to throwing all her official looking mail into the stove, so she never knew she was being left money. Knowing her, she wouldn't have wanted it anyway. Quite the pioneer."

"Poor old Mary! I don't suppose there'd be many as would mourn for her except Tilly. I wonder what will happen to that big house? By all rights it should belong to the surviving daughter, unless she's found guilty of having murdered its owner. You know, it occurs to me that I've not really asked Tilly for everything she knows. She might know a bit more about why Mary went out there in the first place. Would this help you?"

"It would actually, thank you. I'll keep you abreast of developments here. Kind of a sad end, really."

"It surely is," agreed Fripps. "I'd better get on to poor Tilly right away."

"Three minutes are up," said the operator.

"Blast! Mum says hi!"

"Say hi back!" Ames said. He hung up the phone, thinking about Mary finding out her sister, long thought dead, was alive, and making the decision to go in search of her. In that moment, Ames had a realization about himself. More than catching the perpetrator, more than stopping crime, more even than the adventure he expected when he had first thought of becoming a policeman, it was the what and the why. You could think of crime as being the sordid failure of people without imagination, or you could see that it was rooted in lives. It was these stories that interested him. God, he thought. I'm getting more and more like Darling.

SIMS HAD LEFT, and Watson and Anthony sat at their kitchen table. It was nearing dinnertime, but neither had the desire to prepare dinner or even suggest an outing to the pub.

"He seemed okay," said Watson, speculatively.

"I'm not sure how much that means," Anthony replied. "I can see me on the witness stand now, telling them that I remembered that it was actually Jones that killed Evans, and being derided for that, and then being asked why I changed my story. It's the crucial bit. It's what everything hangs on. I'd be about to tell the world that the British government had forced me to lie by threatening to reveal that I am a homosexual. There's not one single thing about that statement that isn't a problem. Not one. No one will buy that the British government would blackmail some-one, and I'd be exposed forever. Even if this policeman didn't pursue us, it would be splashed across the papers, and I'd lose my job and be arrested by some other good citizen policeman looking to impress his superiors."

"We don't really know that."

"You're so bloody naïve, Adam!" Anthony said angrily. "What do you think is going to happen? We're going to get the Boy Scout medal of honour? Are you forgetting that Salford possibly died over this?"

"We don't know that. It was a suicide. That's what they said. Look, I know you only flew with Darling the one time. But I was a part of his crew. He was loyal to us. For God's sake, he saved us that day! I can't let him down, Nev, I can't. I keep thinking that the worst thing that can happen to me is I'll lose my job and get some time in jail, but he could be hanged. Hanged, Neville! On a lie! A man like him! It's just not right."

"It's not up to you, though, is it? It's not just you that has to get up there and be destroyed in a public court. I'm going out." Neville Anthony got up and pulled his blazer off the back of his chair, put his right arm into the sleeve, and then stopped. Watson was sitting in front of him, a picture of utter misery. Neville was running away from what was right, and he knew it. He took his coat off and went around to kiss the top of Watson's head, and then resumed his seat. He folded his hands together on the table in front of him and took a deep breath.

"Of course I'll do it. Of course I will. I'm just frightened," he said in a whisper.

THE NEXT MORNING Watson and Anthony were ushered into Higgins's office, and now sat like bookends, Higgins thought, with their hats on their laps. "Gentlemen," he said.

"I've decided I will speak up if I'm put on the stand," said Anthony. "We've come to tell you."

Higgins sighed. He could have used this the day before. "Very good of you, of course. Top hole. But I've been instructed by my client that you are not to testify."

"What do you mean? Then how is he to be protected?" asked Watson.

"As I told you the last time we spoke, we will go for creating doubt. I will probably put Darling on the stand to tell us what happened. He's very personable. He's bound to win a few over. Sims is no longer convinced of his guilt. I believe he can be induced to say that much at least on the stand. I'm not sure what the government will throw back, but it might be enough."

"That's ridiculous. I'm willing to tell the truth. I don't know how you can stop me." Having screwed up his courage, Anthony was now furious at being opposed.

"Very easily, I'm afraid, Mr. Anthony. By simply not calling you as a witness. Darling is right, in any case. I doubt it would do his case any good if the government lawyers were able to tear you to pieces on the stand. Your way of life, your truthfulness, your hidden motives, or whatever else they would like to suggest would all become fodder for them. I'm very much afraid that your disintegration would blow back onto my client. I think it is best that we keep it simple, don't you?"

THE DIRECTOR PUT down the phone. It was done. She was across and delivered to the Russian side, to a hard-boiled longtime operative called Viktor Aptekar. Dunn did not doubt that her loyalty to Darling and to her word would keep her on track. She was to offer herself as a disgruntled British citizen who wanted to spy on behalf of the Soviets. Feeling a deep and undignified thrill of satisfaction at Darling's defeat in the matter of Lane, the director reluctantly began to think about whether he ought to honour his promise to get Darling out of prison and out of the country. He'd have to come up with a way to smooth the whole business away, of course, but he had no real interest in seeing Darling hang. He wasn't an absolute savage, after all. It was likely that his initial idea, which was to provide a scapegoat should any of the business get out, was perhaps no longer necessary. The party who had seen his operative in Paris was dead, bit of providence there, to be sure, and the others were frightened enough that they would not talk. Anyway, he had what he wanted. He was lighting a self-congratulatory pipe when there was a knock at his door.

"Come!"

The secretary put his head around the door and said, "Someone to see you, sir, from the Yard."

Now what? "All right, all right. Send him in."

Inspector Sims came in and stood before the director's desk.

"Who are you?" asked the director, putting his pipe in the ashtray.

"Inspector Sims, sir. From the basement. I don't imagine you get down there much."

Suspecting a touch of hostility, the director said, "What do you want?"

"I understand you are the puppetmaster, so I came to tell you that as the investigating officer, I find there is only a very weak case to made against Flight Lieutenant Darling, and I shall be recommending such to the judge."

"Who the devil let you in here?" the director said angrily. He was not used to being readily available, or thwarted.

Inspector Sims winked and could not resist the cliché of touching the side of his nose. "Oh, you aren't the only one that knows people, sir. Or things, for that matter. I've come as a courtesy, really. I find that you, or someone here, blackmailed a British citizen into lying, which is inadmissible in court. We'll just leave it at that, shall we? I shouldn't think of going any further with this. You already have one body that I'm not, if I'm honest, one hundred percent convinced is a suicide. I shouldn't recommend you tally up any more. Well then. I'll wish you good day. I'll show myself out." Ha, Sims thought as he put on his hat. They won't be dragging me away from the Yard to slave in the basement of the War Office anytime soon!

CHAPTER THIRTY-ONE

RELIEVED THAT THERE WOULD BE no need to travel to Potsdam, Lane settled into the hotel room she had been provided by, she presumed, Aptekar. It suited his old world, continental style. How a hotel with this level of luxury had survived the war, she had no idea. Perhaps it had been quickly refurbished to meet the needs of high-level party apparatchiks, who would no doubt scorn the more practical lodgings of ordinary people.

She had drawn a hot bath, ostensibly to prepare for the dinner Aptekar was taking her to in the hotel dining room, but in her heart she knew she wanted to wash away all the stink of what she was doing, all the memory of being undercover. It was not for her, and she rebelled at the idea that her intelligence, grasp of languages, and wartime experience only fitted her out for this sordid, underhanded life.

In the bath, she closed her eyes and became aware of a persistent ache in her heart: for King's Cove, for the clean, fresh air of an honest life, for Darling. What had become of him? She didn't know that she trusted Angus

Dunn to do what he promised. Her whole relationship with him had been founded on lies. When she was young, he had skillfully engaged her deepest feelings and woven his dishonesty so thoroughly through them that she had not seen through him at all. She sat up, her eyes open. She had handed Dunn another means of hurting her. He knew that she loved Darling.

Wrapped in the bathrobe the hotel provided, she sat in the dark and looked into the street below, where the street lighting was intermittent and few cars were going by. Hardly any people were walking there, as if citizens knew it was best to be indoors after dark. In London, the end of the war sent people back out into the streets at night—undaunted by the continued shortages, stepping cheerfully over the wreckage to go to restaurants and theatres. Here she could only feel a pall of dark caution. She must put her mind to saving herself, praying that Dunn had honoured his promise. And if he had not? Could she learn anything from Aptekar, who was clearly bent on sweeping her into his orbit by indulging her, on the basis, he had said, of his great regard for her father? She didn't know what the conditions were for real, everyday people engaged in espionage, but she was certain it would not involve the luxury she was being shown now. Would he indulge her questions as well? She would have to try. Everything depended on it.

JONES SAT IN the café, a glass of schnapps in front of him. He wasn't inclined to self-reflection, but he was inclined to self-protection, and he needed to think carefully through his next moves. His East German handler had been angry about the business in England. Chief among his complaints was not so much that he'd killed the bloody fellow, but that he'd jeopardized his ability to move about England freely. The Paris incident was bad enough, but it couldn't be helped. That sort of thing can happen, he'd said. He'd been dismissed angrily like a child told to go to his room. Jones fumed about this now. After all he'd done, all the risks he'd taken.

He drank the fiery liquid without watering it down and banged his glass on the table to get another. Revenge seemed futile. He could not expose his keepers without exposing himself. The director in London at least had not suspected him. When they met in the tenth arrondissement, Dunn believed Jones had been in Paris the whole time. The director had been angry about his being recognized and warned him off any precipitate action, but Jones could not take the risk. He knew those men. They were as thick as thieves. And now that blasted woman. He was certain when he tailed her that she'd lead him to the others, but she'd given him the slip. Well, she didn't know Berlin like he did. Then he'd go back and mop up in London. He had been certain that Salford would be telling someone in no time. And he'd been right. He'd found the letter on Salford's desk. He'd go after Anthony, but for the first time in his memory, Jones was feeling a touch of fear. He knew that if his attempts to tidy up were discovered, he'd alienate the director as well and be finished as an East German asset. He'd have to be careful. He sat looking morosely out at the street. The problem with the letter, he knew, was that it was clear from the wording that Salford had written an earlier one as well. Well, that didn't matter. They'd arrested the man it was written to for murder, thank you, good Herr director. Jones mentally saluted.

Maybe it was time to get out. He would change his name and move into the house in Leipzig he'd inherited from his mother. She, at least, had not lived to see her country and her husband's go to war a second time. His drink came and he nodded at the waiter. Who was he fooling? He'd go mad. Best swallow the drink, the humiliation, and get back to work. He was good at it. He'd go back to Paris. He liked Paris. He felt safe there. But first the loose ends. He put some coins on the table and touched his hat toward the bar.

"Good night," said the barman.

Jones didn't see the movement in the kitchen as he was leaving.

AGATHA BROWNING SAT very still, watching as Ames wrote things down.

"Can you explain to me exactly how your sister came to die?" he asked.

"I didn't mean to kill her. We got into a violent argument. She seemed shocked that I didn't know Lucy had died and began shouting and knocking things about and then came after me. Accused me of living off her money. I would never have guessed she had that sort of rage in her. But of course, I don't know what's happened to her over the last forty years. I honestly thought if I got out, disappeared, everything would go back to the way it should be. I was shocked to learn I was being left money. I could not understand why he wouldn't leave all his money to his widow and children. Of course I would have said no immediately. But I burned the lawyer's letter and forgot about it until Mary turned up at my door."

Ames scribbled something and then said, "Can you just take me through what happened. She came after you, how?"

"She seemed to want to throttle me. We ended up by the sink, and she must have grabbed a knife. I was really frightened now, and I ran outside and wanted to hide in the privy. But she was right there behind me. I managed to wrestle the knife out of her hand, and she sort of lunged at me and I struck out. I honestly didn't think I'd hurt her badly, but I was sort of in shock. I dropped the knife, and she started through the garden and up the hill. I collapsed for a moment, and I think it all came to me at once. Lucy dead of a suicide, my father of a broken heart. I felt bereft. I know they'd been dead all these years, but for me it was fresh. I felt such anger at Mary, that she'd let it happen. I still do, if I'm truthful. Anger at myself too. I caused it all in the first place. I ran after her. She was standing in the trees, exhausted I suppose, and I came up behind her and shoved. It wasn't till then that I realized what I'd done. I went back and got the knife and threw it into the lake." Agatha stopped and looked at her hands. "I think it was the most dishonourable thing I've ever done. Even stealing my sister's man, I might excuse as youthful passion, but I felt certain I'd expiated it by leaving them all behind forever. But throwing that knife into the lake. Trying to cover up what I'd done. That was when I felt shame. You cannot know me, Constable Ames, but I have always been forthright. Unfortunately ruled by passion, yes, but not dishonest."

Ames put his pencil down and rubbed his eyes. O'Brien had been sitting with his arms crossed behind the prisoner, and from time to time had shaken his head in wonder. "Be that as it may, Miss Browning," Ames said. "Laws are meant to keep people from acting on passions. I am formally charging you with the murder of Mary Browning. If you are unable to afford a lawyer, one will be provided for you." He nodded at O'Brien, who got up to escort Agatha Browning back to her cell.

"Oh, by the way, how did the cabin get into such a mess?" He wasn't sure at this point that it was relevant, but he thought Darling might ask it, and he was curious about it himself.

Agatha paused at the door and then looked back at him. "Me flying into a passion again, I'm afraid—this time against myself. I wanted to destroy everything I had. I wanted to run away again, like I had all those years ago. It took me only a little time to realize I'd destroyed everything I had the minute I left my home to meet that man in London."

When O'Brien had delivered her to her cell, he made his way up the stairs to talk to Ames. "I'm a little worried. I don't think she's fully right in the head. She could try to kill herself. I had a cousin who killed herself, and the thing that struck us all at the time was that her own mother had done the same thing years before. I'm wondering if it runs in families, and she ain't got much to live for right now."

Ames pursed his lips. "Jehoshaphat. I didn't think of that. You might be right. Could you take everything away from her . . . belts, scarves, shoelaces. Thank you O'Brien. Whew. There's a lot in this. I wish the boss were back. He'd know what to do."

"Aw. You're doing a passable job." O'Brien said, winking.

ANGUS DUNN WALKED along the Serpentine until he came to the bridge. Here he stopped and leaned on the parapet, looking out at Hyde Park. It was another beautiful day, and like all Londoners, he was not immune to wanting to capitalize on the outbreak of good weather. That he was human enough to want, like all ordinary people, to feel the sun on his face did not surprise him, but a more human emotion was causing him difficulty now: the desire to crow about his victory over Lane in regard to the vanquished Inspector Frederick Darling. The fact that she loved Darling infuriated him though he knew he himself had no use for her other than the one he had put her to.

If he was honest, he looked back on his relationship with her during the war as his very own halcyon days. Her beauty and complete dependence on him were the most tender of his memories. She was a thing apart and had let herself be shaped by him. Of course, he loved his wife and children—though these last were becoming both expensive and mutinous—but Lane belonged to a separate, almost protected part of his own being. To see her love an ordinary person in an ordinary way was a challenge to his sense of his own impact in her life. But he had won in the end. It was really impossible that he should not want, at the very least, to see the expression on Darling's face.

DARLING WAS RELIEVED to be told he was going to the interview room. Higgins must be back with news. He was nearly mad with worry about Lane. He had tried by every means at his disposal to calm himself, if only because he knew how much she disliked his fretting about her safety. In the end, it was history that helped him. She had survived a war doing God knows what; he had to admit he had no idea, but he assumed it was dangerous, given her sangfroid more recently, and she had survived several assaults on her own person since he'd known her. She was tough and smart and a survivor. Just as he arrived at the realization that worrying about her was a way to keep her near him, if only mentally, he was called to meet someone.

He sat down, prepared to show his newfound calm. When Dunn was ushered in, Darling was at once confounded and angry. What should Dunn have to do with any of this? He'd had his fill of Dunn the summer before when he'd marched into his office in Nelson and thrown his weight about. Dunn had had the unmitigated nerve to try to take Darling's prisoner, Lane Winslow, off his hands and back to England with him. Why should he be obliged to endure an interview with someone he disliked so intensely in this trapped situation?

Dunn sat and threw his hat nonchalantly on the table between them and stretched his legs. His wavy hair was beginning to grey at the temples, giving him, Darling thought, a smooth and smarmy appearance. He sat and waited. Damned if he would be the first to speak.

"Darling," said Dunn, by way of greeting. "Is his majesty treating you well?"

"Well enough. Though he is keeping his cards close to his chest," Darling replied.

"You may not need to endure his hospitality much longer. There have been one or two developments."

"So. You have something to do with this whole ridiculous charade. Why am I not surprised?"

"No, please don't thank me. It is Lane you have to thank. In fact, it's thanks to her, really, that you may be shoving off home your name untarnished."

Darling fought a knot of panic. "How so?"

"She obviously misses real work. She came to me, don't you know. We've picked up right where we left off. She's a sharp little operator."

"I don't care for your familiar tone," Darling said.

"My dear fellow! What a lovely colonial sense of chivalry! She and I have been far more familiar in the past, I assure you. In any case, I just thought I'd pop along to let you know that there's a bit of bureaucratic paperwork to be accomplished and then you'll be free to go. I'll have to stand down the court process, and so on. They can be difficult, as they tend to operate free of the constraints that I think are most conducive to national security."

Darling heard little of Dunn's observations about the independence of the judiciary. He was occupied with a wave of wrath that astonished him for its power, and in the next moment seemed to unleash in him a cold and utterly clear sense of control.

He looked at Dunn, tilting his head as if in wonder. "You have vastly underestimated Miss Winslow, once again. It is a mistake I am never likely to make." He knew as soon as he said it that it was not likely to appease his jailer. He struggled to feign nonchalance. "Not the least because you seem to have put her right out of reach. Thank you for your visit. I would invite you to come again, but the flow of guests does not seem to be up to me."

Dunn stood up and dusted the brim of his hat. "You should know, old boy, that she went absolutely of her own accord. Happy to do it. Great girl. We're happy to have her back."

Back in his cell, Darling gave way to a bout of shaking, probably, he told himself coldly, merely the result of the rush of adrenaline he felt at Dunn's provocations. When it was over he knew that he would need to confront both his fear that he might have ruined his chances of getting out of prison and, deeper than that, a growing despair that Dunn had indeed put Lane out of reach.

CHAPTER THIRTY-TWO

THE DINING ROOM WAS BATHED in warm yellow light, and the subdued activity of serving and dining gave the vast room the hushed air of a cathedral just before the start of Mass. Aptekar escorted Lane to a table tucked into the corner of the room, along the windowed wall. Heavy gold and maroon drapes provided a sense of privacy on one side of the table, and the wall directly behind the table was papered in a dark floral motif that flickered in the candlelight. He seated her against the wall so that she might have a view of the entire dining room. It was gentlemanly, she thought, but of course, it also meant that whatever he would have to say would be audible only to her.

"I have taken the liberty of ordering. I hope you don't mind. These postwar times and, I am very sorry to say, the socialist supply system, have resulted in a limited choice of the kind of excellent food one ought to expect at such a place."

Lane smiled. "I am in your hands. As it is, I am not accustomed to such luxury. In London, I am staying in the same room I was in during the war. My landlady must adhere to the limitations of the ration books, so I imagine whatever it is we are getting will be at least as good as that!"

Aptekar talked about the grand hotels of the prerevolutionary days in Moscow, and in due course a waiter approached with a dish that appeared to consist of boiled meat and dumplings in a fragrant soup. A bottle of nearly golden Riesling was produced and poured. When the waiter had put the wine bottle into a silver ice bucket and left, Lane exclaimed, "You see. I was right. Mrs. Macdonald would never extend to dumplings! This smells lovely."

"Now then," said Aptekar. "What should we do? Perhaps we should start with this. When Andrea sent me a message that we were to receive a new recruit potential in the form of a dissatisfied true believer, I was very surprised to find that it was you. Your failure to reply to my letter in Canada last winter convinced me that you had no interest in us. What can this mean? I asked myself. You are not here to find out about your father, since you would have had no way of knowing that you would be meeting me specifically. Though I must add that I am delighted beyond measure to be able to meet you and speak about him. I miss him still."

Lane drank wine and looked out over the diners and then looked back at him. There was no point in dissembling. "I came because of a man. Your counterpart in London has framed the man I love, and being pressed into service seemed to be the only way to save him from the gallows. There. I'm afraid you will ask me to repay the cost of this meal now that you know the truth."

"Ah. You have the same honest streak your father had! Though I assure you, you are much, much more charming. He could be a hard man. But I don't need to tell you that. This man you are trying to save must be an exceptional man to have won your affection."

"I learned something from my father, after all, and that is that there is no point in wasting time with pretense. I do not know if the man who sent me here will honour his promise to free the prisoner, and if he does intend to honour it, how long I must pretend to be his willing pawn. There. As you can see, I will make a lousy double agent. I am not disillusioned with the West and have no great love for the socialist paradise. I want to go and visit my grandparents in Scotland and then go home."

Aptekar shrugged regretfully. "Just my luck! If it is any consolation, I knew it as soon as I knew it was you I was meeting. I am a great admirer of the grand sacrificial gesture, but I also like happy endings. They are nearly impossible to come by in my game. It is the intrigue that keeps me going. I was as happy spying for the czar as I am for Comrade Stalin. I have no illusions that there will be any paradise. He is too inclined to revenge, and I pride myself on the skill I employ staying on the top. Perhaps, one day, I shall be able to retire to a nice little farm. But even that dream is being put out of reach, as the state has collectivized everything. For 'the people.' I'm not over fond of the people and would prefer to live in splendid isolation."

"It sounds to me like I should be interviewing you in a bid to persuade you to come and work for us. I'm sure a nice farm can be found in Sussex for your retirement. This soup is really quite delicious."

"Your father was intelligent but rarely displayed a sense of humour. I see now that a sense of humour takes more than intelligence. It takes some degree of kindness or empathy, perhaps. So then, I wonder if we can find a way to satisfy your handler?"

Lane put down her glass and leaned forward. "What can you tell me about a man named Jones? He was supposed to have been killed in a plane crash in '43, but I now believe he is working in Paris under an assumed identity. It is fairly certain that he is in fact responsible for the death of a fellow airman, the crime for which my friend has been banged up. I believe Jones has been following me. I had to give him, or whoever it was, the slip. Does he work for you?"

"Ah. You know about him. But following you? I would be surprised. Not on our behalf."

Lane sat silently. It was the same thing Dunn had said. Of course there was no way to believe either one of them completely. But if they were right, whoever it was could be acting alone. If that was the case, he would be that much more dangerous. The waiter came to clear the plates.

Aptekar smiled and put his napkin on the table. "Can you excuse me for just a moment, my dear?"

Left alone, Lane began to contemplate the possibility that the Russians, or Aptekar at least, wouldn't want her after all. She sighed and shook her head in a little movement. It was all like lying on quicksand. Nothing could be trusted. It felt as if no move could be made without sinking irretrievably. She looked up and smiled as Aptekar returned.

"You must allow me to have the dessert cart brought over. It would be a dreadful shame for you to miss what is really done well over here." When the waiter had gone in search of the trolley, Aptekar said, "Now then, Jones. His handler is German. He worked as a double agent with the Nazi regime during the war. He, like me, I suppose, had no trouble slipping into new alliances. He is an arrogant man. Arrogant men tend to become too big for themselves. Jones is becoming a liability, I understand. He has been a relatively useful agent. His mother was German and died young. He moved to England with his father but was a troubled man. He joined the RAF, and the Germans found he was quite easy to bring over, really. They appealed to his vanity and the idealized dead German mother. He is quick to kill, again, something that can be very useful. However, he took it upon himself to solve a problem that cropped up when someone recognized him in Paris by going to England and eliminating the problem. He thought he was terribly clever, but he has, as you say in England, blotted his copybook. So. I expect that your people do not know he works for us. This will be something you can bring back?"

Lane leaned back pensively. "At the very least it means that the intelligence they've been getting is false. If they learn he killed a man in England, they may want him to stand trial. I know about this dead man, by the way. His death was declared a suicide."

"We can't take that risk, obviously. Murder is a capital crime. Your intelligence branch will have a great deal of leverage to get out of him whatever he has. No. I think you will want to let us look after it at this end. Oh, you needn't look so distressed! We won't eliminate him. He's become used to an easy life in Paris at our expense. He'll be sent to Siberia. Now what Siberia does with him . . ." he shrugged.

Lane shuddered at the power wielded by this man. Did he mean to let her go back with enough to buy off Darling and herself? She smiled at the waiter who arrived with the dessert cart. "I'll have that, thank you. It looks lovely. And a coffee."

"Ah. The prinzregentorte. Yes, I shall as well, for tomorrow we may die?" He lifted his glass of wine in her direction. "Now then. I think it just possible that I may have something else for you. He is very sure of himself, your director. Too sure. You see, arrogance again. Thanks to information we fed him through Jones, who calls himself Vigneault in France, and his mother's name, Farber, here, he is miscalculating even now about Berlin. The bloc will not long tolerate a Western eyesore in the middle of a socialist haven. Your Jones is busy convincing his British handlers that the focus of the Soviet government is consolidating power in the Baltic. But, and you should trust me on this, my dear, it is looking to make a move on Berlin, eliminating any easy access to the West."

Lane ate in silence for some moments. She thought she would really like to take the balance of her cake up to her room and eat it with a good book, away from this heightened atmosphere of continental manners and deadly information. "My father never ever told us a single word about his work. He was, according to my grandparents, a 'diplomat.'"

"But he was. In the most real sense. It is with him, with us, that most of the real work is done."

"Nor did we know about his colleagues. He never brought his work home. Not even a satchel of papers. It is remarkable that his oldest colleague, and friend, I suppose, was you. I will say now, no matter what happens, that I have appreciated being able to be honest with you."

"My dear Miss Winslow. You will, as you so rightly said at the beginning, be of no use to us. Your heart is not in it. It is a measure of my regard for your father, who, while not an easy man, was hardworking and honest, that I say this. I believe you should go back to England, go to your grandparents, and then take that man you love home again to your new country. I have given you something that is real, which I hope you may put to good use."

Lane looked away, feeling tears beginning to form. She felt a flood of relief, and in the next second, fear that this too was some manipulation. "Thank you. I suppose you mean the business about Berlin. Assuming that what you tell me is true, why are you doing it?"

Aptekar shrugged and smiled. "We are fulfilling your assignment, are we not? For now, this moment, you are a double agent, and I have given you something useful. Besides . . . I am a member of the old guard. My time will come soon, and honestly, a farm in Sussex, or even a flat in London, would not be the worst thing in the world."

Aptekar walked Lane to the elevator and stood vigilantly waiting for it to open and take her up to her floor. She bade him good night as the great brass doors opened. When the operator asked in German what floor she wanted, Aptekar answered for her and then tipped his hat, turned, and walked away.

"Let me out on the next floor, please," Lane said with a smile. She came out onto an open mezzanine, from which stairs curved down toward the lobby. From here she could survey the people moving about, many in evening dress, going into and coming out of the restaurant. No sign of Aptekar. Desperate for a breath of air and a quick walk around the block before she turned in, Lane hurried down the curved stairs and thanked the doorman who held the door for her.

Outside she was hit with a welcome wave of cool night air. Streetlights that glowed overhead near the hotel gave way to intermittently working lights farther down the street. Taking in a great breath of air, Lane turned to her right and walked briskly toward the next street.

"Where do you think you're going then, love?" The voice was right behind her suddenly. She felt her arm grabbed with an iron hand. She turned to try to look at her assailant, her heart pounding. A gloved hand pushed roughly at her face, keeping her from turning her head.

"Let me go!" Lane tried to pull herself free, but this move only tightened his grip.

"Is that likely? I can't believe my luck as it is. I thought I'd be visiting your room. This is infinitely better. Saves the hotel a lot of cleanup." The man had pulled both her hands behind her and was beginning to shove her forward down the darkened street.

Lane swivelled, her eyes looking frantically along the street. Not a bloody soul in sight! If this were London, she could have screamed the place down and scores of people would have seen what was unfolding.

"Are you Jones?" she asked, hoping to stall for time.

"Not anymore." She could hear the smile in his voice. "Now shut up. I don't need you going around blowing my cover. Here we go; we'll just pop in here."

To her horror she saw they had reached a narrow alley that seemed to be almost emanating a thick and grabbing darkness. I'm going to die here, she thought. Suddenly she stopped, bracing her feet and forcing a halt to their stumbling motion toward the alley. With as much violence as she could muster, she slammed the heel of her right foot onto Jones's toes, praying he wasn't wearing thick boots. Jones cried out angrily and his grip on her arms loosened for a split second. She twisted violently. Throwing him against the corner of the building and trying to free her hands completely, she began to scream, "Help!" in English and Russian. Her right hand slipped free and she used it to push at him just as he was righting himself and reaching for his knife.

"Pomogite! Help!" she shouted. Useless in this bloody empty street! He had a hold of her left arm and slashed at her with the knife. She could feel the blade hit home along the side of her chin. She yanked her arm, causing her cardigan to pull loose, and twisted to pull it off her other arm. He tried to reach for her but found his hand full of only the sweater. She began to run. Gasping, she reached the hotel steps and quickly looked back. He had not followed her. She stopped and leaned over, trying to catch her breath, and then looked again down the street.

A dark car pulled away from the alley and sped around the corner.

The doorman ran down the stairs to where she stood. "Are you all right, miss? You're bleeding!" He said with a soft German accent.

Lane shook her head and tried to smile, only that moment feeling the pain on her chin. She put her hand up to it and pulled it away covered in blood. "Someone tried to attack me," she said.

"Hooligans! Please. We will get a doctor." He pulled a large handkerchief out of his pocket and she pressed it onto her chin.

Later, in an office behind the front desk, she sat while the doctor swabbed her chin with something before he applied the dressing. She was exhausted and beginning to shiver.

"I have put three stitches in. I will give you some tablets, and then I suggest you go right to bed. It will sting a bit tomorrow no doubt, and I expect there will be a bruise as well."

"Thank you, Herr Doctor. It was stupid of me."

"You were not to know, madam. I'm afraid we have a fair amount of street crime. The authorities keep promising." He shrugged. "We had this sort of lawlessness after the last war as well."

On her way out she stopped at the front desk. "Can you have a Scotch sent up to my room, please?"

"Certainly, madam. Right away." The deskman watched her as she made her way to the elevator, her back straight, her steps strong, and shook his head longingly. Such a beautiful and brave woman. What on earth could she be doing here alone? And then he picked up the phone.

UPSTAIRS, LANE PULLED back the covers and collapsed onto the bed, waiting to undress until her drink arrived. She was playing the whole attack over and over in her head, wanting it to stop. She felt an utter fool. She had exposed herself to this danger. But then she thought about what he'd said. That she had spared him the trouble of messing up the hotel room. She sat up, clutching a pillow to her chest. He could bloody well come back! The knock on her door nearly made her jump out of her skin. She stood with her face pressed to the door.

"Who is it?"

"It is room service. The drink you ordered." A woman's voice.

Lane pulled the door open an inch, and saw a young woman in a black hotel uniform holding a tray with a glass and a small bowl of ice. There was a cream-coloured envelope on the tray.

"Here you are, miss, and I was asked to give this to you." She lifted the envelope to show Lane.

Lane closed the door and said, "One minute," and went to her purse for a few coins. "I'll take the whole tray," she said, handing the woman the coins.

Back on the bed, the Scotch providing a soothing burn in her throat, she opened the envelope, trying to fight back the anxiety. All she needed was a gloating note from her attacker, promising to get her next time. But it wasn't. She recognized the signature from his earlier communication.

He will not trouble you again. Perhaps I will see you
in Sussex one day. Yours most faithfully, Aptekar.

HIGGINS STOOD IN the judge's chambers, summoned there together with the prosecutor. The judge was scowling and drinking down some powders for his dyspepsia. "Bloody waste of the court's time," he grumbled. "Apparently there is no case to be made against this man Darling. The whole thing is unfathomable. All this moving the man around, the Home Office involvement. They obviously think Great Britain's judiciary is a plaything to suit their every whim."

"But m'lud. There has been a request from the Home Office that we keep him locked up for the time being. There are procedures . . ." The prosecutor looked like a dog watching his bone disappear down the drain. A big trial involving treason could have been the making of his career.

"I don't care if His Majesty himself is dressed in feathers and plimsolls and demanding it. There is no case here, and I'll not have the court being made a mockery of. The law is the law. Now get out of here."

Higgins ventured, "Will my client be released immediately?"

"I have so ordered. Presumably a judge's orders still count with someone. He's to be delivered into your hands, so if I were you I'd get along there and spring him, and leave me in peace!"

SANDRA PULLED OPEN the door and cried, "Oh my God! Frederick! How splendid. Good lord, what have they done to you? You look like a skeleton!"

Darling submitted wearily to being hugged and bundled into the house. He was given a cup of tea, when he longed for a Scotch, and made to sit at the kitchen table, when what he craved most was a bath and some solitude. But the tea, drunk as it was in freedom, proved uplifting, and he could feel his guard let down slightly. Sandra Donaldson was on the telephone to her husband.

"Darling! Frederick is here! They've let him out. It's over! That Higgins is a miracle worker. Yes, yes, I'll tell him."

Darling listened to this and thought about Higgins, who had come for him at the prison. Higgins had been sure of his innocence, had been sure that it was Sims's casting doubt on the whole case that had done the work. Darling had stood on the street, smelling the vaguely unhealthy and glorious smell of a busy city, feeling the sun on his face, scarcely able to believe they would not snatch him back. Knowing, as he walked away to freedom, that they did not because they had Lane.

Sandra was back. "Oh you poor thing. You're really done in. You run upstairs and draw a long hot bath, and push all these clothes out onto the landing. We'll wash the prison right out of them. I think you have clothes in the suitcase, but if not, I'll give you something of Rudy's. He is thrilled. He sends his congratulations and says I'm to give you something proper to drink."

"I think I'll have that bath. I have other clothes, so no need to raid Rudy's. But I'll be very happy to shed these. I've a good mind to throw them in the bin. I'll have the proper drink, and then I think I just need to lie down."

"Oh, of course. You poor dear, help yourself to anything you need. I'll pop out and find something decent for supper. It's such a shame Lane has gone off somewhere. She's not due back for another day or two. She should be here to celebrate with us."

So she should, Darling thought, so she should. He climbed wearily up the stairs, the full realization of what she may have had done for his now meaningless freedom finally sinking in.

CHAPTER THIRTY-THREE

DUNN PUT THE PHONE RECEIVER gently in the cradle, as if not to disturb the silence of his office. He was smiling though he did not feel the triumph he had imagined. He took a moment, his hand still resting on the telephone, to try to understand why. He had what he wanted, after all, Lane back in service. His man in East Germany confirmed that all arrangements had gone exactly as promised, with only one variance. She had been scheduled to go to Potsdam to meet the Soviet agent, but a senior agent had gone to Berlin for other reasons and agreed to see her there. That meeting had gone as planned.

So why this moment of doubt? She was a tremendous asset, and she was a practical girl. She would get over her objections soon enough. The work would reconnect her to the idea of doing something meaningful, an idea she had espoused often enough during the war. A jolt of truthful realization made him jerk his hand away from the instrument and aggressively pile the papers on his desk into a stack. The cloud on his perfect triumph, he knew, was that what he wanted was to have her enthralled with him again, as she had been during the war—dependent on his wisdom and guidance. Instead, the full knowledge that she had consented only because she loved someone else irked him. He certainly had no intention of trying to engage her affections again. He was not a fool. He was suddenly embarrassed by his own juvenile competitiveness. He was being ridiculous. The bloody woman had the capacity to make him ridiculous in his own eyes.

He had toyed, at the beginning of these ruminations, with the idea of leaving Darling locked up just because he could, but now he thought that he could afford to be the bigger man. He would follow through on his promise. He picked up the phone and asked to be put through to his contact at the Home Office.

"You can start the process of releasing him," he said.

"All done, sir. I expect he's at the local as we speak, enjoying a pint."

"What?" Dunn sat up, his brow furrowing.

"He's out, sir. At . . ." there was a pause, "yes, at four thirty this afternoon."

"I didn't authorize this. Who did?"

"I couldn't say, sir. If it wasn't you, I'm guessing it came through the court. I just got a notification saying he was out and no case made."

LANE WATCHED AS the plane circled toward the Croydon airstrip. The neatly unsymmetrical fields of England lay below her, the lanes and roads winding through them. It was beautiful from up here, she thought. I'd be very happy if I were Aptekar, thinking of the prospect of retiring to this green and pleasant land. Not for her though. She pined for her house in King's Cove. She imagined the view now, looking out from her porch over the lake. The blue mountains that edged the blue-green water on the far shore, the sun sparkling like a spray of diamonds. The glorious fresh silence, and the prospect of Eleanor Armstrong's kitchen, Kenny's feet on the grate, lemon oatmeal cookies on a plate. Perhaps now there would be a dog. They had spoken about finally replacing their last one. She sighed. There was much to do before then.

No car was waiting in Croydon because she had not told them she was coming back, and she had asked Olga not to tell them. She bought a ticket for the London-bound bus and settled into a seat near the back of the nearly empty one that pulled up. She wished she knew whether Darling was out. She would call Higgins from a call box at Victoria and then go in search of Dunn. Perhaps the best thing was to go to the War Office. They'd know how to find him. He wasn't expecting her back for several days. She felt a grim satisfaction at thinking about his expression when he saw her.

IT WAS NEARLY seven o'clock when she was in a call box at the station. The whole trip had taken much longer than she expected. Of course she would not reach Higgins, but she had to try. She looked through the window of the call box, watching ordinary people with ordinary lives walking by. Old couples in companionable silence. Young couples holding hands, enjoying the evening. People carrying suitcases and arguing. How lovely it would be to be ordinary again! The phone kept up its fruitless double ring. She wouldn't get anyone. Sick at heart that she did not know Darling's fate, she stood on the street and then realized there was nothing to be done that evening. She set off for Mrs. Macdonald's. Her chin was beginning to ache. She would stop at the chemist and get something.

SANDRA HAD MANAGED to procure a chicken, and while Darling slept an exhausted and anxious sleep upstairs, she baked it with some potatoes and set the dining room table with her special tablecloth, a family heirloom. Rudy had come home with a Victoria sponge from the bakery down the road and a bottle of wine and was now gathering plates from the cupboard.

"I do wish Lane could be here," Sandra said wistfully to her husband. "It doesn't seem right, somehow, without her, after all she's done. I do wish she hadn't gone off without telling us like that."

"I can't believe she just flitted off on holiday. I'm certain it must have something to do with all this. I've never seen a more determined woman." He looked fondly at his wife, who had put on her prettiest blue frock. "I'm glad she didn't drag you off on whatever expedition she's on now. I don't think you're cut out for the life of adventure."

"Steady on! I might be, for all you know. Here, put the salt bowl on the table. You know, I wonder if she's somehow had something to do with his getting out. I mean, there seems to be a connection. She goes away somewhere and he gets out shortly after."

"Ah! Here's the guest of honour," Rudy said, as Darling was coming downstairs. "It's very, very good to see you, old man!"

Darling submitted his hand to an energetic shaking and felt a wave of almost humble gratitude. "This is lovely," he said, surveying the dinner arrangements.

"We're hoping you can tell us how it all transpired. Sandra has the mad idea that Lane has somehow engineered all this. Here. Sit. It's all ready. I can't imagine what you were getting to eat in prison."

Darling smiled. "Not this, that's for sure."

"There's a nice Victoria sponge for our pudding, as well," Sandra said.

"So, how did you come to be released?" Rudy asked after a short spell.

"According to Higgins, it was largely due to Inspector Sims, who felt there was no case to be made after he interviewed Anthony, in particular." Darling could not talk about his appalling interview with Angus Dunn and was, he realized, more than puzzled himself. Why had Dunn said Lane had ransomed herself for him, when Higgins had been quite insistent that circumstances had come up in the investigation that exonerated him completely? Was it Dunn playing games? But if that was true, where was Lane? Or was Dunn in deadly earnest? Had Lane decided willingly to go off and do whatever the hell it was she was so good at? He felt his heart sinking again and knew he had to pull himself together in the face of the overwhelming kindness of his friends.

"And then where's Lane gone off to? Did she tell you?" Rudy asked.

"I have not been allowed to see her since they moved me. I have no idea where she is." The truth of this statement threatened to overwhelm him again.

Seeing Darling descending into an unhappy silence, Sandra said with exaggerated brightness, "So, what is the first thing you'll do with your newfound freedom?"

What indeed? Darling held his wine glass and looked at the contents. Glass half empty, he thought ruefully.

"I suppose I'd better contact my constable and find out how he's getting on. I left him in charge of a murder investigation. He thinks I've been on holiday. Of course, he'll want to know when I'm coming back. Blast." He looked at his watch. "I imagine it is too late to get a wire off. Do you think I can phone through?"

"It will take some time I expect, but we'll set a chair up here and bring you a Scotch. Have some pudding first."

The Victoria sponge dispatched, Rudy and Sandra busied themselves in the kitchen with the washing up, and Darling leaned against the wall of the hallway with the phone at his ear. Within ten minutes and many crackling international exchanges he finally heard, "Please hold. I have your party on the line."

"Nelson Police."

"O'Brien. Hello. Can you put me through to Ames?"

"Is that you, boss? You sound like you're in the bottom of a barrel. How's the holiday?"

"Very good, thanks. Ames?"

"Right. I've been helping him out, you know. Visits to the crime scene, interview of the suspect. That sort of thing."

"Fantastic. I'm glad to hear he's been doing some work. Now can I talk to him? These trunk calls aren't cheap."

"Yes. Right away, sir."

Ames was at his desk writing up his notes. He was still expecting to hear from Fripps, but it was really all over bar the shouting. He had his woman. The phone rang. "Ames."

"Good to know you're at your desk at least pretending to work."

"Inspector! I was expecting Fripps. Good of you to call."

"No need to be sarcastic, Ames. Who's Fripps?"

"Sorry, sir. He's a policeman over there, in a place called Whitcombe, where our body came from."

"You seem to have shown an unexpected burst of initiative, calling England. Did you find out who killed her? O'Brien said you'd been interviewing a suspect."

"She's not actually dead!"

"She looked pretty dead to me. And Gilly seemed to think so as well."

"No, I mean, the dead woman is dead, sir, but she's not Agatha Browning. She's the sister, Mary Browning. I've got Miss Agatha Browning in lock-up. She's confessed. I'm just doing up the paperwork."

"Well, bully for you. Nice work." He meant it.

"Thank you, sir. When might you be coming home? There are still things to sort out here. I wouldn't mind your help," Ames said.

"Ah. I expect it's soon. Let me call you in a couple of days. Is there anything you need me to do at this end?"

"No, sir, thank you. I have Fripps for that. Just enjoy the rest of your holiday, and say hello to Miss Winslow if you see her. I imagine she's in Scotland now with her grandparents. She was pretty helpful, by the way, all the work she did with the birth certificates and so on. But I expect she told you that."

She hadn't, he thought sadly, hanging up the phone. How unsurprising that she'd been helpful. Bloody helpful woman, she was. If only she were in Scotland! The momentary normality he'd felt talking to Ames was washed away in a second. He'd have to accept that she'd left his sphere, gone off back to a world he knew nothing of that had been trying to pull her back since he'd first met her. He'd have to get a ticket and go back home. There had still been a wash of light when he'd begun his call, and now that night settled over the city, Darling was standing in darkness in the hall. He felt paralyzed. He knew he would have to leave, and yet some mad rebellious part of him knew that Lane would never walk meekly back to something she professed to hate.

"Good call to your constable?" Rudy had come into the hall and was in the process of pulling his jacket off the hook. "The night is young. Why don't we go off to the local for a pint? Sandra has some sappy radio drama she wants to listen to in peace and quiet."

Darling shrugged. "Sure, why not."

THE MINUTE THEY were out the door, Sandra took up the phone and, peering at the number Lane had given her for the rooming house, put in a call.

"Mrs. Macdonald. Good evening. I know Miss Winslow is away just now, but did she tell you when she is coming back? This is her friend Mrs. Donaldson."

"No, not exactly, lovie. I think she said a few days. It's been two. I'd expect her back maybe tomorrow or the next day."

It wasn't much to cheer up Darling, but it was something, anyway. "Okay, thanks, Mrs. Macdonald. Bye now!"

Later, when Lane had come home unexpectedly, Mrs. Macdonald remembered to tell her about the phone call when she'd come down for her hot cocoa at ten. "Oh, by the way, someone called Mrs. Donaldson called to ask me when you were due back. I said in the next day or so. I wouldn't telephone her now, it's late, but I'm sure she'll be very pleased to hear from you in the morning."

LANE STILL COULD not reach Higgins in the morning and set out instead to the War Office in the hopes of tracking down Dunn. She managed to find Captain Hogarth and asked for her help in finding Angus Dunn. As it happened, the director himself was there, railing at someone for letting Darling go before he'd been authorized to. Dunn had been called away from this meeting by news that a Miss Winslow wished to speak to him.

Puzzled, and feeling as though things were becoming unravelled, Dunn stormed into the room where Lane had been told to wait. She sat with self-contained stillness, her legs crossed, her hat on her lap. She looked at him expressionlessly when he came in. The dressing on her chin and the angry bruise that reached up into her cheek startled him.

"I didn't expect you back so soon. But I understand some Soviet agent was able to see you in Berlin," Dunn said trying to match her mood. "What happened to you?"

"Oh, this? Your man Jones. And I did see the agent. A fellow quite high up. I was surprised," she said coolly. "I have one or two items of interest for you. Have you released Darling?" She tried to say this neutrally, as if it were merely part of a business transaction they'd made.

High up? But of course, his contact had said "a" Soviet agent happened to be in Berlin anyway. Perhaps they were getting desperate . . . why would someone that high up in the organization want to interview a potential defector? "What items?"

"Although it irks you, no doubt, to have anyone having any cards at all, I believe I'll keep mine until you answer my question about Darling."

"Yes, then. He's out." May as well retain the illusion that it was his doing.

Lane looked down, trying to hide the rush of relief that was threatening to bring on tears. Composed again, she looked up. "Good." Why had she not called the Donaldsons? He would have gone there! She scarcely had the patience for the end of this interview. "I can tell you that you've backed the wrong man in Jones. He's working for them, not you. He tried to kill me, actually. It was very unpleasant."

"That's preposterous. All of it. Why would you think Jones is working for them?"

"Why indeed? And further to that, though you probably know this, he was the one who pushed Salford off the platform into an oncoming train. The Soviets are finding him a liability. They are taking him out of circulation. I'd like to think it was because he tried to kill me in Berlin, but they were already feeling uneasy about him. They feel, and one can hardly blame them, that with a murder charge hanging over his head here, you could probably pump a good deal of information out of him if he decided to try to take refuge in England. They want to avoid that."

Dunn turned away from her and walked to the window, his hands behind his back.

"I know. It must be very disappointing to find you've been systematically fed misinformation. I wonder if you are as a good judge of character as you think you are? However, I'm satisfied I've done my job. I should mention that the Soviets are making plans to do something about Berlin. They don't like it sitting there in the middle of their sphere of influence. There now, was there anything else?" Lane got up, took up her handbag, and started toward the door. "Oh, yes. If you play your cards right, you could get a major Soviet asset over here. He'd like to retire here, I expect."

At this Dunn turned, his face hard. "That's it then?"

"I'm afraid so," she said lightly, going out the door. Darling was out and her heart had wings.

CHAPTER THIRTY-FOUR

LANE STOOD ON THE DONALDSONS' doorstep, her heart beating, and with a moment's fearful hesitation, she knocked on the door. The door opened and he was there, his white shirt open at the collar, hair falling over his eyes, and one hand in his pocket.

"I heard you were out," she said, and was enveloped in a fierce embrace.

KENSINGTON PARK WAS at its dramatic best. The sun shone down, making great pools of shade under the trees, and in the distance heavy blue-black clouds were gathering for an afternoon rain, creating the effect of making every colour more intense: the grass greener, the sky a deep cerulean. The air had the thick, uneasy heat that only a good storm could abate.

"I'd better go back. Amesy claims to need my help. He doesn't, of course."

"Ames can wait, surely? I want you to meet my grandparents. They will spoil you unmercifully and fatten you up."

"Maybe I should. Look at the mess you get into when I'm not around to save you." He reached over and touched her cheek softly above the bruise. "I should thank you. I'd still be in prison reading bad detective fiction if it were not for you. Bit of a turn-up really. A change from me trying to rescue you, only to find you'd done it yourself," Darling said.

"No change at all, as it turns out. My quixotic offer to sacrifice myself to some project for that ass Dunn was completely unnecessary. Your colleague, Sims, whom you won over completely with your manly forthrightness, is the one who apparently secured the rescue. He discovered that Anthony was being blackmailed and was able to get the truth out of him. But Sims made it very clear that he was convinced of your innocence the minute he met you."

"You could have fooled me," said Darling. "When we met he treated me like someone who still held the smoking revolver in my hand. He said he was astonished that I would not tell him why I'd done it. No. I'm afraid you must take credit. I know it was you who tracked down those men and got the truth. And, sitting here in the sun with you, my liberty ensured, I cannot say I am particularly unhappy about being rescued."

Lane looked down. "Now you are saying I am small-minded to dislike being rescued by you?"

Darling looked distressed. "Certainly not! Never. I accept that we are troubled by different things. I, for example, don't mind being rescued, but I have had real difficulty with feeling the very foundations of my life shaken. My sense of security about the future is in tatters. I never felt like this during the war. I mean, I knew I could die, but we all did. It was a kind of universal condition. But finding myself suddenly alone, in a cell, put away unjustly by forces far beyond my control . . . I don't know. I just can't seem to get my equilibrium back."

Lane took his hand and kissed it and then sat looking across the sweep of lawn. The clouds, though darker, did not seem to have advanced.

"At least tell me," Darling said, turning to look at her, "that you put that idiot Dunn in his place."

She smiled and shrugged. "You have asked me the one thing I cannot tell you."

"You did. I knew it. You've done it to me often enough with far less provocation. By the way, I told him he had completely underestimated you. I told him that it was a mistake I was unlikely to ever make. There. That is the same as saying I love you, only less mushy."

She smiled. "I too will never underestimate you. Are you sure about Scotland? I hate to turn up empty-handed."

"You can bring them some chocolate. Why don't you invite them out to Canada?"

"It's a long trip. I don't know if they'll be up to it."

"If they are your grandparents, they are like twin oaks, I am sure, hardened by being pushed around in their own home by Bolshie officers."

"It seems easy being here because we are here now, but when we go back to Canada, a trip to England will seem far away and impossible and something undertaken once a decade. They may be oaks, but even they will have to die sometime. Please say you'll come. Ames can wait another couple of days."

Darling sighed and looked into the eyes of this impossibly beautiful woman. How had he deserved her? "Will they demand to know if my intentions are honourable?"

"We'll see. Before we go I'd like to take everyone out. The Donaldsons, Higgins, your crew. I have money left over because I didn't have to get you out of hock. I'm thinking of Claridge's or the Ritz. We could do it tomorrow if I can get a table. And then I'll leave the next morning. I don't think I can stand around saying goodbye to you again."

"Is Claridge's as expensive as it used to be? I could never afford it during the war."

"Absolutely. And I can afford it. Perhaps there are some things I can tell you that I learned about my father."

He stood up and pulled her to her feet. "Then let me take you to dinner tonight, and you can tell me. A little Italian place somewhere so we can compare it with Lorenzo's. It'll give Sandra Donaldson a night off from fussing about me. And I might go to the pub with Sims before I leave. He may have one or two tips."

THE PLATFORM WAS wet at the station in Peebles, as though it had just suffered a deluge, but the rain had stopped, and people waiting for the train were looking skyward and folding up their umbrellas. Lane felt like a small child, looking eagerly out the windows to catch sight of her grandparents as she made her way through the car.

"There!" she said, pointing. Darling ducked to look and saw an elderly couple, comfortably upholstered, looking anxiously toward the compartment doors.

"He has a fine moustache, your grandfather," he commented. "If anything, it makes him more frightening than I imagined."

"Laneke!" It was her grandfather. He reached up to help her down, taking her suitcase and then putting his arm around her. "Look, Mother, isn't she lovely? But what has happened here?" He touched his own chin so as not to hurt hers.

"It is nothing, Grandpapa. A little cut when I tripped."

Lane's grandmother swept her into her arms and then stood her at arm's length to look her up and down.

"Thin. Too thin. Did you have a good journey, little one?"

Darling watched these proceedings from a few feet away. It was so extraordinary to see Lane in the context of a family. He had become used to seeing her as a creature unto herself who had suddenly materialized in his life fully formed and ferociously independent, like that mythical goddess on a shell . . . what was her name? And now she was someone's "little one."

"Frederick," Lane said, "come and meet my lovely grandparents. Grandpapa, try not to frighten him. He can only stay for two days, and then he has to go back to Canada. I would like him to have happy memories."

They took the trap, which travelled along a winding road through the village, over a stone bridge, and up a sweeping hill. They arrived at a cottage with a stone fence around a spacious garden overlooking the countryside, which seemed to fall below them in waves.

"What do you think?" her grandmother asked.

"It's lovely. To think of you living here will make me so happy ever after!"

"I'm sorry, Mr. Darling, about the rattling ride. We don't keep a motor car," her grandfather said. "No one to drive the thing, you see."

"On the contrary, Mr. Johnson, I have never ridden in a trap. I found it relaxing after all the train changes and the smell of coal. It's very beautiful here."

LATER, IN THE kitchen, Lane sat at the table watching her grandmother chopping potatoes. "Why don't you let me help?"

"No. I enjoy it. Judith comes in during the week and does all this sort of thing and won't allow me into the kitchen at all. Your Mr. Darling is exceedingly good-looking."

Lane put her head down to hide the blush she felt rise up her face. No one else on the planet could make her blush, she thought. I am a sixteen-year-old again. "You know, Gran, I don't even think about that."

"I'm absolutely certain that is rubbish for a start. If I had that around the house, I'd never take my eyes off him. Do you think I picked your grandfather solely because my parents hated him?"

"Gran, I don't have him around the house. And anyway, how do you know he is not just my friend? He is just my friend. He had to come to England on business, and I was coming to see you. I thought I'd bring him along. That's all." Best not to say he'd been in the clink and charged with murder.

Putting down the knife and potato, her grandmother

looked at her. "All that matters, my Laneke, is that he is worthy of you. That he is kind, that he appreciates and understands this heart he has captured. Does he?"

Lane shook her head, suddenly unsure. "When you love someone, that is sometimes sufficient to make them seem worthy. I know this. He loves me without wanting me to change. We live thirty miles apart, and he knows I cannot leave my house, and he has never asked me to. I once thought I loved a man, and he ordered every part of my life, and I thought that meant he loved me, but it only meant he controlled me. This man only wishes I were not so, I don't know, reckless, I suppose."

"Then I must take his side on that, at least. Don't worry. I'll find out. It won't even take me the two days."

"Oh God," Lane muttered. "Poor Darling."

WHAT A LOT of things we can feel at once, Lane thought. She was sitting in the garden drinking tea and eating shortbread the next afternoon. Darling had gone upstairs with her grandmother to fetch a box of photos. She dreaded the grilling he must be getting. Her grandfather sat beside her, his black cane resting against his leg. She ached to be home, but her gran's lavish hugs and endearments warmed and repaired her in ways she never imagined. That first night under her grandmother's roof she had nestled into the bed in the spare room looking out the open window into the dark, her whole body in the embrace of a deep sense of home.

"Do you miss Bilderingshof, Grandfather? I've been a little afraid to ask you. You lived there since you were a child, did you not?"

"I was born there. The only time I left was when we were sent to school in England. I suppose I miss it. It got a bit crowded with all those Russians. Had to wait in line to pee. It's better here. I have the garden. And now I have you, my Laneke. Your gran was so happy when we got your letter. You know how she likes to make a fuss." He looked at her conspiratorially. "Do you think he's all right up there with her alone?"

"He's a big boy. He's a policeman. I'm sure he's faced worse."

"A policeman! Well, I never," he said, glancing back toward the door.

"Not your local bobby with a helmet under his arm. He's what you'd call a detective inspector here. He's very good at his job. He'll be able to handle her."

"I don't know. I've seen her disarm generals. The Russian officers were extremely glad to be rid of us. She didn't care for them acting as though our house was theirs, and she told them so very often. Of course, in the revolution, the aristos are out and the people are in. I'll tell you something, no 'people' will ever see the inside of our old house."

Darling came out carrying a box, looking, Lane was relieved to see, no worse for wear, followed by her grandmother who caught her eye and gave her a broad wink behind Darling's back.

They cleared the tea things onto a silver tray, and her grandmother began to take the photos out. Lane picked them up one by one. Can you go back? she asked herself, or was the past just this vast sepia space that lay where it had been captured, on horseback, having tea with great uncles she scarcely remembered, holding a balalaika she could remember playing very badly, on the leaf-covered verandah of a house she would never see again. You could look there, but you could not reach in, pull it out, see it again as it had been.

"Look, Inspector Darling, here is a picture of our Laneke as a girl. Is she not beautiful?" her grandfather said, handing him a picture of her at seventeen, posed on the porch in a white summer dress and bare feet. Darling looked up inquiringly at Lane at being so addressed.

"I had to tell him, otherwise he might think you were a moocher," she said.

"Tell him what?" asked her grandmother.

"Our guest is nothing less than an inspector in the police force in Canada." Her grandfather gave him a pat on the back. "Now then, what do you think of that?"

"Frederick knows exactly what I think," her grandmother replied, smiling. She took up another photo. "Look, here's your father, God bless him, when he first met your mother. So handsome. She was quite taken up by him."

"I don't understand. Why would she have fallen for such a hard man, when all she knew at home was love?"

Her grandmother smiled sadly and stroked the photo. "He was not as bad, perhaps, before she died. She was a stubborn girl, your mother. Intelligent and independent. But full of laughter and kindness. I think once she committed in her heart to him, she felt she had done a good thing, could fill in what he lacked. She had a romantic view that people of opposite characters attract one another. It is not a view I subscribe to. He had excellent manners and gave her everything. But he was secretive and away a great deal. His work in the diplomatic corps. I believe that she began to sink under him. When she died in that awful epidemic, it was perhaps a merciful escape. And he had the good sense to bring you and your sister to us. He was not a bad man, Laneke. You mustn't think that. But . . ."

"But?"

"But I worried from the beginning. The only time I saw that old light in her eyes was when she was with you girls. It is too bad your sister was only a baby when she died."

Instead of anchoring her, the trip into the past unsettled her. To hear her mother described as full of laughter made her wonder about herself. Was she full of laughter? What good had it done her mother, to have her laughter stilled by a man?

She felt her hand taken and looked up to see Darling watching her with concern. This move was not lost on her grandfather, who smiled at his wife.

"Now then. Why don't we forget about the old days? They weren't much to write home about anyway. Why don't you tell us how you met?"

It was no good keeping secrets about absolutely everything, Lane thought. It becomes a habit that eventually drives everyone you love away. "Pour us all some more tea, and I will tell you. He arrested me!"

CHAPTER THIRTY-FIVE

___

Whitcombe, November 1908

TILLY STOOD WITH HER HAND on her mouth, her breath choking in her throat, watching two men from the village bring in Lucy's body. No one spoke. Mr. Browning stood resolutely looking away from Mary, who was weeping inconsolably.

"Oh, Tilly!" Mary cried, and Tilly took her into her arms.

Later, in the garden, Tilly had come out with a shawl for Mary, and asked her if she wanted to come in and have a little supper.

"Tilly, how could she do it? I keep imagining myself at the top of the cliff about to fling myself off, and even in my imagination I cannot see myself able to do it. What was in her, or not in her, that allowed her to drop like a stone to her death?"

"I reckon that grief takes everyone differently, Miss Mary. Our Lucy, well, she was always like a butterfly in the sunshine. She never thought anything would change or that anyone who loved her would hurt her. For some reason she never did come back from that."

"I never thought anything would change either. Not anything. I thought it would always be the four of us here, happy as clams. Why should I have lived and not them?"

"I don't know, miss. I reckon it's the will of God."

"It's not the will of bloody God! It's the willfulness of bloody Aggy. And then she went and died without seeing what she'd done. I could never forgive her, not if I was standing at the gates of heaven."

"Miss. It's cold out here. Why don't you come in?"

Mary did not move. "If you want the truth, I never thought any of us would even get married and leave till Lucy fell in love with that dreadful man. We all tried to be happy for her, didn't we?"

"We did, miss."

"Father's not well."

"No, miss. Please come in now."

"You know what I see now? It will just be you and me and the ghosts in this house in the end." Then she turned to Tilly. "You're younger than me. You will get married, and then it will just be me. Promise me you'll come to see me if that happens. There's no one else who knew Lucy."

"And Miss Agatha," said Tilly.

"Nobody knew her. Nobody," Mary said, turning away.

ELEANOR ARMSTRONG SLID open the wooden post office window with a bang and locked it into place. Angela was at the screen door calling to the boys to wait before they gave Mr. Armstrong's horse an apple. "Do you think Kenny will mind?" She asked Eleanor.

"Good heavens no. I got some news this morning," she added after a moment.

"Well, go on. Don't keep me in suspense. It had better be about Lane!"

"It is. They phoned in a wire. She's coming back in a week."

"Oh, thank goodness!" Angela exclaimed. "I was honestly afraid that if she went to England she wouldn't come back here."

"I know something else as well," Eleanor said coyly.

Angela was about to protest at being strung along in this fashion, when Gwen Hughes came in, banging the screen door. "Your horse is going to be as fat as a blimp at the rate those boys are feeding it," she remarked.

"Eleanor was about to tell me something about Lane. She's coming back in a week."

"Oh, about that inspector, I suppose," Gwen said.

"Gwen! You listened!" Eleanor said, frowning.

"I didn't mean to! I picked up the line to order some feed and I chanced to overhear that bit."

"What about the inspector?" Angela cried, in an agony of curiosity.

"Only that he was over there at the same time and is already back," Eleanor said, with a repressive glance at Gwen, who had been about to speak.

"Ha! I knew it! She's always pretending there's nothing in it. Horrors, I hope they haven't married. I wanted to be there!" Angela said.

"I was only going to say," said Gwen, still embarrassed about being caught eavesdropping, "that we should go and tidy up her garden. I've had to split some of our bedding plants, so we could bring those along. What do you say?"

"I think it's a splendid idea. I'll bring lemonade and the boys can help with the weeds."

"I bet they can," said Gwen.

"DAD," SAID DARLING. He was standing on the wooden porch of his childhood bungalow in Vancouver. His father, wearing a white shirt and suspenders, looked at him, leaning forward a bit, as if his eyes were troubling him.

"I didn't know you were coming. Come in."

His father was a taciturn man, and Darling dreaded visits because he ended up having to fill the silence and feeling like some sort of chatty ingénue. He rather preferred his image of himself as a man of not few, but at least only necessary, words. But of course, recently, with Lane, he had not found that to be true either. In fact, everything seemed now to be upended, and perhaps his visit to his father, while certainly fulfilling a filial responsibility, was a way of going back to the beginning and trying to rebuild that sense of security he felt certain he had constructed for himself since the war, until Lane, until a murder charge in London.

"Thanks. How are you keeping?" He came in and put his suitcase down. "Place looks the same."

"Go on up to your room. How long are you staying?"

"I thought a couple of days." He said this tentatively, aware that this was no longer his house.

"Long as you like. Your brother's got engaged. Couldn't reach you on the phone to tell you."

"I've been in England. In London. I'm just on the way home."

Later, over coffee in the sparse and obsessively tidy kitchen, his father said suddenly, "Did you go to Piccadilly? I went there when we first arrived. I wanted to see it because of the song. We all gathered there in throngs before we shipped out to France. I wrote about it to your mother."

Darling's desire to re-establish his sense of familiarity and security was dealt a blow by this speech, which was the longest he'd ever heard his father make. His father was looking at him, the large dark eyes Darling had inherited now rheumy with age. His father spent his retirement from the engineering firm poring over his stamp collection for hours. No wonder his sight was going.

"I guess I knew you fought in the Great War. You never talked about it."

His father shrugged. "After Piccadilly it was all downhill." He put a spoon of sugar in his mug of coffee and looked out the window that gave onto the back garden and the apple tree that had now grown taller than the house. "I wasn't as badly affected as some of the fellows, but I still dream about it sometimes. I dream about being caught on this roll of barbed wire. One of my friends bought it like that right in front of me. In my dream I can't tell if I'm me or him. Funny, after all this time, to still dream. I guess I came out no worse because I had something to do."

Darling watched his father, and then said, "What do you mean, 'something to do'?"

"I guess I mean that I wasn't just handed a gun and told to go fight with it. I was in the army corps of engineers.

357

We had, I don't know, problems to solve. I think it maybe kept me from thinking about what was going on so much."

"I hadn't thought of it that way. Perhaps it worked for me as well. I think it still works, being a policeman. Problems to solve." He paused, and then thought, what the heck? "I had to go back because they reopened an investigation into the crash I had in '43. Turned out someone reported he saw me shooting one of my own men. Suddenly I was in prison, getting ready to face a trial. I felt like I was trying to climb a sand dune and just going farther down with the sliding sand. I didn't, obviously. Shoot someone, I mean. The witness made a false statement. Now I'm back. The result of good police work, I'm happy to say. But it has shaken me up somewhat. You don't expect your world to be turned over like that."

His father reached over and patted Darling on the hand once. "Glad it worked out. I felt all at sixes and sevens when I got back." Darling could see that his father had collapsed this return from England from the one two years before, after the fighting. "You have to have someone to turn to. I turned to your mom and then you boys. There's no other direction to go but forward."

"I miss Mom," Darling said. "I wish she could meet . . . the person I might turn to . . . and John's fiancée for that matter. What's she like?"

His father smiled for a moment, which lit up his face. "Atta boy. There's no other direction." He got up, pushing his chair carefully away and then replacing it under the table.

I got my meticulousness from him, Darling thought.

"I'll give your brother a ring. See if he and that girl can come over. She's okay. I think I like her. He does, that's what matters. Then we can go to the butcher and get some pork chops."

AMES WAS FEELING a bit like he had when he'd gone off to police training in Vancouver when he was nineteen. He'd come home feeling changed, more grown up, and was anxious about his parents not seeing that and just treating him like a boy, as they always had. He got to the police station early. He wanted to tidy his office, to feel like he was in charge, at least in his own space. He looked anxiously at his watch. Ten to eight. Darling would be along any minute. He heard the sound of the door opening from the street. O'Brien called up the stairs.

"You in already, Ames? I guess His Nibs is due back this morning."

"Yup. Any minute," Ames called back. Then he heard the door again.

"O'Brien." Darling said by way of greeting, and then started up the stairs. Ames stood up and then moved firmly to the hallway.

"Ames. Good to see you." Darling reached out and shook his hand and then, much to Ames's amazement, smiled. "You better not have had your feet up on my desk."

"No, sir. Only on my own. It's good to have you back, sir. I don't think the others were too keen on my being in charge."

"They looked all right to me. Seem to have survived your reign of terror."

Ames smiled. "Very funny, sir."

"I'm going to hang up my hat, and then I want you to tell me about your case."

"SO, I HAVE Father Lahey coming in today. He is going to take charge of Mary Browning's funeral. She'll be buried in the cemetery near his church. In the meantime Sergeant Fripps over in Whitcombe will be handling that end of the business. I'll take Agatha Browning along to the funeral. It turns out the old lady left her property to the maid, Tilly. I think that's all, sir. Oh, except Sergeant Fripps invited me to come over to visit him one day. He says his mother was pretty excited to learn her son was on the telephone to a policeman all the way over in Canada. She wants to meet me."

Darling looked through the papers Ames presented to him. "Not bad," he said. "Clever of you to get the inspiration that the dead woman might not be Agatha Browning after all. But don't go patting yourself on the back too much. After all, the murderer came back to tell you all about it. In fact, a child of eight could have solved this. Had breakfast?"

"No, sir."

"Go get your hat and get this junk off my desk." Darling handed Ames back his file.

Ames finally asked the one thing he'd been dying to ask from the beginning. "How's Miss Winslow, sir? Did you see her while you were overseas?"

"A bit, yes."

Ames smiled happily as he left Darling's office. At least that was still a go. "Atta boy," he said under his breath.

"Ames, did you just say 'atta boy'?" Darling said, following him into the hall.

"No, sir."

"Good thing. I won't allow that sort of familiarity till after your promotion."

ACKNOWLEDGEMENTS

I THINK IT'S ABOUT TIME TO thank my mother. Of course she's no longer here to accept those thanks, but they are heartfelt nonetheless. Her young (and, to me, unknown) self was the original inspiration for Lane Winslow, the framework upon which I built some of Lane's character, and certainly her exceptional beauty. But more and more, my mother's crazy courage—not just during the war, but after, when I was still a small child dependent upon her for stability and sandwiches—are a constant source of wonder to me. Even though I have given Lane a complete life of her own, I like to think that if my mother were to wander back from the great beyond and get her hands on one of my books, she might recognize herself a little.

A deep thanks as well to my manuscript readers, including Sasha Bley-Vroman and Gerald Miller, who have been generous with their time and kind in their support and encouragement to get it right.

My husband Terry is my constant sounding board, idea sharer, and enthusiastic supporter. He always knows what really matters in life.

Finally, the glorious Touchwood team—Taryn, Tori, Renée and Colin—deserve not just my abiding gratitude, but enormous martinis.

IONA WHISHAW was born in British Columbia. After living her early years in the Kootenays, she spent her formative years living and learning in Mexico, Nicaragua, and the US. She travelled extensively for pleasure and education before settling in the Vancouver area. Throughout her roles as youth worker, social worker, teacher, and award-winning high school principal, her love of writing remained consistent, and compelled her to obtain her master's in creative writing from the University of British Columbia. Iona has published short fiction, poetry, poetry translation, and one children's book, *Henry and the Cow Problem*. *A Killer in King's Cove* was her first adult novel. Her heroine, Lane Winslow, was inspired by Iona's mother who, like her father before her, was a wartime spy. Visit ionawhishaw.com to find out more.

Turn the page for a preview of
the next Lane Winslow mystery,

A SORROWFUL SANCTUARY

PROLOGUE

Friday, July 18, 1947

WHEN THE SHOT CAME IT deafened him. He fell backwards, down, down, until he lay rocking, facing the night sky, wondering who had been hit. Above him stars whirled like a carousel in the moonless dark, and he felt himself smile at their antics. There was the Great Bear, its north-pointing star, still in the maelstrom, a sign just for him. He closed his eyes but felt the rain on his face, wet, falling, as he was. How had he mistaken the rain for stars? He opened his eyes, trying to will the stars back, trying to hear something besides the din reverberating in his skull. He did not hear the urgent whispers or the pounding of the running feet, nor was he aware of the man hiding in the water under the pier, shivering with cold and terror because he had seen it all. He could not remember any moment in his life before this one had engulfed him.

"**HOW LONG HAS** it been?" O'Brien said into the telephone. It was first thing Saturday morning, and the desk sergeant at the Nelson Police police station was having a difficult time with a caller. He was leaning heavily on the counter, prepared to take notes, but already impatient at the unnecessarily panicked tone of the woman. Young men rarely went missing. Gadding about, more likely.

"He went to work yesterday and he hasn't been back. It's not like him. If he's planning to stay away, he always tells me. He writes down the phone number if there is one, and tells me exactly when he'll be back."

"How old is he, ma'am?" O'Brien wrote *Friday* in his notebook and underlined it.

"He's twenty. And he never misses work. Mr. Van Eyck at the garage has no idea where he is."

"Are you sure he hasn't gone on a bender with some friends, or gone off to see a girl?"

There was a longish silence. "Are you going to help or not? I want to talk to somebody." The woman sounded desperate and angry.

"I'll put you through to the inspector," O'Brien said. Let him deal with it. It was time he got back into the swing of things after his little holiday in London.

Darling was at his desk reading through the notes about an affray at the local hotel bar the day before. Both men had spent the night in jail and had been released that morning, rumpled and smelling of stale beer. They'd fought over a woman. A bigger cliché was difficult to imagine, Darling thought. He earnestly hoped she would drop them both. The ringing phone triggered a hope that some real meaty case was in the offing, or better yet, that it was Lane Winslow calling.

"That fellow I was just talking to is a useless lump! Are you going to help me or not?"

Not Lane, then. "If I can, madam. Tell me what's happened."

"My son, Carl, is missing is what's happened. He went off yesterday. He comes home from the garage at noon every day for his meal, only he never came back at all, and he's not been seen since. As I told that imbecile a minute ago, it is not like Carl. I'm his mother. I should at least know what is and is not like him, and this is not."

Darling was sympathetic to this phenomenon. In his experience, people not behaving like themselves was something to pay attention to.

"Can you tell me your name and where you live?"

"Vanessa Castle, and I live near Balfour. We have a poultry farm. My husband is dead, no surprise, and I'm running the farm. Carl works at the garage. He left in the morning, like usual, put on his hat and went to work. Only he didn't, because Van Eyck doesn't know where he is. He was quite offensive. He asked why I thought he should have seen him."

"And how old is Carl?"

Barely containing her impatience, Mrs. Castle snapped, "Twenty."

"You're worried something has happened to him," Darling said, wanting to get away from the barrage of questions.

"Look, he's always been a good, straight boy. Doesn't drink, even after he signed up near the end of the war and was with those other fellows in training. He used to come home on his leave and tell me some hair-raising stories about how they all behaved. He never did go overseas, but he liked the work on the vehicles and got a job at the garage. I called one of his friends from school, but he's gone up north to some mining camp. You have to believe me—what's your name again?"

"Inspector Darling."

"You have to believe me, Inspector Darling, when I tell you, Carl would never go off and not tell me. He was none too happy with his dad's treatment of me, and he's kind of tried to make up for it."

"I imagine you've contacted anyone he knows?"

"That's not a long list. I had to wrestle the name of the mining outfit from his friend's mother, but I finally got through to him and he hasn't seen or heard from Carl."

"His friend's mother was not willing to tell you where her son was?"

"No, she was not. Kept telling me she didn't want her son involved."

That's odd as well, Darling thought. "Did she say involved with what?"

She hesitated. "I asked her what she meant, and she said something about it just being better that her boy got away from all that. The war is over, she tells me. Best leave things be, she tells me. Then she rang off. The idea that Carl is 'involved' with anything is ridiculous."

Darling noted her hesitation. "Did he belong to a club, go to a legion or anything?"

"He went into town sometimes, after work, but he isn't

a drinker. He'd always come home early."

There was that insistence again that he didn't drink. "And you've checked the hospital?"

"They don't have him. I wanted to be relieved when they told me that, but I'm more frightened than ever."

"Did he go off in a car?"

"Yes, his dad's old Chevrolet. Yellow, about ten years old. Are you going find him?"

"I'll need the licence number if you have it. Then I can get on to my colleagues in the RCMP, and my constable and I will come out to see you, if we may. Look at his room and so on. Please don't tidy up or touch anything till we get there."

"I don't know the licence plate. I'll look for it." She didn't sound hopeful.

Darling took down her address, resisted being reassuring, and called down the hall to Constable Ames, and was rewarded by silence.

"Where's Ames gone?" he asked O'Brien irritably.

O'Brien shook his head at the phone receiver. "You said he could have the morning off, sir. He's helping his mother move some furniture."

"Why can't she get moving men like normal people?" It was a rhetorical question, but O'Brien seemed to feel it wanted an answer.

"Because that's what sons do for their moms."

Darling hung up his phone and thought about sons and their mothers. He never had opportunity to do much for his own mother. She had died an agonizing death of cancer when he was sixteen. To this day he couldn't think clearly about what that had meant to him. The shock of her suffering and the finality of her absence had seared itself into his young mind, and he had stored the memory, tightly sealed and unexamined, into the farthest recesses of his consciousness. His father had once called one of his high school friends a "mama's boy" and had made an unflattering observation that at least he, Darling, had been saved from that by his mother's death. All he really felt he'd been saved from was understanding women, and perhaps—he thought of Lane Winslow and swallowed—giving himself freely to a relationship without fearing that it would all be taken away.

Glancing at his watch, he saw that the morning was nearly over, and he was feeling a little hungry. He'd have to wait for Ames anyway. "I'm going next door for a quick sandwich. Tell Ames to meet me there." O'Brien saluted and got back to the crossword puzzle he kept under the files he was meant to be working on.

"Good morning, Inspector. No trusty sidekick today?" the waitress at the counter said. Darling knew April because Ames had gotten into a lot of trouble with her the year before when he dropped her for his current flame.

"He's helping his mother move some things. I expect him here soon, though, so get your game face ready."

"A regular fair-haired boy, then. Honestly, I stopped being mad a long time ago. I just love to get his goat."

"Me too. I admire your technique."

April beamed engagingly. "What can I get you?"

"A grilled ham and cheese and . . ." The sound of the door opening caused him to turn. Ames was taking off his hat and advancing cautiously to where Darling was sitting. "And whatever he's having. Make sure he gets the bill."